HE CAME IN HER DREAMS

It was a long time before Julie fell asleep . . .

A fragrant breeze caressed her cheek, smelling of wild roses. The sweet scent of newly scythed grass filled her lungs. A large rowan tree stood before her, the orange berries a rich contrast to the lush, dark green leaves.

Under it stood a man.

His face was turned toward her, but the shadows hid his features. Julie didn't need to see. Her heart knew her love without sight or words.

Silently they came together. Their bodies melded into one.

Love looked at her from his gray-black eyes and rained down on her from his warm lips as they touched her cheek, her chin, her mouth.

Her arms clung to him, wrapping around his shoulders, her fingers treading through his hair. She held him to her, moulding herself to the hard angles and hollows of his body which seemed made to accommodate her curves and swells.

Together they soared. Together they finally subsided. Limbs entwined, hearts beating strongly as one, the love flowed between them like waves of shimmering heat rising into the air.

Julie woke with a start, searching for Ian. They'd just made love. Where was he?

AMBER KAYE

HAUNTED BY LOVE

ZEBRA BOOKS
KENSINGTON PUBLISHING CORP.

Indeed this very love which is my boast,
And which, when rising up from breast to brow.
Doth crown me with a ruby large enow
To draw men's eyes and prove the inner cost,—
This love even, all my worth, to the uttermost,
I should not love withal, unless that thou
Hadst set me an example, shown me how,
When first thine earnest eyes with mine were crossed,
And love called love. And thus, I cannot speak
Of love even, as a good thing of my own:
Thy soul hath snatched up mine all faint and weak,
And placed it by thee on a golden throne,—
And that I love (O soul, we must be meek!)
Is by thee only, whom I love alone.

Elizabeth Barrett Browning
Sonnets from the Portuguese

Prologue

Ian Duncan Macfie gazed out the window, his feet spread apart and his hands locked behind his back. The black morning coat pulled where it buttoned across his broad chest, and his cravat was too tight for his comfort. Even his shirt points, while not the excessive ones of a dandy, were too high for his liking. This whole situation was too formal to suit him.

Turning on the balls of his feet, he wondered for at least the sixth time where Douglas, Campbell of Cashlie, was and how much longer the man would keep him waiting. Ian was here to request the hand of Campbell's oldest daughter, and this wait did not bode well.

Ian's lips twisted in cynical amusement. He was in the prime of life and poor, while Campbell's child was on-the-shelf and wealthy. What better match could there be?

And Ian needed the money desperately.

"Macfie," a loud, hearty voice interrupted Ian's thoughts. "Sorry to keep you waiting, but my tacksman needed my attention. The man will continue to plague me about these new methods of agriculture even though he knows I have no interest."

Ian angled around to look at Campbell. The older man was red faced and red haired with sparkling blue eyes that were becoming decidedly cool by the second. Ian knew how this meeting would go.

"Sir," Ian said, bowing slightly and keeping the disappointment from his voice with an effort. His success in gaining an heiress was too important to let the man's coolness deter him. "Robert is a good tacksman. He's studied in Edinburgh and knows the value of improved farming, especially now."

"Well," Campbell said and cleared his throat, "you may be right about Robert's knowledge, but hard times are here to stay with us. But that's not what you're here for."

Ian turned a dull red at the tone of contempt in Campbell's voice, but he drew himself up proudly, his head held high. No man, not even the father of the woman he hoped to marry, would make him cower. "No, sir. I've come to ask for Isabel's hand in marriage. While I am not a wealthy man, I can support her comfortably and I can give her an old and honorable name."

Campbell's eyes narrowed into blue slits as he moved to sit in a well-upholstered chair positioned behind a massive mahogany key-hole desk. From his place of authority, he cleared his throat again.

Foreboding hung over Ian's shoulder. Campbell's actions spoke louder that any words just what his attitude was about Ian's suit. But Ian needed the dowry too much to allow even his pride to make him recall his offer for Isabel's hand. Too many people depended on him.

"Aye," Douglas Campbell said slowly, as though considering each word before uttering it, "your father has an honorable name. There've been Macfies at Colonsay as long as there have been Campbells at Cashlie. I won't be denyin' that. And if a name were all my Isabel would be having with her marriage, then you'd be the best of the lot. But there's more to consider."

Ian stood his ground and raised his head higher. He knew the next words. He'd heard them spoken not three months ago by the father of another heiress. His shoulders knotted in spite of his determination to meet rejection stoically.

Campbell continued, "I would be a gentleman about this, Macfie—for your father's sake if naught else." His eyes slid away from Ian's face only to return immediately, blazing with righteousness. He spoke softly. "I don't think you're the right husband for Isabel."

Ian nodded, his eyes hooded by heavy lids to keep from showing the old man the disappointment and fury coursing through him like a raging Highland river. "Thank you for your time, sir."

Isabel Campbell had been his last hope of marrying a Scotswoman. Now he must face defeat—something he couldn't afford to do.

Without another glance at the Campbell sitting behind his fortress-like desk, Ian quit the room. It was almost a relief to have the thing over with. Striding through the hall, be grabbed his quirt from the heavy oak Elizabethan table and pulled open the massive door without waiting for the butler. Failure rose like bile in his throat. He stepped outside and took the reins of his stallion from the wizened man holding them.

"Let's be on our way, Jamie," Ian said, swinging himself into the saddle, his hands tight on the reins.

"Aye, laddie," the old man said, nimbly climbing onto the back of the gelding whose leads had been in his other hand.

As Ian urged his stallion to greater speed, the cool, clean air of the Highlands invigorated him. Hair blowing in the wind, muscles extended, Ian lost himself in the exhilaration of pushing himself and his mount to the utmost.

Finally, Ian began to slow down. At a trot, he turned around and headed back to Jamie who wasn't as rash in his older age.

"Breath deeply, Jamie," Ian instructed, taking in great lungs full of air. "There's nothing better than the Highlands and the smell of heather in the spring. I'd ask no more of life than to live it here."

Jamie smiled in sympathy. "Aye, it do be that way fer every Highlander."

"Yes," Ian agreed, pulling his horse around to match pace with Jamie's. "But times are hard and the land won't support the people living on it. Something must be done." Frustration knotted Ian's belly and anger followed quickly in its wake. He smashed his fist against his thigh, making the spirited animal he rode rear up. "Easy, Prince, easy," he soothed the horse.

"Doon be blaming yerself, lad," Jamie said, his lined face creased until it resembled untanned leather more than human skin. "Ye've done yer best, and now ye must think of something else."

"I know," Ian muttered, "but it doesn't ease my anxiety. We needed the girl's dowry so badly. There was so much I could've done with that money." His jaw clenched until it ached. "We could've started agricultural improvements." He laughed mirthlessly. "I could have done at Colonsay exactly what Campbell is so loath to do at Cashlie. We could build new crofts and a new school since the one at the kirk one is too small for all who want to attend. We could have done all the things necessary to bring Colonsay into the nineteenth century, to make it productive so that the clansmen won't have to emigrate.

"Aye, and we'll still do that, lad."

Ian released his breath in an explosive sigh. "You're optimistic for an old man, especially when this is the second time I've been rejected."

Jamie grinned, showing a missing front tooth. "I know ye, lad. I know that when ye set yer mind to something, ye accomplish it. Now, ye must go to London and woo the ladies there. You're a big, handsome lad, and many's the lass who's looked a second time at ye. And ye be heir to an earldom. Mark my words, laddie, ye'll find yer heiress."

Chapter One

Juliana Mary Stockton stopped deliberately in front of the closed doors and smoothed her hair back into the chignon, as though she hadn't just spent the better part of an hour ensuring that every strand was in place. Then, drawing herself up straight, she ran her hands down the narrow skirts of her pomona green muslin morning dress. The silky feel of the finely woven cotton soothed her nerves.

She didn't want to enter the library. Inside, her father, Joshua Stockton, self-made merchant prince, was accepting the offer of a Scottish peerage in exchange for her hand in marriage to the holder of that title. Her dowry and her body for an earldom. Not a bad trade if position was all one wanted in life.

She wanted more. Much more. She wanted love.

She raised her chin defiantly. She'd already spent her first twenty-four years as an unpaid housekeeper and accountant for a man who had begat her but didn't love her. She'd be damned if that same man would sell the rest of her life to another man who would use her the same.

No, she wanted love. And she would get love, even if it meant forcing the Reverend David Worthington to elope with her.

Dear sweet David. Every Sunday in church he preached God's love. After service several months before, Julie had approached him, intrigued by the genuine concern for others she sensed in him. That had been the beginning. Now David wanted her to marry him, promising her undying love and devotion, caring nothing for worldly possessions.

She shook her head to clear it of David and the happiness he promised. David's love couldn't help her right now. She had to enter the library and confront her father and the man who wanted her hand. There was no other choice . . . unless she wanted to face her father's wrath. Head up, she pushed open the door and entered the library.

Her gaze went immediately to her father who sat behind a large desk covered in papers. Joshua Stockton was as stocky as his name implied, with a face that was more jowl than cheek and more chin than not. His green eyes, eyes the same jade green as Julie's and the only trait they shared either physically or mentally, settled on her.

She met his look squarely.

"Julie," her father said, "you should've been here ten minutes ago."

Flinching at the rebuke, she drew herself up straighter. Her father never hurt her physically, only made sure that she always knew when she hadn't met his standards. Long ago she'd learned to live with his exacting measures that cared nothing for the person she was. But she'd never managed to completely reconcile her need for love with Joshua Stockton's inability to give it.

No, she corrected herself, her father didn't withhold his love. There wasn't any love to keep from her. For reasons she didn't know and would never be privy to, her father felt no kindness for her. Julie's chest tightened, but she'd learned long ago to ignore the pain. It would eventually subside.

Quietly, in a voice as smooth as fine Scotch whiskey, Julie said, "My apologies, Father. I was unavoidably detained." Even as she made the excuse, she regretted the weakness that made her utter it. Weakness was exploited by those stronger.

"Well, your apologies should be for Viscount Kiloran here. He's the one you've kept waiting."

Julie's attention riveted on the stranger. Her first impression was of darkness and leashed power, lean and sharp as a well-honed sword. Dressed in black, except for a fine white lawn shirt that emphasized his swarthy complexion, he made the breath catch in her throat.

She shivered with the awareness of him as a man; she had never felt such awareness for David.

She was pondering this unsettling feeling when the Scot made a curt bow. His eyes, so like unpolished pewter, mocked her.

He made her uncomfortable, goading her to drop into a curtsy so shallow it could barely be called such. "My pardons, milord."

His firm mouth quirked at the corner, increasing Julie's unease: he would use her mercilessly. More determined than ever, she vowed not to marry this arrogant man. No matter what her father did.

"No apologies are needed, Miss Stockton. I would have waited much longer for a glimpse of your beauty."

His bold words, followed by an even bolder appraisal of her person, sent a blush into Julie's face that was hot and furious. How dare he.

"I regret I do not share your sentiments, sir."

"Julie!" Joshua Stockton roared. "You will *not* speak to his lordship thusly. He is your future husband and you will show him all due respect, as I have taught you to do.

"Father . . ." The words she'd been ready to say died at the glare her parent bent on her.

She wasn't surprised. She'd realized many years before that her father viewed her as a commodity that he could trade or barter at his own whim, much like the spices he imported. Even though she'd long ago resigned herself to this, she couldn't stop the tightening of her chest or the glistening of her eyes at this latest reminder of her father's lack of love.

Joshua Stockton turned his attention from her. "As we were saying, Lord Kiloran, I believe all the papers are in order. That leaves only the formality of your asking my daughter and her accepting."

Stockton leveled a look on Julie that told her plainer than words that if she didn't say yes, she would find herself the worse for her rebellion. His blatant command erased the hurt of seconds before. She should be stronger by now than to let his lack of caring cause her grief.

Her body stiffened in opposition, but she held her tongue. She'd learned through long practice that openly expressing her dissatisfaction got her nowhere

16

and, in fact, only insured that she would end up doing the exact thing she was trying to avoid.

Clasping her hands tightly together, she bowed her head to keep her father from seeing the determination in her eyes. She would not marry this arrogant stranger who looked down at her with disdain. Somehow she would find a way to thwart her father's plan and marry where she had already given her promise, where there was love and a chance of happiness.

Her father intruded on her thoughts, saying, "I will leave the two of you to conclude this business." Stockton rose and moved from the desk toward the door. Turning back, he added, "I will be across the hall when you're finished."

The door closed silently behind her father, and Julie looked once more at the Scot. His hair, darker than a stormy night, was longer than the fashion and brushed back from his forehead to curl roguishly around his shirt collar. He was broad shouldered and narrow hipped. His thighs were powerful muscles encased in black breeches. He looked as wild and dangerous as she'd been raised to think Scotland's Highlanders were. She swallowed the sudden lump in her throat.

"Do I meet your specifications, Miss Stockton?"

The sardonic amusement in his eyes and in his tone chased away her apprehension. She decided nothing would be gained by being mealy-mouthed with this man. "No, sir, you do not."

He raised one winged black brow. "I'm deeply aggrieved. Perhaps if you would care to elaborate I will be able to remedy my shortcomings."

Piqued by his cool sarcasm, she still found herself

17

reacting to his intense masculinity. Warmth, as insidious and scalding as steam, coiled in her stomach. He was everything David was not, and she found him dangerously intriguing. Her confusing reactions only increased her ire.

She drew herself up and met his eyes without flinching. "Milord, you're everything I don't want in a husband. So please be so kind as to refrain from asking for me, because my answer can only be an embarrassment for both of us."

Ian narrowed his eyes as he studied his future bride once more. Tall and willowy, with a deep bosom and curving hips that made him tighten with desire, she excited him so that he wanted no other woman—and very likely, part of him insisted, would never want another woman again.

The top of her golden hair, the same shade as the sun rising over a Highland hill, reached his chin—just the right height for kissing. His gaze lingered on her full, wide mouth. The lower lip was more pronounced than the upper, and he wondered how it would feel under his tongue. His gut clenched in reaction to the sensual onslaught of the idea.

But it was her eyes that caught and held his attention. Slanting upward above her high cheekbones, her jade eyes bewitched him, their depths framed by thick gold-washed lashes that seemed too heavy for her lids. She had a languorous ambience that sent blood to his loins.

Simply, elementally, he wanted her.

He pulled himself up short. More important than the desire he felt for her was his need for her dowry. Nothing must prevent him from getting the settlements Joshua Stockton was prepared—no, eager—to settle on him for his title.

Still, desire coursed through Ian's body, tensing the muscles of his thighs and stomach. He would have Julie Stockton *and* her money.

Julie drew back from the dark emotions blazing at her from the Scot's hooded eyes. She didn't understand them, yet they exerted a potency on her that was drug-like in its intensity. Her palms dampened and she surreptitiously wiped them on her skirts, trying to remain outwardly passive. She couldn't allow this to continue.

She took a deep breath to still her disquietude. "Now that I have explained to you that your suit is not welcome, please be so kind as to inform my father."

"And what if I refuse to do so, Miss Stockton?"

His melodic baritone played down Julie's spine, sending rivulets of sensation rippling throughout her body. Her unwilling, unstoppable reaction to him scared her. She must be blunt.

She looked at him, noticing a muscle twitching in his jaw. He wasn't pleased. "You will only succeed in causing us both unpleasantness, since I don't intend to accept." She saw his eyes become the sharp silver of a highly polished blade and her mouth went dry. He would not intimidate her. "It would appear that my father has already arranged everything to his satisfaction and expects us to do similarly." She took a deep breath. "However, I will not enter into a marriage such as my father proposes. Therefore, I would appreciate it if you would withdraw your offer."

Ian eyed the woman with dawning respect. Anyone

who spoke her mind as forthrightly deserved consideration, even though he could not comply with her wish. "I'm sorry you find me so distasteful, but the decision is not yours to make."

Not yours to make. It always came to this for her. She tried to convince herself that she should be accustomed to it by now, but she wasn't. Especially when it involved this overbearing man.

Julie took a step closer, two pink banners of indignation flying in her cheeks, her hands clenched into fists. But she'd learned long ago that anger accomplished nothing, so she spoke calmly. "On the surface it would seem that the decision is not mine, even though it is my life we are arranging."

He studied her before speaking. She was like a fiery Celtic goddess in her determination to avert a marriage she didn't want. Her burnished gold hair was beginning to form little curls around her face, and the flush on her skin made him long to undress her and see how far the blush extended. She stirred his blood until he almost forgot about the clan and wanted the marriage solely to claim her.

None of his passion colored his voice. "I know this is your life we're arranging, but you are your father's property by English law." *And when we are married, you'll be mine.*

The anger she felt at his demeaning words was too much, even for the control she'd honed over the years. Throwing caution to the wind, Julie moved toward him until his breath was warm on her cheek. "Just because the law gives my father the right to do with me as he wishes doesn't make it right."

Julie was so close to the Scot that his scent en-

20

gulfed her; musk and fine tobacco so faint and yet so masculine that she longed to be closer to him. Julie fought the dangerous compulsion and the anger her reaction intensified until she could speak without screaming. "I may be only a woman to you—chattel to do with as you deem fit—but I am also a human being. As such I deserve consideration." She pivoted on her heel and stalked away to stand in relative safety behind the massive desk her father had recently occupied. From this position, she composed herself. Her gaze met and held his. "I won't marry you."

Ian raised one eyebrow. "Won't? That is a very final-sounding statement about something over which you have no control."

Ian's breath left him in a slow exhalation of appreciation as her eyes flashed, the rivals of the finest pieces of polished jade in his collection. The comparison brought him up short. Her eyes were the rivals of the finest pieces of jade he had owned before necessity had forced him to sell the works of art. It was just one more reminder of how important this marriage was for him. She would marry him even if he had to abduct her.

"You will marry me. That is one thing you may stake your life on, Miss Stockton."

She saw the determination in his dark eyes and the set of his broad shoulders. She wanted to scream her defiance, but knew it would only make the situation worse.

"I won't marry you," she reiterated. "Oh," she waved one hand in dismissal, an attempt at bravado even though her fingers shook with suppressed agita-

21

tion, "I realize that I will be coerced to accept you today, but I *won't* walk down the aisle with you. Of that you may rest assured."

He watched her jockey for command of the situation and admired her the more for it. He could have used someone like her in France, but right now her strength of character was likely to be a hindrance to his goals.

Ian's mouth curved into a cold smile. "I see that you won't be a conformable wife. Be warned that I won't countenance defiance of my wishes."

Julie had thought she could be no angrier, but it wasn't so. "*You* won't countenance defiance? *You* are not my master."

"Not yet." His eyes sparked with danger.

Julie gritted her teeth. "Never."

It was the end of Ian's tolerance. She would be his. In three quick strides, he rounded the desk and pulled her into his arms. He looked down at her upturned face, her eyes wide in astonishment, her pouting lips soft. "This is where you belong," he stated.

Julie stared up at him in frozen shock, her arms pinioned to her sides, her bosom pressed to his chest. Never in her wildest imagination had she thought he would do this. He was a barbarian. A Scot. And he was going to kiss her.

Fascinated in spite of her better judgement, Julie watched his head lower until his mouth was a hairsbreadth from hers. His eyes, glinting in the afternoon sunlight coming through the window beside them, were no longer the pewter that had caught her attention. They were the piercing clarity of polished silver.

Then his lips met hers.

She expected it to be a harsh, domineering kiss. It wasn't. His mouth was incredibly gentle and coaxing, kneading and persuading her to respond until her attention focused totally on the union of their flesh. She didn't want to react to him, but her body betrayed her.

Slowly her eyes drifted shut as he continued to kiss her with small exploratory movements that massaged her lips until they tingled. Without conscious intent, her hands crept up to clutch the lapels of his jacket, whether to keep him from coming closer or to pull him to her, she didn't know. She didn't care.

She felt him shudder against her, and the next instant he put her away from him. Still reeling from the sensations he'd evoked in her, her mind no longer in control of her flesh, she opened her eyes. On his face was blatant male satisfaction at the knowledge that he'd made her respond to his kiss.

More than anything, that look made her realize that no matter how natural his arms had felt around her, he wasn't the man for her. He would never love her. It was a dash of cold water on the smoldering warmth he'd created deep within her.

How had he made her succumb so completely to his kiss? Never in her wildest dreams had she imagined that a man could make a woman melt in his arms, and if someone had told her it was possible, she would have laughed in their face. Yet she had done exactly that. But worse was the inkling that her world would never be the same because of him.

She quelled the disturbing thought and stepped a safe distance away from the hard lines of his thighs and chest, ignoring the cold that washed over her breasts and stomach. She grasped for dignity and the ability to refute her total submission to his embrace.

Haughtily, she lifted her chin. "That proves nothing." Her lips felt tender when she spoke, but she ignored them and continued. "Do not think that because I let you kiss me without fighting that I will marry you."

His smile was slow, sardonic, and superior. "Without fighting? If you wish to believe that, it is your prerogative."

Julie gritted her teeth, striving for calm in the wake of her shattering response to him. "Well, then, our little discussion is at an end." She walked around the desk, away from him and the urge to be in his arms.

His smile widened, but there was no amusement in it. It was a baring of teeth, as primitive as if he'd slung her over his shoulder and absconded with her. He circled the desk until he stood in front of her. His gaze held her captive even though he did not touch her.

With a voice low and clear, he said, "You will marry me, and we will finish what we have started."

Chapter Two

You will marry me and we will finish what we have started. The words rang in Julie's head as she watched Ian Macfie go out the door.

Unconsciously she fingered her lips which still tingled from his kiss. Even in her innocence she knew the kiss had been chaste by anyone's standard, and yet . . . and yet her complete body had thrilled to it. She had never seen the man until thirty minutes ago, but at his touch her senses had flared into a white heat.

This was not good. The short time she'd spent in his company had shown her that the Scotsman would be as domineering and demanding as her father. Essentially, her marriage to Ian Macfie would be the same as though she had never left her father. The only difference would be that with Ian Macfie she would bring a rich dowry, while with her father she did the work of a housekeeper and accountant for no pay. It was all a form of servitude.

Servitude she had already decided to escape by marriage to David. Dear, sweet David, the Reverend

25

Worthington, loved her and wanted her as his help-meet, not his servant. David was the man she would wed.

Taking her courage in hand, knowing that what she was about to do was outrageous, Julie sat down at the desk where so short a time ago she'd attempted to take refuge from Ian Macfie. With quick, jerky movements, she pulled a sheet of paper from the drawer and dipped a quill in ink.

David, she penned, her heart beating rapidly, *you must come immediately. Something has happened that could change our plans if not stopped.*

Julie reread the note, then, satisfied that it conveyed the urgency she felt, she sanded, folded, and sealed it. Too impatient to wait for the butler to answer her summons, she opened the library door and looked out cautiously.

The door to the sitting room was open, but she didn't hear voices. Ian Macfie was gone. Releasing the breath she'd held, Julie went into the hall and found one of the maids waxing the banister.

"Susie," she said, "please take this to the Reverend Worthington's rooms. Don't wait for a message. There's no need."

"Yes, mum," the maid said, bobbing.

"Thank you, Susie. And take this. It will come in handy when you have your next holiday." Julie pressed a copper into the girl's hand along with the note. It wasn't much, but it was all she had and she knew Susie would make good use of it. Her father paid the servants enough, but he certainly was not generous. He firmly believed in a body earning a body's keep, but no more.

And there were things for Father's daughter to be busy doing. Next week's menus were still to be planned, the linen had to be inspected, and the business books needed to be balanced. Julie ran her fingers through her hair, disrupting her perfect chignon. She shrugged. Impeccable grooming was a detail she couldn't afford when there was so much work to be done and so little time to do it.

By the next morning, the Reverend David Worthington still hadn't answered Julie's summons. She was becoming frantic. Should she send David another message?

She stared at the silver spoons laid out on the sideboard. She was supposed to be inspecting them, a job she usually enjoyed because the rich sheen and satiny texture of the utensils were an aesthetic delight, but today her concentration was elsewhere.

A growling meow and the pressure of a feline body twining between her skirts finally drew Julie's attention. She glanced down and smiled at Pumpkin Cat.

Julie stooped to scratch the cat's ears. "What are you doing here?" she asked softly, as the animal's purr increased in volume. "You know that if Father sees you, he'll have you thrown out."

For answer, Pumpkin Cat rose on her hind paws so Julie could rub under her chin. Shaking her head at the animal's single-mindedness, Julie picked the cat up and carried her back to the kitchen where Joshua Stockton wouldn't go. Pumpkin Cat had been a stray, starved and near death when she first jumped through the basement window a year before. In that time, Julie had grown to love the now overweight cat with an intensity that was reciprocated by the feline. Julie was taking no chances on losing her companion.

Julie was giving Pumpkin Cat one last scratch when someone coughed behind her.

"Mum," Susie said, "Lord Kiloran is waitin' upstairs. He says he's come to take you drivin'."

"Who?" Because her mind was on David, Julie stared at the girl as though the maid were speaking another language. Single-mindedly, she asked, "Did you give my message to Reverend Worthington?"

"Mum?" Susie asked back, now as confused as her mistress.

"The message yesterday. Surely you took it." For an instant, Julie hoped it hadn't been delivered. That would explain David's lack of response.

Light dawned on Susie's rosy face and she nodded her head. "Oh yes, mum. But the reverend weren't there. I left it with his landlady."

"Oh." Disappointment weighed Julie down before she brightened up. David had probably been out attending parish duties. He must have her note by now and would be coming to her soon.

"Mum," Susie swallowed, bringing the subject back to the present, "Lord Kiloran is upstairs waitin' to take you drivin'."

"Tell him I'm not home." It was the only excuse Julie could think of that a man of Ian Macfie's ilk would accept. She strongly doubted that a polite refusal would deter him in the least, and she had to be here in case David called.

"Yes, mum."

Julie stood rooted to the floor watching the door close behind the maid. Even though she had no intention of driving out with Ian Macfie, just the knowledge that he was in the house made her pulse flutter. She wanted to run and hide from his disturbing influence.

She was being silly, and she knew it. Yet ever since that disgraceful kiss, she'd been prey to the unsettling desire to repeat it. It was an inclination she knew she must fight. Desire was no substitute for love.

David offered her love, and she wanted love more than anything else in the world. Love lasted for eternity and enriched one's life, making it worth living.

She knew what it was like to grow up without love. Her mother had died in childbirth, taking with her all the love and comfort a mother would have given her child.

The kitchen door banged open, making Julie jump. Her melancholy fled in the wake of Joshua Stockton's mottled purple face. He never came to the kitchen, so she knew instantly that there would be no arguing with him.

"Holed up like a rat in a trap." His thick brows formed a bar over his eyes. "Julie, you *will* go driving with Lord Kiloran, just as you *will* marry him."

A massively built man, he always made Julie feel as though she were shrinking into nothingness whenever he exerted his power over her, probably because nothing she said or did ever seemed to make a difference. Where there was no love there was no consideration or understanding. Still, because he was her father she would obey him on the issue of going driving with the Scot.

"Yes, sir." Knowing that he wouldn't leave until

29

she did, Julie moved past him and went up the stairs. His heavy tread was close behind.

"Lord Kiloran," Stockton boomed, "the maid was mistaken. Here Julie is, ready to go."

Julie met the hard look her father bestowed on her, but instead of feeling intimidated as she was meant to, and usually did, she found herself pitying him. It was as though she saw him in a new light.

There was gray in his yellow hair and sagging lines around his eyes and mouth that she'd never noticed before. He wasn't a young man anymore. And now, in the twilight of his life, he'd been offered the goal he'd never stopped striving to attain: a peerage. Oh, not one for himself, but one that would be handed down to the issue of his body, her children and his heirs. She knew he wasn't going to let anything keep him from attaining that goal.

Her father's determination was formidable at all times, but Julie realized that in this situation he would be ruthless. If only the fulfillment of his desires wouldn't mean the demise of her own, she would gladly aid him.

But Joshua Stockton's happiness depended on her marrying the Scot, and she knew that would be a union based on convenience—Ian Macfie's convenience. The knowledge did nothing to soften the look she gave her betrothed.

Once more he was dressed all in black except for an immaculately white shirt. Once more, his swarthy complexion and black hair were in startling contrast to his clothing. And his eyes, a warm pewter gray this morning, contributed to his distinctive coloring.

A *frisson* of excitement shot through her at his masculinity.

"Good morning, Miss Stockton."

When he took her hand and put it on his arm, Julie thought her limbs would melt from the heat of his touch. Her voice huskier than usual, she murmured, "Good morning, Lord Kiloran."

Ian's arousal increased. Julie Stockton's deep, raspy voice created in his blood the same slow burn fine malt whiskey created in his gut. He wanted her more than he'd ever wanted a woman—and he would have her. With her he would save his clan.

For the first time since he went to Spain, determined to give his services to Wellesley in the Peninsular War, he had it all. But too much had happened since Spain. He'd lost too many things he held important, lost the respect of other Highlanders, to be easy with what seemed like a *fait accompli*. Any second he expected to lose it all. Pessimism dampened his ardor, but his pride rose up to fight. This time he would win.

He glanced down at Julie, walking by his side, and he wanted to crush her to his chest. He wanted to bind her to him forever. And he would. But first, they had a ride to take and then a marriage to consummate.

Julie's eyes widened at sight of the carriage. The vehicle was sleekly beautiful: glossy black with thin red stripes. The seat squabs were the same shade of red as the stripes, and in the traces were two high-stepping ebony geldings, champing at the bit to be off. It looked precarious at best and dangerous at worst. Perspiration dampened her palms in their blue kid gloves, while anticipation accelerated her heart-beat.

Ian put his hands around her waist and easily lifted her into the phaeton, chasing the trepidation of the ride from her mind. It was replaced by the thrill of his fingers lingering on her waist, making her pulse speed with the heady titillation of his proximity. She flushed and smoothed her dress in an effort to calm her rapid breathing, not wanting him to see his effect on her.

"Are you trying to ruin my day, Miss Stockton?"

Her eyes flew to his. "I beg your pardon?"

The corner of his mouth quirked up, but his face was serious. "I asked if you are trying to ruin my day."

She wasn't sure what he was up to, but found his intense scrutiny disconcerting, coming as it did on the heels of her response to his touch. "I don't understand what you mean. I'm certainly not trying to ruin your day."

"Then why do you look as though you're staring into the abyss of hell?"

"Oh," she laughed nervously. He'd mistaken her attempt to disguise her reaction to him as displeasure, and she certainly wasn't going to disabuse him of that assumption. "I've never been in a high-perch phaeton before, and it is certainly higher than other carriages."

Amazement was written all over his face. He said, "Never been in a phaeton? I thought all Londoners had ridden in one of these. In that case, I'm honored to be the one to introduce you to the thrill of perceived danger." His smile turned sensual. "Just as I intend to introduce you to other pastimes that are spiced with equally dangerous enticements."

Julie looked at him warily, unsure whether his last words were alluding to pastimes in which he'd already begun to educate her. "Danger is a dubious pleasure, my lord, and one I would prefer to avoid in any disguise." But secretly and against her better judgement, she instinctively longed to experience everything she knew he had to offer.

He laughed outright at that. "Most things in life are dubious. But enough of carriages. Call me Ian. That milording is for people who aren't betrothed." He paused, becoming serious, his gaze lingering on her lips. "Not for people who have tasted each other."

She gasped and her gaze flitted to his mouth. Its firm curves reminded her more potently than memory of just how he had tasted: fresh, with just a hint of the brandy he'd shared with her father.

The uneasiness between them was palpable as he stood on the ground beside the carriage, his tanned, finely shaped fingers resting nonchalantly on the side panel of the phaeton. If she moved her hand, it would rest on the top of his black hair. He was too close. She would do anything to lessen the tension, even call him by his Christian name. "Of course . . . Ian."

"There," he said moving around the carriage, "that wasn't so hard. And you'll soon find the ride is more enjoyment than discomfort, too. Trust me."

His autocratic assumptions about what was and wasn't going to please her blew from her confused mind the treacherous longing of seconds before. Ian Macfie was not for her. David never dictated to her or insisted that she do things that made her uneasy. David was concerned about her.

Her memory of David evaporated when the Scot leaped into the carriage, causing the well-sprung vehicle to rock, and David was irrevocably ousted from her thoughts when the Scot's thigh touched hers. Sparks of heat licked up her leg to settle like butterflies in her stomach. She squirmed away until she was sitting on the edge of the seat.

A quick glance over the side showed Julie that she ought to move back toward him a little—it was a long way to the ground. Instead she clutched the side with one hand and clenched the other in her lap.

Just as she took a deep breath to steady herself, Ian tossed a coin to the tiger who'd been holding the horses in check. The man moved aside, and Ian signaled him not to jump up onto the back.

They were going to be alone. Julie's heart thumped with a mixture of dread and anticipation. She dreaded that he might take liberties as he had in the library, and simultaneously she anticipated those very liberties. Her weakness for the physical delight he gave her was shocking, and must be overcome.

To calm herself, she said in a credible tone of nonchalance, "This is a very striking vehicle, mi . . . Ian. Did you bring it from Scotland?"

"No," he said, his voice harsh, "I didn't bring this from Colonsay. For one thing, Highland roads aren't good enough to safely drive a carriage of this type on them. Secondly, I haven't the funds to purchase a farm cart, let alone a high-perch phaeton."

His blunt speaking and the underlying frustration she sensed in his words made her regret the impulsive question. She should have known he wouldn't be trying to marry her, a merchant's daughter with more dowry than looks, if he weren't in need of money.

"I'm sorry for my thoughtless question," she said. contrition lowering her voice until it was barely audible.

He glanced at her and the frown that had lowered his eyebrows lightened somewhat. "It doesn't matter—or it shouldn't. But you'll be my wife soon, so you might as well know the worst."

She bit her tongue on the refutation of their marriage. She despised his assumption of their marriage; still, she admired his honesty about his reason for marrying her. He might be a fortune hunter, but he didn't cloak it in fulsome compliments that meant nothing.

He gave her a quizzical look, but traffic picked up and he spent the next fifteen minutes maneuvering them through the heaviest of the early morning travelers. When they reached the turn into Hyde Park, which was deserted at this early hour, he asked, "Would you care to take the reins?"

She shook her head no but then realized he couldn't see her. "No," she mumbled. Then, deciding to make a clean breast of it as he seemed wont to do, she added, "I don't know how to drive a carriage."

He glanced at her before returning his attention to the road. "Is that by choice?"

She didn't want to confide in him, and she didn't want him to confide in her. Any knowledge of him, of his hopes and dreams, would weaken her resolve to prevent their marriage, as would opening herself to him.

But she didn't want to fight him the rest of the outing, either. So with a resigned sigh, she said, "No, I would prefer to know how. It ... it seems exciting, but I've never had the opportunity." What she didn't add was that her father considered anything that didn't pertain directly to managing his household or his business to be a waste of her time.

"My poor little Sassenach," he murmured. "You've lived a sequestered life. Never ridden in a phaeton and never driven a carriage."

"I don't need your pity," she stated. Pity was something she'd felt for the first time this morning when she'd seen her father as the old man he was. She didn't want this strong, magnetic man beside her to feel such a mewling emotion for her.

"I don't pity you, Sassenach." His voice roughened. "Far from it."

Heat suffused her face at the implication of his words, and she was thankful for the cooling breeze. Suddenly, she didn't want to know what he felt for her, so she asked, "What did you call me?"

"Sassenach?"

"Yes. What does it mean? Is it Scottish?" Much to her chagrin, she wanted the word to be a term of endearment. Surprise at her wish hardened her mouth, and she pointedly looked away from him.

"Sassenach is Scottish, and it means someone who's not Scottish."

She thought about that. Wed to him she would be an outsider, not only to his people, but to him, or he would never have called her Sassenach. Surprisingly, she found that it hurt to realize just how little he thought of her as a person. More than ever, she knew marriage to the virile Scot wasn't for her.

"I see," she said and sat a little straighter, refusing to let disappointment show in her voice. "A term you use for foreigners."

He scowled. "You'll be my wife."

"Your wife, whom you call a Sassenach. That doesn't speak well for my position." Her heightened sense of not belonging began to turn into anger at the situation he intended for her. "Why don't you marry a Scotswoman and be done with it?"

He pulled the horses up sharply and jerked his head in her direction. His eyes were as hard and as cold as the metal they resembled. Julie shivered in spite of the warm sun.

"Because none with money would have me."

The blood drained from her face at the clipped words, and her hands turned cold. Her question had hit a sensitive subject, and she knew she should stop, but she had gone too far to quit now. She had to know.

She licked dry lips. "Why?"

"Why?" he repeated softly.

"Yes," she whispered, her gaze firm on his stony features as she gathered her courage. "Why?"

His mouth moved into a rictus of a smile. "You don't intimidate easily do you?" His teeth flashed in the sun, a brief baring that did nothing to alleviate the hard angles of his face. "None of the ladies I chose to wed would have me, because their fathers forbade them to."

He couldn't have surprised her more if he'd said Napoleon was invading England. He was a peer, heir to an earldom, and the most magnetic man she'd ever seen. What had he done to turn those fathers against him? Was he a criminal? She knew very well that members of the aristocracy could commit murder and no one would do anything about it. But even though she had only met him twice, she knew instinctively that he was no criminal. He was too proud for that lowly occupation.

She asked the fateful word again. "Why?"

Controlled fury flowed from him in waves. "Because, my inquisitive *Sassenach,* I am a disgrace to the name I bear. I didn't fight Napoleon during the Peninsula Wars. That is an act of cowardice no Highland laird will accept."

Indignation at the treatment he'd been accorded swamped her. These Highlanders were archaic and bloodthirsty, their prejudices unjust. "Didn't fight Bonny? A lot of men didn't fight him. Why should that make you unacceptable?"

A bitter chuckle rumbled from his throat. "Because in the Highlands a man who is worth anything at all will enter a regiment and fight. Since 1745, the Highlands has manned more than eighty regiments. Our fighting men are all we have to sell. Not to fight is a stigma no Highland laird will tolerate in a son-in-law."

She began to understand the humiliation he'd been through before asking for her, and part of her regretted her intention to refuse him, which would humiliate him the more. She squashed the weakness. His problems weren't worth sacrificing the rest of her life for.

"So," he continued, his voice harsh, "I came to

London and met with an associate of our Edinburgh solicitor, who told me about your father. You know the rest."

Yes, she knew the rest. He was bound and determined to wed her regardless of her own wishes. The plight she found herself in, and his part in it, washed away any vestige of sympathy for him.

"Well," she said, "I think you're making a mistake to seek a wife so cold-bloodedly, particularly when I have been very plain about my unwillingness."

He flicked the reins, urging the horses into a sedate walk before replying. "I seek what I must have. It just so happens that a wife comes with it."

"Oh!" she gasped. "Cold-blooded was too kind a term. Avaricious would have been more appropriate."

His face darkened. "Much more appropriate, and it would behoove you not to forget it."

The muscle in his jaw twitched, and Julie felt great satisfaction in knowing that her shaft had hit home. He even urged the horses to increased speed although the thoroughfare was becoming more crowded as the day warmed.

For the first time since entering the carriage, she looked around. The strollers and occupants of the other vehicles were all dressed in the height of fashion, the ladies carrying parasols to protect their complexions and the gentlemen sporting canes to enhance their images. As a merchant's daughter, Julie felt distinctly out of place among this privileged class. She would ask to be taken home.

"Lord . . . , Ian, would you mind—"

"Farley!" The name burst from Ian as he caught sight of a man dressed in a bottlegreen coat. He urged the horses forward until they were abreast with the newcomer. "Farley, old man, I thought you were on the Continent."

Astounded at the joy in Ian's voice and the friendliness mirrored on his face, Julie turned curious eyes on the man named Farley. He was slim, not as tall as Ian, with flaming red hair and electric blue eyes. On his arm was a fragile lady dressed all in pink muslin who didn't look a day over seventeen.

"Farley," Ian continued, ignoring the inquiring gazes of passersby, "we must get together before I leave London."

Under Julie's inquiring gaze, Farley's countenance changed from surprise to frigid disdain. Then, just as Ian got the horses stopped and the carriage stationary, Farley turned his back to them and led his companion down a side path without saying a word.

The man had given them the cut direct.

The blood drained from Ian's face, and his mouth hardened into a thin line.

Bewildered, Julie blurted, "Why did he do that?"

Ian bit out, "He's Scottish."

"That's no excuse!" Julie was affronted at such rudeness.

Before she could say more, Ian whipped the horses into a canter. The abrupt start threw Julie back into the squabs where she grabbed the side with one hand and her hat with the other. Soon they were past the pedestrians and slower carriages.

In no time they had completed the drive and were on their way out of the gate. Ignoring the curious stares of people who had seen Farley give them the cut, Julie held her head up proudly and noticed out of the corner of her eye that Ian did the same.

Then, with a flick of his wrist that would have been the envy of any whip, Ian turned the phaeton to the left. They were on their way back to Julie's.

She watched him surreptitiously, noting his inflexible hold on the reins as the black leather of his gloves stretched over his knuckles. Against her thigh, she could feel the bunched tightness of his muscles. He was taut with carefully controlled anger that she sensed came from pain.

"Ian," she began tentatively, "that man. . . . Farley, was wrong." The Scot growled at her, but instead of intimidating her it strengthened her resolve to discuss this with him. "Don't think you can scare me off this subject, milord, for I intend to speak my piece."

At that, he pulled the carriage to a stop, heedless of whoever might be either in front of them or behind them. Not saying anything, he scowled at her.

Julie gulped in spite of herself, but she knew what he was trying to do. He didn't want her sympathy and she didn't intend to give it. But she would give him understanding.

Hesitantly, ready to pull back at the least sign, she put her hand on his arm. "I know Farley cut you—it was because of what we talked about. You didn't fight Napoleon. That still doesn't make his action right. I've only recently met you, but already I know you're no coward. You didn't fight because you had good reason not to. Farley and his kind are too blind to see that."

Even as she watched him, earnestly hoping he would listen to her and put Farley behind him, she saw his eyes blaze until they were silver flames. Julie thought she would be caught up in them and burned to cinders. She closed her eyes to shut out the fire in his.

"Julie," he said, his voice low and exultant, "look at me."

She opened her eyes, leery of what she might see, but unable to resist his command. The look in his eyes told her more clearly than words that he intended to kiss her. Her stomach twisted, and her hand on his arm shifted to his chest as he moved closer.

"Milord . . . Ian, it was nothing. I only spoke what anyone with sense would know. You're no coward, and . . . and . . ." Just the idea of his lips on hers was more heady than any dozen glasses of sherry with dinner. Already she could feel the pressure of his mouth on hers—and he hadn't even touched her. Dazed by the intensity of her longing for his kiss, Julie shook her head. She had to stop this. "Just because I defend you doesn't mean I'll marry you. I won't."

For an instant, his eyes darkened, then they lightened and he said, his lips a whisper away from hers, "Yes, you will, Julie. You will marry me."

She pushed against him to no avail. "I won't. And," she gasped, "we're in the middle of the road. People will see."

"I don't give a damn," he said, closing the scant distance between them until his chest pressed against her bosom.

His mouth took hers. Need as hot and sharp as lightning struck Julie when his warm lips met hers.

42

His free arm wrapped around her, pulling her into his embrace so that her head fell back onto his shoulder.

Exultation surged through Ian. She responded to him as no woman ever had.

He devoured her with his mouth, wanted to possess her completely. Never had a woman aroused him to the point where he was unable to stop himself, and when she parted her lips, the hot blood flowed through him until he was ready to complete what they had started. He wanted her, here, now; all thought of propriety turned to ashes by the fire she stoked in him.

Julie felt Ian shudder under her palms, and she clung to him fiercely. He was her only security in a world spinning out of control.

When she thought she would suffocate, and would have gladly done so rather then end the kiss, he lifted his head. She forced her eyes to open. Even in her innocence she recognized the desire he made no effort to hide.

"You're mine, Sassenach."

Chapter Three

She'd responded to him like a harlot. Julie put her cool palms on her hot cheeks, trying to dispel his effect on her.

Here it was twenty-four hours later, she was in the kitchen trying to preserve cherries, and she couldn't stop thinking of Ian Macfie. What hold did he have over her that made her toss all her inhibitions to the wind with nary a consideration? Surely it wasn't all physical pleasure. It couldn't be. It had felt so right to be in his arms that at the time there'd been no shame.

"Excuse me, mum."

Julie whirled around. "Oh, it's you Susie. What can I do for you?"

The maid bobbed a curtsy. "I was sent to tell you a gentleman's here to see you."

Instantly wary, Julie asked, "What is the gentleman's name?"

Susie turned an uncomplimentary beet red. "Mr. Stockton says you're to come right up, mum."

Julie regarded the young girl. It must be Ian Macfie coming to take her to Gunter's as he'd said he would. There was no sense in refusing, her father would simply come and fetch her. "Tell Lord Kiloran and my father that I will be there as soon as I freshen up. I'm quite sure neither would appreciate my showing in all my dirt."

"Yes, mum." Susie bobbed another curtsy and scurried off.

Julie took a quick look around and sighed. Cook would have to finish preserving the cherries. She untied her muslin apron and noticed dark red stains on her fingers, aware that she might very well have matching stains on her face.

She sighed in exasperation. Crimson splotches on her hands and chin were all she needed, and all because she'd been mooning over the Scot. Since coming into her life, he'd turned her world topsy-turvy.

Absent-mindedly folding her apron and putting it away, Julie pondered her uninhibited response to the man. Never before had she longed for a man's touch as she found herself wanting the Scot's. He was in her thoughts constantly, becoming a normal part of her daily routine. Something had to be done.

Before leaving, she bent down and stroked Pumpkin Cat's sleek fur. Purring noisily, the feline arched her back under Julie's hand, obviously wanting more. Julie chuckled. She didn't have the time; Ian Macfie wasn't a patient man.

Taking the backstairs slowly, Julie couldn't stop herself from fingering the sensitive flesh of her lips, still slightly swollen from yesterday's kiss. Thank goodness he'd stopped, but part of her wondered what it would be like if he'd continued. What came next? She had no idea, and found the mystery intriguing in spite of her determination not to wed him.

Was she a wanton? She'd never thought so before. David's kisses—no, pecks—had never excited her as Ian Macfie's did. She'd thought all kisses were cool and slightly boring—until the Scot.

She reached the landing and turned to go to her own room. Things were rapidly getting beyond her ability to direct them, and she knew they wouldn't be improved by seeing him today. She had to do something.

She had to write David another note. He must not have received the first, for she was certain he would never fail her if he knew of her plight.

She penned another short missive before changing clothes. This one was more urgent than the last, for the situation was deteriorating rapidly: *David, Come quickly. I need you. J.*

She would have Susie deliver this immediately. No one else in the household must know she was sending messages to David. The other servants would be bound to tell her father, and then the fat would be in the fire.

Twenty minutes later, Julie entered the sitting room.

"About time you got here, girl," Joshua Stockton boomed, rising from a large gold damask chair. "Lord Kiloran's been waiting going on half an hour."

"My pardons," Julie said coolly. This time she refrained from making an excuse. Excuses, she'd found in dealing with her father, were always construed as signs of weakness. Her physical response to Ian

Macfie was vulnerability enough; she would not compound it with emotional frailty as well.

Ian rose and moved to take her arm. "Now that you're here, it's time we left." Glancing over his shoulder at Stockton, he added, "I shall return her this afternoon."

Stockton could have been rubbing his hands together in glee from the look on his face. "Whenever you deem it right, my lord."

For all her father cared, Ian Macfie could abduct her and ravish her. Pain constricted Julie's throat. Then, resolved not to let her father's callousness hurt, she squared her shoulders.

When she and Ian were outside, she noticed that the vehicle was yesterday's phaeton. On a more pleasant note, she said, "I believe I may get used to that contraption."

He smiled as he lifted her in. "You'd be amazed at the number of things you can become accustomed to if you set your mind to it."

Julie flushed, reading in his sparkling eyes that he was really referring to his kisses. She wasn't helped by the fact that he kept his hands on her waist longer than necessary, heating her skin even through her dress, corset, and chemise. It was unnerving, the way his touch sent her mind and body careening down rebellious paths.

She couldn't breath again until he finally released her. "Well, my lord, there are some things I've no intentions of becoming used to," she said, struggling to control her voice.

Instead of replying, he rounded the carriage and got in, flipping a coin to the same tiger as the day before. With a deft flick of his wrist, Ian set the team in motion.

"I'm glad to hear that you are mistress of your own inclinations, which brings me to yesterday."

"What?" His abrupt change of topic nonplussed her. What was he up to?

"Yes," he continued, paying marked attention to his driving. "I've been thinking about your response to my kiss. You seemed to enjoy it considerably."

"How dare you!" The cad! "A gentleman wouldn't mention it."

"I'm no gentleman, and the sooner you understand that, the better for both of us." His hands tightened on the reins and the horses faltered, making the carriage sway from side to side.

Julie grabbed the seat, all her anger at him evaporating in her fear of being turned over. It took all her composure to say dryly, "You'd do better to keep your temper in check. I've no desire to wind up under this vehicle."

"And I've no desire to see you there." He got the horses settled down and the phaeton going smoothly. "As I was saying, I've been thinking about yesterday and remembering how good you felt pressed to me— and I think that you've been remembering it too."

She flushed. "Don't be any more arrogant than you already are. I most certainly have *not* been thinking anything of the kind."

He turned to her and asked softly, "Haven't you? Haven't you been wondering what it would feel like to have me touch your breasts? I have."

"What!" Automatically, her hand rose to hit him, but she managed to stop herself in time. "If you weren't driving, I would slap you for that. But I don't want to be the cause of your oversetting this vehicle and hurting us and the horses. However, I wish you would refrain from speaking your lewd thoughts. I do *not* share them."

"I believe you do, but I will stop for now. As you said, it's dangerous to do so when driving."

Julie tore her gaze away from his, and pressed a palm to her chest, trying to still her rapidly beating pulse. What was he doing to her? Never had she even considered a man touching her bosom and now she couldn't stop thinking about it. She had to escape him before it was too late.

Arriving at Gunter's and seeing all the fashionable patrons did nothing to make Julie want to become part of them by aligning herself to the Scot. The proprietor sat them at a small table for two near a window, and Ian ordered two ices. For a while it was so busy with people, mostly couples coming and going, that neither spoke—something for which Julie was grateful. She was afraid of what he would say.

A waiter brought their orders to the table. Julie took a small bite of her ice. She had no idea what to expect, having always considered ice to be something used in keeping food fresh, not for eating.

"This is delicious," she said, surprise enthusing her voice.

Ian shook his head in mock concern. "Sassenach, you *have* led a very sheltered life and right in the middle of London, too."

Julie bristled. "I've had more important things to do than gallivant around amusing myself."

"I know," he said, sounding as though he genuinely did. "You've been your father's unpaid house-keeper."

Her mouth would have fallen open if not for the spoonful of ice in it.

He almost grinned at her, but the angles of his face were too sharp to soften into an expression so boyish. "I have eyes to see and ears to hear. Best you remember that."

If not for the threat inherent in his last words, Julie would have made the mistake of thinking he sympathized with her plight. "I never thought you were deaf and dumb, milord. Merely domineering."

"Darling," a throaty contralto said from just behind Julie's left shoulder. It was followed by a hush that was almost palpable. Looking around to find the source of the voice, Julie's eyes met the velvety brown ones of the most beautiful woman she'd ever seen.

The woman was petite, but perfection in proportion. From the top of her chestnut curls to the tip of a green satin shoe peeking out from gossamer muslin skirts, the newcomer was incomparable. She had a small, heart-shaped face with sloe eyes and sulky red lips which parted into a dazzling smile.

"Ian," the stranger said, "when did you get back into town?"

Ian, his face void of any emotion other than polite greeting, rose and took the hand the woman held out to him. "Louisa," he murmured.

Both Ian and the woman completely ignored her frowning escort who moved to procure a table, leaving the tableau to settle itself. Julie, watching it all, realized with a flash of insight that this beautiful

51

woman must have once been Ian's mistress. There was no other explanation for the knowing look in the woman's eyes as they rested first on Ian's face, then moved downward to his broad shoulders and narrow hips. Julie would almost swear the newcomer licked her lips.

"Ian, I'm delighted to see you again. It's been such a long time."

The woman's voice was thick and sweet like honey, and like honey Julie thought it clung with cloying strength. She didn't even know this woman, and she didn't like her. Intuitively, Julie knew she wasn't to be trusted.

"Louisa," Ian said, interrupting Julie's dark thoughts, "I would like you to meet my fiancée, Miss Julie Stockton."

Julie rose and took the fingers the woman held out. They were cold even through the pomona green leather gloves the woman wore.

"And, Julie," Ian continued, "I'd like you to meet Louisa, Comtesse de Grasse."

"How do you do?" Julie inquired, her tone as cool as the air in the shop.

"Very well, thank you," the comtesse said. "But I see that Paul has gotten us a table. If you will excuse me." The comtesse seemed to float away. Over her shoulder, she said, "Ian, I insist that we get together—for old time's sake."

Julie searched Ian's countenance for any reaction to the woman's invitation. She couldn't detect any, but then she didn't really know the Scot that well.

They both sat down again, but the outing was spoiled for Julie. She had no intention of marrying the Scot, but that didn't make it any easier to be confronted with a former mistress who sounded as if she wanted to take up where they'd left off.

However, she wasn't about to let Ian Macfie think she was discomfitted by the woman. Brightly, she asked, "Is the comtesse an emigré?"

His eyes contemplative, Ian didn't answer immediately. Once more, Julie found her temper beginning to fray around the edges, and she was on the verge of asking to leave when he finally spoke.

"It's time we left." He stood and offered her a hand. "I'm sure you have plenty to do before our wedding."

Disconcerted and not a little irritated by his blatant refusal to answer her question, Julie ignored his hand and rose by herself. "Yes, it is time we left, and I do have plenty to occupy my time, However, none of it is related to the fact that we are not going to get married."

Chin up, she walked past him without even checking to see what he thought of her words. She didn't care what he thought. She was standing on the curb, one foot tapping impatiently, when he finally came out. Without a word, he helped her into the phaeton, and without a word, she allowed him to do so. His hands didn't linger on her waist, and her body didn't respond to the heat he generated—or so she told herself.

They were at her door before either spoke. As he helped her down, Ian said, "I'll see you tomorrow."

Julie, her emotions already a riot of contradictions, stared coldly at him. "You're an arrogant, self-centered beast, and it will surprise me very much if you see me tomorrow, for I don't intend to be home to you."

He had a lot of nerve to tell her she would see him tomorrow when he couldn't even be bothered to answer her one question about the woman. Well, she would not see the Scot tomorrow, or any other day. Before he could do more than raise his eyebrows in mock surprise, she swept past him and in the door.

Ian watched Julie flounce into the house and knew he'd done nothing to further his cause. The outing to Gunter's had been planned to woo Julie, not anger her. He knew not answering her question about Louisa would not make Julie more amenable to his suit, but . . . Louisa was his past and a large part of what he wanted to forget. None of it was Julie's concern. He would simply have to use more drastic measures to ensure that Julie Stockton married him, whether she wanted to or not.

The clan, his people, needed the money Joshua Stockton was prepared to settle on him when he became Julie Stockton's husband. And he wanted Julie Stockton with an intensity that dwarfed any memory of other passions. She would be his—body and soul.

Late the following afternoon, as Julie took a deep breath of the garden's rose scented air, she congratulated herself on avoiding both her father and Ian Macfie for the better part of the day. Now, hidden under an arbor of climbing red roses, she felt secure from detection. This was her hideaway where no one ever found her.

She came here when she needed a quiet place to

think, and right now she needed to decide what to do about Ian Macfie's persistence. She had thought David would help her, but she still hadn't heard from him. Of all times for him to fail her, this was the worst. David would marry her. Then not even her father could force her to wed the Scot.

In spite of the warm afternoon sun, little shivers skipped down Julie's spine. Her father would disown her if she married David, but that would be preferable to wedding Ian Macfie. The Scot didn't want her, only her money . . . and, perhaps, her body.

Yes, her body enjoyed Ian Macfie's attentions. There was something about his mouth on hers, his hand on her waist, that sent all her resolve and maidenly modesty flying away as though they'd never existed. In fact, just thinking about his touch caused her breathing to quicken and her stomach to tighten in tiny, pleasurable spasms.

She buried her face in her hands. How could she want him this way?

"Sassenach," *his* voice said just before he put his hands on her shoulders and turned her to face him.

Her heartbeat accelerated—with irritation, she told herself. "How did you find me?" she demanded.

He grinned, his eyes warming. "I'm linked to you, Sassenach, and there's nothing either of us can do to change it." Then he shrugged as though sloughing off an unpleasant chill. "I don't really know. I just started walking and my feet led me here."

A cool breeze made her tremble. His finding her was merely chance. "Well, then, you are better than most—no one else has ever found me here. But I'm sure you didn't seek me out to explain how you did it."

"No, I came to spend time with you."

She raised an eyebrow. "To spend time with me? That isn't necessary."

Without asking permission, he sat beside her, so close his thighs brushed hers. Lightning shot up her leg in burning pleasure at the intimate contact, and she scooted as far away from him as the small iron bench would allow.

Ian angled so that he could watch every expression on her face. "I consider it important that we become better acquainted. After all, the first of the banns was read yesterday. There are only two left before we wed."

Anxiety made her frown and her voice sharpen. "Read yesterday?"

"At service last evening."

Fury at his high-handedness bunched her hands into fists. He was worse than her father at doing things without consideration for her. "You move quickly and with little regard for my feelings," she stated flatly.

His face tightened into hard lines. "I do as I must."

She glared at him. "Then be warned that I will do likewise."

His eyes narrowed to blazing slits. "You will do as your father says, and after our union, you will do as I say."

Julie surged to her feet, intending to stalk away from this autocratic, unfeeling beast. She was only one step away when his hand fastened around her wrist.

Pointedly, she looked down at where he held her prisoner; she raised her eyes to his. The implacable determination she read in the tense lines of his face caused her stomach to churn.

Slowly, inexorably he drew her near. Julie knew he intended to kiss her, and possibly more. It was the last thing she wanted him to do. She was too susceptible to him and too determined not to wed him for her to be this responsive to his touch.

"Let me go," she said, the words barely above a whisper. Her heart pounded in her chest, almost painful in its intensity.

"I can't."

Ian stared into the depths of her eyes, seeing her uncertainty and anguish over what he was about to do. He wished it didn't have to be this way, but he needed to ensure that she married him. Memories of Colonsay, harsh and barren in the winter, its people gaunt from hunger, assailed him. He needed to marry an heiress. Julie Stockton was the heiress he wanted. He knew without a doubt, like he knew when a storm was coming in over the Atlantic, that what he felt for this woman would last a lifetime. Right now, he had to take her in order to keep her.

Julie saw his face turn harsh, his jaw jutting and his eyes narrowing. She didn't know what he felt for her, but she realized that he was determined to go through with what he'd started and there was nothing she could do to stop him. But she would try.

As his arms closed around her like a band of iron, Julie's chest rose in rapid, shallow breaths. "Milord . . . Ian, let us discuss this."

"It's too late for that, Julie. I can't take the chance that you will get out of this marriage. I cannot."

Julie stared at him with widened eyes. Their bodies were chest to chest, hip to hip. Heat, insidious as smoke, curled through her limbs to gather in her abdomen. He was like a spark to her tinder. She didn't understand why it should be so, but neither could she ignore it.

"Ian ..."

"I won't hurt you, Sassenach," he said just before his lips took possession of hers.

Julie's equilibrium spun away as his mouth consumed her. His tongue slid along her lips, dipping into the crevice between them, teasing and demanding.

"Open to me, Julie," he commanded against her soft flesh.

She shook her head, freeing her mouth from his. "No," she panted softly. Pushing against him with her palms on his shoulders, she reiterated, "Please, let me go. You don't need to do this to me."

His eyes bored into hers. "Don't I, Julie? You intend to prevent our marriage. I intend to see that it takes place."

The planes of his face hardened until his cheeks and jaw were drawn sharply in the fading evening light. Julie knew her pleas were futile. She beat on his chest with her fists.

"You can't do this—I won't allow you," she gasped.

"Won't?"

He caught her hands and imprisoned them in one

of his. With his free hand, he cupped the back of her neck and moved her inexorably to him.

Julie fought her own desire to experience the physical delight she intuited that he could give her. She wasn't wanton. She wasn't.

Ian's mouth slanted over hers, passionately and completely. He groaned into her throat. "Julie, Julie, I want you so badly. It's a fire in my loins that can only be quenched by possessing you."

She sighed as his words sent waves of desire tingling to her toes, negating every thought she had of resistance. For a brief moment, insight told her that their union was inevitable; to fight it was to fight the passage of time. Her resolve weakened and her body molded to his.

The warmth of his flesh made heat radiate throughout her limbs, turning them weak. Her rebellion seeped away, and she finally admitted to herself that she was lost. She no longer had the energy to deny him. She had used it to fight herself and failed.

Through the thin muslin of her gown she could feel the buttons of his shirt against her engorged breasts. One of his thighs pressed between her legs, rubbing her in a way she had never imagined possible, sending heat shimmering straight to her core.

He freed her hands and placed his palm against her bosom, just where her breasts began to swell. His touch was a brand, burning her with the intensity of her reaction to him. He released her mouth and her head fell backward to be supported by his hand at her nape.

Slowly, so slowly that Julie's fingers clawed into his shoulders, Ian's mouth moved down her neck until he nuzzled where the material of her bodice met the hollow at the base of her throat. Then, just when Julie thought she could know no greater passion, his hand lowered from the beginning swell of her bosom to cup the aching mound. His thumb flicked roughly against the point of her nipple, sending rushing flames to burst inside her.

His leg parted hers and his knee pressed against the apex of her thighs; his hand squeezed her breast with the same rhythm as his knee massaged her. Julie thought she would faint from the intensity of the pleasure.

"Julie," he groaned, lifting his lips back to hers.

Deeply, he plumbed the sweetness of her mouth, his tongue moving with the erotic rhythm of his hand and knee. She sagged against him, wanting to lose her identity in his embrace.

With one powerful surge, Ian swooped her into his arms and laid her on the iron bench they had sat upon only minutes before. Kneeling beside her, he cradled her head on his arm and kissed her with exquisite longing.

Julie's world was turned upside down, and she clung to Ian as the only reference in a reality of burning conflagration.

"So sweet," Ian murmured against her open mouth.

Her fingers clutched at his shoulders and pulled him closer until his chest crushed her breasts. The closeness, the heat were like nothing she had ever experienced. Vaguely, she wished that this intense feeling of exploding passion was all there was to love. Then she need never search further than this wild Scot.

"Ian," she moaned as his hand stroked down her hip and thigh, smoothing the soft muslin of her skirts.

His fingers rubbed her quivering flesh through the barrier of her clothing. Moving lower, his hand slipped under her skirts to skim up her calves, tickling her skin through the transparent thinness of her silk stockings. Before she realized what was happening, his palm was stroking her outer thighs, coaxing her nerves to respond. Then his fingers kneaded her inner thighs, moving higher until they reached the core of her womanhood.

Julie tensed at the unfamiliar touch, and tried to push him away. "Ian," she gasped. The word was swallowed by his mouth as he thrust his tongue deeper, sending shudders ripping through her body.

"Trust me," he murmured, his fingers massaging her until her legs parted and he could touch the swollen flesh of her deepest portal.

Julie stiffened in shock. She tried to squeeze her legs shut, but only succeeded in trapping his fingers against her most sensitive core.

"It's all right, Sassenach," Ian said, his mouth moving over hers with a possessive intensity that increased the delight of his fingers moving over her nether lips.

"Please stop . . ."

Her protest died as his tongue plunged into her mouth, and his finger surged into her woman's sheath. Julie sucked hard at his tongue as she tightened around his finger. Slowly, inch by inch, he withdrew both only to repeat the motion.

"Ian . . ." Julie moaned, beyond herself, beyond reality.

"My God," he groaned, moving more rapidly now. "I want to bury myself in you, Sassenach. You're so warm, so very beautiful."

Julie's back began to arch, and her chest rose in rapid breathing as he increased the friction. Something was just on the edge of her experience. She didn't know what it was, but she knew only Ian could give it to her.

"Ian," she moaned again, moving with his finger.

"That's it," he coaxed, inserting another finger.

Julie felt herself stretch to accommodate him, and her pleasure became more intense. His thumb moved across the swollen nubbin buried in her heated flesh as his fingers thrust in rapid strokes.

Her body went rigid. Julie sensed she was on the brink of an explosion.

"Sassenach," he groaned. "I have to have you. I can't take any more. I'm aching for you. I want you to pulse around *me.*"

Her thighs tightened to keep him a prisoner.

"Greedy," he murmured, his thumb rubbing against her. "Does that feel good?"

Her upthrust hips were his only answer.

"God," he groaned, "I can't take any more of this."

Ian pulled away just enough to undo his breeches. His manhood sprang forward, heavy and engorged. He ran his hand up her legs, pushing her skirts until they bunched around her hips.

For long seconds, Ian feasted his eyes on the bounty of her womanly flesh. His shaft pulsed with each thudding beat of his heart, but he held off, savoring the exquisite anticipation of knowing that soon he would bury himself deep in the moist heat of Julie's eager body.

Cold evening air hit Julie's fevered flesh like ice water. What was she doing? How could she behave as such a wanton?

Shame, hot and furious, engulfed her.

Yanking desperately at her skirts, she rolled off the bench, landing with a jarring thud on her knees. The graveled path sent shooting sparks of pain up her legs. Frantic, she glanced at Ian, who stood as though frozen, watching her.

His face was hard lines and hungry eyes. Her gaze lowered. His manhood stood in full splendor, large and thrusting. An overwhelming urge to reach out and touch him in that most private of places swamped her. She wrenched her gaze away to keep from caressing him. Shame at what she'd allowed him to do to her was a hot mask on her face. "What have we done?" she cried.

Ian quickly secured himself then grabbed Julie by the shoulders and hauled her to her feet. "We have almost made love."

Julie began to shake all over as the meaning of his words sunk in. "You tried to seduce me," she accused him, nearly weeping.

He laughed, a harsh ragged sound. "And I almost succeeded."

She stared at him. "Succeeded?"

"Yes," he said, his eyes blazing with triumph. "In seconds you would have been completely mine. There would have been no way for you to escape me."

Shocked understanding held her motionless. "You

intended to take me, right here in the garden in broad daylight where anyone could have found us. You planned to seduce me so that I would have to marry you."

His head jerked in an assenting nod. "No one would have discovered us. You said yourself that you're never found here."

"That doesn't matter!" Anger, such as she had never known, roared through her, but her voice was deadly calm. "You must want my money badly to do so dishonorable a thing."

He flushed a deep red and his mouth thinned. "I need your dowry more than you will ever be able to comprehend."

She laughed, a choking bitter sound that was wrenched from her chest. "Money. Never love. You are exactly like my father. All you want from me is the money I'll bring you." She twisted from his slackened hold on her shoulders. "Well, Lord Kiloran, you thought to trap me so that I had to marry you. You failed. I'll never marry you now."

Chapter Four

She'd elope before marrying that Scot.

But she had to reach David to elope. Soon.

She dared not trust the Scot to be honorable enough to keep his hands from her, and her own body betrayed her at the loathsome creature's every touch. Another note had to go to David.

Julie's fingers shook as she reached for a piece of stationary from the neat stack sitting on the edge of the library desk. Clenching her traitorous hands into fists, she squeezed her eyes shut.

Ian Macfie was ruining her peace of mind. He made her want things she hadn't known existed: fire and passion. But he did not make her feel loved.

Determination squared her chin as she began yet another missive to David. When a blot of ink obscured her name, she crumbled the paper with a vicious disregard for paper cuts. She paid the price. A thin, painful line of red welled up along the palm of her hand. She stared at it without immediate comprehension, the burning discomfort insufficient to pull her whirling mind out of the vortex Ian Macfie's seduction had plunged her into.

She had to escape the Scot. She had to—but the only way she knew to escape was by convincing David to elope. With luck they could be in Gretna Green within a week.

Exhausted, confused, and more close to desperation than ever before, Julie rubbed at her aching eyes. Perhaps she should just go to David's rooms. She had sent two notes already and not heard back.

"Julie," Joshua Stockton's voice boomed from the opened doorway.

Her head jerked up. Taking in the purple cast of his features and the flashing green of his eyes, she thought her plan to elope was discovered. As he strode in the room to stop in front of the desk, she forced her distraught emotions under control.

She was perceiving threats that didn't exist. If her father knew what she planned to do, he wouldn't have halted in front of the desk. He would have come over it and dragged her to her room and locked her up until the wedding.

Her fingers stroking nervously along the smooth shaft of the quill, Julie made herself respond without quivering. "Yes, Father?"

"Viscount Kiloran will be here for dinner tomorrow night. See that we aren't disgraced by our table."

She nodded, knowing that to do aught else would only create problems and tirades she didn't have the energy to withstand. Besides, if things went as she fervently hoped, she wouldn't be here tomorrow.

"I'll do my best, Father."

Stockton's eyes narrowed and his lips pursed, wrinkling his ample jowls. "Are you ailing?"

Immediately, Julie realized her mistake. She'd been too passive and agreeable where always before she'd fought the inclusion of the Scot. Her smoothing of the quill extended to the silky feathering.

"No, Father. I don't wish Kiloran to sup here, but since you've made it abundantly clear that he's always welcome—even allowing him to have the banns called without notifying me first—I see no point in continuing to fight you."

The mention of the banns brought crashing in on her all her grievances with her father, with the Scot. She gazed at the man in front of her. Dislike for her, his only child, made his bearing resemble the stubborn stance of a bull, and his countenance mimic the ruddy fullness of an overripe tomato. Unbidden the questions came to her mind. Had he ever loved her? Had he even loved her mother?

Against all reason, Julie realized that she had to ask those questions. They had lain just below the surface of her emotions for all the long years of her life. Now that so many things were on the brink of changing, she had to finally know the basis for her father's mistreatment.

She couldn't just flee with David—not without trying to make her father see the injustice of this forced marriage; this marriage without love. She wanted to reach her father, just once. Just once she wanted to believe that he cared for her and would put her well-being first.

And perhaps, a tiny voice insisted against the wall of pragmatism erected many years before in an effort to save herself from any more emotional pain, just maybe, she could reach her father. There might be a small chance of showing him that the marriage of convenience he was pushing her toward was wrong—especially if Joshua Stockton had ever loved his wife.

Before all the past hurts inflicted by her parent could rear their fearsome heads, Julie rose and took a step around the desk. Even so, she couldn't ask the questions directly. Her eyes beseeched her father. "Father ..." she swallowed hard, "you must have loved my mother. You wouldn't have wed her otherwise. Please don't force me into a marriage without love. I can't believe you would give me to a man who cares nothing for me."

Shame stained her cheeks at her craven inability to ask the questions directly. But it was the best she could do with Joshua Stockton towering over her, his shoulders hunched forward and his mouth a snarl. Her heart beat erratically, and her body felt as though it were strung up to dry. She wasn't afraid of the physical threat, but of the emotional devastation if he called her a sniveling fool ... if he hadn't loved her mother.

"You stupid girl. Whatever gave you the idea that love was necessary for marriage?"

Her hand lifted to ward off the verbal blow even though she knew that nothing could dull the brunt of his contempt and rejection. "I ... I ..."

"You are like all your sex. Mewling bitches."

He hated her. Had never loved her mother, even though he didn't say so. He didn't need to.

Her throat closed on the tears that she wouldn't

shed. Her chest constricted painfully until she had to gasp for breath. He hated her.

In spite of the devastation, she forced herself to speak—to ask the question that moments before she'd been unable to speak. "You hate me. Did you hate my mother as well?"

He forced himself under control with a visible effort that made his large body shudder. "Your mother was a means to an end. Nothing more. Just as you are. Your mother brought me her dowry to build my business and now my wealth will buy a title for my grandson." A smirk stretched his thick lips. "You will give Kiloran the money he seeks."

His eyes stared coldly at her, making Julie's skin turn clammy. To think that she'd hoped against hope to gain his love, to make him understand how important love was to her. She'd been a fool.

Seeing the disgust and dismissal written all over her parent's face, she knew that she would never willing subject herself to marriage with a man who thought of women as chattel—and that was exactly what Ian Macfie thought of her.

Neither would she give that man children to suffer as she'd been made to suffer by a father who cared nothing for her. Nothing.

Drawing herself up proudly, she spoke with utter calm. "I see now that my questions were foolish. You've never shown the slightest sign of affection for me. You've never spoken of my mother or kept a memento of her. I should have realized without asking."

She moved past him to the door. But she couldn't leave before saying one last thing. "You've always made it a point to succeed at whatever goal you set yourself, regardless of anyone else's feelings. You never quit—but this time it won't be easy for you. I will see to that."

"Impertinence!" A thunderous look darkened Stockton's heavy features, and he took a menacing step closer to her.

She'd come perilously close to pushing him beyond his tolerance, yet she was glad she'd spoken her feelings. It felt as though a suffocating weight had been lifted. His words sounded the death knell on the last ounce of hope that had somehow managed to hide itself in her heart. Nothing said that a parent must love its child or that a man must love his wife. She'd been naive to think so, but she wouldn't be naive enough to marry Ian Macfie and condemn herself to purgatory for the rest of her life.

Without a backward glance at the man who'd used her as an unpaid servant when he should have given her love, she left the room. The quill fell from her grasp, the shaft broken in two.

Julie picked up the portmanteau in one hand and the straw basket containing Pumpkin Cat in the other hand. Stealthily, she moved down the hallway.

It was past midnight and the candle sconces on the walls cast eerie shadows on the floor that climbed up the walls to the ceiling. She shuddered at the wavering elongated figure of herself as she hurried to the stairs. If she were imaginative, she could have very easily construed the pictures to be ghosts following her footsteps, ghosts of all the things she'd wanted in life: a mother to cherish her; a father to protect her; a husband to love her.

What she was doing was foolhardy and possibly even dangerous, but she knew that after throwing down the gauntlet in the library her father would make anything else impossible. If she didn't run to David in person now, there would be no other opportunity to reach him.

Still, she couldn't prevent the shudder of apprehension that rippled down her spine. This was an action from which there would be no turning back.

She paused and took a deep breath to slow the fluttering in her chest. Pumpkin Cat prowled from side to side in the basket, bumping against her thigh and meowed indignantly.

A door closing nearby made her jump. The abrupt action unsettled Pumpkin Cat who gave a meow of protest and shifted, causing the basket to bump heavily against Julie's thigh.

"Susie!"

"Mum!"

Julie's startled gaze met Susie's equally surprised one. The servant had a look of satiation about her; puffy lips and languid posture told Julie the girl had been involved in dalliance. Julie wondered if her eyes had held that glow after Ian had kissed her.

Julie pushed the thought aside. She was fleeing to David. Conjectures about Ian and the effect he had on her traitorous body were out of place and unwelcome.

Julie gathered composure like a desperate man gathers courage. "Susie, I need your company. I'm going to the Reverend Worthington's room."

The maid's mouth fell open. "Mum?"

"Yes," Julie said firmly, "and I need your company."

Susie swallowed hard. "Yes, mum."

Julie was glad for the servant's company as they neared David's rented lodgings. The hair on her nape tingled as she registered the change in neighborhood. While her father didn't live in Grosvenor Square or places favored by the aristocracy, his house was in a well trafficked area of London, even at night. David's rooms were located in a working area where pubs dotted the corners, their inhabitants still coming and going.

Julie dodged a pair of men coming out of one such pub, their raucous laughter following her. Pulling the hood of her cape tighter to hide her blond curls, she shivered in spite of her determination. There was a reason ladies weren't supposed to travel alone, and even though she had Susie behind her, the girl didn't engender security.

Julie quickened her footsteps until the basket holding Pumpkin Cat beat against her thigh with a staccato rhythm. Behind her, she could hear Susie's labored breathing.

David's rooms were above a baker's shop and already the aroma of fresh bread wafted from the open windows. At least she wouldn't have to bang on the door until she awakened the landlady. Some of the anxiety driving Julie lessened at the realization, even as the desperation that had driven her to flee her home tightened the knot in her stomach.

She circled to the back of the building with Susie trailing her, and rapped on the heavy wooden door standing ajar to let in the cool morning air. Susie hovered at Julie's elbow, glancing around fearfully. Julie's apprehension increased.

"Mum, you shouldn't be doin' this."

Julie already knew that, and shot the servant a dampening look.

"What yer be waitin'?" a voice sounded behind her.

Julie's head whipped back around. The woman standing in the doorway was as big and round as one of her loaves of bread. Flour dusted the heavy face and covered the white apron that wrapped around an ample waist.

Julie swallowed down the lump in her throat. "Ma'am, I apologize for interrupting, but I've come to . . . to see the Reverend Worthington."

The baker's eyes narrowed as she studied Julie from head to toe. "Are you one of his flock?"

"Uh, yes." It *was* true.

"Funny time to be seeking a man of the cloth." She peered closer, her gaze going to the basket holding Pumpkin Cat and then to Susie hovering in the background. "Yer ain't running away, are yer?"

For some absurd reason, Julie hadn't anticipated this interrogation and now found herself perilously close to giggling; either that or collapsing onto the flagstone step. She had to calm down. There was still David to get through.

Inspiration struck. Using her free hand, Julie dug into her reticle and brought forth a shilling. The well endowed baker looked greedily at the coin and Julie knew she'd done the right thing.

"He's on the second floor. Go past the fireplace— the stairs are on yer left."

With unspoken accord, Julie held out the money and the woman took it.

The steps were dark and narrow, winding steeply up past the first floor where Julie assumed the family lived, and continued on. The second floor was little more than an attic, with the stairs ending abruptly at an ill made door.

Julie knocked tentatively at first, then with more force when no one answered. *Please be here,* she prayed. She felt Susie shifting weight on the step behind her, causing the lightly packed portmantaeu to bump into the back of her calves.

"Sorry, mum," Susie muttered.

In spite of her anxiety, Julie smiled at the uncomfortable girl. If this was difficult for her to do, it must be hard for Susie also—especially since the servant still had to return home.

Just as Julie prepared herself mentally to trudge back down the stairs, defeat slumping her shoulders, the door creaked open. He was here. The air left Julie's lungs in a whoosh of relief.

Sleep still blurred David Worthington's features and his fine brown hair lay in mussed wisps around his narrow face. His tall, thin frame was wrapped in a plain, black robe of broadcloth. His brown eyes, so gentle and serene, gazed at her in confusion.

Her heart swelled with affection for this compassionate man who would give her a lifetime of love and quiet devotion. "Oh, David, I'm so glad you're here."

"Miss Stockton. Julie, what is the matter?"

Instead of answering, Julie stumbled into him, her fear and exhaustion causing her to trip on the last step. His arms closed around her with soft support as he helped her into the room.

It was a single room, shabby but neat. A small fireplace stood in one corner with a small brass kettle resting on a trivet in the middle of the dead embers. Clothing was neatly folded on the room's only chair, a heavy book on top. Everything had its place.

Julie smiled. It was so like David.

He led her to the chair and carefully lifted the clothing and book and deposited them safely on the bed before returning to her. Julie sat gratefully.

Next he took the portmanteau from Susie. In his soft, melodious voice, he said, "Susie, go down and see if goodwife Bread will part with a pastry." He pressed a coin into the maid's hand.

Julie watched him with adoring eyes. "David, you're so wonderful. Only you would be so considerate and caring of a servant's feelings."

He smiled, a kind gesture that accentuated the concern in his gaze. "What is wrong, Julie?"

His compassion was her undoing. All the pent-up emotions of the last week overwhelmed her: the confrontation with her father; her unsettling response to a strange man's amorous advances. She crumbled in upon herself, her shoulders slumping and her head dropping as tears coursed her cheeks.

"Oh, David, it's been horrible. I was afraid I'd never reach you in time.'

"Calm yourself, Julie. Surely it cannot be as bad as you are making it seem."

Coming closer, he patted her on the shoulder. Julie

75

longed to burrow into the warmth of his embrace, to feel his arms close strongly around her and keep her safe from the emotional storm that had tossed her about until she no longer knew her true self. But before she could rise up and move into him, David stepped away.

A small prick of disappointment jabbed her, but it was quickly gone. David was not a demonstrative man. He would never hold her against her will or maul her like the Scot had done.

"Would you care for some tea?"

Julie shook her head no. "Tea won't solve this problem." She rose and moved to him, her hands held out. Hesitantly he took her fingers lightly in his own. "David, we must elope."

"What?" His eyebrows rose and his long, patrician nose quivered. They were the only signs of his surprise.

"Yes." She nodded vigorously. "We must leave immediately for Gretna Green. If we are quick, we can be there before my father realizes that I've fled to you."

He released her fingers in order to lace his own together behind his back as he stepped away from her. "I do not understand, Julie. I thought we were to go on as we have been until I get my own living."

She followed him, anxiety making her voice shrill. It had never occurred to her that he might not be willing to elope with her. "We were. We can't now. Father is trying to marry me to a *Scot*."

"Mr. Stockton is forcing you to wed?"

"Yes, yes," she nodded vigorously. "Ian Macfie is heir to an earldom and Father wants the title in the family. If you don't save me, I'll be dragged to the altar with a man who doesn't love me. A man who only wants to use me . . ." Her voice died away to an agonized whisper. "A man just like my father."

David rubbed reflectively at his jaw with one long, bony finger, a gesture that Julie always found restful and endearing. But not today. Right now the gesture only served to heighten her anxiety and she found herself becoming irritated with him.

"David, we must act."

He gazed at her, his large brown eyes soulful. "I did not realize how impulsive you could be, Julie. This is a trifle sudden."

His withdrawal was obvious in the tightening of his thin lips and the tensing of his narrow shoulders. Julie forced herself to return to the chair, but she couldn't make herself sit down. She was too agitated to remain still.

Pumpkin Cat's indignant howl broke the tension. Chagrined at forgetting her pet, Julie rushed to free her. Pumpkin jumped from the open lid of the basket to pause at Julie's feet. With a measured lift of her chin, the cat surveyed the room before jumping to the narrow cot that served as a bed. She paced the lumpy mattress several times, clawing as she went, before leaping back to the floor. She glided to Julie and sat down to lick her sleek orange fur.

David watched the cat in fascination. "You must be serious, Julie, to have brought your pet."

Pumpkin Cat's solid weight leaning against her lower legs gave Julie the comfort David had not. Reaching down, she stroked the cat behind the ears in slow movements that made the feline arch her back.

77

"I would never leave her behind."

"I see."

Julie straightened her back and watched David as he moved slowly and methodically around the room. In another man, she would have described the action as pacing.

Her tongue felt glued to the roof of her mouth, and her hands began to shake in the folds of her skirt. Still, she said nothing. To push now would ruin any chance she had of converting David to her way of thinking.

"Perhaps Mr. Stockton would reconsider if I told him of our plans."

Julie almost laughed, so intense was her disappointment. "The first of the banns was read last Sunday."

David's eyes widened momentarily before resuming their normal passivity. "Mr. Stockton is your father."

"David!" Julie's muscles bunched in an automatic urge to fling herself against David's chest to cling at the lapels of his robe. She caught herself up short. Emotional volatility wouldn't win David to her side; only reason would prevail.

"David," she began, forcing her voice to a calmness she didn't feel, "I thought you didn't believe that women are the property of their fathers or husbands."

He had the grace to blush. "Yes, normally I do not. But we are discussing marriage here. It is a solemn institution of Church and State and no woman should go against the better judgment of her father in such a momentous choice."

"But if I don't, we won't be allowed to marry. Once the banns have begun, it is nearly impossible to stop the marriage." She took a deep breath. "Please, David—if you love me as you've professed, then you must escape with me to Gretna Green. Once there all we have to do is declare our marriage in front of witnesses." Her voice caught and she swallowed hard. "Otherwise, I'll spend the rest of my life with a man who cares nothing for me or the children I'll be forced to bear."

"You must give me a few minutes to consider," he finally said. "And," he smiled wryly, "allow me to get decently dressed."

At least he wasn't saying an outright no. There was still a chance.

Gathering up Pumpkin Cat, who purred with contentment at the physical closeness, Julie left the room. Downstairs she set the cat on the floor and took a seat beside Susie at a large oak table.

"Are we going home, mum?"

"Not yet. Reverend Worthington is changing."

Susie nodded her head. "That rattled he looked at the sight of you."

Julie smiled, but it was only a thin stretch of lips. Her heart was pounding painfully. She ran her hand across the smooth oak of the table. The satin texture, devoid of roughness or splinters, slid along the tips of her fingers, relaxing her.

She was still doing so when David appeared.

In his left hand he carried a small, well-used carpetbag. Relief rushed through her like a tidal wave. He was convinced.

Soon she would escape the Scot forever.

Soon she would be his forever, Ian told himself as he ascended the steps to knock on Stockton's front door. It was opened by a little serving maid. At sight of him her face flamed scarlet and then blanched to the whiteness of bed linen.

He grinned quizzically at her. He had many effects on women, but most didn't regard him as though they'd just seen a ghost. "Relax, girl. I've no intention of beating you just because you were late in answering my summons."

She bobbed a curtsy that sent her off balance.

She must be touched in the head, he decided. Nothing else explained her blatant fear of him.

"Do you intend to let me in, or must I wait for your mistress to come?"

Susie turned a sickly shade of green. "No, milord." She bobbed another curtsy. "Please come in, milord."

Ian gave her another curious glance and then dismissed her. Stockton had some queer servants, but then, most people did.

"Kiloran," Stockton boomed, his voice preceding him as he came from the library. "Glad to see you."

Ian shook hands and followed the older man back to the library. Stockton stopped at a table and picked up a decanter of brandy. Ian noticed that his host's hand was not as steady as he remembered. Something was wrong.

"Care for brandy?" Stockton asked.

"Please."

Ian took the proffered glass and took a drink, concentrating on the burn of the liquid as it slid down his throat. Casually, he glanced around the room but saw nothing out of the ordinary. Yet tension held Stockton's shoulders rigid and emanated from the man in waves.

"We have a bit of a problem."

Ian's right eyebrow rose. "Such as?"

Stockton gulped the last of his brandy and poured himself another full glass before meeting Ian's eyes. "But nothing that can't be resolved."

Ian took another sip, his concentration never wavering from his host. "Everything can be resolved. For a price."

"Yes." The older man stopped, his face turning a blotched purple. He pulled at the collar of his shirt with a thick forefinger and then turned away from the intensity of Ian's study. Under his breath, Stockton muttered, "When I get my hands on her, I'll beat her within an inch of her life. The ungrateful slut!"

"What do you mean?" Ian wasn't sure if he'd heard correctly.

Stockton turned back, his green eyes jade shards. "There's no polite way to say this, Kiloran, and I respect your common sense too much to mince words. Julie has run away."

Ian felt like someone had punched him in the gut. "What the bloody hell are you trying to say, Stockton?"

The older man's Adam's apple bobbed. "Don't worry. We'll find her. She can't have gone far. She doesn't have anywhere to go. And when I find her, I'll chain her to the bed until your wedding. The ungrateful little snit."

Ian's hands clenched. She had run away rather than

marry him. The pride he thought he'd learned to control long ago, after all the contempt shown him by his fellow Highlanders, rose in his breast like a raging lion.

"Damn her! Damn her to hell!"

Chapter 5

She was his, by God.

Ian felt the muscle in his right eyelid twitching, yet no matter how he willed himself to calmness it wouldn't stop, "Do you know where she might have gone, Stockton?"

Joshua Stockton shook his head like an enraged bull about to attack. "There's no one. She can't have much money—unless . . ." Stockton stormed from the room.

Without asking, Ian poured himself another drink and downed the fiery liquid in one vicious gulp. He would find Julie Stockton if it was the last thing he did. Without her dowry, the Macfie Clan was doomed to starvation or forced emigration. He wouldn't allow that. Never would the Macfie's do to their people what Sutherland was doing to his clan. Never.

"She took the housekeeping money," Stockton bellowed, his body shaking with rage. A cruel smile curved his lips. "But she won't get far on it."

Ian studied his future father-in-law and for the first time registered the hard cast in Stockton's jade eyes and the deep lines in the man's jowls. Perhaps Julie had good reason not to want a marriage without love. It appeared that her father had not used her well. That would change once they were married.

She was betrothed to him and she would marry him.

"So," Ian said, "she has money, but not enough to go far. But how far?"

"Depends on her mode of transportation."

Ian rubbed his jaw. "Is there anyone who might have seen her leave? A servant?"

Stockton frowned.

Ian paced to the window, remembering each of the servants he'd met during his visits. "What about the girl who answered the door? Short and blond with an ample figure and a breathy voice."

"What servant is that?"

Ian turned around to look at Stockton. The man didn't even know his own servants or what jobs they did. "Where are the kitchens? I'll find her." He had lost all patience.

He found her easily enough. She was cowering in a corner in the kitchen, her face gray and white as burnt-out ashes.

Sympathy blunted Ian's anger. "Girl, I won't beat you—but you must help me."

Rising, she bobbed him a curtsy that was barely more than a dip. "Milord."

Ian forced himself to speak soothingly. "What's your name?"

"Susie, milord." She bobbed another nervous curtsy.

"You know Miss Stockton is gone. That's why you were so nervous when answering the door."

She nodded, watching him out of rounded eyes that reminded him of a trapped animal watching its death descend. What kind of man was Joshua Stockton? Or what did this girl know that she was afraid to divulge?

"Do you know where your mistress went?"

Her gaze darted away from her and her shoulders hunched. She knew.

"I won't hurt you, Susie, but you must tell me."

She gulped. "W-will you hurt her?"

Ian's eyes narrowed as anger coursed through him. What had Julie told this girl? "Of course I won't hurt Miss Stockton. I'm going to marry her." *But I will tame her.*

"That don't mean nothing."

"What do you mean, Susie?"

"The master is her father, but he hurts her. All the time."

The girl was going to be difficult, but it was for Julie, and Ian found within himself a respect for this drab servant who wouldn't be intimidated. Against his will, he developed a curiosity about how his betrothed could engender this type of loyalty.

"I have an idea, Susie. If you will tell me where to find your mistress, I will take you with me. You may even come with us after we are married."

The servant considered that, then slowly nodded her head. "She's gone with the Reverend Worthington."

Ian watched carefully for any signs of lying, such as shifting eyes or nervous ticks. There were none.

85

Carefully, his temper under extreme stress, he asked, "Who is the Reverend Worthington, and why did she go to him?"

As though she sensed the danger in him, Susie backed further into her corner. "You said you'd not hurt her . . . nor me."

Ian swallowed hard. "I won't. My word means something to me."

"They've gone to someplace in Scotland. To be married."

Fury such as he'd never known surged through Ian, making the blood boil in his veins. His fist pounded into a nearby oak table, sending bowls flying through the air.

"Damn her to hell."

Hell must be like this, Julie decided as she tossed for the umpteenth time in bed. It wasn't even because the Bell Inn in Stilton was disreputable. It was the continuing dread of being caught. She had wanted to catch the next mail coach, but David had insisted on stopping to rest the night.

Agitation drove Julie to throw back the covers, disrupting Pumpkin Cat from a cocoon of duvet. The cat cast Julie a grievous look accompanied by a short meow before rising up to knead and bunch the covers. Satisfied that everything was once more as it should be, Pumpkin Cat subsided with a contented purr.

Julie scratched the now satisfied cat under the chin before donning her wrap to ward off the heavy chill that permeated the room. She pulled back the heavy chintz curtain and looked through the grimy panes of window glass down onto the coach yard.

The moon, not yet retired from the dark sky, provided enough light for her to see the activity still going on. Several booted and spurred post boys ranged through the dust, preparing for the arrival of the mail coach. A private vehicle, by the coat of arms on the side, had just pulled in and ostlers were changing the team.

She sighed. She had to get some sleep, otherwise riding in tomorrow's stagecoach, possibly even on the top, would tax her beyond her endurance. It had almost done so today.

A lone rider swept into the yard, catching her wavering attention. Because of her distance from the activity and the deception of the silver light, she couldn't make out the man's features, but his bearing struck a nervous cord. Her hands went cold and her fingers fumbled at the latch holding the window closed.

"Hellfire," she cursed under her breath as a fingernail broke on the latch. Then the window opened and she leaned precariously out, the night breeze cooling her clammy skin.

The rider sat proud and tall in the saddle, showing no sign of fatigue even though his mount stumbled as it came to a stop. The set of his shoulders, the angle of his head, all spelled disaster for her plans. He took off his beaver and the moonlight glinted like silver on ebony hair.

How had he found her?

She backed into the room, stumbled and caught herself on a table. The last thing she wanted was for the Scot to catch her. Ian Macfie would ruin everything.

But would that be so bad? a small voice asked. Already her pulse was pounding and her senses were alert as neither had been throughout the journey with David.

She squeezed her eyes shut, trying to ignore the tiny question of doubt. David was the man who loved her and would protect her.

David was on the third floor. She had to find him.

Whirling around, she dashed from the room. She took the stairs two at a time, her breath laboring between stiff lips. Frantic, she pounded on the first door she came to, hoping it was the one David said he was sharing. Her summons was answered by a tousled man who frowned hugely at her.

She peered around the man and saw on a nearby chair the same robe David had worn when she'd come to his London rooms. Without waiting, Julie darted around the individual and sped to the large bed where David was just beginning to awaken.

"David!" She grabbed his arm and shook him. "We must be gone. Hurry. The Scot is here!"

Eyes unfocused by sleep, nightcap knocked askew by her handling, David levered up on the elbow that Julie didn't have. "Miss Stockton. Julie, calm yourself."

"Oh, David!" Her fingers bit like vises into his flesh. "Ian Macfie just rode into the yard. He's come to stop us!"

Grimacing, David disengaged her hold. "Surely you are mistaken. The rooster has not even crowed."

Julie stared at him, wondering what it would take

to galvanize him. "I tell you, I just saw the Scot. He will make me marry him unless we leave before he finds us here."

David's soulful brown eyes flickered with an emotion that in another man she would have named distaste. But David loved her. He was merely concerned that in her agitation she not harm herself.

"Please calm yourself, Julie. You must be mistaken. Surely your father would not send this man after you. It is not proper. Perhaps, in your anxiety, you mistook the figure of your father for the other man?" He lay back against the pillow, pulling the covers up to his chin, his gaze wavering from her face.

"Of course not," she answered with mounting impatience.

"Well," his attention reluctantly came back to her, "then you must be letting your imagination run away with you. I am quite certain that your father would come after you and not send a single man."

Her jaw tensed and she glanced away from him as she fought to control her temper. She knew who she'd seen. David would not believe her.

He sighed. "Please, Julie, if you will go outside for but a minute, I will dress and escort you back to your room. When you are dressed, we can find a private parlor and discuss this."

He thought her overwrought. He didn't believe her. He wasn't going to flee. Ian Macfie would find them. Dread ran through her veins like ice. She had to escape. Her eyes pleaded with David. "Please! We must leave before he finds us."

David patted her hand in a gesture she knew was meant to comfort her but which only succeeded in angering her. "There now, Julie. I am sure that everything can be worked out in a reasonable manner. It has been a long and arduous journey."

She gaped at him, biting down hard on the frustration bubbling up within her. David was a cautious man who didn't rush into anything . . . including love. That was one of the traits that drew her to him, that made her feel she would be safe with him. Now she would have to trust him to protect her from the Scot, because it was abundantly evident that David didn't believe they'd been found.

Bowing her head in hard held submission, she left the room and waited, rubbing her hands together. When David emerged, closing the door on the vituperative condemnation of the man Julie had forgotten about in her extremity, she allowed him to lead her down the flight of stairs to the second floor.

Ian heard their footfalls before he saw the yellow flicker of candlelight. His breath hissed between grinding teeth. If he lived to be a hundred, he knew he would never forget this moment.

She was dressed in a blue robe that billowed behind her, outlining the lush fullness of her bosom and hips. Her breasts rose and fell with each breath she took. Her hair flowed like ripe wheat around her shoulders, one hand raised so that she could stroke and twirl the silken strands that beckoned to him. Another man's arm held her.

The anger that had been simmering in Ian below the level of active thought steamed into scalding fury. The crop in his hands cracked in two.

Julie jumped at the splintering sound. Her gaze flashed from the floor at her feet to Ian's face.

"You!" Julie breathed, freezing in place. Even knowing that he was here, did nothing to lessen the alarm his violent action churned up in her breast.

He made her a mocking bow. "In the flesh."

She turned frantic eyes to the man beside her. "David, you've got to keep him from taking me."

Ian's temperature rose. He'd be damned if anyone, let alone this unimpressive specimen, would keep them apart. She was his, even if he couldn't trust her not to run away. He'd soon remedy that.

Ian stared coldly at the figure beside Julie. The man was slender, not much taller than she, with fine brown hair cut short and a pair of eyes that would put a saint to shame. David, or so she'd named him, patted absent-mindedly at her hand which clenched his forearm with white knuckles.

"Sir," David said, "I do not believe we have been introduced. However, Julie seems to know you and even claims to know why you are here."

The gentle, reasoning tenor wouldn't normally have vexed Ian's patience, and there was no threat in the solemnity of posture or expression of face to do so, either. But the man was a rival for Julie's regard, and Ian felt the hair rising on his nape. She was his, and he would fight in any way necessary to keep her.

Ignoring her, knowing that to look at her would only infuriate him further, Ian said, "Miss Stockton knows exactly why I'm here. Joshua Stockton sent me to fetch her."

David's brows rose. "I beg your pardon."

"Yes, do that," Ian responded with sarcasm.

"I cannot believe that Julie's parent would do such a scandalous thing to his child. No loving father would so besmirch his only daughter's name and reputation." As though unaware of the two people standing so close, he murmured, "I thought for sure that he would come himself."

Ian saw Julie's face blanch as though she'd been struck. He might be livid at her attempted elopement, but he would have never betrayed her trust this way. "You blathering idiot," he spat.

"I beg your pardon?" Worthington inquired.

"You've already done so. You might try begging for hers after what you did." When the Reverend continued to look confused, Ian added, "Leaving a note with instructions."

Worthington had the grace to turn a bright pink. His eyes shifted from Ian to Julie. "I thought it for the best."

Compassion softened Julie's expression. "I know, David. How could you know my father would do this?"

Worthington's shoulders sagged with relief. "Exactly."

Ian snorted. "I've had enough of this mutual understanding. Let go of her arm, Worthington, so that she may dress properly and pack her bags. We're leaving immediately."

The Reverend released Julie, but she didn't release him. Ian's chest constricted with near explosive anger at her stubborn clinging to a nonentity who didn't have the gumption to stand up to an adversary in order to do as his woman wished. It was the last thing Ian needed while he was trying to maintain some perspective on her actions.

Ian took one step forward and ripped Julie's fingers away from their hold. Accidentally, he crushed her bones, bringing a small exclamation of pain to her lips.

"Beast!" she cried.

He met the flashing green of her accusing eyes with cold contempt. "Name calling so soon?"

"Bastard!" she answered.

Ian flung her from him. "Get dressed. As for you," he rounded on Worthington and saw his rival cringe backward, increasing the disgust he already felt for the weakling, "we have things to discuss."

Ian sensed, rather than saw, Julie enter her bedroom. Without a backward glance, he strode down the hall, never doubting that her paramour would follow. Reaching the private parlor, he moved inside. Worthington followed.

Before the other could speak, Ian stated, "Stockton almost didn't get your note. The maid wasn't going to hand it over. I convinced her to give it to me. It was very helpful." Ian's eyes narrowed into stormy slits as he watched the tell-tale paling of the other man's face. "Next time you betray someone's confidence, I suggest you ensure that the person you enlist is capable of the action you require."

Worthington's chin began to tremble. "I am a man of the cloth. I could never marry Miss Stockton without her father's permission."

"You're a sniveling coward."

Ian watched the man's lips whiten around the edges and felt great satisfaction. The emotion surprised him by its intensity. Never before had he enjoyed an opponent's suffering, not even when that opponent had been a Frenchman during the wars.

"Sir," Worthington drew himself up straight, "it is true that I intended for Mr. Stockton to catch us. When that occurred I planned to explain the circumstances to him. I still intend to do that. You have helped by delaying us so that it will be that much easier for Mr. Stockton to reach us. For that I must thank you."

"Are you dense as well as weak? Stockton has no intention of following you. As far as he's concerned, this is my affair."

"I beg your pardon?"

Ian gritted his teeth. "Do *not* start that again." Mentally he counted to ten and concentrated on unknotting the muscles in his shoulders. It was a technique he'd perfected during the countless nights of danger spent skulking in French alleys. It wasn't as effective as he remembered. "Joshua Stockton has given Julie Stockton to me in marriage. My title for her money. I even have a letter signed by the man and witnessed by the same bishop who provided the Special License I carry."

David Worthington's mouth pursed.

"I see that you're beginning to comprehend the situation."

Worthington turned away from the sardonic amusement Ian made no effort to hide. Ian could almost feel sorry for the man; duped by a woman who was a stronger personality than he. When he and Julie were wed, he'd be damned if she led him around like a gelded bull.

The Reverend wrung his hands and furrowed his brow, then, as quickly as the consternation had descended on him, it disappeared. "If what you say is correct, and I have no reason to doubt your word, then what do you plan to do now that you have found us?"

"I intend to ask the landlord to direct me toward the parson in this area as soon as Julie is packed. She's already shown herself to be devious and unscrupulous when it comes to dealing with me and the wedding contract I've reached with her father."

Worthington stared at nothing. "You say Mr. Stockton is in favor of this union?"

Ian flexed the cramping muscles in his neck. This man was becoming a bore, or perhaps he was dimwitted. "I have the letter."

He reached inside the pocket of his coat and brought out the paper with Stockton's signature. He added the Special License.

The Reverend took both sheets and perused them. "The Bishop's signature is very distinct."

Ian's eyes flashed like lightning over a stormy loch. "Did you doubt my word?"

Worthington glanced up. "No, sir. But one should always be sure."

"A worthy trait, I'm sure."

If Worthington noticed the sarcasm Ian took no trouble to disguise, it didn't show on the Reverend's serene countenance. "I can see my duty, Viscount Kiloran."

Even as Ian sensed that Worthington was about to capitulate, his skin became charged with electricity. He hadn't heard the door open, but he knew it had and that Julie stood in the threshold, listening to every word.

Worthington continued, "The least I can do to ease

Miss Stockton's distress over this marriage is to perform the ceremony myself."

"What?"

Julie's sharp, agonized question rang in Ian's ears, making his muscles clench in sympathy. The man she'd risked everything to marry was betraying her once again. But the weakness only lasted an instant. She had run from him, nearly taking from him the only means he had to help the Macfie clan. No, any sympathy he felt for her was negligible after what she'd almost done to him and his people.

Angling around so that he could see her face, Ian said, "Don't you wish to thank Reverend Worthington for this kindness? It will make it easier on us than having to go out into the dark morning seeking a parson."

Her jade eyes opened wide in hurt bewilderment. She came into the room, stumbling on the rolled-up corner of the area rug. Ian sprang to catch her elbow. She shook off his hand with a vehemence that tightened his jaw.

She went straight to Worthington and looked him straight in the eye, her full lips speaking words Ian didn't want to hear, but couldn't bring himself to shut out. "David, I thought you loved me. We were going to marry. What has changed that now you will even go so far as to wed me to another man?"

The pain she made no effort to hide colored every word, and every word of her love for another man was like a sharp knife in Ian's chest. His shoulders hunched to ward off the unexpected emotion. Just as quickly, he squared them.

She belonged to him. Her father gave her to him.

The Macfie clan needed her wealth to survive. That was all. If she loved another man, he could feel sorry for her, but it didn't mean anything to him. It didn't cause the wrenching in his gut.

"Please, David," her soft, pleading voice continued to torture Ian, "please don't do this. The Scot," with her hand, she made a choppy gesture in Ian's direction, "will make my life a living hell. He doesn't care about me. But you do, and I care for you. Don't you remember how we were going to work side by side in the parish you'll soon receive. Have you forgotten how we planned to love and cherish one another as we strove to make the world a better place for those less fortunate than we?"

That was it. Ian took two rapid strides forward and yanked her away from the gutless man she wanted. "Stop it. Have you no pride, woman? He's made it plain as the nose on his face that he does'na want ye. Be done with this groveling."

She twisted like a wildcat in his hold. "Who are you to speak of pride? A man who has none?"

Her words cut like swords, but he closed his ears and held on to her thrashing body. She was so close that he could smell the woman's musk coming from her heated flesh. One of the pins fell from her hair, releasing a sun-bright strand to caress the flushed rose of her cheek. Ian wished the Reverend Worthington anywhere but here.

"Be still, Julie. You do nothing but make a bad situation worse. I've your father's signature confirming my right to you. Worthington knows this, and he won't go against a father's legal authority over his daughter." His eyes caught and held hers, compelling

97

her to stop struggling. Slowly, like water that drips on rock until a crack forms, his will dominated hers until she quieted. "You've lost this battle, Julie. Truth to tell, you never had a chance."

Her gaze faltered and her head sank. In that instant, Ian wanted to gather her to his chest and hold her until her despair faded. He wanted to protect her from the world, himself included.

She lifted her head, her eyes cool as the finest green jade. "I may be forced to wed you, but I'll never share your bed or give you children. In that I will thwart both you and my father."

At her vituperative declaration, all thought of comforting her seeped from him to be replaced by a cold fury that made the blood pound painfully in his temples. The urge to shake her was so great that he took several steps away.

In carefully measured tones, he said, "You will live to regret those words."

Chapter Six

Ian entered the Inn bedroom without knocking. She should be ready by now.

"Milord," Susie bobbed a curtsy.

For the first time since his wedding and the departure of David Worthington an hour before, Ian allowed himself to smile. "I see your carriage arrived without mishap."

"Yes, milord. Horrible ride, that." She bobbed another nervous curtsy. "Miss Stoc ... I mean, her ladyship, is ready."

Ian glanced in the direction Susie's nod indicated. Julie was propped in bed, several large pillows supporting her back, the covers pulled to her chin, and her glorious hair falling like sunlight onto the white linens.

Beside her a large orange tabby raised its head and regarded him with wide yellow eyes. Seeming to take his measure and find nothing worthy of alarm, the cat rested its head on the tops of its front paws.

Ian couldn't help smiling. At least the feline thought him harmless.

"You may go now, Susie," he said, unable to keep his response to his new wife's beauty from deepening his voice. "And thank you." He smiled at the maid, a genuine appreciation that lit his eyes and made her own widen in surprise. Her reaction amused him further, fitting as it did the cat's response to him.

But the humor fled when he looked back at Julie. Her golden brows were a bar across her flashing jade eyes, and her usually full pink lips were thin white lines. He nearly turned and left the room. It was what he would prefer, rather than fight with her as he knew they would. Before he could, she spoke.

"How dare you come in here without asking. Must you make a mockery of everything by pretending to love me on our wedding night?"

His brows rose. "Who spoke of love?"

The skin around her eyes tightened. "You never did. Therefore, you have no place in this room."

On cat-silent feet, he moved to the bed until he towered above her. "Not only do I belong in this room, but I belong in this bed. With you."

She paled. "I'll never let you touch me."

"Never?"

"Never."

He had wanted her from the beginning. Seeing her lying on the bed, her golden hair fanned around her face, her eyes dark with anxiety that mimicked the arousal of passion, he wanted her until it was an ache that started in his loins and spread to every part of his body.

"You, Viscountess Kiloran, have no say-so in whether or not I touch you. You gave up that privilege when you fled with your paramour full knowing that your father had promised you to me."

She sat straight up and leaned toward him until less than a foot separated her face from his chest. "That was Joshua Stockton's bargain. Never mine."

She was a woman with a will and determination, qualities he admired even though they irritated him at the moment. "As your father, he had the right to give you where he chose."

Her jaw clenched. "I've told you before. I am a human being, not chattel to be given away at a man's whim."

"You are my wife. And I intend to make very sure that you stay that way."

Without another glance at her, Ian turned and began to unbutton his coat. When he pulled off his shirt, he heard her sharp intake of air.

"What are you doing?"

He glanced over his shoulder. Beneath the protection of the blankets, her bosom heaved with such indignant breath. Above the covers, her skin was tinted a delicate shell pink. Ian felt his need for her, that rampant emotion he'd fought from the first, surge into a consuming throb.

Meeting the defiance in her flashing eyes, he suddenly realized that he wanted more. The memory of her indignation for his sake in Hyde Park softened the sharp edge of his desire, making it no less potent, but sweeter. She had championed him with the same fire and spunk she showed him now. She was a woman worth keeping.

Looking away, trying to master the urge to make

love to her that threatened to overpower him, he answered, "Exactly what you think."

"You can't. I won't let you."

The rising panic in her voice was more effective than any cold bath to quench the desire that had been pulsing in his loins moments before. This wasn't the wedding night he'd hoped to one day share with his bride, but it was the one he had to have.

The warmth caused by the memory of her support ebbed. Wearily he began to wonder if he could even go through with the ordeal before him. He pivoted on the ball of his foot and moved to the bed. At least she wouldn't be scared by his arousal, since there was none.

Julie watched him move toward her, clenching the sheets with hands as white as the linen. The sight of Ian naked did strange things to her. His hair, like midnight velvet, hung in heavy folds around his head. She quickly averted her eyes from the forbidden curiosity that drew her gaze downward. It was much safer to look at his face, or so she thought. But his eyes were dark and stormy like the sky during a thunder storm. Any minute she expected lightning to strike her.

He effectively aborted her study by picking up Pumpkin Cat and depositing her on the floor. The feline protested in no uncertain terms, her howl of irritation running up the scale.

Ian bent over and scratched the cat behind her ears before saying to Julie, "Move over."

"Never."

He sighed heavily. "You're becoming as repetitive

as that milksop you tried to coerce into marriage."
Looming over her, he repeated, "Move over."

"I won't share this bed with you."

Flinging the sheet from her, she rolled over to the
other side of the bed and jackknifed into a standing
position. Equally quick, Ian lunged across the mattress and grabbed her wrist, yanking her off balance.

"Oh," she yelped, falling backward onto the rum-
pled covers.

In a flash, Ian pinned her legs with his and her
chest with his. He knew his weight was making it
hard for her to breathe, could see it in her gasp for
breath and could feel it in the agitated rising and
falling of her breasts beneath him. But he'd reached
his limit.

"Let me go," she rasped through gritted teeth. His
body pinned her helplessly to the bed but increased
her determination to fight him.

Inexorably, he pushed her arms above her head
where he held them against the pillow with one of
his. Gently, but firmly, he said, "When you settle
down, Julie, I'll get off you."

"I won't let you make a mockery of love. I won't
let you do to me what you did in London."

He raised one eyebrow. "Make love to you and
make you like it?"

She turned away from his mocking gaze, feeling
the stain of shame creeping over her flesh. "You'll
have to force me."

"Perhaps. But mark my words, I will take your virginity tonight." With one hand he grasped her chin
and forced her to face him. "Should you ever run
from me again, there will be no means for you to ob-

103

tain an annulment. Our marriage will be in body as well as on paper, and no bishop in the land will grant an annulment under those circumstances. Do you understand?"

For long minutes, she stared wide-eyed and defiantly into his eyes. It was a contest of wills, and he knew it. If he allowed her to win, he would lose everything he'd spent his entire life working to achieve. If he let her go tonight, tomorrow she would run away again. If he didn't bed her, take her virginity, she'd have grounds for an annulment. No marriage, no money. No money, and the clan would perish.

Julie was the first to look away. She would never admit it, not right now with his naked body pushing her into the softness of the mattress, but if he didn't take her tonight she would flee in the morning. It was galling that he knew it, too.

Realizing that this was as close to capitulation as she was willing to go, Ian said, "Too bad you don't want to enjoy this." He truly meant it. "But it won't stop me, Julie. You have left me no other choice. I have too much at stake to allow you to browbeat me the way you did David Worthington."

Her head whipped around and she looked coldly at him. "Rape me."

"It bloody hell won't be that."

She had thrown down the gauntlet, and by God, he intended to pick it up. He didn't want to break her spirit; she'd need it on Colonsay, but he needed to tame her.

He lowered his head until her dilated pupils were black mirrors in which he saw his own determination

104

reflected back at him. Still watching her, he closed the distance.

It was a domineering kiss, a contest of wills. He could force her compliance, and he saw that she knew it. When all the air was sucked from her lungs, he ended the kiss.

"I'll make you enjoy this," he vowed.

Julie laughed, but it was forced and made her throat ache. Worry that he might succeed in his threat made her hands break out in a cold sweat. Where would she be if he made her like this? She knew. She would once more belong to a man who would use her for his own gains without any consideration for her feelings. Again she would be without love, only this time there would be no possibility of escape. One didn't escape from a husband.

Still lying on top of her, Ian saw the fine blue lines that traced patterns on her eyelids when she closed her eyes to the sight of him. A tiny pulse beat in one of them, racing as his heart raced. Against his chest, the hard pricks of her nipples sent jolting flashes of pleasure directly to his loins.

He wanted to bury himself so deeply inside her that she shivered with the same desire raging over him. To taste her swollen lips and dine on the fine wine of her breath. He wanted all those things with an intensity that scared him. But what scared him even more was his overpowering need to have her respond to his loving. He wanted her to desire him as he did her.

Ian spent long minutes breathing deeply, trying to regain perspective. She was his wife, an heiress with money he needed badly. Even if nothing more came of their union, the money to save Colonsay would be enough. He didn't have to have the passion and support he knew her capable of. But he craved it.

His need for her was almost fatalistic in its intensity. It was as though they belonged together, no matter what differences brought them to this point.

A drop of perspiration fell from his cheek to where her left breast began to swell. It coalesced, caught in the flickering yellow light of the bedside candle like a many-faceted diamond laid on her satin smooth skin.

Ian stared at it. Bending forward, he extended his tongue so that the tip touched the drop. It tasted of salt and the passion it came from.

Her eyes opened. Caught by the passions rioting through her, obvious in the changing green of her irises from pale to deepest jade, Ian longed to give her the independence she wanted. He couldn't, but he could give her physical satisfaction.

"Sassenach," he said softly, breaking the spell that had held him. "I don't want to hurt you. With your help, I can make you enjoy this."

Julie tensed under him, her fingers curling and her arm muscles bunching. His words were too true. She was weak enough, susceptible enough to his physical caresses that she never doubted his ability to make her enjoy their union. But that would be the first step in the complete loss of her dream. If she succumbed to him now, she would never find the love she'd spent her life seeking.

Through drawn lips, she said, "Let me go."

"I can't, and you know it."

With his free hand, he smoothed tangled strands of

hair back from her face. Straddling her, his weight still holding her, he began to ease the transparent folds of her nightrail from her shoulders. When she refused to raise her hips so that he could pull the material the rest of the way, he ripped it. The shriek of tearing muslin pierced the air.

He ignored her gasp of indignation. He took both her hands in one of his and wound the silky muslin around her wrists so that she was snugly bound. Then he pulled her arms above her head and secured her to one of the bedposts.

"Just say the word, Julie, and I'll undo these."

She glared at him.

There was no other way. He had to insure that their marriage was inviolable and that her money came to him. Still, he'd hoped for more.

"Have it your way, but I'll make you want me before we're done no matter what you think now."

"Bastard."

He stopped, his lips inches from hers. "Your vocabulary leaves something to be desired. I'll enjoy hearing other words from your lips soon."

As she opened her mouth, to heap further curses on him he was sure, he kissed her. He kissed her until her chest rose and fell beneath him. Only then did he stop for breath.

"You're mine," he whispered.

Looking into the swirling depths of his passion-dilated pupils, Julie saw the inevitability of their union, but she would fight it to the end. No other way was open to her. He was the wrong man for her. He didn't offer her love; only lust.

Her legs shifted and her chest twisted as she tried to get away. "I'm not chattel."

"As good as."

Her complete body jerked in denial.

She had spirit, like a fine mare. The last thing he wanted to do was break her. She'd need her strength to survive Colonsay.

Ian inched down, careful to keep one leg heavily across her thighs. The last thing he needed was for her to geld him with her knee. It might have been a mistake not to have tied her ankles as well, but the idea of binding her completely didn't sit well with him.

Level with her chest, he studied her, noting the sheen of light perspiration that coated her flesh from their struggles. Under his fingertips he could feel the barely perceptible jumping of her muscles as she held herself aloof from his touch.

He smiled, a slow, lazy acknowledgment of how hard it was for her to ignore the sensations created by caresses. "Stop fighting, Sassenach. You know what we do to each other. You know that you want me. We nearly did this before and you liked it—you wanted more. Tonight we're going to complete what we started in London."

Julie stifled a sob. Everything he said was true. From the first, she'd been drawn to him. What he was doing to her this instant was the culmination of that attraction. Her body knew it even as her heart denied it.

His grin widened as he traced the outline of her ribs where they strained against her creamy skin with each breath of air she took. Lightly he flicked his tongue against the ridge of bone, felt as well as heard her sharp intake of breath.

Immensely satisfied, he spread his palm flat, pressing gently, his thumb rubbing circles just below her last rib. He felt an increasing arousal just as he had in the rose garden.

Even here, hundreds of miles from that idyllic setting, she smelled of fragrant, spicy tea roses. She reminded him of a proud yellow rose, its petals curled tightly into a bud, protecting its core from the harsh world. But soon, that tight bud would unfurl as he warmed her; soon heat would spread her petals wide for his most intimate kiss.

Ian swallowed the groan rising in his throat as his shaft swelled and throbbed. He couldn't wait forever. His body wouldn't let him.

He palmed the silken heaviness of her right breast, kneading her swollen flesh. His thumb moved back and forth over the dark nubbin of her nipple, making her chest move rapidly in short, shallow gasps.

He wanted to see passion creep slowly over her features until her eyes glazed with desire and her pupils widened into endless black wells of sensuality. He wanted to see passion in her face, in the depths of her eyes where she couldn't lie to him. They were closed so that she couldn't watch what he was doing to her. It frustrated him.

Leaning down, he took her nipple into his mouth and sucked. The air left her lungs in a whoosh.

He looked back at her countenance. The angles of her cheeks were sharply drawn, the skin over the bones pulled taut. Her eyes were open, staring at the ceiling.

"Look at me, dammit."

She continued to look at the ceiling, refusing to acknowledge what they both knew he was doing to her body.

He bit her nipple. Not hard, but enough to elicit another gasp from her. His tongue laved over the sensitized bud, and his hand cupped her to hold her better for his ministrations.

It wasn't enough. Watching her every expression, he lowered himself until his buttocks met her thighs. His erection stood arrogantly obvious.

Her gaze flicked to him and down. Her brows rose in twin golden peaks. She caught her lush lower lip so that her teeth gleamed in the flickering light and felt the heat rise in her. Not even that time in the garden had she realized just what happened to his body. The part of him that made him a man was full and thrusting where it lay along the slight rise of her belly.

He shifted his weight and his shaft skimmed across her flesh, like satin. Shimmering waves of warmth spread from his caress to every part of her body.

The lids of her eyes lowered, as though weighted down by the heavy thickness of her gold-tipped lashes. It told Ian what she would never admit: she wanted this.

He smiled.

She released her lip so that it formed a soft, pink pillow. He wanted to touch it with his tongue, taste the honey of her mouth.

Unable to resist the temptation, he bent down and touched the ripe fullness gently with his mouth. It was like sinking into eternity. His shaft was pillowed by the rippling softness of her belly as he kissed her. With his teeth, he caught her full lower lip and pulled gently, molding her mouth to his.

Julie twisted under him. "Oh, God, stop this." The words were torn from her, barely above a whisper. Passion shot through Ian at the surrender implicit in her plea. She wanted him in spite of herself.

"When I'm through, Sassenach. When you lay beneath me, your skin warm and slick from our lovemaking."

"That will never happen. It can't." But Julie knew that her body would welcome him.

Her struggles increased. She arched her back so that the silken smoothness of her stomach pressed and rubbed against his hard need. "Sassenach, if you don't stop squirming, I'll have to take you now."

A soft moan came from her parted lips and Ian longed to swallow it with his mouth, to plunge his tongue into her hot depths in unison with his shaft plunging into her hot womanhood. Soon. But first he must pleasure her.

She twisted several more times so that Ian thought he would go crazy denying himself the ecstasy she could give him. Suddenly she subsided, but the damage had been done. He was too aroused.

His back arched and his neck corded as he strove for control. To keep from taking her that instant, was the hardest thing he'd ever done. Spying for England in Paris ghettos had been child's play compared to this effort of will.

"You've undone me, Sassenach. Never has a woman enticed me so that my shaft rules my mind."

Her breath came in small panting gasps. "Do it and

be done. You've made it plain that you mean to debase me with your body., Get it over with."

His head jerked up. How dare she call this debasement! His eyes caught and held hers. In the black depths of her regard he saw arousal and denial. In the drawn angles of her cheeks and jaw he saw hunger and starvation.

"Damn you, Sassenach," he said softly. "Before I'm finished with you, you'll be melting around me, crying out for the passion you're capable of."

So true, she thought, *so true.*

She bucked under him, trying to dislodge him as a wild horse attempts to unseat the man mastering it. "Never," she hissed between gritted teeth.

He laughed.

Enough of playing with her.

Still straddling her thighs, he moved downward so that his buttocks slid along her legs. His hands skimmed the firm flesh of her ribs and hips.

"Feel my fingers on your skin, Sassenach? Now I'm going to massage the little rounded mound of your stomach." He brought his thumbs together across the expanse of her lower abdomen and began to rub circles into her quivering flesh.

Her muscles clenched tightly. It felt so good. Too good.

"It feels good, doesn't it!" He echoed her thoughts. "Next I'm going to take my thumbs lower."

The anticipation caused by his words sent tingles radiating downward, down to the place he would go. Julie bit her lip to stifle the moan rising in her throat. He moved his hands lower so that he could stroke along the golden furred mound. Her skin became moist and hot.

"That's it, Julie. Enjoy this because this is only the beginning."

"Let me go. Please," she whispered.

"No." Determination hardened his resolve. "You're mine now, and I mean to keep you."

Ian realized that her continued request to leave him was making his neck and shoulder muscles tighten until they were like corded rawhide. Still stroking her, he mentally forced himself to relax. She could never escape him, and after tonight, no court in the land would grant her an annulment.

He would prove to her once and for all that she was his. Forever.

Inexorably, he pushed her thighs apart and then knelt between them so that she was open to him, his to delight as he saw fit. She was perfection.

He smiled in anticipation of the pleasure he was about to give her.

When his tongue touched her, her hips shot upward.

"Stop!"

It was an order, rife with unspoken meaning. He smiled as his tongue glided deeper.

"You taste like salty honey," he murmured, holding her immobile while he ran his tongue along her satin folds.

Julie thought she would explode. The things he was doing to her eclipsed anything that had gone before. Never had she thought pleasure this intense was possible.

Ian heard her soft moans above the roaring in his

ears. When he delved deeper, she contracted spontaneously around him. She was as tight and smooth as his tortured dreams had led him to remember. She was ready for him.

He lifted away so that he lay beside her on the bed. Nuzzling her neck with his mouth, he dipped deeply into her.

"Sassenach, don't fight me. Please."

He nibbled on her ear lobe, wanted to nibble on her lips but her head was turned from him.

"Let me give you pleasure, Julie. You want this. Your body is wet for me. You've wanted this since that moment in the garden."

"No," she said softly, knowing she lied.

But her lips were swollen, her eyes smoldering jade jewels, and her body was flushed with desire's heat. He moved deeper, felt her contract around him even as a moan ripped from her.

"Julie," he whispered into the delicate shell of her ear, "Promise not to fight me and I'll release your hands. Let me love you, Julie. Let me do to you what we both want."

She twisted to look at him. He moved within her and her eyes opened briefly before resuming their darkness. Ian reached out with this tongue and traced the fullness of her lip. He dipped into the hollow between her lips, then deeper.

He caught and held her mouth with his own. He ran his tongue along the smooth ridges of her teeth. He sucked her tongue into himself. And all the while his fingers moved over her moist skin.

"Do you want me to release you, Sassenach?"

Her answer was an increased dewing.

He knew she was ready and would no longer fight him. With a groan of frustration, he withdrew from her heated depths. As his hand went to untie her bounds, the scent of musk wafted to his nostrils, intensifying his erection which already strained against the round curve of her hip.

He undid the tie and brought her hands down. Kissing each finger, he massaged her lower arms from wrist to elbow. He licked one of her palms, followed it by a kiss and closed her fingers around it.

He met the question in her eyes with one of his own. When she didn't protest, he took her hands and laid them on his shoulders.

"Open your legs for me," he commanded, helping her to do so by kneeling between her thighs.

The baring of her secrets to him made her skin turn rosy from the line of her beautiful golden hair to the very portals he contemplated. Tenderness for her vulnerability welled up inside Ian. She was his, and he would protect her with his life.

With deft movements, he quickly brought her to the peak of arousal she'd been at before he released her. All the while, her hands lay docilely on the bed where they'd fallen when he settled between her legs. He knew he'd succeeded in bringing her to the peak when her fingers curled into fists. She gave no other indication, not even a moan.

She was as tough and as determined as any Highland lass. But he was determined to have her writhing beneath him.

He doubled his efforts, lying at length between her thighs as he enticed her. "Feel me, Sassenach?"

Her hips began to move in unison with his ministrations and her back arched slightly. Soon, he thought.

Ian repositioned himself so that he was kneeling and her legs were draped over his thighs and around his waist. He continued to stimulate her, watching through narrowed eyes as her eyes opened to gaze at him. Her pupils encompassed the irises. Her lips were full and ripe as a fully open rose.

Angling so that his entry would be smooth, he stroked and rubbed until he felt the quivering of her belly under the palm of his free hand. Only then did he plunge into her, shifting his weight so that he now lay upon her.

Her whimper of pain was swallowed by his mouth. He drove his tongue forward even as he stopped his penetration. She'd been shocked enough.

Not until he succeeded in drawing her tongue into play did he speak. "It won't hurt again, Sassenach. I promise you."

Julie felt him deep inside her. Nothing had prepared her for this total penetration. She was stretched and full, the brief flare of pain gone; replaced by an urge to move. Instinctively, she knew that this was the way to the pleasure his fingers and tongue had only hinted at.

Her eyes drifted open. The passion in them was his undoing.

Covering her with his body, taking her lips with his, he began the undulations that would take them to the pinnacle of earthly bliss. As his hips increased their rhythm, her palms rose to his shoulders and slid to his sides.

Her nails scored him as she strained to pull him

deeper, keep him pressed to her for longer periods. She was so close to experiencing something she hadn't known existed. Every portion of her sensuality longed for that experience. She writhed beneath him, seeking purchase that would satisfy her needs. He felt her straining to reach the explosion he was a whisper away from attaining himself.

His momentum escalated into near violence as sensations wracked his body, burnt his nerve endings. Like tongues of fire, desire flared through him from every place their bodies touched. It raced along his skin, leaving a burning intensity in its wake that only she could extinguish.

He groaned with the effort to hold himself back, then realized that she was whimpering in her own need for completion. Bending down, he kissed her. Her lips opened beneath his and she sucked in his tongue, her cries for completion counterpoint to his moans.

His release moved through him like scorching talons, raking and rendering his flesh raw, and even as he came apart, he felt her joining him, her womb tightening around him until she sucked from him every drop of life he had to give.

It was over too soon.

"Sassenach," he murmured, his sweat-drenched body sliding off of her. "I could make love to you all night." He grinned at his boyish enthusiasm, amazed at his rejuvenation powers; for his shaft was still strong enough to continue pleasuring her.

He nuzzled her neck, one hand cupping her left breast. Her neck tasted lightly of salt, and the satiny sheen coating her skin made his thumb glide easily over the tight nub of her nipple.

Without a word, Julie reached up and removed his hand. She felt no anger—her flesh was too satiated for that, and she knew that her traitorous body would welcome him again and again. The things he'd done to her, made her experience still resonated in her limbs.

But not now. Not yet. First she had to come to terms with the demise of her dream.

Never would she find a union of love. Ian Macfie had seen to that. From now on, her life would be filled with passion, but never love.

Never love . . .

Chapter Seven

Julie retched the last of her dinner over the side of the boat into the choppy gray waters of the Atlantic Ocean. Overhead, thunder clouds rumbled ominously.

A male hand proffered a damp cloth as she tried to right herself. The way her skin tingled and flushed told her without her having to look that the good samaritan was *him*.

"Thank you," she muttered as she shrank away from his touch, averting her eyes. If he disappeared this instant, she wouldn't mourn her widowhood.

She clenched the cold rag in hands that shook. Why did he have to be the man to make her body shiver and her senses sing? Why was she a whore in his arms, wanting his caresses even knowing there was no love behind them?

God, she wished she knew.

He stood up in the boat, making it rock dangerously. Julie grabbed the side with one hand and Pumpkin Cat's basket with the other. As it was, the feline's indignant meow was loud enough to be clearly heard over the crashing of the waves against the prow.

"I know, I know, Pumpkin," Julie crooned, holding the container securely in her lap.

The Scot glanced down at her. "Your cat doesn't seem any fonder of our mode of travel than you."

Julie stared stonily at the insensitive brute, noting, in spite of herself, the way the wind whipped his black hair back from his strongly chiseled face. It emphasized the sweep of dark brows over eyes that matched the turbulent waters in color and depth. His cheeks and jaw were as stark and forbidding as the sea cliffs they approached. This land fitted him.

She only wished that he had never come into her life; never touched her with his fingers that left fire in their wake. She would spend the rest of her days remembering the feel of him in her, and she would curse him every hour for the yearning he'd created in her.

She was ten times a fool. With his one act of seduction, a seduction that she should have been able to resist, he'd taken from her all chance of happiness. Now she was bound to him. No judge or priest would allow her an annulment now. If she screamed force, they would laugh in her face. A man had every right to take his wife against her will.

Her skin burned. He hadn't taken her against her will. Not in the final, ultimate possession. No. She'd begged him. Her shame at her own weakness only served to increase her ire at him.

"Your lordship," Susie said diffidently from where she sat beside Julie, disgusting Julie with the hint of worship she heard in the servant's voice, "will we be traveling by carriage on Colonsay? Seeing as how we left Mr. Stockton's carriage on the mainland."

Ian smiled at the little maid. "Nothing so grand, Susie."

The lurch of the boat hitting bottom ended the questions. He jumped out along with the men who'd done the rowing and the three of them, water up to their knees, pulled the boat onto the beach.

Julie's cheeks reddened as she saw where the waves had wet the Scot's breeches up to his loins. Beneath the once unfashionably loose clothing, she could see the ripple of his thighs as he strained to get the boat onto dry land. The fact that the juxtaposition of wet to dry fabric emphasized the part of his anatomy that he had wielded with such devastating effect less than a week prior only deepened her mortification and sense of ill-usage.

The men talked among themselves as they hauled the boat onto shore, distracting her because she couldn't understand them. The words flowed melodically, but enigmatically. It had to be a different language, but she knew not what. Not that the words they spoke mattered.

What mattered was the patches covering the islanders' clothing and the deeply etched lines in their thin, weather worn faces. They were poor men.

The Scot worked well with them. He didn't shirk any of the hard labor required to pull the boat ashore and they didn't spare him. A team, that's what they resembled. She began to understand a little of the Scot's determination to have her money.

"Welcome to Colonsay," Ian said, ending her musing as he offered her his hand.

121

Julie raised her chin an extra inch and ignored him, determined to get out on her own. Intent on maintaining a chilled distance, she paid no heed to what she was doing. She swung her leg over the side of the boat, and as she did so her dress got caught on the handle of one of the oars, and her skirt pulled her up short. Her foot couldn't find purchase in the shifting ground beneath her, and she lost her balance to sprawl face first into the warm sand. Or she took it to be sand. Never in her life had she actually seen the stuff, only read about it in books.

"Oh!" Her exclamation of surprise got her a mouthful of sand. The sound of ripping cloth and the realization that she'd torn her skirt heaped anger on top of discomfort and indignation. It didn't help that she had to spit the gritty stuff out of her mouth.

Ian Macfie was the first to reach her. He hooked his hands under her arms and lifted her without strain. The movement caused some sand to go down her throat, making her cough.

Chest aching, Julie shook herself free of him, hating the hot pricks of desire caused by even so casual a touch. "Leave me be. Haven't you done enough? I don't need your help. It's your presence that has gotten me into this hell hole."

He stepped abruptly away, hands falling to his side, eyes as inscrutable as the gray rocks rising majestically behind him. "Have it your own way," he replied. Over his shoulder, he yelled, "Jamie, give her ladyship the docile mare. She doesn't need any more excitement for one day."

Julie glared at the man's back as he helped Susie from the boat and then lifted Pumpkin's basket out.

She would die before admitting that she couldn't ride a horse. Joshua Stockton had considered riding to be an expensive hobby of the aristocracy.

Sand settling in the valley between her breasts distracted her. She set about brushing the insidious grains from her dress and wished there was a private place she could go to clean them out. They were even in her hair, as she found when she reached up to smooth a stray wisp back into the chignon.

"Here, milady," a gruff voice spoke from behind her.

Julie whirled around, wondering if the man had seen her fiddling with her bodice. The gleam of amusement in his brown eyes made her think he had.

"Thank you," she murmured.

Taking the reins, she looked at the horse. It seemed tame enough, but how was she going to mount it? As covertly as possible, she looked around to see if anyone else was doing so. The only other horses were hitched to the cart, with the exception of Ian's giant stallion.

And how would she ever carry Pumpkin Cat's cage if she were riding?

She handed the reins back to the wizen little man. "I'm afraid that I will have to ride in the wagon. There is no way I can carry my cat's basket if I'm on this horse." She watched for any tell-tale trace of emotion on the gnarled face that would tell her he knew she couldn't have ridden the mare even if her life depended on it. There was none.

Jamie dipped his head in acknowledgment. "Aye, lassie, that do be hard."

He accepted her statement with no argument. It

was the first time in her life that someone had listened to her and not told her to do something different. She liked him, even though she suspected that he knew her failing very well and she gave him a genuine smile. His smile in return warmed her heart. "So, if you don't mind, Mr . . . ah . . ."

"Jamie."

"Jamie, I shall just get Pumpkin and find a seat on the wagon."

Julie made her way to the boat, her feet slipping backward with every step as the sand made walking more difficult than normal. Pumpkin's basket wasn't where she'd seen the Scot set it.

"Where's my cat?" she asked.

Ian glanced at her. "I've put the basket just behind the wagon seat. It won't slide that way, but from the sounds of it," he paused, a wry grin softening the stern set of his mouth as Pumpkin Cat's plaintive howling rose above the wind and waves, "your cat doesn't appreciate my kindness."

"Of course not. She's never been in a basket before, let alone for days on end."

Concern for her pet drew Julie's brows straight as she rushed to the cart as best she could in the tricky sand. She pulled the basket from where the Scot had wedged it between two trunks, trunks Susie had packed and that had come with the maid in Joshua Stockton's carriage. Julie put the irritating reminder of the past week behind her and opened the basket lid. Pumpkin stuck her head out immediately and cried a heartrending plea for attention. Julie lifted the animal out and cuddled Pumpkin to her breast and crooned softly, all the while stroking the silky length of orange fur on the cat's back.

"What a fraud," Ian stated, drawing near.

His uncomplimentary assessment of Pumpkin added to Julie's already deep resentment of the man. "You are obviously a boor."

He threw back his head and laughed. The sound rang from the surrounding cliffs. "That cat has got you cozened."

He reached forward and with his forefinger, scratched under the cat's chin. Pumpkin, liking the caress, stretched her head out to allow better access.

Disgusted, Julie looked away. Even her cat succumbed to the beastly Scot's touch.

"If you don't mind, milord, I'll put your newest admirer back in her basket." Not waiting for a reply she didn't care to hear, Julie gently lowered Pumpkin back into the wicker prison.

Pumpkin didn't go willingly. She splayed out her legs so that her paws landed on the rim then arched her back, the hair standing on end. After several efforts and numerous scratches on the back of her hand, Julie decided to concede defeat and carry the cat in her lap.

"Let me," Ian Macfie said, reaching past, his hands completely circling the cat's middle.

It wasn't even a fight. Pumpkin submitted to the Scot's authoritative tone and gentle handling and went quietly into the basket.

Julie frowned. What was it about the man that every female he touched, human or animal, submitted to his domination?

Not wanting to examine the phenomenon too

closely, she moved away. Lifting her torn skirt, the sight of which irritated her the more, Julie climbed onto the wagon's straight board of a seat.

"You can't sit there," the Scot said.

She angled around to look at him. "And why not?"

His head jerked in the direction of a rock studded path that led seemingly straight up the side of the cliff. "Use your eyes, woman. The path is too steep to make the mules haul more weight than absolutely necessary."

Chagrined, she looked away from the frosty gray of his eyes. Again he made her feel the fool, and a selfish one at that.

Stiffly, she climbed down, back straight.

"Doon be mindin' the lad," Jamie's brogue came softly from her left. "He be havin' a difficult time o' it." He grinned knowingly as he looked from one to the other.

As much as she liked Jamie, she didn't appreciate his telling remark. It wasn't her fault Ian Macfie's life wasn't peaches and cream. She hadn't asked to be forced into this marriage and abducted to this unwelcoming island.

The wind had risen and the sand was beginning to blow, stinging her eyes. Overhead the storm clouds looked ominously dark. To her left, the road, if it could be called that, looked steep and treacherous, with tufts of green grass growing along its side. What she could see of the cliff top seemed to be densely covered in trees, none of which she recognized.

She sighed heavily and turned to start the trek. Pumpkin Cat's piteous meow stopped her. Tired though she was, she couldn't leave Pumpkin in solitary misery.

Once more she reached for the basket. Strong hands were there first, lifting the feline and her carrier from the wagon.

"You'll be exhausted long before you reach the top. I meant what I said about your not being able to ride." He nodded to the mare who stood docilely by chewing on a clump of marsh grass. "There's still the horse."

Julie searched his countenance for any clue that he was intentionally goading her. She found nothing, only the well defined angles of bone that threw into relief the brooding darkness of his eyes and brows.

In a small voice, willing to give up the fight because of the energy she would need just to walk up the cliff, she said, "I can't ride."

One black brow rose. "Can't ride?" he repeated.

"Do you think this is another attempt on my part to make your life miserable? I said I can't ride, and that's exactly what I meant."

His mouth curved into a sardonic grin. "Initially I thought you were trying to provoke me. Hmm ..." he rubbed his chin with thumb and forefinger, "I never expected it, but it makes sense. You can ride with me."

She made no effort to hide the revulsion his statement caused. "Never."

His grin widened until it was insulting to her in its intensity. "You said that once before."

"Beast," she said, quietly and distinctly, for their ears only.

"Your description of me, Sassenach, leaves much to be desired."

He set Pumpkin's basket on the ground and walked away. Julie stared at his back, willing him to trip and fall for his arrogance. When he didn't, she bent and lifted the cat.

"Mum—pardon, your ladyship," Susie said, materializing out of the growing darkness, "I'll carry it."

Julie smiled. "Thank you, Susie, but I couldn't ask that of you. You're as tired as I am, and Pumpkin is my pet, not yours."

Jamie reined in his sturdy Highland pony next to them. "The wee lassie looks fashed. Here, lass, ride pillion wi' me."

Susie's eyes got round as saucers. "Thank you kindly, sir, but I couldn't."

"Ach. Doona be thinking ye'll burden me pony. 'Tis a right bonny lad he be."

Before Susie could protest further, Jamie grabbed her arm and hauled her up. It was either comply or find herself prone in the sand. Susie, always sensible, leaped up and grabbed Jamie's upper arm, swinging her right leg out and around. She landed with a firm plop.

"Right well doon." There was smug satisfaction in Jamie's voice.

All Highland men must have a need to dominate, Julie decided as she watched Jamie ride away with Susie hanging on securely to his waist. But she wouldn't be so easy to master as Susie. No, she wouldn't be.

Determined to hold her own, Julie picked up Pumpkin's basket and began to climb up the rutted pathway. She'd be damned if she would give the Scot the satisfaction of seeing her flounder.

They were just past the half way mark on the trail to the top, and Julie felt as though the muscles in her legs were on fire. With every upward step she took, pain shot through her legs, making her think that the next step would be her last. Pumpkin prowled her cage, making the already unwieldy basket an instrument of torture as it banged against Julie's leg.

Then the storm broke.

A clap of thunder, a flash of lightning, and the Scot appeared in front of Julie as though conjured up from the raw elements venting their fury all around her. His great black stallion reared up, front legs pawing in the air as though mauling a physical enemy. Julie started backward, losing her footing on the now slippery track.

"Stubborn woman," he spat. Before she realized his intention, he reached down and swooped her up, basket and all. "I'll not have my wife arriving at Colonsay Castle looking as though I've beaten her and driven her through hell."

"I've been to hell already. This is purgatory."

The arm around her waist tightened, bringing her close to his chest, but he said nothing. Pumpkin's carrier was in his other hand.

Straddling the horse in front of Ian, Julie was exposed from ankle to knee in front, further up in back. His thighs and knees pressed against the back of hers, scorching her bare skin. Every time he used his legs to control the stallion, the bunching of sinew and muscle sent tiny pinpricks of sensation marching up her body.

As though to cool her inflamed flesh, the wind-driven rain buffeted then. Above, thunder rumbled and lightning cracked. Even with the Scot's cape covering them like a tent, she was soaked to the bone, and although she detested the man holding her, he was warm. She could feel the rise and fall of his chest against her back and the heat of his body penetrating the layers of clothing between them. There was something solid about him, and, against her will, she found herself feeling safe. Nothing would be able to harm her while the Scot held her. It was an unsettling thought, so she concentrated on the discomforts the journey provided.

Water ran in rivulets down her face and the wind bit into her cheeks. The pungent scent of moisture and sulfur filled her nostrils. But not even the horrendous weather could dampen his effect on her. Heat, insidious as unwelcome smoke, curled in her belly.

His hand, where it wrapped around her waist, was too close to her newly awakened breasts, their cold tips straining against the fabric of her bodice. Her body, that traitorous instrument of passion, longed to have his fingers move up . . . or down; it mattered naught which way.

"Would that you were more like your cat."

"What?" What was he talking about?

"Unlike her mistress," he said, his breath hot against her ear, "Pumpkin settles down when I handle her."

Did he know how his touch affected her? Had he felt the tightening of her nipples or the clenching of her stomach? Surely not.

"You make no sense. You haven't touched Pumpkin."

A chuckle rumbled in his chest, sending vibrations from her back downward.

"You're right, but she knows I would if I could and that I would protect her, so she's stopped pacing in her cage—which makes it a lot easier for me to carry her basket, hold you on Prince, and ride with no hands."

"You make yourself sound a paragon. Which," she paused to blow away water that was dripping from her nose to her mouth, "you most definitely are not."

He laughed aloud, the sound competing with the steady patter of rain. The thunder and lightning were letting up, but the sky was still gray and ominous.

In front of them, the track turned and Julie realized that they were no longer climbing the cliffs. It appeared to her rain-blurred sight that they were traveling through a dense forest, but that too ended.

As she squinted into the shadow rich darkness, she could just detect the outline of a massive building that appeared to be made of stones. Then they were on a road of some sort, possibly a bridge, made of more stone. The horse's hooves rang with each step and the wagon's wheels clanked noisily with each roll.

Halting the horse in what Julie took to be a courtyard, Ian swung gracefully down and set Pumpkin's cage down. He reached for Julie's waist and before she could stop him, he grabbed her and lifted her off.

His hands burnt like hot irons. But when she looked up at his face, framed by wind-whipped strands of wet hair, his eyes were as cold as the stone of his castle.

"Welcome to Colonsay Castle, Viscountess Kiloran."

"And a sorry welcome it is," a booming voice said from the massive oak door that had swung open without either Ian or Julie being aware. Julie started away from the Scot's disturbing embrace.

Framed in the golden light of numerous candles stood a man of above average height. She could tell nothing else since the illumination came from behind him, but his voice had been kindly.

"Hurry up, hurry up lass," the man boomed again. "How like you to keep the lass out in this God-forsaken weather, Ian."

Ian's answer was a laugh. It was apparent that neither man thought ill of the other.

Obeying Ian's push on the small of her back, Julie ran up the stone steps to the entry. Entering the hall was like walking through a curtain of fire and light until she was inside, and the fire and light were now the warm flow of an earthy womb. She felt as though the world had been in some way altered. A shiver ran her spine.

The man whose voice had welcomed her stood before her . . . all six feet of him. He was a bear of a man, with a thatch of red hair sticking out like a broom and blue eyes glowing merrily, although she could easily imagine them flashing fire and brimstone. Bushy russet brows and a falcon's nose dominated the ruddy face in spite of a square jaw and thin lips that were stretched into a wide grin. Across the bridge of his nose and high cheekbones was a smattering of freckles which did nothing to lessen the impact of his looks. His was a countenance of diverse parts, thrown together until they worked.

If this was Ian's sire, there was none of the father in the son. But in his own way, this man was as overwhelming as his son. Even the plaid skirt he wore, made of red and green wool and matched by socks that reached his knees, did nothing to blunt his masculinity. Julie immediately realized it must be the forbidden kilt that the Scots had lost the right to wear when they lost the Battle of Culloden to the English in 1745.

Before she could do more than gape at the sight, Ian was behind her with Pumpkin's basket.

"She's brought a familiar, too, Father."

The big man's voice moderated somewhat and the sparkle fled his blue eyes. "Doona speak of things like that, Ian."

Ian laughed at Julie's bewildered look. "These are the Scottish Highlands and Islands, Sassenach. Here many things you modern Londoners scoff at are still believed in."

Julie felt her eyes widen and knew she was a fool to let their teasing get to her. Surely they didn't believe in witches and familiars.

She was saved having to inquire by the arrival of a woman. A woman as forceful in her presence as the man whose arms she went into. It was she Ian took his looks from.

Tall and statuesque, with a buxomness that hovered on the border of plumpness without going over. Black hair with silver wings at her temples wound around her proudly held head in a crown of braids.

However, while Ian's eyes were either the cold metal of a sword or the unpolished gray of thunder clouds, his mother's eyes were the warm gray of sunlight on pewter, and her full lips were curved into a smile of unconditional acceptance.

"Welcome, daughter," Ian's mother said.

The softly rolled r's surprised Julie. Admittedly, her acquaintance with Highlanders was limited to Ian and Jamie, but she hadn't expected to hear the accent on the tongues of the Earl and Countess of Colonsay.

Yet, burr or not, there was no mistaking the acceptance in the eyes of both her new in-laws as they looked at her. It obliterated the fear of rejection that Julie hadn't consciously known she felt until that moment. The sagging relaxation of shoulders she'd held tight against exclusion told her clearly just how much she had dreaded this moment.

"Father, mother," Ian said, "this is my wife, Julie Stockton. Julie, my parents: Lachlan and Mary Macfie, the Earl and Countess of Colonsay."

Julie curtsied, glad to show respect for these two compelling people.

"Come, come, child," Lady Macfie took Julie's hand and pulled her up, "you're one of the family. No need for that." Her voice was melodically lilting, the hint of accent beguiling to Julie's ears.

"No need for that, family or not," Ian's father stated.

Lady Macfie smiled tenderly at her husband, making no effort to hide the love and adoration she felt for him. Turning back to Julie, she said, "You must be exhausted. I'm sure my scapegrace son drove you unmercifully." She bestowed a warm glance on Ian to counteract the name she'd used, as though anyone could doubt the affection this woman had for her men.

"Thank you, my lady," Julie answered.

"Now, child, you must call me Mary." Her look softened. "I doon imagine mother would come easily to your tongue this soon."

Wistful longing tugged at Julie, but she pushed it aside. It was too much to hope: that here, on this island hundreds of miles from London in a country she'd heard only bad of, that here of all places, she would find the love and acceptance of a mother that had been so long denied her.

"Thank you, Mary."

Lady Macfie nodded her head, an imperceptible movement, that acknowledged Julie's implied reluctance to use the endearment. "Come then, Julie. I will take ye to the room you and Ian will share. I'm sorry to say that it's the same one Ian has always used, rooms being hard to come by in a stone castle that hasna been renovated since it was constructed in the fourteenth century."

Julie searched her tone for condemnation of the living conditions, but found only matter-of-factness.

"Love," Lachlan Macfie protested, "We had glass installed in the windows!"

Lady Macfie laughed up at her husband, for tall as she was, she only reached his shoulder. "Only after I threatened to nurse yer first born in the stables because it was less drafty there, and I did'na want the Macfie's heir taking a chill."

Everyone laughed at that, even Ian, who seemed to enjoy the loving camaraderie his parents displayed so openly. Longing tugged at Julie's vulnerable heart. Their's was the marriage she'd once dreamed of sharing with David.

"Come along, Julie," Mary said.

Julie followed her mother-in-law, determined to become friends with this imposing, yet warm woman. They walked briskly through the remainder of the foyer, which was really a very large, rectangular room. Hung on every available wall were woolen blankets in the same pattern as the earl's skirt. Julie realized that the red and green plaid, shot through with thin stripes of yellow and white, must be the Macfie tartan. Interspersed with the tartans were weapons arranged as ornamentation. They were polished to a high sheen and very dangerous looking. Much like her husband. He had the gloss of civilization, but only barely.

Julie shivered at the blatant display of violence and the insight it provided into the Scot, nearly failing to duck her head when Lady Macfie led her through a stone archway and into a very narrow passageway of stone steps, worn in the middle from hundreds of years of footsteps. They climbed in a spiral pattern, passing by several dark openings.

Just when Julie decided that her legs could take her no higher, they exited. The candle in Mary's hand illuminated stone walls and a three foot long passage that ended in a door which stood from ceiling to floor, large enough for two men to go through abreast.

The iron hinges protested as the door swung slowly open to reveal a room as large as the entry several floors below. Julie felt as though she'd stepped back in time several hundred years.

Wrought iron sconces, each holding several lit candles, dotted the walls and provided a mellow glow. Tartans hung on each wall here, too. A fireplace spanned the length the outside wall, orange flames jumping in its belly. Pulled up to this warmth was a large, plain, yet elegantly formed square table. Beside it were two equally simple but well-formed armchairs.

Julie's gaze traveled further, only to stop at the bed. It was a massive piece of furniture that took up one complete wall. Seemingly built into the room, its straight lines and sturdy design spoke of utility. At the foot was a large clothes press, equally simple, yet beautiful in that simplicity.

In all, it was an imposing room, yet welcoming with its warm yellow light and simple luxuries.

"Ian's bedroom and, now, yours," Ian's mother said.

Julie gulped at the finality of those words.

Chapter Eight

The massive oak door opened, its iron hinges screeching. Julie jerked to a sitting position, dislodging Pumpkin from the spot where she had curled up against Julie's waist. The cat's indignant exclamation echoed off the walls as she arched her back. Kneading the bunched counterpane, the cat circled back into an orange ball, this time on the pillow beside Julie.

"What are you doing here?" she demanded.

Nonchalantly, as though he barged into his own room every day carrying a tray laden with tea pot and accessories, Ian strolled in and set his burden on the large table. "'Tis my room, after all, and my bed in which you're resting." He set the tray down. "My mother sends her concern. She hopes this will help put things to rights."

Julie's stomach rumbled. The smells of freshly baked scones and brewed tea were heavenly. Until now, she hadn't realized how hungry she was. But why did he have to be the bearer?

"Where's Susie?"

"She's in no better shape than you." He flashed her a knowing grin, showing predatory white teeth in the light of the candle that sat on the sturdy table where he'd placed the tray. "Jamie's seeing to her comfort."

"He's too old for her."

"Hah! You tell him that. In Jamie's opinion, a man is never to old as long as he can rise to the occasion."

Julie flushed. "Your crudity is out of place."

He shrugged. "Not between a man and his wife." He slanted her a look from beneath lowered brows.

Ignoring it, Julie rose and went to the table, sitting in the heavy armchair Ian pulled up. There was a crock heaped with clotted cream and another brimming with strawberry preserves.

"Would you care for some tea?" she asked. He might be a boor, but she wasn't going to emulate him.

"Thank you. Three lumps of sugar."

"Three?" She did as he requested. Handing him the cup, she surreptitiously eyed his physique. He didn't carry an ounce of fat on him.

Grinning at her subtle scrutiny, he said, "I work it off."

The challenging gleam in his eyes told her louder than words what he meant by "work," and it was a subject she didn't want to discuss. She took a sip of her own strong, plain tea. It was hot enough to form blisters on her tongue.

She put it down and sat up straight. Awkwardness descended on them like a plague. There had to be something to say while they ate their repast. "Your parents both speak with an accent."

"True."

Exasperation made her motions jerky as she spread preserve on a scone. "Why don't you?"

Leisurely, he helped himself to a scone, mounded it over with strawberry preserve and then doubled its height with clotted cream. "I didn't go to school in Edinburgh."

"Where did you go?" she asked pointedly, watching as he took a big bite out of the confection. "You have berries and cream on your chin." The words slipped out before she consciously thought about them.

His eyes narrowed to sparkling slits that seemed to caress her lips as he wiped his chin. "I went to Eton and then Oxford."

She gulped, feeling the heat rising in her stomach at his blatant perusal. "You lost your accent there? But how?" Either this conversation didn't make sense or he had her so upset that she couldn't concentrate— she didn't know which.

"Aye, I was the only Scot who spoke like he came from the Highlands. All the others had been reared to speak as the English. It behooved me to lose the burr before first term was up."

"Ah," now she understood. "They ostracized you."

His grin was insouciant. "That too."

"But what else could they do?"

"You'd be surprised. But enough of that, it's too depressing. Suffice to say that for the most part I speak like an Englishman."

She'd heard tales of the indignities the aristocracy put up with at school, but they'd been few and vague. Could it be true? "Did they beat you?" she asked, unable to quell her curiosity.

His grin widened. "When they could catch me."

Indignation welled up in her. "How dare they do such a thing!"

He laughed outright. "Oh, they dared quite a bit." He popped the last bite of smothered scone into his mouth and chewed with relish. "But they got little pleasure from it."

Looking at him, his broad shoulders and well-muscled arms and legs, she could easily imagine that the school bullies hadn't enjoyed his reprisals. No, he was a man who held his own, as she knew so well.

Pumpkin Cat took that moment to voice her request with a piteous meow. Julie couldn't help smiling. "All right, I'll pour you a bowl of cream," she murmured.

"That cat lives a life of pampered luxury," Ian said, but his mouth was curved upward.

Seeing that he meant no criticism, Julie's attitude of defense melted. "She's been a good friend to me."

"And you to her," he replied graciously.

Embarrassed by the praise, something she'd heard so little of, Julie rose, clutching her robe tightly around her waist. Better to end this conversation. Besides, she was tired. It had been a long and arduous journey here.

Her gaze darted to the large bed and back to the man resting at his ease, his eyes inscrutable. "Where are you going to sleep?" she asked, though even as she voiced the question, she knew the answer. He'd shared every bed with her on the journey here. It was highly unlikely that he'd stop now. Still, it was worth a try.

His lips parted in a wolfish grin. "I'm going to sleep in *my* bed."

The words, spoken with a knowing gleam in his eyes, made Julie's face heat. What he really meant was, "I'm going to make love to you." And she wanted him to. Anger at her weakness strengthened her legs which threatened to buckle under her.

"You mean you'd force yourself on me again?" Try as she might, instead of sounding cold she sounded breathy.

His gaze rolled over her, taking in her heaving bosom and pink stained cheeks. "I don't think I'll have to do much more than touch you, Sassenach."

Mortification at his accuracy only increased the color in her face. She had to fight him, and physically he would win.

"Don't make a mockery of our marriage, Scot. You and I both know you didn't marry me for love. Leave off this coupling."

One black brow rose. He set the candlestick he'd just picked up back down on the long table.

"Why we married doesn't matter. You're my wife. I want you . . . you want me." He took a step nearer to her. "You're the one who makes a mockery of this by denying your desires."

Dismayed at how easily he'd turned the tables, she said, "Mockery? All you wanted was my money and now you want my body. This is a mockery of everything marriage is supposed to mean."

"Are you talking about love?"

Twisting the ties of her robe, she nodded.

He closed the distance between them and lifted her into his arms. "Poor little Sassenach. I've spoiled your dreams, but give me the chance and I'll give you a new one."

"Filled with lust."

Laying her on the bed he slipped the robe from her shoulders. "That's a start."

"I'm a woman, Scot. A flesh and blood woman with feelings. I matter. I wanted love in my marriage. You took that from me. I *will* have respect."

"Then admit that you want what I have to give you. When you deal honestly with me, then I'll respect your wishes."

"You care nothing for my feelings."

His gaze moved over her, his eyes darkening to the gray of smoke stoked from a deeply burning fire. "You're wrong." He started undoing his shirt, revealing a tangle of hair that spread across his chest and arrowed down the ridged hardness of his belly. "I'm very concerned about how you feel—"

"To your lecherous hands."

He grinned. "You know me well, *wife.*"

A blush, so hot it scorched her skin, rose at his words. It was a double entendre, and she knew it from the way his concentration lingered on the swell of her bosom which no amount of covers seemed able to hide from him.

"Much to my regret."

He laughed, the rich sounds echoing in the high vaulted stone ceiling of the medieval room. "But not to mine."

She bit her tongue.

The pool of light coming from the candle flame on the table, shone like a beam on his lips. His fingers moved smoothly on the tabs of his breeches, mesmerizing Julie.

Her mouth went dry.

He stood, the shirt open and white against the swarthy sheen of his skin, the breeches undone and black against the tantalizing outline of his loins. Sitting down, he worked the unadorned Wellington boots from his feet until his buff-colored stockings revealed well-muscled calves. When he stood up to pull off his shirt, the breeches slid downward with tantalizing slowness.

Julie gasped softly.

The golden glow from the candle played hide and seek with the angles and planes of Ian's body, showing the broadness of shoulder, the leanness of hips. The skin of his chest was burnished bronze, his nipples a darker copper. His waist and ribs were shades of shadow, narrowing to . . .

Ian eased out of the last of his clothing. Julie couldn't make herself look away. He was magnificent. Frightening.

She realized that she hadn't really seen him that first time. She had fought too much and he'd been too determined not to let her escape for this kind of prelude.

Feet planted at shoulder width, his thighs rippled with lean muscle. Further up, the bold desire he made no effort to conceal was highlighted in tones of gold and black. Thrusting proudly up from a bed of gilded ebony, his manliness called to her, beckoning with memories of the final dissolution of resistance that it had worked once before on her.

The breath caught in Julie's throat. Butterflies

swirled in her stomach. Her fingers fretted with the bed covers, smoothing and bunching the finely textured wool plaid.

Her eyes met his. Neither spoke to break the palpable tension in the room.

He moved to the bed, a sleek tomcat, muscles flexing and contracting. He looked down at her. His eyes were deep pools of an emotion she recognized as passion. He wanted her. And to her shame, she wanted him.

Throwing back the cover, Ian revealed her in her thin muslin nightrail. It lay across her body, a gossamer barrier to his perusal.

Julie felt her breasts tighten and swell as his gaze lingered. She shut her eyes to close out the sight of him, standing full and proud, but she couldn't keep from peeping at him, drawn by the unashamed masculinity of his body.

His head lowered and his sight drifted slowly over her stomach and loins like a caress. To her chagrin, Julie moistened in anticipation of the act she told herself she didn't want.

"You're a beautiful woman."

Even as he said the words, his hands came out and his fingers closed over her swollen breasts. His thumbs caressed the dark skin of her nipples, sending jolts of hunger to her womb. She wanted to feel his hands inside her and then that part of him that made him male. She wanted his lovemaking, and it infuriated her.

"Stop it." Her voice was a squeak that tried to be a hiss. "Stop it now." She swatted at his lingering, pleasuring hands.

His lips parted in a wolfish grin. "You don't mean that."

She squeezed her eyes shut. "I do."

Still, he didn't withdraw his touch. "I'll wager anything you like that if I dip into you, I'll find you hot and wet. For me."

The low growl of his voice, another indication of the arousal he wore so arrogantly, made liquid heat run down her spine to pool in her belly. She opened her eyes and stared defiantly at him. Her hands locked around his wrists, and she tried to push him away from her burning skin.

"I won't let you do this to me."

His eyes darkened until they were as black and as thunderous as the sky that had drenched them just hours before. His tongue moved hungrily, suggestively over his mouth.

"You can't stop me."

"I'll hate you forever."

Sardonic amusement harshened his features. "What do I care? As long as you move under me, kindling to the torch I wield, you can loath me and it'll matter naught."

She looked up into his passion-dark eyes, her body betraying her with every touch of his fingers on her skin, and knew that for now she would have to accept his word. For much as she fought it, she wanted him as badly as he wanted her.

Ian gazed down into her passion-sated eyes and knew that she'd enjoyed their loving as much as he. Her limbs lay beneath him, warm and relaxed.

"Tell me you liked it," he demanded, moving off of her but pulling her flush to his side.

Her eyes met his defiantly. "Did I have any choice?"

"Yes, dammit, you did." Releasing her, he rolled over and landed deftly on the floor.

Her mouth tightened as she pulled the covers protectively over her naked flesh. "Not much. In case you hadn't noticed, you're much larger than I."

He glared at her, the sarcasm she laced her words with slashing him like a whip. "In case *you* hadn't noticed, you were moaning and thrashing under me like a bitch in heat."

She gasped, her face going chalk white.

In that instant, Ian knew that if he stayed they would get into a fight from which neither would emerge unscathed. Pivoting on the ball of his foot, the cold of the stone floor penetrating all the way to his gut, he grabbed his robe and stalked out.

Outside the closed door, Ian belted the robe securely as he took deep calming breaths. He wanted her to admit that his lovemaking was something she wanted—that she longed for him as badly as he did her.

He laughed, a harsh sound in the cold stone hall. What could he expect after forcing her to marry him and then seducing her against her will. Oh, her body had been willing, but her spirit had not.

That left him two options. To leave her alone or to seduce her until her body ruled her heart and she melted around him. Given those choices, he knew what his decision would be. She was his.

Almost he turned and went back to her. It was

what he wanted, but he knew she wouldn't welcome him—not now.

No, he shook his head and moved purposefully to the stone stairs. He'd go for a ride. So what if it was past midnight? He knew Colonsay like he knew his own face, every crag and wrinkle a well-traveled path.

Reaching the foyer, he yanked open the front door, the sharp screech of iron hinges grating on his already severely tested nerves. The cold wind hit him full force. Only then did he remember that he wasn't dressed.

His riding clothes were in the bedroom. With her.

"Damnation," he swore furiously into the darkness.

He slammed the door shut. In just that short a time, he was soaked through. The satin of his robe clung in a sodden caress.

He stalked through the entry and into the library. Once it had been a closet, but his grandfather had renovated it, taking the small, dark room and building floor-to-ceiling bookshelves that sat on hinges which allowed them to be rotated around to show yet another set of books. In a small alcove, glassed over, were three empty shelves.

Ian turned away from the sight of the special display case that had once held his jades. His jaw stiffened. What were jades compared to a person's life? Nothing.

He sighed. This wasn't a good homecoming.

Sitting at the small desk where the estate business was attended to, he saw a cream vellum envelope propped against a silver ink well. Find spidery writing addressed it.

It must have been sent before she saw him in Gunter's. What was the Comtesse de Grasse doing, writing him here? One of the cardinal rules of their business was not to involve his family.

Anger flooded him. Anger at *her,* at himself, at the situation he'd made of his life.

He ripped open the envelope and read its contents. A short bark of bitterness escaped him to echo against the stone walls, not softened in here by tartan plaids. She wanted him to come to London. Rumors about Napoleon were rife and the Home Office needed him.

He rose to throw the damn thing into the fire. It deserved no better. If the British Home Office needed him to spy again, then the British Home Office could contact him. He would consider it then.

But there was no fire in this room. He ripped the missive into tiny pieces that could never be put back together again and let them drift slowly into a trash can.

Chills ran his spine as he watched the cream-colored paper float downward. He told himself it was his wet clothing, reminding him of the woman he'd left upstairs.

Julie was his future now, not the Comtesse de Grasse and the British Empire, and Julie would be the death of him. Either through an inflammation of the lungs or frustration. She was a mixture of defiance and sensual warmth, a juxtaposition of traits that he'd never before seen in one woman. She intrigued him.

She was fiercely independent, yet loving to those she cared for, even to a cat. And she was loyal, whether the person she gave that loyalty to deserved it or not, such as Worthington. He'd betrayed her trust and she'd still forgiven him. Ian shook his head in amazement.

All those qualities—every one traits he prized. She was as precious as the jade her eyes reminded him of. It was an unsettling thought, triggering responses and emotions in him that he didn't want to become subject to.

He'd rather think about the physical pleasure she gave him; it was more straightforward in its effect on him. He chuckled, feeling the tightening in his loins.

All he had to do was close his eyes to see her. Bloody hell. He didn't even have to do that.

In his mind's eye he saw her: long hair falling like molten sunlight; long legs going on for eternity . . . to the little bit of heaven he ached to sample.

With short, jerky movements he poured himself a glass of whiskey. It burned all the way down to explode in his stomach. Julie made him explode.

He lifted the decanter to pour another round. No. He slapped the glass down. He wasn't a drinker, and no woman was going to make him one. Cursing her with each breath, he retraced his way up the stairs. When he came to the floor where Julie slept, he paused. It would be very easy to turn into the corridor and enter his bedroom. It would be even easier to get into bed with her and repeat what he'd already finished once. Just the idea made him swell and ache.

He couldn't sate himself. Her jade eyes flashing defiance, her chin upraised to fight the next battle she perceived was coming, her face soft with concern for someone else; she made him want her. No matter how he tried, or how many times he made love to her, he couldn't exorcise the need for her from his soul.

Chapter Nine

Julie woke to Ian's hand on her breast and mind-numbing lethargy that left her pliant to his ministrations. Only after he'd accomplished the task his hand had started, did she fully rouse.

He was right. She was a bitch in heat when he caressed her.

What would David think? Tender, esthetic David, who hadn't even allowed his gaze to fall below her chin. Perhaps she was better off married to a man like the Scot.

Her head ached. She no longer knew what was right for her: Love, or lust. It seemed that was the only choice left to her, and she had lust.

Ian left the bed, making the mattress bounce. The movement called her back to the present situation.

He glanced at her, his cool scrutiny taking in her flushed face and tangled hair. Knowing he should let it be, but unable to do so, Ian said, "Admit you enjoyed that as much as I did."

She turned away from his burning gaze. "You're being repetitive."

"You're being stubborn."

She pulled the sheets around her and stood up, feet spread apart. "And you're not?"

He took in her stance, defiance screaming from every inch of her tense posture. Not only wasn't she broken, she wasn't even tamed. He wanted to shake her until she admitted it. His hands clenched into fists as he resisted the urge.

Instead, he left the room without a word. He didn't trust himself to speak to her. Once again her refusal to admit that she belonged to him had driven him almost to the brink. The fact that he craved her admission of need only infuriated him the more.

Outside, he took great gulping breaths of air, the scent of heather inundating him. On the breeze was the hint of salt water. Clouds scuttled across the aquamarine sky of morning.

He entered the stable and went directly to the stall where Prince was kept. Several deft movements later and the stallion was groomed and saddled.

"Eh, laddie, be ye goin' off wi'out yer bride?"

Ian scowled over his shoulder at Jamie who stood with his hands on hips, mouth curved into a grin at Ian's expense. "Leave off, Jamie. I've not the temperament for it this morning."

Jamie guffawed. "If she's na' interested in yer bed, then mayhap ye should make her."

Ian's scowl deepened. "Leave off, I said. My marriage bed is no concern of yours."

Leading the restless stallion from his stall, Ian swung gracefully into the saddle. A flick of the reins and Prince was off with a powerful contraction of muscle and sinew.

From behind, like the wailing of a harpy, Ian heard Jamie's retort. "'Tis the concern of anyone who has to put up wi' yer sour puss, laddie."

Ian let the horse have its head, as needful of exercise as his mount. When both beast and rider were totally winded, Ian reined in to a walk and pointed the stallion's head in the direction of the peat bog. Like as not, there would be men there digging peat for this winter's fires. He would help. Nothing calmed him like heavy physical exercise. And after almost bedding Julie against her will, exercise was something he needed badly.

Ian jumped from the saddle and left Prince to munch on anything edible he could find. The odor of decaying vegetation permeated the air as Ian strode closer to the working men. Most doffed their hats or pulled their forelock in acknowledgment of him. Ian smiled back and picked up the shovel one worker had set aside while he rested.

Ian dug into the peaty ground with a vengeance. He would labor until the burning in his blood turned from desire to exhaustion. He would toil until his shoulders ached from heavy lifting, not from the need to hold himself back from the lush curves his wife withheld. He would exorcise her spell over him in the only way he would allow: by working until he had no energy to walk, let alone make love.

Damn her. Damn the ache that started in his loins and spread to every inch of his body like a bloody disease.

Sweat rolled down the small of his back, soaking his shirt and making the waistband of his breeches scratch his skin raw. Blisters formed over the calluses on his palms.

He stopped, removed his shirt and threw it on the pile with the other men's. Stretching his sore back, he wiped his arm across his brow, removing the sweat that continued to run into his eyes, making them sting almost as badly as the virulent desire for Julie made his blood burn.

When the cart was full, he joined the others in taking it around to several crofters. They reached the last cottage in the late morning, and Ian sent the others home. This last one was his responsibility.

Julie sat in the cart, holding onto the sides as the shaggy little Highland pony pulled them along the rutted path. Overhead the sun peeked through skittering clouds and a gull reeled and soared to its own music. Heather, its rich purple flower still to bloom, blanketed the rolling moors in the forest green of its leaves. Occasionally, in the distance, she saw the fleeting trail of smoke coming from a solitary house. This was a desolate and lonely land, yet, it brought her a peace and awareness of things beyond her self. She began to understand why Ian was so determined to save it.

"Just over yon hill is the cottar we're visiting."

Mary Macfie's rich tones and barely rolling r's brought Julie's attention back to her traveling companion.

"What is a cottar?" There were so many new words that Julie sometimes wondered if these Scots spoke the same language she did.

Mary smiled. "I forget that you're not from here. A cottar is a tenant. They till the land, raise sheep and cattle." Sadness entered her eyes. "Many of them don't even do that. They're too poor to own animals."

They crested the gentle rise and Julie saw below them, like a white jewel in the midst of a verdant blanket, a long rectangular house. Golden thatch gleamed in the sun. Outside a man labored, carrying something that was only a black mass at this distance, from a wagon to the side of the whitewashed walls. Even though she couldn't make out the details of what he did, Julie recognized who did it. Ian.

Was this where he'd gone after storming out of their chamber? But why?

Pulling up in front of the door, Julie saw that what Ian was transporting looked exactly like black bricks. And it smelled.

He looked wild and free. His hair clung to his forehead in damp tendrils. His shirt was open at the neck and black curls caressed the collar. Perspiration had molded the muslin to his chest, accenting the broadness of his shoulders and revealing the dark aureoles of his nipples. Julie's mouth went dry.

Ian put down his load, wiped his hands on his breeches and came to help. As he lifted his mother, Julie watched the sinewy twining of his forearms, revealed by the rolled-up sleeves of his shirt. Butterflies took flight in her stomach.

Not wanting him to touch her, Julie jumped down on her own. The feel of his hands on her, so intimately, would only increase her own unwilling awareness of his masculinity.

"Thank you," Mary smiled at her son. Reaching up, she smoothed back one clinging look that fell into his eyes.

Julie wished she could have done that. The penchant to touch him came over her in the oddest moments.

"Gran is waiting for you," he said, taking his mother's hand and leading her to the open door.

Julie was given only a searing glance, the curve of his mouth implying an almost mocking regard, and left to follow as she wished. A quick look around showed a cow grazing nearby and several chickens pecking at seed. The black stuff that Ian had been moving was piled against one wall, reaching from ground to roof.

She ducked and entered the cottage. Inside was a dirt floor and the stink of animals. Two stalls lined one side. On her left was an opening. She went through that into a short hall that passed an open room with a butter churn and ended in a larger room. One wall had a fireplace, a pot of what smelled like mutton stew simmering over the coals. A wall hutch took up one side, sturdy earthenware plates and bowls adorning it. Drawn up to the fire was a rocking chair holding an old woman.

To one side of the woman was a spinning wheel, the spindle covered in what Julie took to be gray wool thread. On the floor nearby was a wooden bowl of fluff, raw wool taken directly from the sheep.

Ian's mother sat on a stool at the woman's feet. Ian towered above them, a look of great tenderness softening the arrogant planes of his face. Both he and the women were in profile to Julie, and there was no mistaking the strong line of jaw and proud angle of head the three shared.

Understanding dawned on Julie. This old woman, living in a poor crofter's hut, was Ian's grandmother. Mother to Ian's mother.

Julie nearly collapsed. Never had she expected this. But it helped to explain Ian's obsessive determination to better the life of his crofters.

He squatted down so that his face was level with the two women's and began to speak in the same flowing language that he'd used with the men who'd rowed them here. She imagined it to be Gaelic. Only right now, instead of smiling as he'd done with the islanders, he was frowning, his brows a black bar. Yet, even as she sensed the anger he held in check, she also saw tenderness and protectiveness in the way he touched the old woman's shoulder and worry in the clouding of his eyes.

Her heart ached to have him treat her in just that way. If only he would show her kindness and concern. Instantly aghast at such a wayward thought, she turned away from the scene. The last thing she needed was for Ian Macfie to be nice. She was already more susceptible to him than was wise.

She must have made a noise, for Ian stopped in midstream. She could feel the heat of his scrutiny on her and, reluctantly, she turned to look at him. Heat flared between them, making her mouth go dry. Then he said something more to his grandmother. The old woman turned to look at her.

Nervousness held Julie motionless except for her fingers, which stroked over her muslin skirt. What if Ian's grandmother didn't like her?

The old woman's smile was like sunlight after a storm, lighting her smoky gray eyes to clearest silver. "Welcome," she said.

Standing, Ian came to Julie with his hand out. "I apologize for speaking Gaelic. English is a second language to Gran." There was a trace of irritation still in his tone, but he offered no explanation.

Warmth from Ian's palm seared through Julie's glove even as she wondered about the discussion that had made him angry. But she wouldn't let his ire make her manners poor.

Julie smiled and stepped toward the two women. "Thank you," she answered with a gracious smile.

Mary Macfie drew Julie down beside her on a second stool that had materialized from a dark corner. "Julie, this is my mother, Margaret Fraser. Born and raised in this very cottage. Her babes were born here, and her husband died and is buried here."

The last sentences were pointed, and Julie wondered if it had something to do with the conversation her entrance had interrupted. Still, it was none of her business.

The morning passed too quickly as Ian's gran and mother showed Julie how to card and spin wool. When they finally left, Mary Macfie and Julie in the cart and Ian on Prince, Julie began to worry about the old woman.

"Is she all alone?" she asked Ian.

Ian, using his thighs to control the frisky stallion who tried to canter instead of keeping pace with the plodding pony, gave her a narrowed look. "My grandfather died ten years ago. And Gran should move to higher ground. This place has already

160

flooded once in her lifetime, but Grandfather was here then."

Mary gave her son a depressing look before adding, "Doon worry, Julie—she'll be all right. In spite of Ian's worry, the chances of the burn overflowing its banks and rising to the cottage are slim. And there are people nearby should that happen."

Julie looked around at the surrounding moors. In the distance was a stand of trees, their green tops swaying in the breeze. Between them was an emerald spread, threaded with a sparkling blue stream. The nearby people were quite a distance, to her mind.

"Doesn't she get lonely?"

Ian laughed, a short bark of sound. "Leave it to a city girl to think about loneliness. Sometimes being surrounded by people is more lonely than any other place on earth."

Mary Macfie gave her son a sad look of understanding. Julie intercepted the glance and felt contrite at asking her question. She remembered how Ian had been snubbed in Hyde Park by a man he'd thought his friend. Without further comment, Ian spurred Prince and the two of them sped toward the forest.

"I'm sorry," Julie said quietly. "I didn't mean to hurt him. I just didn't think."

Mary Macfie laid her hand briefly on Julie's before returning it to the reins. "Doon fash yourself, child. Ian has many burdens to carry, but only he can learn to do it gracefully."

"And I'm just another problem." The words were out before Julie realized it. Before now, she had thought that this marriage of convenience was inconvenient only for her.

161

Mary sighed. "Yer not to blame. Ian is man enough to make his own decisions. He didn'a have to marry you. There were other heiresses available, I'm sure. He chose to marry you. However," she smiled, a soft accepting smile, "you have complicated matters. I think yer more lovely and more challenging than he imagined."

Julie looked sharply at her mother-in-law. Mary was smiling tenderly at her, honesty shining in her gray eyes.

"Why couldn't he marry a Scot?" Julie asked, fidgeting with the folds of her shawl she'd put on to ward off the slight chill. "That was a silly question. Pardon me. No one would marry him. He told me that in London."

"No, they wouldna. Not a Scot. And, headstrong that he is, Ian decided that it was his duty to get the monies needed to keep the clan Macfie on Colonsay."

Ian was headstrong, all right, but he was more than that. She'd seen him work beside the common people, and she'd seen him angry from the inability to do what he thought best for his grandmother. Yes, he was headstrong, but she was beginning to realize that he was so much more. He was a complex man and an admirable one; in his own way doing more to help others than David Worthington. It was a sobering thought.

As though reading her mind, Mary continued. "Ian is stubborn as all the Macfies, but he's honorable and he cares about this island and the people who depend on it for an existence. Colonsay isn'a prosperous. The land near the sea is too salty to be farmed, and our crofters have been prolific. There are more mouths to feed today than fifty years ago. Not that that is truly the problem ... but a part. The Macfies lost everything except their titles when they supported Charles Stuart in the 1745 Jacobite uprising." Her eyes took on a faraway look and she allowed the pony to stop and munch on a rare clump of grass. "The Macfie should have married for money."

In a hushed voice, Julie finished the unspoken words. "Instead he married for love."

Mary nodded her head. "Yes. He married a crofter's daughter. Had I been stronger, I wouldn'a have wed him. But when I realized I was heavy with Ian, I couldn'a let my child be born a bastard. That's when I gave into Lachlan's demands that I make our union legal." A soft smile made her beauty shine through the years of age that had put crow's feet at her eyes and brackets around her mouth.

"But you have love," Julie said, envying Ian's mother. "You have something more precious than any gold."

"Aye, we have that in abundance, and for that bounty I thank God every day of my life." She flicked the reins and clicked her tongue at the pony. "But it doesn'a put food on the table of a starving family."

"So Ian sacrificed himself and made a marriage of convenience." Try as she might, Julie couldn't keep the bitterness from her voice. "At least he did it for a good reason. If I must live a loveless life, it will help to know that I'm doing it so that others can survive."

Mary's face was full of sympathy. "Never forget that love can exist anywhere ... and often comes when we least expect it. I certainly never thought that the laird of the island would want me—a crofter's daughter. But he did."

Julie eyed the Highland pony with trepidation. This might be her third lesson, but she was still far from comfortable on a horse. If there was any other means of quick, relatively easy transportation around the island, she would have taken it instead of lessons. But weeks on Colonsay had driven home the fact that it was foot or animal.

Taking a deep breath and squaring her shoulders, Julie entered the stall and began to tack up. She was adjusting the stirrups when a sound made her look over her shoulder.

Ian lounged against the wall, his arms crossed over his chest, emphasizing the breadth of his shoulders. One unruly lock of hair dipped over his right eye. Her fingers itched to push it away.

To banish the weakness, her voice was harsh. "What are you doing here? You're supposed to be supervising the planting."

His grin, a sardonic parting of well-shaped lips, did nothing to ameliorate her dislike of him being present during what had to this date always been an humiliating experience . . . the pony being more in control of their lessons than she.

"Watching. I've hired a factor to supervise the daily running of the land."

A succinct reply and so much like everything he said to her these last days. Julie rose, her exasperation barely contained, and pushed the loose strands of hair from her forehead.

"Well, there's nothing interesting going to happen, so you should be about your other business."

Instead of leaving, he shoved off from the wall. He came several steps closer and checked the saddle girth.

"You did a good job," he acknowledged.

"Thank you."

He angled a noncommittal glance at her as he straightened up from his inspection. "How long has Jamie been teaching you?"

Did she detect anger in the clipped accents? No, it couldn't be. Why should he care if Jamie taught her when he was too busy to do it himself?

"This is my third lesson. Susie and I have both been learning, but Susie didn't finish her work today so Jamie told her to come this evening."

"I see."

She didn't think he did, but it didn't matter. If he would move, she'd take the reins and lead the pony outside. But Ian didn't move, and she didn't want to take the chance of touching him. Whenever that happened, no matter how much of an accident it was, it seemed to inflame him.

Their eyes met, and suddenly, Julie felt as though she were smothering. The small stall seemed suffocatingly tiny. Her breathing felt labored and ineffective.

His gaze moved from her eyes downward. One hand reached out and he ran a finger along her lower lip. Her mouth parted and her breasts swelled against the tight material of her habit. She closed her eyes to shut out the hunger she knew would be in his, hoping to keep him from seeing its twin in hers.

"Lass," Jamie's tenor penetrated the thick morass of desire that was building around Julie and Ian, ". . . 'tis time and past." His footsteps shuffled through the hay, thudding on the packed earth and stopping abruptly. "Ach, and did I be knownin' yer husband was wi' ye I wouldna ha' come."

Julie flushed hotly and rounded on the wiry man, intending to berate him. The flash of wicked mirth in his brown eyes forestalled her. Jamie, the mischief-maker, knew exactly what he was saying.

With an almost gallant flourish, Ian moved away, opening a path for Julie to reach the reins without touching him. Her relief was short lived.

"I'll give you your next lesson." He slanted a challenging look at Jamie. "I've no doubt I'll be a better teacher."

Her hands closed tightly over the leather reins, in-advertently jerking at the bit. The pony snorted and shied.

"I'll also show you how to handle a horse more gently."

"I dinna show her that," Jamie interjected.

"Neither would it have happened," Julie said, indignation squaring her shoulders, "if I hadn't been taken unawares. Until now, I had thought you too busy."

No sooner were the words out than she would have gladly bitten her tongue to stop them. She didn't know what had come over her. Never, never would she have spoken thusly. Not only was Jamie listening avidly to every word exchanged, but she'd vowed to herself never to let Ian know how she longed for his presence at her side in this strange world to which he'd brought her.

"I'm never too busy for my wife. She only thinks I am." His eyes deepened from silver to smoky gray as a satisfied grin creased his lips. His step was almost jaunty as he left.

"There'll be no livin' wi' the lad now," Jamie said in a very put-upon tone. Under his breath he muttered, "Not that that'll be any different from the last months."

Julie heard it all. The inference that she was the cause of the Scot's irascible temper only increased her dissatisfaction with the entire situation.

"Ach, and I've nearly forgot to give ye this." Jamie pulled a much creased paper from his pocket. With exaggerated movements, he tried to smooth the sheet. "'Tis fer ye."

Puzzled, Julie took the offering. Turning it, she realized that it was a letter. In the poor light of the stables, she had to squint to read the address. *Viscount Kiloran, Colonsay Castle, Colonsay.*

"This isn't for me." She handed it back to Jamie, who took it with a look of chagrin that did nothing to hide the curiosity in his eyes. "But you knew that, didn't you?"

He took a step back at the accusation in her words. "Nay, Why should I be givin' ye a letter meant fer yer husband?"

"Why should you indeed, unless you know something I don't."

Before he could move out of her reach, she snatched the letter from his slack grip. But it had been too easy and she knew he'd meant her to get it back. This time she studied the envelope. It was heavy cream vellum and very expensive. The writing was flowing and spidery, done with a fine quill. She raised it to her nose. Her nostrils flared at the heavy scent of patchouli.

Handing the letter back, she asked coldly, "Who is she?" It never entered her mind that Jamie wouldn't know the answer.

"The Comtesse de Grasse."

She hadn't expected the answer, though once the immediate shock was gone and her hands were no longer trembling, she found that she wasn't surprised. It explained the Scot's behavior at Gunter's.

Allowing the reins to fall from her nerveless fingers, she walked off. The riding lesson could wait.

Julie stalked in the front door and smack into pandemonium. Boxes littered the flagstone floor. The Macfie and Mary were circling an embracing couple that turned into Ian and a red-haired nymph. First the comtesse and now this. The rake.

Pumpkin Cat meowed a greeting from her perch on a highly polished cherrywood trunk before jumping gracefully to the ground. Instead of coming directly to Julie, Pumpkin twined herself around Ian's legs, leaving an orange fringe on his dark pantaloons. Julie fumed at this further evidence of her cat's increasing desertion into the Scot's camp.

Did the man mesmerize every female he met? And who was the doxy disengaging herself from his arms?

The woman stepped away, flashing a set of straight

white teeth and a smattering of freckles across high cheekbones. Dancing blue eyes looked from the Scot to Julie.

Even though the newcomer was a good foot shorter than Ian and several inches shorter than Mary Macfie, Julie belatedly recognized her as the sister who was supposed to be in finishing school at Edinburgh. She was the spitting image of the laird of Colonsay.

The young woman stepped toward Julie. Her bright eyes lit with merriment, she said, "I'm Fiona, and you must be Julie." Then she stopped and exclaimed, "No wonder Ian married you. Your eyes are the same color as his precious jades."

Julie felt herself blush, the heat rising from the neckline of her plain dress to the roots of her hair, which was pulled severely back to facilitate the riding she'd planned to do. A quick glance in Ian's direction showed him watching her with inscrutable eyes.

"I'm pleased to meet you, Fiona." She wanted to ask what the young woman had meant about "jade", whatever those were, but didn't dare. Perhaps later.

Not taking the hand Julie held out, Fiona flung her arms around Julie's shoulders and hugged. "I'm so glad to meet you at last." She cast a quick look at her brother. "Ian's written me so much about you that all I know is your Christian name."

The mild sarcasm didn't appear to bother the Scot. An indulgent grin creased his tanned cheeks.

"Children," Mary said complaisantly, obviously used to playing the moderator between the two.

"Now if only Duncan were home," the Macfie boomed.

"I know," Mary said wistfully. "But we mustn't be greedy. 'Tis seldom enough that we have two."

Fiona released Julie and moved into the warm embrace of both parents. Next Ian stepped into the loving circle.

From her spot on the outskirts of the group, Julie watched the affectionate exchange. Her chest constricted painfully. How nice it would be if she were included.

As though hearing her unspoken wish, Ian looked up. His eyes met hers across the expanse separating them.

"Julie," his deep voice said softly, "come join us. You're part of the family."

Mary and The Macfie joined their son's request. Tears Julie refused to shed blurred her vision. She hadn't expected to be asked, and not by her husband. Yet he'd sensed her isolation and offered her inclusion.

She took a hesitant step forward, her heart softening toward him. Perhaps he did care for her.

Fiona turned and added her smile to those of her family. For a split second, Julie thought she detected sadness in the blue depths of her sister-in-law's gaze; then it was gone. Joining the group, Julie decided it had been her imagination.

She'd seen in Fiona's eyes the melancholy that haunted her own heart. Or had until now. Now there was hope.

* * *

Long hours later, the new arrival situated in her old suite and everyone fed and tired, Julie stood in the room she shared with Ian. In her fingers was the letter from Louisa, Comtesse de Grasse. She still hadn't confronted Ian with it. There hadn't been an opportunity. Now she doubted the wisdom of doing so.

It would be so easy to throw the heavy vellum paper into the roaring fire. Only a few seconds, and the words, along with the enticing scent of another woman, would disappear in smoke. So easy.

She turned away from the temptation. Not to destroy the comtesse's letter was harder than Julie would have thought. Particularly now.

Ian had showed her a consideration and kindness she had never expected from him. He had included her in his family. That was precious. It was what she had always dreamed of . . . what had led her to elope with David Worthington.

She feared that whatever was written in this letter would destroy that reawakening dream. But she couldn't destroy the letter, either. It was for Ian, not her. It would be dishonest not to give it to him.

Sighing, she placed the letter on the table, next to a lit candle. Ian would be sure to see it when he came in.

He did.

Picking up the letter, he looked at Julie where she sat by the fire, Pumpkin Cat curled in her lap. "Where did this come from?"

The frown on his face was fierce, and Julie was sure it was directed at her. Immediately, her hackles rose. "Your trusty servant gave it to me by mistake."

He raised one black brow. "Jamie?"

171

She nodded, determined not to let him intimidate her. No matter how much she longed to build on the glimpse of heaven she'd seen earlier in the evening, she wasn't going to grovel.

"Then you can be sure it was no mistake," he stated.

"I know that."

Ian ripped open the sheet and scanned the contents before tossing it into the fire. His face remained impassive except for a tick at his right eye. Without telling her anything, he began to undress.

In a calm, hushed voice, she asked, "Are you going to explain to me?"

Neatly folding his shirt, he looked at her. "There's nothing to tell."

Her hard-won composure disintegrated. Julie jumped to her feet, dumping Pumpkin Cat unceremoniously on the floor. The cat howled her indignation, but Julie was too distraught to pay attention.

"Nothing to tell? A woman writes to you, and from Jamie's attitude has *been* writing you, her scent drenching the paper so it's obviously not business, and you say there's nothing to tell. I saw the way she looked at you in London."

A smile slowly made its way across Ian's features. "You're jealous."

"I'm not."

He took her shoulders in his hands. "Look at me." When she refused, he lifted her chin with a finger. "You're jealous."

She lowered her lids, covering her eyes. She was afraid of what he might see in them. "I'm not, but neither will I stand by and let you carry on with another woman. We may have a marriage of convenience, but it doesn't have to include infidelity." The words tripped from her tongue as she tried desperately to form a reason for her unreasonable refusal to accept his dalliance with another woman.

He laughed out loud, a sound of mirth and satisfaction. "Sassenach, you have great faith in my prowess. A compliment indeed."

Bewildered by his words, she did look at him. Joy lit his eyes, turning them to a fine, clear silver.

"Even with as long a shaft as you seem to think I have, I could not possibly make love to a woman in London when I'm here at Colonsay."

She was tempted to leave it at that, for it was true. But she couldn't. Something she couldn't comprehend drove her on.

"No, but you could very easily go on a business trip that took you to her."

Shaking his head in disbelief at her stubbornness, he pulled her to his chest where he cradled her against his warmth. With one hand, he touched the heavy gold-washed lashes she used to shadow the emotions in her eyes.

"I would never do that to you, Sassenach. A man will lust after many women during his life, but only one will bind him to her forever."

Julie looked into his eyes, searching for the truth of his words. Did they mean more than he said? She didn't know. She had to accept them for what they were: no protestation of love, but acknowledgment of something between them that might—with hope and understanding—become love.

Chapter Ten

Julie swung her leg over the pony's shaggy back and slid to the ground, her knees nearly buckling under her. It had been a harrowing ride, what with her lack of experience and the heavy basket she'd had to balance. But it was done and she wouldn't have not done it, no matter how hard.

Inner thighs throbbing, she walked shakily to the wooden door in the side of the whitewashed cottage. She knocked loudly and waited.

A thin woman answered, her shoulders hunched and her face stark with lines cutting deeply into the skin of her cheeks. But she smiled at Julie and dipped an awkward curtsy.

"Milady?"

"I've brought some things," Julie said, hesitantly holding out the laden basket. She didn't want to offend the family, but she knew they needed the food badly. The woman's husband had been recently drowned in a boating accident.

"Thank 'ee." There were tears glistening in her

worn, blue eyes. "Would ye be havin' time to take a cup a tea?"

Julie smiled. "That would be welcome." She knew that the tea offered was hoarded by the crofters and only used for special occasions because of its expense, but she also knew that to refuse would be to insult the woman.

Stepping inside, the first thing Julie noticed was the smell of porridge. A black pot hung over the central fire; inside it simmered oats and water, the Scottish staple. Ian had told her that poor Scottish youths often went to Edinburgh for college with no food other than a sack of oatmeal. A poor land.

Julie accepted the cup of tea, but was careful not to drink more. It was one thing to accept hospitality, another to abuse it. She also kept her visit short.

On leaving, she lightly touched the woman's workworn hand. "If there's anything you need, please let me know."

The woman nodded, but Julie knew the crofter would never dare to approach her. Still, she'd had to make the offer.

Mounting the pony once more, Julie grimaced at the renewed aching of her inner thighs. It would be a long ride back to Colonsay Castle. She might even walk part of it.

Later that day, at loose strings, with Ian and his father riding the land and the few servants and household chores required by Colonsay Castle being superbly handled by Mary Macfie, Julie wandered through the stone rooms looking for occupation. She would even have polished the silver, but it had all been sold years before to buy grain.

With a sigh of discontent, Julie looked around the foyer, spying the door that led to the library. It was the only room on the bottom floor that she'd yet to explore. There might be a book to help her through the rest of the day until Ian returned.

It was an unsettling thought that thinking of Ian's return perked her up and made her step lighter. But it was so, and she could no longer deny it. Pausing with her hand on the doorhandle, she wondered how long she had felt this way. She thought it might have started when Ian drew her into the warmth and love of his family the day Fiona returned.

Even the Reverend David Worthington was no longer a specter in her marriage bed, not that he had ever been a detriment to her response to Ian's caresses. No longer did she suffer remorse over her avid response to her husband's lovemaking.

Ian's lovemaking. She relished it, though she would cut her tongue out before admitting it to him even when he pestered her for a verbal response.

She smiled tenderly, remembering his persistence just this morning. As usual, he'd insisted on ordering her to say how much she enjoyed his loving. As usual, she had refused. He had too much power over her happiness, a man who'd made no vow of love to her, to give him that final power.

No, she wasn't ready for that final relinquishment. Not yet.

Bent on concentrating on something besides the Scot, Julie pushed open the library door. A soft hiccup greeted her entrance. Surprised, having thought

177

the room empty, she scanned the small area. A blaze of copper beckoned from the top of a wingback chair.

Since Lachlan Macfie was with Ian, it could only be Fiona. Julie's surmise was confirmed when Fiona peered around the side, her blue eyes awash with the tears trailing down her cheeks.

"Fiona." Julie rushed forward, her hands stretched out.

Fiona clutched Julie's fingers. "Julie, I'm sorry to worry you. I . . . I thought I'd be safe from discovery here."

Julie was contrite instantly. "Oh, Fiona, I didn't think anyone was here." Julie squeezed her sister-in-law's fingers and then released them. "I'll leave." The stricken look that came over Fiona stopped her. "That is, unless you'd like someone to talk to."

Fiona's smile wavered, but it was genuine. "Please, Julie. I'd like that."

Sinking to the floor, her skirts protecting her from the cold stones, Julie said, "Then I'd like to listen."

The story tumbled out of Fiona's trembling lips. "I met a young man. I thought he loved me as I love him." She shut her eyes, tears seeping from below her thick red lashes. "I was wrong. He thought that being Lady Fiona Macfie, I was also an heiress. When he found out differently, his allegiance shifted."

She opened her eyes and met Julie's look with a wry twist of her mouth. "I was stupid. I see that now. But it doesn't erase the pain of his desertion, for I truly loved him."

Julie's heart swelled with sympathy. Love hurt. Acting instinctively, she gathered Fiona into her arms

178

as she would a small, suffering child, and for long minutes they stayed that way.

Finally, the sobs wracking Fiona's body subsided and she pushed gently away from Julie. Wiping her eyes with the sleeve of her dress, she smiled. "I needed that. But now I'm going to put it behind me. A Macfie is strong."

Julie returned the grin. "And stubborn."

"That too," Fiona agreed.

Both women burst into peals of mirth, a release from the intense pain of earlier.

Wiping the tears from her eyes, Fiona asked, "But what brought you in here, Julie? Not to hear my sad tale."

Fetching a handkerchief from her skirt pocket, Julie dried her own eyes. "No, I came looking for something to do. I thought I might find a book."

Fiona gave her a considering look. "It's not easy being married to the heir and living in the parent's house. You're betwixt and between, neither mistress nor guest."

Julie nodded. It was an apt assessment, but she didn't want to get into the discussion. It would be disloyal to Mary Macfie who had taken her in and treated her as a cherished daughter.

"True, but I'm resourceful," she answered. She stood and smoothed her skirts, which had creased from sitting on the floor. She looked around the room, trying to decide where to start her book search, when her attention was caught by a small, empty set of shelves. Stepping over to them, she realized that they were closed in glass. "What is this?" she asked.

179

Fiona joined her. "That's where Ian's jade collection used to be."

Julie digested this, seeing the sorrow etched on Fiona's face. "What happened to Ian's collection?"

Fiona forced a smile. "Colonsay is not thriving. Ian sold his valuable jade to raise money, but it didn't last."

Bewildered, Julie asked, "But if you're so poor, how did Ian come by a collection of jade that was worth so much?"

"A gift from a distant cousin who died in the East Indies."

"How long ago did Ian sell it?" She knew it couldn't have been more than several years. When the money ran out he'd started searching for a rich wife.

Fiona confirmed it. "Two years ago, but Colonsay is a bottomless pit."

Julie stared at the empty shelves, absorbing the melancholy loss they symbolized. Ian had forfeited something precious to him in order to save something he valued more highly.

Impulsively, she asked, "How hard would it be to find some of the pieces?"

Fiona's eyes widened, then she appeared to seriously consider the question. "Hard, but possible."

"Let's start." Julie wanted to give back to Ian something he valued. He'd married her to save his beloved island and the people who depended on him. Now she wanted to give him back the jade that he had treasured. It would be her personal gift to him.

* * *

Days later, Julie bent at the waist, a knife in one hand as she struggled to cut the kelp free of the rocks. It was backbreaking work and she'd been at it since noon. But it had to be done. They needed the kelp to burn on the fields to fertilize next year's crops. Ian had tried to hire laborers from neighboring islands, but no one had been willing to come. Not with harvest so near.

Straightening up, she sighed and knuckled the small of her back.

"Are you finally willing to admit that this is no job for a gently reared lady?" Ian's voice said from nearby.

She looked up and saw him throw yet another handful of the slimy, smelly stuff into the wagon. They were lucky to have the vehicle. The crofters, already gone for the day, had carried their kelp in creels, or woven baskets, on their backs. When she'd protested the harshness, Ian had reminded her that there were few horses and wagons and that he'd provided all the Macfie had. They just weren't enough.

Julie vowed to work harder. If the islanders could keep going and with less food than she, then she would be no slouch. She'd stayed with Ian to finish gathering what his grandmother's and the Laird's crops would need.

But he was right about her lack of fitness for the heavy labor—it was pure stubbornness that kept her going. She lifted her arms high above her head and stood on tiptoe trying to pull the kinks out of her spine. Surreptitiously, she looked at Ian from under her lashes.

He'd stopped cutting the kelp and was watching

her, his perusal moving slowly over her. Blushing at his intent regard, she turned her back to him and went to sit on a nearby rock. It jutted into the bay, a stage overlooking the white-capped North Atlantic. Beneath her perch, the waves hit and broke into foaming cream. Gulls reeled and screamed above them. A salty breeze blew in off the ocean, cooling her flushed skin and blowing away the reek of fish.

"Storm's on the way," Ian said.

"How do you know?" she asked, bewildered as usual by his ability to forecast the weather.

He threw another batch of kelp on the wagon then shrugged, setting the muscles in his back rippling. Sweat glistened on the well-delineated ridges. "Don't know. Just always been able to."

"Another family gift," she muttered, wondering if all the Macfies had hidden abilities that couldn't be explained by modern science. Suddenly the breeze seemed too cool.

He gave her a quizzical gaze. "I've also lived on this island all my life, Sassenach. I know the feel when the wind off the coast is bringing in a storm. There's electricity in the air and a bite in the temperature."

It was a reasonable explanation, a comfortable explanation.

As though to confirm his prediction, the wind whipped up, lashing at Julie's face and plastering her skirts to her legs. The sky darkened with slate-bellied clouds as the sun disappeared. She hugged herself, trying to get warm in the sudden chill.

"Julie," Ian's voice rose above the wind, "we need

shelter. It's going to get worse before it gets better, and it's coming in fast."

She turned and saw him fighting against the incoming storm to reach her. She began to clamber off the rock. He was there to catch her waist and lift her down to the shifting sand. With his arm around her shoulders, he half guided, half dragged her to a large fishing boat drawn well up on the beach. It was one of the two he'd bought to start the men fishing for herring during the summer months after the crops were planted and awaiting harvesting.

"Nothing will move this hulk," he said, throwing back the tarp that covered the boat to keep out rain and unwelcome visitors.

Before Julie could lift her skirts to climb inside, Ian picked her up and deposited her safely on the bottom. He followed her in and pulled the tarp back over the boat, tying it down.

The inside was dark and musty, with the scent of salt mingled with aged wood and the distinct odor of fish.

Julie smiled. What else would one smell in a fishing boat? The arousing musk of a man who'd worked hard, especially when that man's arm was circling your waist and your head was resting against his bare shoulder. Ian hadn't put his shirt back on, but left it outside in his haste to get her to shelter.

It was a natural sort of intimacy, and for the first time since her marriage, she felt completely at ease with him. She felt as though the two of them belonged together: in this cramped boat; on the beach cutting kelp for the people of Colonsay; in bed . . .

She rubbed her cheek against him, reveling in the

feel of crisp hairs. "Ian," she murmured, "you'll get cold without your shirt."

He chuckled, a rumble deep in his chest that vibrated through her skin. "There's no chance of that while you're in my arms."

Warmth suffused her, starting deep in the belly and spreading to every part of her body. Proximity to him was more potent than any aphrodisiac. It had been even when she resented him for forcing her into marriage, but with mild surprise she realized that she hadn't resented him or their marriage for some time now. When had it begun to dissipate? She didn't know.

He stroked the soft wave of her hair where it fell loose from the chignon. His lips whispered across her brow. His tongue flicked against the delicate shell of her ear, and his warm breath moved against her skin, lifting the tiny hairs at her nape and sending shivers skating down her spine.

She turned into his caress, wanting this sharing with him as she'd never wanted it before. She didn't pause to think about the emotions flooding her, but deep down she knew that her feelings for this Scot were undergoing a transformation

Rain pelted the tarp, the sharp staccato an echo of her own heartbeat. Wind rocked the boat. Ian's mouth found hers.

A hungry kiss, it spoke of need and denial. He moved over her, teasing and massaging. Her head fell back, supported by his arm. His tongue wet the edges of her lips. It tickled and tingled and made her want to open up to him, and with a sigh of pure pleasure, she did.

Ian plunged in, exulting in her open response to him. He slid his tongue over the rough grooves of her teeth, then the smooth satin of her inner cheeks. A tight, hard knot formed in his gut.

"It's been so long," he murmured, nipping at her full bottom lip.

"Since last night?" Grinning, she took bold action. Her hand brushed across the obvious result of his arousal. "Mmm," she murmured wickedly, "most definitely."

"Minx," he replied, the air leaving his lungs in a whoosh.

Completely satisfied with his response, Julie threaded her fingers through his hair, the damp tendrils clinging to her flesh like silken bonds. He'd allowed it to grow longer here on the island where there were none to dictate fashion. Falling to his shoulders, waving around his square jaw, it became him in a wild, indomitable way that attracted her.

"I have to feel you, Julie," he said.

Still, unable to see her expression in the blackness of the tarp-covered boat, he waited before acting. He didn't want to seduce her against her will. She deserved better than that. He wanted her to respond to him this once with all the passion she possessed.

Sensing his hesitation, Julie smiled a secret smile he couldn't see. His restraint showed respect for her as more than an object that he'd married. Perhaps there was a chance for them. Perhaps he would bring her what she wanted more in life than anything else . . . love.

Please, God, let it be so.

She ran her fingers down his neck, across his

shoulder and along his arm until she reached his hand. She took it in her own small hand and put his palm against her aching breast in reply to his unspoken question.

His touch was a hot brand on her skin.

Lightning flashed through the thick tarp, eerily highlighting the taut angles of Ian's face. Right behind, thunder cracked, vibrating through the wooden hull.

His thumb rubbed across the tight bud of her nipple. The coarse weave of the crofter's blouse that she'd worn to work in separated their flesh, yet added a new dimension to the caress: a rough, untamed quality that increased Julie's response.

She arched her back and pressed the full weight of her bosom into his palm. A soft sigh escaped her lips.

When he drew away, she felt cold and bereft. Bewildered, she asked, "Ian, why are you stopping? I'm not fighting you this time."

He laughed. "No, you aren't, but I don't like the barrier. It's too rough for your skin, and I can't feel the tight puckering of your nipple that I know exists."

Heavy heat suffused her as his nimble fingers undid the strings at the neck of her bodice. He brushed over her skin along the line formed by her chemise.

"I didn't think you had a corset on," he said in a gratified tone.

Delighting in his gossamer touch, she sighed. "How would you know?"

Slipping beneath her chemise, he cupped the orb of her breast. The breath caught in Julie's throat.

"Because, love, you're too well endowed to go without a corset and not show it. Your lovely breasts swayed with each step you took today, and every time you bent over, your blouse fell open, giving me a very tantalizing glimpse."

If it hadn't been too dark for her to see the expression on his face as he said the words, Julie knew she would have blushed a hot red. As it was, in the anonymity of darkness, she found his words strangely erotic.

It was heightened by his teeth catching her lower lip as his fingers simultaneously caught her nipple. Fire flashed from both points to center in her abdomen, tightening her muscles. She wanted him to love her.

Ian felt Julie responding to him. Her breast, a satisfying, smooth mound of flesh in his palm, seemed to swell as her nipple hardened. Her chest rose and fell beneath his fingers. The urge for more sent the blood to his head, causing a roaring in his ears to rival the storm that had sent them seeking shelter.

Slipping the blouse from her shoulders, he caressed her skin, marveling at its smooth texture, as fine as the silk chemise still between them. Even after all these months and all she'd been through, her body was as ripe and as exciting as when he'd first made love to her.

He feathered his lips over her cheek and down the side of her neck, absorbing her small gasps of pleasure. With one arm, he lifted her onto his lap. He bent his head and licked a trail from the finely wrought cords of her neck to the swelling satin of her bosom. One aching stroke and her breast was in his mouth. The texture of silk between their skins was exciting.

He sucked deeply of her hot flesh. Her soft moan made him harden painfully. Soon. Soon she would be his.

Julie wondered if her world was exploding. Her body was.

She twisted in Ian's embrace, trying to get closer and finding the confines of the small boat frustrating and uncomfortable. This wasn't the way it had been on their wedding night or any of the times before when he'd laid her out and made her want him against her will. Now she wanted him . . . and there was no way to accommodate their coupling.

Ian groaned as her derriere rubbed his inflamed loins. If he didn't have her soon, he'd cheat them both of the ultimate pleasure loving brought.

Lifting his head to take a deep, calming breath, he realized that the heavy, pounding rain had stopped. There was no thunder booming in his ears, only the soft patter of what he knew to be an island sprinkle. It was always thus after a storm.

He set Julie on the rough boards of the boat bottom and undid the tarp. Droplets of moisture beaded on his face, but no torrential rain. A soft, iridescent fog swirled over the deserted beach.

He looked down at Julie. Her face was radiant and flushed with desire. She was as ready as he. His chest swelled with an emotion he wouldn't analyze.

Unexpectedly words tumbled from him. "You're all I want," he said, the force of his feeling making the words a vow.

She smiled and lifted her arms to him. "And I, you."

Stooping, he took her face between his hands and

gently, reverently kissed her. "Sassenach, I want to make love to you, but not in here."

She nodded, understanding darkening her jade eyes. "On the beach," she whispered.

He laughed. She'd learned to be as wild and free as his beloved Colonsay. "Yes. On the beach. In the heather. Anywhere we choose."

Her husky laughter melded with his. "In our bed?"

"Even there—but not now. I can't wait that long."

Julie's eyes widened at the rakish cast of his features. A wicked grin crooked his mouth. His eyes were the deep gray of the storm that had just passed. Dark locks of hair fell over his brow, giving him a devilish look that heated her blood. She reached up and pushed the strands back, then stroked the strong bones of his brow and forehead.

When her hands fell away, he murmured, "Touch me again."

She obeyed as he cradled her in his arms and carried her to a secluded spot. She stroked her fingers through his hair, separating and lifting the wet waves that fell to his square jaw. He was so thoroughly masculine. Even the thick pelt of lashes framing his eyes were purely male, and his lips, while fully formed, were chiseled and firm to her touch.

He grinned, biting gently on the finger she'd traced his mouth with. His white teeth gleamed in the fluorescent light of sun dappled mist.

"Perfect," she said.

"You are."

"No," she smiled. "You. You're perfect."

He gazed solemnly at her. "For you."

Silent, she put a finger to his lips. There were no

words she could speak to say what was forming in her heart. Not now. It was too soon and he didn't love her yet. But she had hope.

He sucked the tip of her finger into his mouth, swirling over the sensitive pad with his tongue. Bolts of lightning shot through her.

A small gasp escaped her. "Everything is so intense, so . . ."

He chuckled, a rumble deep in his throat and chest that communicated to her where their bodies met as he held her against him. "So special," he finished for her. "This only happens once in a lifetime, Sassenach."

She nodded, wanting to speak of the love for him that she'd just discovered buried in her heart. But she didn't.

He set her down and disappeared into the damp mist that swirled up from the ground like smoke. It was as though he'd walked into a different world where she could neither see him nor follow him. Cold arrowed down her back.

Then he reappeared from the shrouding fog, indistinct at first, then solidifying as he came closer. Heat returned to her paralyzed limbs.

In his hands was the tarp. He spread it out on the sand where clumps of fairy flax and lady's bedstraw mingled with the sand dunes to provide privacy from anyone coming down the cliffs behind them.

He lifted her onto the tarp and she looked around at their natural boudoir. The soft swish of seagrass mixed with the silken caress of warm rain that had started to gently fall.

"We're well protected from prying eyes, but not the elements," she murmured to him.

"Only madmen and fools would be out in this wet weather," he said, the melodic lift of brogue telling her how completely his emotions were involved.

"Or lovers," she added softly against his lips.

"Aye. Or lovers."

His mouth moved over hers, taking possession with a tenderness she had only begun to see in him. Perhaps it had always been there but she'd been blind to it. She thought it had, but for others more than her. Now it was for her.

Divesting himself of clothing and boots, he stood before her in all his magnificence. Feet apart, he was a conqueror . . . and he was hers.

She rose up onto her knees and ran her hand up his leg, feeling the coarse black hair that helped to make his body so different from hers. She stopped when she reached the outward swell of his buttocks and grinned mischievously up at him.

He looked down at her, his pupils dilated and his lips drawn back. She was teasing him and knew it. She wanted to hear him tell her he could take no more.

Turning her head, she brushed her lips against the skin of his outer thigh. Under her fingers, his muscles became hard knots. She smiled and ran her tongue lightly along his moisture-slicked skin, exploring the mix of warm autumn rain with his personal taste. It was mildy salty and intensely arousing. Before she realized what she was doing, she rubbed the tight buds of her nipples against his legs. Her knees weakened, lowering her so that her mouth slid along the front of his thighs.

A groan wrenched from Ian as the touch of her mouth ignited him beyond anything he'd ever known before. The soft caress of her lips on his legs, so close to his aching shaft, was exquisite torture. If she moved her head to the left only a fraction, her tongue could . . .

He squeezed his eyes shut and clenched his hands to keep from grabbing her shoulders and positioning her where he wanted her. Never again would he force her to do anything she didn't want. Never.

But, damn, it was hard.

Julie sensed that he was tightly drawn, like a bow ready to let fly. She was unsure what to do next. And yet . . . and yet, instinct bade her move to the left, toward the center of his masculinity.

Eyes wide with apprehension . . . anticipation . . . uncertainty . . . she slowly turned. There it was, so close that if she stuck her tongue out she would taste it. Hard and thick, it looked smooth as satin. Was it?

Ian thought he'd go out of his mind when her head turned and her eyes took in the state of his arousal. What if she tasted him? Sweat broke out on his forehead and his heart hammered in his chest.

Fascinated, Julie watched as the light rain fell in droplets from his distended shaft. One drop hung, a tiny prism in the misty light. Hesitantly, in slow motion, her tongue reached for it. With the tip, she caught the water, grazing his flesh.

"God, Julie."

The fervent force of the words took Julie aback.

TO GET YOUR
4 FREE BOOKS
MAIL THE COUPON BELOW.

Heartfire Romance

FREE BOOK CERTIFICATE

GET 4 FREE BOOKS

Yes! I want to subscribe to Zebra's HEARTFIRE HOME SUBSCRIPTION SERVICE. Please send me my 4 FREE books. Then each month I'll receive the four newest Heartfire Romances as soon as they are published to preview Free for ten days. If I decide to keep them I'll pay the special discounted price of just $3.50 each; a total of $14.00. This is a savings of $3.00 off the regular publishers price. There are no shipping, handling or other hidden charges. There is no minimum number of books to buy and I may cancel this subscription at any time. In any case the 4 FREE Books are mine to keep regardless.

NAME

ADDRESS

CITY _____ STATE _____ ZIP

TELEPHONE

SIGNATURE _____ ZH0693

(If under 18 parent or guardian must sign)
Terms and prices subject to change.
Orders subject to acceptance.

GET 4 FREE BOOKS

HEARTFIRE HOME SUBSCRIPTION
SERVICE
120 BRIGHTON ROAD
P.O. BOX 5214
CLIFTON, NEW JERSEY 07015

AFFIX
STAMP
HERE

Against her breast, his legs buckled before he caught himself. Leaning away, Julie looked up at his face.

His eyes were tightly shut, his mouth a bared line of tension, his jaw clenched. Moisture ran in rivulets down the crags of his cheeks but he didn't seem to notice.

Like the sun rising on a perfect morning, she realized what the caress of her tongue had done to him. Exultation rushed through her, bringing with it a sense of complete power. She had something he wanted. Something she could use to do to him what he'd done to her. To take him to the brink of cataclysm and over . . . if she chose.

It was a heady feeling.

Shrugging out of her chemise, she rubbed her bosom against him as she slipped down lower onto her haunches. The muscles in his legs flexed and rippled. When her face was level with his straining loins, she stopped.

Ian's fingers bit into her shoulders.

Deliberately provocative, she inched closer to him. Her tongue flicked out. He flinched. Laughter gurgled up in her. Her mouth opened and closed gently around him.

The air left Ian's lungs in a whoosh. His hips jerked. What she was doing to him was like being dipped into fire.

"Julie," he moaned, his body radiating heat. "You can't do this."

Instead of answering, she began to experiment. Remembering the rhythm he set between them, she began to move in imitation.

"For heaven's sake," he said through clenched teeth, "you're a devil, Sassenach; nay, a witch."

In response, her fingers trailed along the rough skin of his bare legs.

"Enough," he panted, "or there will be none left for you."

She knew he was slipping deeper into the physical abyss of sensual delight. A little more and he'd be hers. Her tongue swirled around the silken head of his shaft.

Ian could take no more. With swift precision, he took her face between his hands. Inserting one finger in the corner of her mouth, he forced her lips apart and quickly extricated his shaft. Just as quickly, he pulled her up and undid the band of her skirt. Several economical motions and she stood before him naked.

Rain drops hit her shoulders, and without her blouse to absorb them, drifted down in tiny streams on either side of her breasts. Ian ran his hands up her ribs, sliding along her moist skin. His touch burned her so that Julie thought for sure that the water would be evaporated.

He lowered her to the tarp and followed her down so that they lay flush to one another. Droplets pearled on her lashes and dewed her flushed skin. Her hair lay around her like floating silken ropes.

He ran his palm down her flanks, puddling the water before him so that it ran in rivulets down the vee formed by the apex of her thighs. Unable to resist that path, his fingers trailed after the moisture.

Julie's heart pounded. Heat consumed her body. Her limbs felt heavy and yet charged with energy. It was the way he always made her feel. She wound her fingers into the heavy hair at his nape and pulled him to her. Their lips met, hers parting to the sweet invasion of his tongue. Her body molded itself to him, the warm rain resting in the valley formed by their fused flesh.

His mouth played with hers, teasing her and then retreating. When she could take no more, her hands stroked down the rigid knots of his shoulders, down the rope of muscle on each side of his spine.

"Ian," she whispered, "take me now. Enter me."

He laughed, an exultant shout of success. "Soon, sweet. Soon."

He smoothed his palm down her chest to cup her breast. Flicking it with his thumb, he brought it to a hard peak.

"Ian," she murmured, arching against him.

"Mmm," he said, bending down to lick the nubbin with his tongue. "What do you want, Julie. Tell me."

She gasped as fire slicked along her nerves. "I . . . have."

He sucked gently, then harder. His teeth nipped her. "No, not exactly. Tell me exactly. Spell it out."

"Devil," she said.

His palm slid down her ribs and over her flanks, then back up to her waist. Silken water rode in front to fall over the soft mound of her belly.

"Tell me, Julie," he commanded.

His hand rode the swell of her stomach, pressing and rubbing in circular motions. Moist warmth that started deep in her womb radiated out to every portion of Julie's body. The heat that he'd started was building to an inferno that threatened to consume her.

She would swear that steam rose from where he touched her flesh.

Her legs fell apart, eager for his penetration. Her hips moved against his loins, pressing and caressing his swollen shaft. Her fingers arrowed to the tip of his manhood.

"This, Ian," she said softly, closing her fingers around him, "I want this. Inside me."

Her bluntness caused the blood to pound painfully in his erection. He tightened to an almost unbearable knot.

"Open further," he commanded.

She did as he said. With unerring precision, he positioned himself at the portal. Unable to wait for him, Julie surged upward, forcing him into her. A cry of delight escaped her as he slid in. She felt whole, completed.

"Oh, love," he groaned, taking her mouth with his. He nibbled at her, interspersing each kiss with words. "This is where you belong. Around me."

His tongue plunged in and his loins pounded forward. Julie lifted to him, opening to his exquisite invasion.

Heat built in her as his motions accelerated. Their bodies met and retreated, the soft slapping blending with the gentle glide of warm rain on their hot flesh. Fire ignited in Julie's womb, exploding outward in waves of flame that engulfed her that burned her to cinders, only to cool and rise again as Ian's thrusts quickened.

In one empowering surge, he took her with him into a hot blaze of release.

Later, as her breathing returned to normal, Julie

opened her eyes. The ground around them was shrouded in mist. She would swear that their desire for one another had made the steam that swirled around them like the atmosphere of another world, another place.

"It's as though we've left earth for a strange new world," she said in wonder. "The fog has surrounded and hidden us as effectively as the stone walls of Colonsay Castle."

Rising on one elbow, he gazed down at her satiated face. Her eyelids were heavily languid and her lips were full and pouty. "As though we've gone to Fairy."

"A whimsical description."

He grinned. "Doon be thinkin' I'm daft. There's a legend aboot this beach. And I'm thinkin' ye should be hearin' it."

She smiled back at him. "Aye, and yer brogue be coming on strong."

"Long ago, there lived a laird of the clan Macfie. On one dark midsummer eve, he came to the shore to see the selkies dance."

"To see the what?" Julie wasn't sure whether the tale was humorous or frightening. So many things about Scotland were unsettling.

"To see the selkies, or seals. People believe that on special nights, the seals come on shore and shed their skins in silky folds to the ground, becoming human-like maidens. Then they dance and sing in the moonlight until the stars set."

It was a strange story to Julie's London-bred ears, and she wasn't sure she liked it. But neither did she want to break this thread of communication that had started between them.

"As I was sayin' before being rudely interrupted," he smiled at her, "a Macfie laird came to the shore looking for a maiden to take to wife. Seal-wives are beautiful and faithful—as long as a mon can hide her seal pelt from her." His eyes twinkled. "For the seal-wife longs to return to the sea no matter how many children she's born her earthbound husband, or how much she loves him. The sea has a siren's call."

"Is this a children's fairy tale?" she asked, hoping to dispel some of the unease caused by the story.

"Ach, 'tis that." He grinned hugely. "Well, this Macfie had many children by his seal-wife, but of course, she found her hidden pelt and returned to the sea. He was heartbroken, but their descendants have always had special powers. A gift from her magical blood."

"And is this to explain your ability to foretell the weather?"

He raised one brow. "Perhaps."

"And is that the end?"

"Aye, and a sad one. To lose one's love is nay a happy thing." He wore a mock-sad expression.

It was a sad tale, indeed, Julie thought. Even though she and Ian had just made love, she felt as though a shadow had passed over them, leaving emptiness in its wake. To dispel her unease, she reached up and traced the line of his upper lip.

He drew back, his mouth puckering. "Doona be takin' advantage of me like that. It tickles."

"If that's taking advantage of you, I shudder to think how you'd describe what you just did to me."

198

A roguish grin showed his teeth. "That was making love, wife."

And she believed him.

Chapter Eleven

Outside, the wind-driven rain beat against the solid stone walls of the castle. Julie huddled deeper into the warmth of the wool Macfie tartan she'd pulled from the bed. It was past midnight and Ian still wasn't there.

Worry was beginning to eat at her, turning her stomach into a slowly churning mass of anxiety. Where was he? The family had eaten dinner hours ago and he'd left shortly after that to go check on the horses.

A sound from the stairway stopped her wondering. She opened the door, the tartan trailing behind her in a train of red and forest green.

"Oh," Fiona gasped, one hand going to her throat. "You surprised me."

Julie looked at Fiona's startled eyes and pale complexion, which accented the flaming highlights of her unbound hair. Ian's sister was beautiful in a wild, untamed way.

"What are you doing up this late?" Julie asked.

Fiona's mouth twisted in a grin. "I might ask the same of you."

Julie sighed. It was a fair retort. "I'm worried about Ian. Why hasn't he returned?"

"Because the storm has turned worse. He's helping the crofters." The finality of the words drained what animation Fiona's features had possessed. "I . . ." She looked away from Julie's study as though making a decision. "I feel as though he or someone I love very much is in danger."

Julie pondered the words and their possible meaning. Stranger things had happened, if she believed any of the tales she had heard over the past months.

"Are you trying to tell me you're fey?"

Fiona's blue eyes flashed defiantly. "Fey . . . a hunch. Call it what you will. It's my blessing and my curse."

Julie gave one nod of understanding, not sure whether she believed her sister-in-law or not. But then, she'd been apprehensive all night herself.

"If you're restless, Fiona, we could get some warm milk. I'm unsettled myself, and we could discuss this."

A clap of thunder roared before Fiona could respond. It was so close Julie could imagine the furniture shaking as the sound reverberated through them, just as her own body was throbbing. Lightning flashed, its jagged edge close enough to the window that the electricity made the hair on her arms raise. Close behind was another boom of thunder. Julie shivered and pulled the tartan closer.

Together she and Fiona descended the stairs to the kitchen level. It was quieter here, being half below the ground in what had originally been the castle's storage area. They got their milk, but before they could begin talking, Susie barreled in, her brown hair sticking out in disarray.

"Oh, milady," she wailed, "Jamie says the storm is washing away the land."

One glance at the distraught servant told Julie things were worse than she'd imagined. Jamie, for all his maneuvering, wasn't a man to exaggerate.

Keeping her voice calm so as not to further agitate Susie, Julie asked, "Where is Jamie now?"

Susie wrung her hands. "In the stables, moving the animals to higher ground."

The stables were on lower ground than the castle, but Julie had never thought they would flood. Unbidden, an image imprinted on her mind: A small white cottage nestled in the fold of two mountains, a small burn running beside it. Only in her picture, the small stream was overflowing its banks, the water rising inexorably to the unprotected home.

"Fiona," Julie breathed in fearful enlightenment. Could her grandmother's danger be what drew Fiona Macfie out of bed this late?

The other woman's blue eyes widened in comprehension. "Gran. I must go to her."

"We both must."

Rushing from the room, Julie said over her shoulder, "Susie, tell Ian where I am when he gets home. We'll need his help."

Long, agonizing minutes later, Julie was scrambling onto the back of her pony. Beside her Fiona was taking up the reins of her mount. The animals were the only way they could get through the morass

the ground was rapidly becoming as the water continued to pour down.

"Ach, lass, this be wrong," Jamie protested, a
slicker hat shading his face from the fretful glare of
a rush light stuck into a holder on the stable wall.
"Ye canna even ride tha' pony proper."

Julie glared at him. "There's no other way. Ian is
gone. You have to move the animals. Lachlan's heart
is bad and the other servants have gone to their fam-
ilies. That leaves the two of us. We're all there is."

"Aye, Jamie," Fiona added her voice. "Julie is
right, and the ponies are the only way. A wagon's
wheels would be stuck before we got out of the
courtyard. Now be done with this. There's no time."

Urging their mounts on, they left Jamie shaking his
head in the stables behind them.

A flare of lightning limned the castle grounds in
stark relief. Seeing the exit, they made their way toward it. The boom of thunder echoed through their
bodies. Water soaked Julie to the skin in spite of the
slicker she wore.

Fiona led the way. Even though Julie had been to
visit Ian's grandmother numerous times, she didn't
think she could find the hut in this weather.

Julie raised her hand in front of her face and all
she could see was a darker outline against the black
night. How Fiona knew where she was going she
didn't know.

The wind roared past her ears and the rain pelted
her back and head. The pony stumbled, throwing
Julie to the side. With wet hands and numb from
cold, she clung automatically to the pony's mane,

gritted her teeth and kept going. Her pony's instinct kept him close to Fiona's.

Time passed without conscious thought. It seemed like days of travel even though Julie knew it was only minutes before they began angling downward. Though she still couldn't see more than a few feet in front of her, she knew they were headed into the valley where Margaret Fraser's cottage lay.

Lightning flickered and flashed, and below them she saw the white-washed cottage. No smoke came from the chimney, and no light warmed the darkened windows.

Please, God, have her be all right. She means so much to Ian.

They had to cross the burn before they could reach the cottage. Always before the stream had barely gone above the pony's fetlocks, but this night the water came up until it touched Julie's ankles, and she shivered with cold.

Fiona was first down and banging on the door by the time Julie had tethered the ponies. There was no sense in giving the animals a chance to flee, though she wouldn't blame them if they tried to get out of these elements.

Julie added her shoulder to Fiona's. Together they lunged against the swollen wood of the door until it gave way, creaking open to reveal inches of water inside that seeped into their boots.

Shouting to be heard above the storm, Julie said, "Isn't it waterproof?"

Fiona laughed, an hysterical sound that sent shivers down Julie's spine. "A thatched roof? Not in weather like this."

"We must find your grandmother." Julie took command, doubting that Fiona could be rational under the circumstances. "Start looking for her while I get us a light to see by."

She found an old oil lamp and grabbed the tinder sitting beside it in a small metal box. She had to crouch under a table to find a spot where moisture didn't drip from the ceiling. After several aborted attempts, the wick caught.

Julie put the glass cover over the flame and shielded the opening with the top with her hand. She held the lamp high.

The bier was a mess of sodden hay and oats. Two sheep and one cow with her calf huddled in the drenched stalls. The water had deadened the smell of manure, but it had increased the musty scent of wet animal hides.

"Julie!" Fiona's frantic shout came from the other end of the rectangular building.

Julie splashed her way across the floor, wondering how long the roof would hold before coming down on top of them. Fiona was in the kitchen room, hunched over a still figure.

"Is she . . ." Julie couldn't say the words.

"She's alive. I think she slipped and fell, hitting her head on the hearth. There's a lump."

Julie wiped a strand of hair back from her face. Water ran in rivulets down her cheeks. "We have to get her out of here. The roof will collapse any time now." Her voice was strangely calm and steady.

Fiona nodded.

Staggering against the sodden weight of her skirts, Julie took the old woman's feet and Fiona took the shoulders. Hunched over like broken laborers they stumbled and sloshed down the narrow hall. Never before had this small dwelling seemed to go on endlessly. Sharp jabs of pain radiated out from the small of Julie's back. Her feet had long since become numb.

Outside at last, they hitched the dead weight of Ian's grandmother over Julie's pony. "Fiona, mount your pony and get her out of here," she said.

"I can't leave you here. I'll ride with Grandmother, I'm smaller than you are."

Julie shook her head no. "That's still too much weight for him. We should have brought an extra mount or taken a horse." She sighed, closing her eyes against the continuing downpour. When she opened them, Fiona had lashed her grandmother's body to the pony.

From inside came the plaintive moo of the cow followed by the frightened bleating of a sheep. Her plan to follow right behind Fiona and the ponies evaporated.

"Go on, Fiona. Before the creek becomes too deep to ford."

Accepting the logic of Julie's directions, Fiona clambered onto her pony. "Keep right behind us, Julie. Hold onto the pony's tail. That will help you through the water."

Again Julie shook her head and shouted to be heard above the punishing rain, "I'm going back after those animals. They're too dumb to leave the only place they know and soon that roof will come down, drowning them or killing them outright." She sighed.

"Julie," Fiona screamed, "you can't. Ian would

never forgive me—I'd never forgive myself if something happened to you. They're only animals."

"They're alive, Fiona. I can't leave them to die." Julie turned determinedly away from Fiona's agonized words. "And Ian will be here soon. I know it. Go!"

Julie turned toward the cottage and never looked back. She plunged through the doorway and headed for the kitchen and the lamp she could see hazily through the dark. Moisture beaded on the walls where her fingers pressed to keep her balance against the drag of her sodden skirts and the push of the deepening water. Droplets plopped on her head.

She grabbed the lantern and hurried back to the bier. Hanging the lamp from a hook on the wall, she pulled at the heifer. When the animal wouldn't move, she switched her attention to its baby. She linked her arms around the calf and pulled, then sobbed in frustration and fear as the infant fought her strength. There was so little time.

Lightning cracked just outside the door, illuminating the entire room in a cold white glare. The huge brown eyes of the heifer looked at her in fear and reproach. Thunder split the air, making the cottage shake and Julie's entire body throb.

Soon. Soon the roof would go. She could feel it in her bones, hear it in the creaking of overloaded beams.

At last the calf moved and followed her. The mother inched forward. Somehow, Julie didn't know how, so desperately intent was she on just functioning, she got the animals out. They huddled around her like pitiful children waiting for guidance.

She'd hoped Ian would be here by now. He wasn't. It was up to her. Julie straightened her back.

Another flash of lightning showed the stream had risen in just the short time since Julie had sent Fiona home. It was now a raging torrent that would be dangerous to ford, but there was no other way. The back of the cottage was built against a crag that Julie knew she couldn't scale.

Tugging on the calf's ear, Julie headed for the water. The current sucked at her skirts. The cow balked as the water swirled around their legs.

"Hellfire!" Her strength was no longer enough to force the animal against its will. She got behind the calf, put her hands on its rump and pushed. "Move, damn you."

The animal started forward, water up to its chest. Soon, Julie knew, it would have to swim. Its mother would have to take them from there; Julie still had the sheep to contend with.

They were even less inclined than the cows. Julie grabbed one by the ear and yanked. With a bleat, the animal jumped in. The other two followed.

The last sheep knocked against Julie. Her foot slipped on the slick mud of the bottom and she fell to her knees. Water swirled around her waist, lapping in icy waves at her chest. The breath froze in her throat as the current caught the folds of her cape, billowing out the material and sending Julie over backwards. The chilling water filled her nostrils and mouth as she tried to scream.

She thrashed and came to the surface, fought to gain a foothold again. In that instant, lightning flashed. With her last desperate attempt to stand, she saw the roof of the hut light up, flames licking skyward. Before the rushing stream that was now more of a river pulled Julie under again, the fire was doused.

Ian saw the stark slash of lightning and knew it came from the glen where gran's cottage nestled. Urgency moved like fire through his blood. He dug his knees into Prince's ribs. The valiant animal's hooves churned the wet ground into mud pockets as horse and rider plunged into the retreating storm. Ahead, Ian could barely make out the outline of something moving in the pale light of dawn.

The outline began to take shape, and Ian saw it was two ponies with riders; one sitting and one lying across the saddle. He urged the stallion onward.

"Julie!" he shouted.

But even as her name left his lips, he knew it wasn't so. The upright figure was too small to be his wife. When the hood fell away to reveal the gleam of red in the pale light he groaned.

"Ian! Ian!" Fiona screamed and waved, pushing her exhausted pony to greater lengths.

Prince slid to a halt in the slick earth, his ears flattened. Ian leaned forward and squinted into the now diminishing rain. He knew that the storm was almost spent, but it didn't help. Not now when someone was hurt and he didn't know where Julie was.

"Ian!" Fiona yelled, her voice cracking. "Ye must go back. Gran's wi' me. Julie stayed to free the animals." The brogue of her heritage broke through her control. "Ach, Ian, I fear for her."

Ian didn't wait for more. Prince reared in response to Ian's knees. Between his thighs, Ian felt the horse's chest expand as they plunged forward.

Rider and mount crested the hill. In the faint dawn light, the glen lay below, a ravaged green sward. Galloping down, heedless of danger to himself or animal, Ian prayed.

Let her be alive. I promise to make it up to her for everything. I'll let her leave. Even that, if only you let her live.

On the periphery of thought, he registered the heifer with her calf and the three sheep. They stood passively munching on a drenched clump of weedy grass.

He scanned the burn, its volume greater than he remembered ever seeing it. This storm had been a bad one.

His attention caught and riveted.

A prone figure floated on the top of the slowing water, its arms twisted around a log jammed against the shore. Waves lapped at its waist while its hands clenched clumps of sod. Wheaten ropes of wet hair streamed around the head and lay mired in the nearby brown earth.

"Julie!"

Her name tore from his numbed lips. Horror like nothing he'd ever experienced before accelerated his heartbeat. Blood pumped through his veins in rushing waves yet he felt frozen.

"Oh, God! Julie!"

He was beside her, gently pulling her from the water's icy embrace. He turned her and cradled her in his lap, rocking back and forth, murmuring her name.

He smoothed back her sodden hair. Her face was as pale as ivory. The delicate blue lines of veins showed clearly on her closed eyelids. Her lips were white as a Highland snow.

But she breathed.

Her chest rose and fell, water gurgling in her lungs. Galvanized into action, Ian laid her prone on the ground and pulled her arms above her head. Straddling her back, he put his palms below her shoulder blades and pressed. It was several times before water trickled from her mouth. Coughs began to wrack her body as more water came out.

"That's my love. That's it, Julie." He crooned to her, willing her to survive, to fight.

Only when the coughing subsided and she lay like a limp doll did he gather her back into his arms. Tenderly he wiped the dirt from her cheeks and pushed her hair back from her forehead.

Her eyelids fluttered open and her lips moved in a smile. "Ian. I knew you'd come."

She spoke so softly he barely heard. Joy filled him. He held her tightly to his heart, willing the heat of his body to penetrate the cold, wet layers of clothing that separated them.

A sigh of contentment whispered out from her pale, pale lips. Ian's chest swelled with all the emotions he couldn't put into words and she was too sick to hear.

Holding her firmly in his arms, he rose and went to Prince. The stallion lifted his head and nickered a question.

"She's all right, boy," Ian answered, setting her

gently on the animal's back. "Everything will be all right. But we have to get her home and get her warm before she catches an inflammation."

Chapter Twelve

"Nooo . . ." The scream broke from Julie's cracked lips. She thrashed in a wet cocoon that squeezed the air from her lungs. She plunged into the abyss, gasping for breath. She was drowning. Icy water dragged at her skirts, pulled at her shroud.

"Julie," a deep, commanding voice penetrated the terror. Warm flesh took her clammy hands, sending reassurance flowing through her chilled body to her heart. "Julie, love, ye be fine. I'm here."

A cool cloth eased some of the fire in her face. A touch like that of ghostly fingers caressed her hot cheek. Contentment, security, claimed her. Julie tried to smile at Ian, tried to open her eyes. Nothing.

Nothing . . . into nothing . . . into the abyss again. Julie spiraled downward, her mouth open but no sound came out. Ropes held her captive. She fought them.

"Shh . . . , love." The same warm voice reassured her. Sanity began to return, the fear of the unknown depths receded. She knew that Ian wouldn't let anything happen to her.

215

The next time the nightmare came, she held it at bay herself. In her hand shone a bright star, its light beating back the darkness of fear . . . of death.

She took a great gulp of air. Her eyelids felt as though they had been sewn shut, but she forced them open. But even when the flickering candlelight burned to her very brain, she still couldn't see clearly.

Something was horribly wrong. The fear that had dogged her dreams crept along the edges of her mind. Ian appeared to be sitting beside the bed—where she seemed to be laying—and there were tears in his eyes. Was this part of her night terrors?

She tried to rub her eyes, but her arms and hands were bound by something soft yet unyielding. She blinked again.

Ian still sat beside her, his eyes moist. The expression on his face was as though he'd lost the most precious thing in his life.

Memory flooded back. The storm. The raging river. Being dragged under.

Had Ian's grandmother died? Was that why he cried? Oh, Lord, had she?

The urge to comfort him overwhelmed her. "Ian." She tried to say his name, but it came out an unrecognizable croak.

"Julie." He bounded up, his face transformed by joy. "God, how ye've fashed me."

Agitation made her chest rise and fall in painful labors. She seemed unable to get enough air. She forced the worry aside. Ian needed her.

"Is your grandmother all right? Did Fiona get her to safety?"

"Aye."

Hearing the lilting brogue, Julie knew just how worried he'd been. She just didn't understand why. If everyone was well, why was he upset? She tried again to free her hands from what she now realized were heavy covers.

Her brows puckered in irritation at her own helplessness. "Ian, I can't seem to get untangled." Even to her own ears she sounded petulant, but she couldn't help it. She felt trapped. She pushed the apprehension away and concentrated on him and the agony he must be feeling. "Ian, why were you crying if everyone is all right?" She continued to fight the blankets that seemed to lie like massive stones on her chest.

He smoothed the covers over her fluttering hands and then pulled them back so that she was free. Solemnly he watched her. "I thought I'd lost you."

She blinked, trying to assimilate the meaning of his confusing words. "I don't . . . I'm right here. Why would you cry over me?"

A smile softened the harsh lines of his cheeks. "Ye've been verra sick. An inflammation of the lungs. I . . . we thought you would die."

Julie gulped and closed her weary eyelids. "You would have had my money without the burden of me for wife." She whispered, more to herself than to him. But he heard.

"Damnation!" The oath catapulted from him. He surged up, dropping her hands as though they were peat coals. Striding across the room, he reached the massive stone fireplace, turned and paced back to the bed.

He clenched his hands. "I thought you were dying,

217

Julie. I thought I'd lost you." He leaned over the bed and took her shoulders in his hands. "I thought I'd lost you and I discovered that I loved you."

The crags in his jaw and cheeks seemed deeper than she remembered. His eyes were a dark gray, darker than the storm that was her last memory. She longed to believe him.

Wonder filled her voice. "You were crying for me? You love me? Me?"

He shook with bitter laughter, shaking her through the grip he still retained on her shoulders. "You, Julie. I've loved you from the moment I saw you in your father's library." His mouth twisted in a self-mocking smile. "I was just too stubborn and too stupid to realize that the blood flowing hot in my veins was from love, and not lust alone."

He released her and turned his back on her. Running shaky fingers through his black hair, he pivoted around to face her again. "Can you forgive me, Julie? For forcing you into this marriage. For making love to you against your will? Can you ever forgive me?" His eyes were a black, agonized window on his soul's misery. "I'd do anything to recall what I've done to you. When I thought I'd lost you I realized that nothing else mattered. Not Colonsay, not the Macfie clan. Nothing."

She didn't need to see the moisture glistening in his eyes or the pallor of his swarthy complexion to know that he spoke from the heart. Still, love had never been hers and it was difficult to imagine it being hers now. Her instinct was to deny what he said. The pain of believing only to realize later that it wasn't so would be more than she could bear.

Pleating the damp sheets between trembling fingers, she said softly, "You don't have to say those things, Ian. I know you're grateful about your grandmother, but I didn't save her. Your sister did."

He was on the bed beside her before she could move away. His thigh scorched hers even through the covers and her gown. He grabbed her hands in his, holding until she murmured in discomfort. He released her immediately.

"I didn't mean to hurt you, Julie." His eyes searched her face, lingering on her cracked lips and heavy eyelids. "You're still not recovered. I didn't mean to tell you. Not yet. But I couldn't help it."

She gazed at him, wondering why he continued to persist in offering her paradise. "Please, Ian, don't."

He turned to look at the peat fire burning brightly across the room. He swallowed and his Adam's apple moved in heavy response. "I can understand if you don't want my love, Julie. God knows I never did anything to make you want it."

The suffering she sensed in him was too much. Reaching out, she tentatively touched his arm. Like a flash his gaze was back on her.

"Don't berate yourself. You did what you thought necessary." She smiled, a bare movement of parched lips. "If you hadn't taken me that first night, I very likely would have tried to run away again."

Taking her nervously stroking fingers in his warm grasp, he lifted them to his lips. Careful not to miss one, he kissed the tip of each finger before holding them securely.

"Then you'll give me a chance to start over? To prove to you that our marriage can be one of love?"

Again foreboding nagged at her, lurking in the dark shadows of the happiness that was beginning to creep over her. He was offering her everything she'd always dreamed of, and yet she couldn't trust it. "I . . . I don't know, Ian."

He took a deep breath. "Then I give you your freedom. If you can't love me or give me the chance to make you love me, then I give you the opportunity to find the love you want with another man."

Ian watched her, noting the paleness of her face and the astonishment that widened her eyes. Would she believe him? Would she accept his apology? But even more importantly, would she leave him? He had to give her that choice, no matter if it was the hardest thing he'd ever done in his life. The love he felt for her wouldn't let him do anything else. But, God, if she left him, he didn't think he could bear it.

The tightness of his voice and the bleakness in his black eyes told her how difficult it was for him to offer her that gift. The most precious gift one person can give another.

With this gift, he was giving her the one thing she wanted most in life. He was giving her love.

She bowed her head and the tears began to fall; at first like dew on her cheeks then like a cleansing rain. When she lifted her face to his, she was radiant.

"I'd like to try, Ian."

Ian tried like hell not to take advantage of Julie's recovering weakness. But it was hard. Damned hard.

Even sick, her skin so pale it was like moonlight on a Highland loch, he wanted her. Her eyes were sunken, their lustrous jade color a shade lighter, and her voluptuous lashes exotic Japanese fans. She made his blood heat until it swelled his nether region to painful intensity.

But he was no ravening beast: no Nessie out of Loch Lomond waiting to devour innocents who crossed his path. Yet, when the rosy tip of her nipple peaked through the fine muslin of her nightrail, he was nearly undone.

He groaned and turned away from temptation. He moved to the fireplace, ostensibly to stoke the slowly burning peat, but really to adjust his breeches.

"Ian," Julie's soft voice came from behind, sending gooseflesh up his arms, "are you all right?"

His groan deepened. This wasn't the first time this situation had occurred since she'd regained consciousness. He had a horrible suspicion that it wouldn't be the last, either.

"I'm fine, Sassenach," he said, poking viciously at the innocent coals.

When he turned and strode back to her side, Julie noticed that he walked with a decidedly ungraceful gait. Puzzled, she asked, "Ian, why are you listing?"

He grimaced. "Observant," he remarked dryly.

Julie understood that there was something she was missing. Her gaze swept over him, from broad shoulders in a loose fitting lawn shirt open at the neck to tighter than normal knit breeches. He was aroused. With that realization came a gratified blush.

He chuckled as the delicate pink of comprehension moved from her forehead to her rapidly rising bosom. "You're as embarrassed by my lack of consideration as I am chagrined by it."

Sitting beside her on the bed, he took both her hands and raised them to his lips. He dropped butterfly flicks of his tongue on each fingertip.

Anticipation sent tendrils of warmth sparking along Julie's arms. Delicious memories of their lovemaking made her limbs lethargic.

The dilation of her pupils told Ian clearer than words that Julie was responding to him. It would be so easy to continue, and it would feel so good after weeks of denial.

He squeezed his eyes shut on the sight of her interest. His voice turned husky. "Don't look at me like that, love. You're still too sick for where this will lead."

She twinkled up at him. "Then why have you started us down this path?"

He shook his head. "It wasn't my doing." He released one of her hands and with his forefinger lightly flicked the pink bud of her nipple that still insisted on peeping out from between the gossamer folds of her gown. "This rogue has been tempting me with promises of ecstasy."

She laughed in delight. She felt a delicious abandon, a sensation she wasn't accustomed to but was finding most interesting. She even felt less tired than moments earlier.

"Then perhaps you should gratify it," she taunted him.

His attention focused with painful intensity on her. His voice fell to a throbbing hush. "Are you truly inviting me to make love to you?"

"Yes."

The word caressed his cheek like a fairy's hand. It

was a promise of everything he wanted in life. She wanted him and was doing nothing to hide it. It took all his will power and years of training as a spy to be able to refuse the promise in her eyes.

"I can't, love. Not yet."

"Why not?" It was a plaintive cry from the heart. Julie had begun to trust that he truly was beginning to love her, that they could find love in this marriage.

Smoothing wispy tendrils of gold from her face, Ian traced the outline of one brow. "Not because I don't yearn to."

"Then—"

"Shh . . ." He put a finger to her lips, stopping her protest. "Because you're not well yet, and I love you too much to risk causing a relapse by my baser urgings."

Her doubts evaporated as quickly as they'd surfaced. He was trying so hard to make up to her for the past.

He leaned over, his mouth moving over hers, and sucked gently at her full lower lip. It was a tender promise for the future.

The future was indeed rosy, Julie decided as the cart bounced to the rhythm of every pothole in the path. Sunlight dappled through the stand of oak, yew and birch they were traveling through. The fresh scent of ocean air, never far from any location on Colonsay, invigorated her.

"When will we arrive?" she asked Ian. "I want to see your grandmother's new croft."

He grinned down at her and flicked the reins, urging the shaggy little Highland pony to a quicker trot. "I was afraid this trip would be too much for you."

"Nonsense," she retorted, on her mettle. "I'm perfectly recovered and would be even stronger if you didn't coddle me so."

He smiled tenderly at her and took one hand off the reins long enough to tuck a stray strand of hair behind her ear. "I want to coddle you." He grimaced. "I want to do so much more—and the more I pamper you the sooner you'll recover and then the sooner I can have my lecherous ways with you."

Her laughter rivaled the trill of a sparrow. Ian slanted her an approving glance. She had gained back some of the weight her illness had cost, and she had a flattering glow in her cheeks.

He was just about to kiss her when they crested the hill. On the edge of a copse, the sun shining on its whitewashed walls, stood his gran's new croft. He grinned ruefully to himself. One didn't make love to a woman, even his wife, within sight of his grandmother. Neither did a man enter his gran's house with a bulge in his skintight breeches.

Pulling up in front of the house, Ian jumped down and went to the well. Confused, Julie watched as he drew up water she knew was like ice and dunked his head into it. He came up sputtering and shaking his head like a great beast.

When he came to fetch her down, his grin was deprecating. He shrugged and lifted his hands palm up. "I couldn't go into my gran's house in the state I was in."

A peal of laughter escaped Julie. "You unrepentant

224

rogue. That will teach you not to make love to me when I offer."

He shook his head, spattering her with drops of ice water. She gasped and tried to slide across the wagon's seat. His arms shot out and grabbed her, pulling her until their chests met in a hot fusing of desire.

Her breathing quickened and her pulse pounded painfully at the base of her throat. Reaching up, she tangled her fingers in his wet hair and pulled his head down to hers.

"Ahem!"

They flew apart. Julie almost tumbled over the opposite side of the wagon, but Ian's hands caught and held her.

Giving Julie a quick look, he turned his attention to the doorway. "Gran, you startled us."

Margaret Fraser chuckled. "Aye, so I see. But coom in, I've tea and oat cakes."

Julie, her face flaming, allowed Ian to help her down. Using his arm for support, she made her way to the new cottage. While she could walk alone, it felt good to have his strength under her fingertips.

Right by the door, Julie's attention was held by a tree, its green leaves and orange berries a striking contrast. "How lucky to have this lovely tree standing right where you built your cottage."

Behind her, Ian coughed. In front of her, Margaret smiled knowingly.

" 'Twas no luck, that," the old woman said. "I made Ian plant it. Full growed."

Julie turned a curious look on her husband. He met her appraisal openly, but she sensed a reluctance in him. She turned back to Margaret for her answer.

"I'm afraid I don't understand."

In her careful English, Margaret answered, " 'Tis a rowan tree."

When Ian's grandmother paused as though expecting a reply, Julie, at a loss for anything more, said, "It's beautiful."

Margaret chuckled. "Ye dinna ken. 'Tis protection against witches and evil. No Highlander would be wi'out."

The old woman was having a joke, Julie thought, but the steady perusal of Margaret's gray eyes and the firm line of the woman's age wrinkled mouth denied it. Julie resisted the urge to rub the gooseflesh rising on her arms. Instead she ducked and entered the house. Inside, the cottage was identical to the one that had been ruined by the storm. Down the hall that ran the entire length of the building Julie could see the swinging tail of the cow and hear the swish of hooves in hay. In the main room where they stood was a central fire, a cabinet with dishes, a box bed and two wooden chairs. A stool stood near the spinning wheel.

She smiled. Ian's grandmother was a stubborn woman. Ian was lucky he'd gotten her to change location. It was obvious he hadn't been able to get her to allow him to provide any of life's luxuries.

The old woman poured scalding water from a pan directly into cups with tea and added a plain plate with a flat oat cake. She put a dollop of fresh butter and preserves on the side.

The tea was strong and the cake textured, much like the woman serving them. Julie couldn't help but admire her husband's grandmother. Margaret Fraser did what she wanted.

Julie let the musical flow of the conversation soothe her. Even though it was a fortnight since the storm, she was still not fully recovered. A tickle started and before she realized it, a fit of coughing took her.

Ian hastily poured her a fresh cup of tea and urged it on her. Julie tried to drink, knowing the hot tea would ease her throat, but it was several minutes later before she could finally force the coughing to stop.

Ian gently wiped the tears from her eyes before giving her his handkerchief. "Julie, Gran apologizes for monopolizing the conversation in Gaelic, but it's easier for her to speak."

Margaret nodded her grizzled head. "Aye. I doo my thinking in Gaelic. But I want to thank ye, lass, for saving my animals. Ian tells me 'twas ye who thought of me."

Julie sat up and brushed the oat crumbs from her lap. "Thank you, ma'am, but it was Fiona who 'saw' the danger. I only figured out that it must apply to you."

"Ah, Fiona's gift," the old woman sighed.

Ian shot Julie a look from under his brows. Did she believe in it? To change the focus, he added, "And she saved your life, Gran."

The old woman shook her head, a strange smile on her lips. "Nay. I dinna hear the bark of the *Cu-sith*. 'Twas not my time."

Ian groaned and looked at the ceiling, willing his grandmother to stop this baptism of fire. Strange things happened in the Highlands—he knew that—

but he didn't want to scare Julie. She needed time to adjust from her London ways and to absorb the ambiance of the land and people here.

Julie watched Ian's reaction to his grandmother's words. "I'm afraid I don't understand," she said.

Margaret laughed, and this time Julie found the sound very like a cackle. It made the hair on her nape stand up.

"The *Cu-sith* be a fairy dog. To hear its bark is to hear yer own death." Her shrewd gray eyes, wrinkled into deep folds, watched Julie without wavering.

Julie smoothed her palms down the length of her skirt several times until finally resting her hands on her knees. "How interesting," she replied.

Ian, seeing the nervous gesture he was learning to anticipate from Julie when she was agitated, rose to his feet. He kissed his grandmother's weathered cheek. With a hand to help Julie up, he said, "It's late, and Julie isn't fully recovered yet from her illness."

Shortly, they were in the wagon, bumping over the land in the direction of Colonsay Castle. Julie pulled her wool shawl more tightly around her shoulders and gazed into the distance. Purple heather covered the moors while pink and lavender bathed the horizon as the sun set.

"This land is strange," she finally said.

"Aye, it is."

"Do you believe everything your grandmother was saying?" Her curiosity was too great for her not to ask the question. Ever since the storm and Fiona's ability to foresee danger, Julie had been finding herself starting at the merest sounds.

228

Ian cleared his throat. "I think that there are many things which we can't explain."

She smiled in spite of her unease. "Then you believe that what your grandmother said is possible."

He shrugged, accidentally pulling on the reins and causing the pony to stumble. The wagon lurched and Julie had to grab the side of the seat for support.

Cursing under his breath, Ian reached for her. "My bloody clumsiness. If anything had happened to you."

Julie gazed up at him from the protection and security of his arms. Even now, his warmth engulfing her, she found it hard to believe that the love she'd always sought was hers. It made her ache with fear for life's frailty.

Wrapping her arms around his neck, she pulled his mouth down to hers. Their lips met, tongues mingling, flesh clinging. Hunger such as she'd never known swamped her.

She wanted everything he offered. She wanted to feel him in every part of her, body and soul.

The kiss seared into her heart.

When Ian finally broke away, Julie took a great breath of air. The cold dampness dragged into her lungs; and a coughing fit doubled her over.

"Love," Ian said, encircling her with support as she coughed in dry heaves. "I shouldn't have let you seduce me. You're not well enough for lovemaking, let alone here on the moor in the cold evening air."

Julie's eyes watered and perspiration beaded her brow. As much as she wanted to lay down in the fragrant purple heather and welcome her love into her body, she knew he was right.

"Mayhap, you have failed to heat my blood

enough." It was a weak attempt at raillery, but worked.

He laughed and put his handkerchief to her nose. "Blow."

"Give me the handkerchief. I'm able to blow my own nose," she retorted.

"Stubborn Sassenach," he murmured, giving over. "I only want to care for you." On a pragmatic note, he added, "But staying here isn't helping."

With a flick of the reins, he put the pony in motion again.

Julie feasted her eyes on his profile as they moved into the sunset. The breeze, redolent of heather and salt, lifted his long hair off his forehead, accenting his high brow and nose. He wore no coat and his shirt was open at the neck, revealing crisp black hairs that she knew angled down to a flat belly. The breath caught in her throat.

He was physically magnificent, and his heart was generous. Her own heart swelled with love and longing. He was everything she'd ever dreamed of, and to think that once she'd thought she hated him.

She'd been a fool. God had given her a chance at true happiness, and she would take it.

Chapter Thirteen

Ian's gaze swept the crowded schoolhouse. Every crofter on Colonsay was here to listen to the new factor. Archibald Paterson was a good man, educated at Edinburgh and dedicated to improving the crofter's yield, having been a crofter himself before Lachlan Macfie sent him to school.

A slow smile transformed the rock hardness of Ian's jaw and released the tension in his shoulders. The islanders were responding to Paterson's words. Soon, with God's help and Julie's dowry, Colonsay's farmers would be able to grow enough potatoes and oats to last through the winter instead of The Macfie, his father, using money he didn't have to import grain from the mainland.

Together, he and Paterson would be able to bring Colonsay and the Macfie clan into the nineteenth century. That alone would take some of the pressure off his father and maybe even improve The Macfie's heart condition.

Lachlan Macfie chose that moment to stand at the podium and add his support to the new land management Paterson was pushing. "I'll give every man, woman, and child in here seed for this new way of planting."

Ian snorted. As if they hadn't been doing that for the last ten years. And cut the rents owed on the crofts to almost nothing. No one else in the Highlands and Islands was doing this. Many were following Sutherland's example of forced emigration or discussing the benefits of clearing out the small farmers to make way for more profitable sheep. It made his stomach knot with anger.

So intent was he on what was being said that Ian didn't realize Jamie was behind him until the gnarled man laid a hand on his arm. "Laddie, there be someone ta see ye."

From the way Jamie's bushy eyebrows wagged, the person had to be a stranger. He'd have told Ian the man's name otherwise. Strangers were rare on the island, especially now that fall was coming on and the Atlantic was getting rougher and the climate cooler.

Leaving the schoolhouse and angling in the direction Jamie's shaggy head and darting eyes indicated, Ian's mouth went dry. A big, burly man with sandy brown hair worn long and pulled back from prominent cheekbones into an old-fashioned queue stood leaning against the stone side of the only inn. He wore a nondescript brown jacket and laborer's loose pants, but his cold, pale blue eyes met Ian's without a flinch.

It'd been two years since Ian had seen Jacque DuBois. The Frenchman hadn't changed. Perhaps thicker in the shoulders, but that could be the coat.

What was he doing here?

Ian frowned, not wanting to find out, but sensing that it had to do with Louisa's letters. Once the three of them had been a team, where each player's life depended on the others. Then Napoleon was captured, and they'd each gone their separate ways—until lately.

With a backward glance to see that all was well, as though the cheer of approval meant anything else, Ian sauntered over. Careful not to appear curious or upset, he moved with easy grace, alert to anything untoward. Jacque was not a man to appear out of nowhere for no reason.

"Welcome," he said in French when he was close enough to speak without worrying about his voice carrying to other ears.

Jacque DuBois smiled, a stretching of thin lips that did nothing to warm light blue eyes. He answered in the same language. "A cold and inhospitable island you own, Ian."

Ian nodded. "I never pretended differently."

Ian watched a muscle twitch in the other man's jaw. Both knew he was referring to the Frenchman's allusions to higher birth than he truly had. It was DuBois' only weakness. Or so Ian had once thought, before he realized why the man wanted to claim birth he didn't have . . . before he'd found him with Louisa.

"Louisa sends her greetings. She wonders why you never answered her letters. It's not as though she is trying to come between you and your new wife." DuBois' eyes took on a gimlet light that reflected nothing of what he felt.

Ian caught the change in expression and wondered why he still trusted this man, even after learning that Louisa was sleeping with both of them—a situation rife with problems at any time.

He had come upon them one night when returning to the warmth of Louisa's bed himself. Entering through the door she never locked, he had seen a mountain of a man, his naked buttocks to the door. Around the man's waist were wrapped Louisa's slim white legs. Grunts and screams had mingled as the two coupled with abandoned passion, unaware that there was a witness.

Only after closing the door and bolting from Louisa's house had Ian realized that the huge man had been Jacque Dubois. That was the end of Ian's liaison with the comtesse. His emotions had never been involved with the woman, and in the line of work the three of them had pursued, a *ménàge a trois* would have been deadly. Still, that was in the past, and there was no sense in withholding his reasons for ignoring Louisa's summons. "Her letters have nothing to do with me. You know that."

DuBois shrugged, a shifting of muscle and bone that lifted his shoulders to his ears. Not Gallic in any way, but very effective in pointing out the strength inherent in the man. "She thought that if you were needed you would come back into the fold."

Ian's eyes narrowed. The inflection of underlying bitterness didn't escape him. "I don't want anything more to do with spying or the Home Office."

DuBois checked the area around them. "You are very free with your words here."

The slight disapproval made Ian laugh. "This isn't

France, and there isn't a war on. And besides, the people here speak Gaelic. Very few manage English. French is beyond them in spite of the Auld Alliance which didn't reach here anyway after '45."

The Frenchman's mouth thinned further. "There is always the possibility of being overheard. You've grown careless."

Ian's hands fisted, but when he spoke his voice was relaxed. "That part of my life is over."

"Don't be so sure." DuBois darted a look around. "Bonaparte is said to be plotting his escape from St. Helena."

Ian shook his head in denial. "He's already escaped Elba once and we've already won Waterloo. The Little Emperor's power in Europe is broken. This is nothing but a politician's nightmare."

DuBois' gaze held Ian's like a magnet holding iron. "So . . . you won't come back."

Ian met the look openly. "No. I won't. My life is here now."

"What if the Home Office sends for you?"

Ian took a deep breath, held it for a count of ten before exhaling. "Then I would have to reconsider. However, two letters from Louisa and a visit from you, no matter how ill-conceived, aren't enough to convince me that there is any real danger."

Dubois' heavy face, never easy to read, registered nothing of what was going on in his brain, but Ian knew the man as well as he thought anyone could. He'd once saved Dubois' life; it was many years ago, on another continent.

The Frenchman didn't speak a farewell, he just disappeared. One minute he was lounging against the stone wall, the next it was as though sea fog had swallowed him whole.

Several buildings away Julie blinked. She hadn't seen the man speaking with Ian leave, yet he was gone. Who was he?

"Ian," she called as she came up behind her husband. He whirled around as though startled. But when she saw his eyes they were a calm silver. "Who was that man? I haven't seen him before. Is he a friend of yours?"

Even as she asked the questions, unbidden came the memory of Farley giving Ian the cut direct in Hyde Park. This man hadn't looked like that: he wasn't fashionable in any sense. But one never knew about the aristocracy.

Ian stood staring at her for long minutes. Julie sensed that there was more to the meeting than she'd originally thought, and it wasn't anything to do with long lost friendships.

Inexplicably, she knew he wouldn't answer her. The need to wipe her damp hands on the simple weave of her linen skirts overpowered her. She stroked them down the roughened smoothness of the material, thankful they weren't silk. Silk didn't fit here on Colonsay with its rugged simplicity.

In carefully measured tones, he answered, "He was an acquaintance. Nothing more."

Julie noted the opaqueness of his eyes and knew he lied. The man was more than that. The fine hairs on her nape rose, and she felt as though a cold finger of air caressed her skin. A thoroughly unpleasant sensation. Unbidden, it reminded her of the meeting at

Gunter's and the beautiful Comtesse de Grasse whose letters still followed Ian.

When she spoke, her voice was waspish and she was glad of it. "Like the lovely comtesse, no doubt."

His brief, almost imperceptible start told her that her shot in the dark had hit home. Was he still interested in the woman? She'd thought that was in the past, particularly after the last several weeks.

Ian's expression cooled and the pain of betrayal constricted Julie's throat. Even after all the attention and consideration ... protestations of love ... the comtesse still had a hold over Ian.

Exasperation mingled with determination in the twist of Ian's mouth. "I told you once before. Louisa is not your business."

Bile was an acid taste in her mouth. "Was he her latest *letter?*"

He had the grace to redden. It didn't make her feel triumphant—it only increased the tightness in her throat until she thought she would embarrass herself with tears.

She was spared that humiliation, at least, by Ian. Unlike the strange man, Ian didn't disappear into thin air. He stalked off.

Julie slumped against the wall so recently occupied by the woman's cohort. Her fingers curled around the smooth stones and squeezed hard.

Ian had said he loved her. He'd said that without her life wasn't worth living. He'd offered her her freedom.

She took deep breaths of the clean ocean breeze, glanced up at the raucous cry of a gull. A shout of appreciation reached her from the open door of the school house as the crofters voiced their approval for what The Macfie, her father-in-law, intended. The open honesty of Colonsay and its people permeated her senses.

Ian was like this land and its people. He had to be. She couldn't be that wrong. He was honest and free, and if he said he loved her, then he did. She had to believe that. It was what her heart told her and her soul intuited.

However, there was something serious about this visit from the comtesse's emissary. Her letters had been arriving with increasing frequency; this visit was the culmination. Ian would explain it to her, or she would make him miserable.

With a determined and unladylike bounce in her step, Julie followed slowly in the direction Ian had taken. At the door to the school, she peered in.

Crofters were standing and sitting, their heads raised in avid interest, their thin frames covered in patched clothes. Archibald Paterson, the factor Ian had hired, was finishing his talk. Lachlan Macfie beamed satisfaction. His complexion had a ruddy color that reminded her of her arrival. He looked healthy. If she didn't know better, she wouldn't realize that he had a weak heart.

Before she could dwell on the subject, the session ended. People stood and talk rose in ever-increasing volumes. Ian shoved off from the wall and headed toward her.

His hair was swept back from his high brow and strong nose, accentuating the clean, strong bones of his face. Even frowning, he was the most virile and attractive man in the room . . . and the Scottish bred masculinity like the British bred cool composure.

The look he sent her brooked no denial as he took her hand and positioned it on his forearm. She complied willingly. He was her husband and she would trust him. She loved him.

She gave him a brilliant smile. Taken aback, he paused in mid-step.

"Julie?"

She increased her smile. "Husband?"

He smiled back, tentatively at first and then completely. "I thought you'd be angry with me over DuBois."

"Should I be?" Glad at his slip in using the man's name, it was all Julie could do not to gloat.

"No, love." He bent to lightly kiss her lips. "Dubois is nothing to us. But you look exhausted. Let's finish this and get you home to some rest."

Her smile turned demure. "I am a trifle tired." And she realized that she truly was. This was the first time in ten days that she'd left the castle. "When we are home, you can tell me more about DuBois. I'm sure it will be very enlightening."

He frowned at her, but before he could protest or even open his mouth, she led him out into the dusty street. She positioned them so that they could greet every person leaving the school house.

The first crofter approached, hat in hands, head lowered to thank them for everything they were doing. The poverty of Colonsay was heart wrenching and the gratitude of the people overpowering.

Behind him came the family of Malcolm Macfie.

There were five children, ranging from a baby to a ten year old. Julie's heart went out to them.

"Thank ye fer the basket," Malcolm Macfie said deferentially. Beside him his wife smiled shyly.

Julie's first inclination was to make light of the food she'd taken them, but she couldn't. She wouldn't hurt their pride. To act as though her gift were nothing would be to belittle further what small amount of sustenance the parents could provide.

"You're most welcome." She smiled at them, including the toddler who clung to his mother's skirts and the ten-year-old boy who held the toddler's other hand.

The older boy returned her smile. She knew his name was Malcolm, in honor of his father whom he resembled even to the gaunt lines of fatigue and undernourishment that lined his forehead. So young. Her heart ached for all of them, but she knew better than to show it, to shame them with pity.

Thank God for the money her father had so generously provided to buy a title for his heirs.

But a title was only worth the good it could do others, Julie decided hours later. Julie studied the room she and Ian shared. She'd seen it many times, but never before had she truly appreciated it and what it stood for: the solidity of the Macfie clan and their determination to care for their own. That was something she was beginning to understand.

"Milady," Susie exhorted, "it doon be right, you doing yer own hair."

Julie smiled at the servant's beginning brogue.

"But I want to, Susie. You're not really a lady's maid, and we both know you don't enjoy it." It was also relaxing. The smooth motion that started at her crown and flowed to the end of her hair near the small of her back gave her something to do with her hands.

Susie drew herself up straight. "I promised his lordship to care for you. That was why he brought me."

Julie laid the brush down, her thoughts skipping back in time. "That seems so long ago."

Turning on the chair, she studied the little maid. Since coming to the island the girl had blossomed. Bright red roses adorned her cheeks and extra weight padded her chest and hips. Her lips always smiled.

"You're happy here, aren't you?" Julie asked.

Puzzled, Susie cocked her head to one side. "Mum? Er, milady? That is, shouldn't I be?"

Julie nodded her head in amusement. "This is your home now. Soon, I imagine, you and Jamie will be tying the knot."

Susie flushed beet red. "I wouldn't be knowin' that, milady."

Julie smiled. "I shouldn't tease you so, Susie. Be on your way. I'm sure Jamie is far from a patient man."

Susie grinned and blushed. "Patience isn't one of his finer points, milady. That be for sure."

The door opened, creaking on iron hinges. Ian stood framed between stone walls the color of his eyes.

"No mon be patient fer what be his by law." A

roguish grin curled his well-shaped lips as the brogue rolled off his tongue.

Julie flushed from the top of her chemise to the roots of her unbound hair. Susie curtsied, almost losing her balance, before skittering past him and down the hall. Julie heard the patter of her feet on the stones become fainter until Ian shut the heavy door. Now no sound came in or would go out.

"Ian, shame on you for embarrassing the girl like that."

He laughed, the sound ringing off the walls. "Mayhap I was a little bawdy for her, but trust me when I say that Jamie will soon put her maidenly blushes to rest."

Ian picked up the brush she'd discarded and began pulling it through her hair. A soft sigh of satisfaction escaped Julie's lips.

"That feels delightful."

Ian's palm followed behind the brush as he continued to stroke her hair. "You enjoy doing this yourself."

Smiling in contentment, Julie asked, "How do you know?"

Face solemn, he answered. "I've watched you. Whenever you're nervous you begin to fondle something; your dress, Pumpkin Cat, whatever's close at hand and silky to the feel. It seems to relax you."

"You're very perceptive," she murmured, not sure whether she liked him understanding that much about her emotions.

He watched her with hooded eyes. "I have to be."

The quiet words reminded her of the afternoon incident. Her pleasure at his proximity and ministrations had made her forget.

Watching him carefully in the mirror, she said, "Ian, who was that man . . . Dubois?"

If she hadn't been studying him intently, she wouldn't have seen the flicker of his eyelids. He gave no other sign that he'd heard. His hands continued to wield the brush without pause.

At last, he replied. "I thought you'd get around to that."

Just as quietly as he, she asked, "Are you going to tell me?"

Still brushing, he spoke, carefully weighing each word. "I can't tell you everything, and I probably shouldn't tell you anything. It's all in the past."

"Please."

His hands stopped, then resumed, as though in that instant he'd made a decision. "I'll tell you what I can . . . what I consider safe."

Julie nodded, glad to have gotten any concession from him. She saw this as another example of the love he professed to have for her.

"Jacque Dubois is an acquaintance. As you already guessed, he's connected to Louisa. In fact, very well connected. He's her lover."

Had he jerked the brush, Julie thought, or was that just her imagination? "Why was he here?"

Ian sighed in exasperation. "The letters. Dubois, Louisa, and I were spies in Paris together. I, because it seemed a better use of my fluent French than leading a regiment of Highlanders in battle." A grim smile twisted his lips as memories moved across his mind's eye. "And even though it brought me disgrace, I'd do it again."

Now Julie understood why he hadn't gone to war. Anger at the derision his neighbors heaped on him made her jerk about in her chair to face him, bringing her hair around to her chest where Ian's hands abruptly halted. "You were a spy, something you couldn't talk about. So when your neighbors accused you of cowardice you had to let them believe it—but now you don't. Why don't you tell them as you're telling me?"

His eyes moved from where his fingers hovered over her bosom up to the fury in her sparking jade eyes. Her defense of him warmed his heart and reaffirmed his decision to tell her.

"At first I was insulted that they could believe me a coward, and my pride kept me from revealing the real nature of my work. That as much as anything drove me to ask for every eligible Scottish heiress before going to London." Still deep in reflection, he put his hands on her shoulders. "But now it seems that for once my pride has held me in good stead. It brought me you."

Stretching up, she kissed him lightly on the lips. "Thank you," she answered.

He gazed down at her for long minutes. His thumb played tenderly along her jaw line. "Thank you, Sassenach."

Seeing the longing in his eyes, Julie knew that if she didn't finish questioning him, soon they'd be making love. Then she'd learn no more, and she had to know. Things appeared to be getting serious.

Quietly, she prompted, "Why was Dubois here?"

Drawing back so that their breath didn't mingle, making him want to get closer still to her, Ian replied, "He and Louisa want me to return to the fold."

"Who are they to ask you?"

Ian considered carefully. There were many things he'd decided Julie deserved to know, but that Louisa had once been his mistress was not one of them. Besides, that hold had been long severed, ever since he'd found her up against a wall, screaming her release as Jacque pounded into her.

"We were once partners. Our lives depending on the skill and discretion of the others." He smiled wryly at her reflection in the mirror. "As you know, Louisa has been sending me letters. Each one asks me to return to London. She, and now it would seem Jacque, seem to feel that our skills as a team are required again."

"Why?" Even though Ian spoke off-handedly, almost callously about the woman, Julie sensed an undercurrent of emotions that made jealousy rear its ugly head.

His eyes met her squarely and without evasion. "I can't tell you that. But I have no intention of going. You may be assured of that."

The small dart of jealousy that had pierced her when he began to speak of the comtesse took root, and Julie knew that the only way to cut it out before it formed into a canker sore was to ask him pointblank what his relationship with the woman was. It was something she was loath to do, but even more reluctant not to. She knew herself well enough to realize that any doubts she had would stand between their chances at happiness.

Taking a deep breath, she asked in a rush of words, "What is she to you?"

Ian noted the pallor of her skin. Fearful of the answer as she was, and she had a right to be, she still confronted it head on. She was a strong woman. His admiration for her doubled. She deserved the truth.

"She was once my mistress—long ago. Our relationship ended long before I ever met you. There's nothing between us now."

But he knew that Louisa wanted to return to their old ways. Even after becoming Jacque's lover, she had made it plain that she wanted to remain his as well. She was an insatiable woman.

His eyes didn't shift away from hers, but Julie noted his irises turning from clear silver to opaque pewter. She realized that he was trusting her to believe what he said; that his liaison with Louisa was in the past and would stay that way.

Could she rise above the aching twist in her stomach and the stab of jealousy that had stopped her heart for an instant? Could she do anything else, loving him as she did? She didn't think so. She would have to trust him. She did trust him.

As he waited for some response from Julie, Ian could feel the tension that held her body erect like the wires that run through a marionette to make it dance. Would she believe him? God, she had to.

Her eyes met his. "I believe that you love me, Ian Macfie."

The tension washed out of him, leaving him weak-kneed and more grateful than ever in his life. Without her, life wouldn't be worth living, and he knew her well enough to know that if she hadn't believed and trusted him, she would have left. Clearing his throat, embarrassed at the intensity of his emotions and unwilling to let them continue, he sought refuge in something he did understand and accept as normal. "Your hair is beautiful, love. After your eyes, it's the thing I noticed most in your father's library."

With one hand, he stroked down the silken length, catching its fineness on the calluses of his palms. He laughed in delight as it clung and twined around his fingers.

"Your hair wraps around me like strands of gold." The poetry of his words struck him as effeminate. Rushing to obliterate them and an image of himself that he couldn't countenance, he said harshly, "Like you were made to surround me."

The blatant, hot sensuality of the last sentence made Julie redden. Ian, satisfied at what he'd done to her, wrapped the rope of her hair around his right hand and lifted it off her neck and shoulders. Bared to his sight, the milky white of her shoulder was irresistible. He leaned forward and kissed her.

Shivers of hot followed by cold slid down Julie's spine. When Ian's mouth slipped along the slope of her shoulder, nuzzling aside the flimsy collar of her wrap, it took her breath away.

The memory of Louisa's pale, perfect face faded along with the wrench of agony that had immobilized Julie at hearing this new knowledge. She lifted her face to Ian so that his lips skimmed her sensitive collar bone, hoping this moment would never end. His mouth found the hollow at the base of her throat where her pulse beat with the rapidity of a hummingbird's delicate wings.

Julie's head fell back, supported by his fist and cushioned by her own hair. Traveling the fine arch of her slender neck, Ian's kiss sent warm heat coursing through her limbs. It was everything Julie remembered, and more. More because now he loved her. And he trusted her as she did him.

His lips found hers and she opened willingly to his exploration. For long, breath-stopping minutes their tongues met and retreated, teasing with the promise of greater intimacy to come.

Ian's free hand moved to her knees and urged them apart so that he could kneel between her thighs. He undid the buttons of his breeches, freeing his tumescent shaft. Pushing up Julie's robe so that he had total access to her, he slid deeply into her.

"Yes," she breathed, needing this union as badly as he did. "Yes, my love."

Chapter Fourteen

Curiosity compelled Julie to follow Ian from the dining room through the hall and into the small library. The talk at dinner had centered around Ian's younger, apparently roguish brother, and she wanted to know more about this latest member of her adopted family. "You never said you had a brother," she said to Ian.

Having taken a seat behind the desk where correspondence was piled awaiting his attention, Ian smiled at her. "You never asked."

Pumpkin Cat chose that instant to come from behind one of the rotating bookshelves and launch herself at him. She landed with a four-footed plop into his lap, her claws extended to maintain her balance.

"Bloody cat," Ian grumbled as he scratched her under the chin. "The least you can do is withdraw your talons from my thighs."

Julie couldn't suppress a laugh. "You two make quite a picture. No doubt she'll be between us again tonight. You spoil her."

Ian raised one thick black brow. "And you don't?"

"Of course I do, but I'm supposed to. She is *my* cat, although she appears to have forgotten that minor detail." She smiled ruefully, not sure she liked having lost a good portion of her pet's affection to her husband. To change the subject, she persisted with her original reason for entering. "Tell me about your brother."

With a resigned look on his face, Ian asked, "What do you want to know?"

Perching on the steps used to climb up to the higher bookshelves, Julie said, "Everything."

Ian petted Pumpkin, causing orange fur balls to roll off the cat and onto his black pantaloons. "You're disgusting," he said to the cat, seeing the hairs that now clung to his once immaculate clothes. Pumpkin purred.

"About your brother," Julie reminded.

"There isn't much to tell. His name's Duncan, he's two years younger than me, he went to Edinburgh University, and he's the captain on HMS Dauntless."

"And," Julie prompted.

His eyes twinkled. "And that's all. Not a very exciting life, I'm afraid."

"Is he married?"

"No," Ian said, turning his attention to the correspondence.

"And that's all you have time to tell me." Exasperation sharpened her voice. If that wasn't just like a man, to only speak the bare bones and leave the rest to be ferreted out from other sources.

Convinced that he'd told Julie all there was, Ian lifted the cat and deposited her on the floor. Pulling up to the desk, he broke the seal on the first letter.

Julie watched him, torn between fascination at the way he could put everything else aside when there was work to be done and irritation that he'd very likely forgotten she was even there. Determined not to be so cavalierly dismissed, she cleared her throat.

He glanced up at her, a frown making him look like a fierce warrior she'd seen in one of the library's books on Celtic mythology. "Is something wrong?" she inquired.

Ian heard Julie's question, but didn't know what to answer. He could feel his right eyelid twitching, increasing his irritation over his failure to control his reaction to this letter.

He looked down at it again. It was in the dark, bold script he knew so well. Masquerading as a friendly note, it contained the two code words that stood for him, Prince Charlie, and a message. The message was embedded in the body starting with the first word, skipping to the eighth, then to the next one and the one immediately following that, and then repeating the pattern. It stood for 1811, the year he'd joined the British Home Office in a very unofficial capacity.

In spite of Louisa's letters and Jacque's visit, he'd never expected to see the code again, yet here it was as plain as black ink and white parchment could make it. Very simply, it said his services were needed once more and that he was requested to *visit* London within a fortnight. That didn't give him much time for travel . . . or farewells.

He meticulously laid the paper down flat and considered his choices—as if he had any. Colonsay might be his blood and Julie his heart, but Britain was his country. A bitter laugh twisted his mouth.

"Ian?"

Julie's question impinged on his ruminations. She'd moved to his side. The worry she made no effort to hide warmed him. He took each of her hands and kissed the palms.

Her fine cheeks pinkened, but she didn't draw away. "Ian, is it bad news? Is the grain you ordered for the crofters not available after all?"

"No, love. Archibald assures me the grain will arrive tomorrow."

He studied her, memorizing each feature. Her eyes were still the green of his favorite jade, but now her fair skin was tanned from the summer spent in the sun. There were tiny golden freckles, just barely discernible, over her nose.

"And none too soon," she replied, "since the bulk of last year's crop went back into the ground. Is it the nets?"

He shook his head. She cared so much for his people, for the Macfie clan. It was evident in the angle of her head; the tension in her shoulders when she spoke of the possibility of disaster.

"The nets to support a fishing fleet for herring arrived yesterday." He pulled her onto his lap and buried his face in the fragrant chignon at the base of her neck. Her hair smelled of roses. "With your money, we'll save the clan."

Her arms went around him and she burrowed closer. "Then what was in the letter?" She paused and then spoke, her voice tight, "Was it another note from the comtesse?"

"No, Sassenach, this wasn't her doing." Or so he thought, but then Louisa and Jacque had warned him that this would be coming. "This is from someone else. Someone I cannot ignore."

She twisted and pulled away so that while still on his lap, there was space between them. He could feel the heat radiating from her and see the pulse throbbing at the base of her throat. He wanted to bend forward and touch that rapidly beating spot with his lips, but knew that if he did he would never stop at that. He wanted to lose himself in the sensation of loving her, of feeling eternity opening up for them. This wasn't the time.

His eyes turned the flat gray of unpolished silver as he fought the urge to love her. Somehow, without revealing the details, he must explain why he had to leave her. Especially now, when they were finally coming together as a husband and wife.

"Can you tell me?" she prompted him when he didn't speak.

His lips moved in the rictus of a smile. "Not much."

The twitch in his right eye increased. He had to think about what to say, how to say it. Setting her down, so that she stood, he rose.

Her hands smoothed down the folds of her skirt, and her eyes followed his every movement. Ian cursed the British and damned the French.

For a brief minute, he took her in his arms and rubbed his hands along the tensed muscles paralleling her spine. "I love you, Julie. Remember that."

Breaking away, he picked up the paper and angled past her toward the fire. He took the tinder box from the mantle and squatted down. In seconds, the letter was nothing but smoking ashes.

Ian returned and took her hands in his, stopping the continual smoothing that her apprehension was causing her to perform. He looked deeply into her eyes and saw the love she felt for him.

"Julie, I love you more than life. The only thing I want is to stay with you."

She nodded, dread tightening the fine white lines around her mouth. "And help the clan," she added.

It was a weak attempt at levity, and both knew it. "That too." He smiled at her, but it didn't reach his eyes. He took a deep breath. "I can't tell you who sent the message, love, but I must leave. No later than tomorrow. I can't even tell you where I'm going, or why. All I can do is ask you to trust me."

Julie stared at him as the meaning of his words sank in. "Tomorrow?"

He nodded.

Her body felt numb, but her mind raced. "And you can't tell me anything."

"The less I tell you, the less chance that you will tell someone else. People's lives depend on this."

"Does this have something to do with that man . . . Dubois? His reason for coming here?"

Ian studied her. Could he trust her? How could he ask her to trust him if he didn't also trust her? He couldn't. He spoke slowly, choosing his words with care. "I believe so. I'm not sure of the reason for this summons. But I can guess."

The hardness in his eyes turned Julie's blood cold. Not even when he'd dealt so ruthlessly with her after her aborted elopement had she seen this quality in him. At least after the first burst of anger at her, he'd treated her with gentle determination. Now, he looked as though he could commit murder if that were required. She swallowed, her throat working as though a lump as large as a boulder were in it.

He continued in a flat voice. "What I'm about to tell you, Julie, must be kept to yourself. Not even my parents know. They imagine, of course, but they don't know."

Julie nodded solemnly, realizing just how close the two of them had become for him to trust her like this. Together they had found what each sought in life, but now something was about to part them.

"The British Home Office needs me again." He took a deep breath as though surfacing after below water for an extended period of time. Then he grinned. "That wasn't easy to admit."

She smiled tenderly at him, pushing back a lock of black hair that had fallen over his forehead. She knew she wouldn't like the rest of what he had to say.

He took both her hands in his and held tight. "I wouldn't leave you otherwise."

"I understand," she said, but it hurt. Just when they'd found each other and the joy they could give to one another, they were to be parted. She had no illusions. "Spying is dangerous."

"It can be."

She forced herself to smile at him. This wasn't the time to burden him with her fears for his safety. "And you leave tomorrow."

"Yes. But I'll return before you even realize I've been gone."

She stared at him, willing herself to accept the inevitable. Smiling again, she said, "We have the rest of our lives."

Ian pulled his wool coat higher around his neck to keep out the biting wet wind. Clouds obscured the moon. Dampness penetrated to his bones. The trip across the Channel to France in the small fishing boat had been long and arduous.

" 'Ere you be, Guv," the rough man said, signaling to the two men pulling the oars. "Don't dare go onto the beach. Can't take no chance on gettin' stuck in the sand and not bein' able to get away."

"Right," Ian grunted.

In the faint light provided by a covered lantern, he exchanged looks with Jacque Dubois. The Frenchman grinned, showing strong, predatory teeth.

"That is why we wear boots," Dubois said, jumping overboard into the knee-high waves.

Ian followed. The cold waters lapped at him, and he raised his coat to keep it from getting soaked. Under his breath, he muttered, "What can you expect from smugglers?"

Dubois laughed. "Nothing more than you pay for."

"That's the truth, in a nutshell."

Before they reached the sand, the small boat was out of sight. The fog blanket that had hidden their approach covered the smuggler's departure.

They clambered up the rocks to the top of a promontory where they were met by a man leading three horses.

"Bon jour," the man said, speaking French. "You made good time."

Ian let Dubois do the talking for them, but listened intently to the rapid exchange. From now on, they would speak, think, and sleep French. Anything else and their disguise was forfeit.

Ian grimaced. For the first time, he cursed his fluency in the language. During the wars, it'd seemed like a good accomplishment. He hadn't minded spying for Wellington. But now when his other skills were equally needed, he found himself begrudging every second that kept him from Julie. To have found the woman he could love with body and soul, and then to have to leave her, was hell on earth.

They were soon mounted and on their way. Their contact disappeared into the surrounding country.

"These are good mounts," Ian said. "They should get us to Paris with time to spare."

Dubois glanced over his shoulder. "Louisa is expecting us in five days. She will know where to start."

Ian grunted an affirmative. The way Dubois had lingered over Louisa's name made him feel uneasy. Out of the corner of his eyes, he watched Dubois. Was the Frenchman still Louisa's lover? Did he resent Ian for having held that position first?

They were questions he'd like an answer to, but couldn't come out and ask. From the beginning of their three-way partnership, they'd respected each other's privacy, trusting one another to use discretion for everyone's safety. He couldn't violate that policy now, even though Louisa already had.

But he would stay alert to any changes in the way Dubois and Louisa acted toward him and toward each other. It didn't pay not to study those around you very carefully.

Right now he was bone tired. It was cold and wet and they would likely meet no one on this deserted path from the sea to the nearest village. With luck they'd find some shelter. Maybe even a hot meal.

Ian sighed. He could hope.

Hope was the furthest thing from Ian's mind two weeks later as he watched Louisa pace her ornate rococo bedroom in the Paris house she'd managed to retain even through Napoleon's reign. Louisa had once said that Napoleon was very lax with surviving members of the *Old Regime,* and Ian knew it to be a truth.

Right now, however, he could care less about how she kept this place. Anger at her simmered in him, but he controlled it, knowing that to release it now would be dangerous and stupid. Being there was foolish enough, but she'd insisted, to the point that he'd feared she would reveal their identities if he didn't placate her. She was becoming a threat to his safety and the safety of their joint mission.

None of this showed in the sardonic grin curling his lips. "You can cut the theatrics now, Louisa. There's no one to see them but me, and they won't change my mind."

"Darling, don't be cruel." She flung herself onto his chest, her face raised to his, her carmine lips puckered.

Ian gazed dispassionately down at her. Her sloe brown eyes, in a perfect heart-shaped face, beseeched him. Her creamy almond skin, revealed by a transparent peignoir, heaved with passion against his torso. Even her coifed chestnut hair, every curl in artful disarray, begged for his attention. She was a consummate actress.

Taking her by the shoulders, he put her away from him. "It's over between us."

She pouted, hands on hips, legs apart. The fire blazed just behind her, shadowing every curve and indentation of her legs and hips, and she knew it.

"How can you say that, Ian? Surely you don't intend to be faithful to that Amazon you married."

Ian's gaze flicked over her. Her rounded flesh had once held great pleasure for him. No more. She was too small and too plump, although many men thought her perfect.

He shrugged, knowing it would do no good to insult her. "I made vows to my wife. I intend to fulfill them."

"Pah!" She snapped her fingers. "That for vows of fidelity. Only the bourgeois are faithful—and that only because they can't afford to be anything else."

She sashayed back to him, her hips swaying, her hands bunching the thin material of her peignoir so that it puckered and pooled at the juncture of her thighs. Ian grinned at the sight. She was as deft as the most high-priced courtesan, only Louisa's price was higher. She wanted a man's soul.

The thick oriental smell of patchouli that she always wore threatened to smother him, its mint overtones at variance with her sultry demeanor. A calculated contradiction. Louisa was nothing like his

259

Julie with her honest passion and clean rose scent. Just the thought of Julie tightened his loins.

"Ah," Louisa purred, reaching out and cupping him. "You are interested." She ran her hand up and down the hardening length of him. "I knew that you couldn't really mean it when you said we would not be lovers again. I knew."

Ian took her wrist in his fingers and squeezed slowly, making her gasp as he removed her hand from his loins. Subtlety was useless with her, particularly when his own body was so volatile as to respond to just the thought of his wife.

"My desire is for my wife, Louisa. You just happened to be present when I thought of her."

It was a verbal slap in the face. Her eyes widened, then narrowed. Her mouth thinned.

"Bastard!" she hissed.

Ian turned away from the hatred that contorted her features, turning her into an ugly caricature of herself, and donned his plain serviceable coat. It had been a mistake to come here. He'd forgotten how stubborn and possessive Louisa was. He wished Jacque well of her . . . if they were still lovers.

"I'll see you in hell for this," she threatened through blood red lips.

Ian studied her dispassionately. Thwarting her was a bad move, possibly increasing the danger he was in, but he would not have sex with Louisa. He wouldn't demean himself or Julie by doing so.

Quietly, he closed the door behind himself.

* * *

Fruitless weeks later, Ian strode over dirty cobbles with long, purposeful steps. The note he'd received earlier from a French urchin indicated that its writer had the information they'd been sent to Paris for: Napoleon's intentions for his next escape from British custody.

The long, low howl of a dog pierced the night. Coming out of the still silence of the black air, it was an eerie, other-worldly sound that made Ian's flesh crawl.

He stopped and glanced quickly around, drawing the knife from the sheath under his left arm. Nothing.

Another low-pitched howl floated on the cold breeze. It seemed to come from his right. An alley stood there, dark and impenetrable. Ian peered in, but couldn't see further than several feet.

He looked around once more. Still nothing.

With deliberate practice, he relaxed the tense muscles in his neck and willed the hair on his nape to lay flat. There was danger enough without borrowing it. Probably the noise belonged to some half-starved mongrel that was foraging in the trash that always littered the Paris streets.

Returning the knife to its leather sheath, he continued. He was on edge, had been since the incident with Louisa. He shook his head in irritation. Only one year separated this mission from the last one, and yet he felt as though the three of them had become strangers.

Several minutes later he reached the rendezvous place. It was near the docks of the Seine—a seedy place, and smelly from fish. Below him the gentle lap of the waves hit the dock piles. Around him was darkness, no lanterns being lit, and the buildings, mostly warehouses, were sealed for the night.

Where was his informant?

Ian moved cautiously, watching over his shoulder as he went, until he blended in with the shadows along the wharf. He'd give the man another five minutes.

As his eyes and nose adjusted, he could tell more about the area. Sails flapped in the breeze, a darker shape in the night. The smell of wet hemp from ropes mixed with the pungent odor of salt and decaying fish.

Docks were a good place to meet unsavory characters—they blended in, but something about this didn't feel right. The informer was taking too long. Maybe he should have told Jacque about the note and asked him to provide cover. But Jacque had been with Louisa.

Ian scanned the area again, his back to a secure wall. He'd count to ten and then, if the informant wasn't here, he'd leave.

One, two . . . At ten, he eased away from the wall.

He didn't like the feel of this. His body was primed as though electricity moved through it, the harbinger of a storm. He slipped the knife from its sheath, holding it out in front, the tip raised.

On feet silent as death, he inched away. Darting glances to all sides, he moved through the area, retracing his footsteps.

The low howl of a hound echoed in the damp air. This time he recognized it for what it was—the baying of the *Cu-sith*, the fairy dog.

Ian jerked around, knife ready. His skin was

clammy. He'd faced death before, but always before he'd known where it would come from.

There was nothing there.

He turned back around, increasing his pace. The sooner he was gone from here, the better.

He didn't hear a thing. The knife entered his back. Searing pain radiated from a spot below his left ribs. A deep, intense burn, it took his breath and buckled his knees. Ian grabbed for the knife in his back. Couldn't reach it.

He willed his right arm to lift his own weapon into a fighting position. Instead, his arm jerked and he fell to the ground. His wrist hit the planking with a sharp crack, knocking the knife from his wrist and across the cobbles, Out of his reach.

He lay on the cobbles, the stench of fish mingling with the odor of human waste. The stickiness of blood seeped along the sensitized flesh of his back, flowed over the ridge of muscle bracketing his spine, and down to his right ribs. It was warm on his cooling skin.

He forced his eyes to stay open and scan the surrounding area. Everything was in sharp detail. What had been pitch was now varying shades of gray on black: the line of a warehouse, the darker emptiness of the alley beside it; the outline of a ship at dock, the lighter squares of muslin sails; the crooked edges of containers piled in small mountains, the murky haze of sea fog.

But there was no movement. The knife wielder had disappeared, confident in his skill.

And rightly so.

Above him, Ian could make out the gossamer body

of gray clouds. It would rain soon. He could smell moisture in the air that hadn't been there before. Soon, rain would wash away the blood that continued to seep from his body as it had washed away the sweat of lovemaking with Julie as they lay on the beach of Colonsay. God, he loved her.

He had to reach her. He tried to rise up to his knees, determined to crawl until he reached an inhabited building. He needed a doctor.

His arms folded at the elbows and he hit the cobbles. It was no use. He knew that.

The rain began. It caressed his face and soaked his clothing. He should be cold, but he wasn't. He didn't feel anything, not even the pain.

The memory of Julie, her body pressed to his, her heat penetrating to his very soul, kept him company. Her face was alight with love. More love than he'd ever hoped to be given by a woman. Love he would never be able to return.

He was dying.

Julie, he cried in his heart. *Julie, my love. Julie . . . Julie . . . Julie . . .*

Julie, my love. Julie . . . Julie . . . Julie . . .

Ian's voice penetrated Julie's consciousness. She could feel his presence, the touch of his warm breath on her neck, the strength of his love. He was back.

Eagerly, she laid down the small shirt she'd been embroidering for the child she hoped to conceive when Ian returned. Twisting around, she looked at the door, expecting to see him framed between the stone walls as she'd seen him so many times.

He wasn't there. Quickly, she scanned the room. Empty.

It must have been her imagination, she decided, as a cold draft of air moved against her flushed face.

At her feet, Pumpkin Cat rose abruptly from a deep slumber and arched her back. Hair straight up, the cat hissed, rearing back and raising one paw, claws distended for attack.

Perplexed by Pumpkin's action, Julie decided to check outside. She stood up and went to the door, opened it, and looked out into the dark hallway. A wall sconce threw flickering golden light on the surrounding stone. But no one moved.

She shook her head and closed the door. Her desire to see her husband was making her hear his voice. But her sense of his presence had been so strong, as though he were standing right beside her, his arms holding her tight to his heart.

She smiled. Perhaps she was having a premonition of his return. She would have to remember to tell him about it. A chuckle relaxed the tension that had held her shoulders tight. Returning to her seat, she picked up the shirt.

"Meow!"

Pumpkin's indignant protest deepened Julie's amusement. "Yes, Pumpkin, I want him to come home, too."

The cat stood on her hind paws, her front paws in Julie's lap. Her yellow, almond-shaped eyes glowed. They seemed to look beyond Julie.

Glancing over her shoulder, Julie saw nothing. "Pumpkin, don't be such a fraidy-cat. There's nothing there. We simply miss him."

Julie set the embroidery aside and picked up the cat. Pumpkin settled into her lap, claws digging as she got comfortable. Scratching under the feline's chin, Julie allowed herself to anticipate her love's return. It was something she'd kept herself from doing, but now it seemed right.

Soon she would be with him, their bodies entwined in physical love, their hearts beating in unison. A great contentment settled over Julie, allowing her to fall asleep in the chair, a glow of happiness radiating from her.

Pumpkin, eyes open, continued to stare at empty space.

So tired, so tired, my heart and I!
Though now none takes me on his arm
To fold me close and kiss me warm
Till each quick breath end in a sigh
Of happy languor. Now, alone,
We lean upon this graveyard stone,
Uncheered, unkissed, my heart and I.
Elizabeth Barrett Browning
My Heart and I

Chapter Fifteen

Tearing at the covering in anticipation, Julie unwrapped the heavy parcel that had just been delivered. Laying serenely under numerous folds of paper was a perfect little green man—the first piece of Ian's jade collection that she had been able to locate and purchase. How delighted Ian would be when he returned.

She wished Fiona could see it, too, having been the one who contacted the owner. But Fiona was in Edinburgh, determined to finish her last year at school in spite of the disappointment in love that she wasn't fully recovered from.

Still, even with just herself to appreciate its unusual beauty, the jade figurine was spectacular. A little fat man, no taller than her index finger, he sat cross-legged, his belly as round as though he'd swallowed a walnut whole. His head was a shiny dome and his face was a happy mask.

Resting in the palm of her hand, the man weighed maybe one pound, and felt cool. Tentatively, she ran a finger over the smooth texture of his head and down to his rotund belly. A silly grin broke out on her face. She could hardly wait for Ian's return.

Intent on studying her acquisition, Julie didn't hear the door open. When a man cleared his throat, she looked up, expecting to see her father-in-law.

Surprise immobilized her. It was Jacque Dubois.

"Pardon, Lady Kiloran," he said, his voice like gravel under foot as he bowed formally to her. "I knocked but no one answered."

She laid the figurine on the desk top. Why was Dubois here? He was supposed to be with Ian. But she knew better than to ask the question. Doing so would tell Dubois that she knew where Ian had gone, and why. She'd promised Ian not to reveal that knowledge.

Instead, she said calmly, as though strange men with French accents invaded the library on a daily basis, "What can I do for you, sir?"

Jacque Dubois stood with his hat brim clasped in his two hands in front of him. In another man it would have been a humble pose. In this man it wasn't.

"I have a message for you, Lady Kiloran. From London."

His blue eyes looked at her without blinking, tightening the knot that had just formed in her stomach. Her voice a croak, Julie echoed, "From London?"

Saying nothing, he held out a simple white envelope.

Sweat broke out on Julie's palms. Suddenly, the

last thing she wanted to do was take that piece of paper. From Dubois' gimlet stare, he realized exactly how she felt, but continued to hold it out.

She met his eyes, seeing nothing in them to indicate his feelings. But she knew.

Fingers shaking, she reached for the paper. In the process of ripping it open, she cut herself, leaving a crimson smear on the pristine sheet she pulled out. The sentences were short and spare. Uncompromising.

"No. I don't believe it." The words caught in Julie's throat. Her head felt light, as though she might faint. "It's not true." Denial rushed hot and pure through her reasoning.

Her fingers opened. The heavy vellum paper, with a streak of crimson emblazoned like a banner across its face, fluttered to the floor. The thick black writing blurred into meaningless jumble.

Julie took a deep breath, trying to still the shaking that wracked her entire body. Striving for control, she looked at the man who'd brought the unwelcome news.

He was watching her in a way that made her think he was waiting for something more. Hysterics, perhaps. She wouldn't disgrace herself or Ian in such a way.

She willed her voice level and pasted a bright smile on lips turned numb. "Surely, this is someone's idea of a bad joke."

He shrugged, setting the loose material of his jacket in new folds on his massive shoulders. "No, Lady Kiloran. I am sorry to say that every word is true."

As though through a long tunnel she heard his words, their French flavor adding to the unreal sensation. Hysteria bubbled up in her, threatened to spill out of her in wild laughter. This was a nightmare and soon she would awaken. That was it.

Surreptitiously, in the folds of her skirt, she pinched the back of one hand with the fingers of the other. It hurt. She blinked to shut out the sight of the Frenchman. When she looked, he was still there. This wasn't a bad dream.

Unbidden came the memory of the night she'd been embroidering the baby's shirt. Ian's presence, his love, had been so strong she'd thought he was in the room with her. He hadn't been; not in body. According to the letter, he had died that night.

Her eyes squeezed shut as the full realization of that night hit her. He'd come to her and for one final time he'd given her the strength of his love.

Fisting her hands until her nails scored into her palms, she forced herself to remain standing. "Then I must thank you for making the arduous journey from . . . wherever you were."

Dubois made a courteous bow. "It was the least I could do."

His attention remained fixed on her. His oblique stare was beginning to make her feel uneasy, as though her thoughts were being pried into. She shook herself to get rid of the unpleasant sensation. Ian had trusted this man. So should she.

Julie looked away, unable to endure the blatant perusal any longer, and to hide the tears that threatened to overwhelm her in spite of her determination not to break down in front of this strange man.

"I know Ian thought highly of you. I'm sure he would be grateful to you for this. I am. And his parents . . . when I tell them."

"I am sorry."

Julie swallowed the lump in her aching throat. "When will his body be returned? He . . ." She paused to stop the quiver in her voice. "He should be buried here. Colonsay meant so much to him."

Dubois' eyes flicked away, came back. "He was buried in France."

"What? What kind of treatment is that for a man who gave his life for Britain? We aren't at war with the French. There is absolutely no reason why his body can't be returned here for burial."

Furious at this insult on top of Ian's death, a death that she hadn't been allowed time to come to terms with, she stared back at the man. There was a look on his face of hesitation mixed with determination. It made her skin ripple with foreboding.

"Lady Kiloran, there is more that you need to know. Something that wasn't in the letter, but that you deserve to hear."

Seeing the tension in the big man, Julie noticed that his fingers had ripped the soft material of his hat brim. Dubois seemed unaware of it.

She licked her lips. "How could there be any more than this? Ian is dead. The British government has already buried him in a foreign land. Isn't that enough?"

"*Non.* The Home Office thinks Ian was a traitor."

"What?" She couldn't believe this. Wasn't it enough that the Home Office had sent him to his death! "I don't believe it!"

"They think he was a double agent—working for the French."

"That's a lie!"

He shrugged, but this time it did nothing to ease the strain obvious in his hunched shoulders. "He was found in a compromising situation."

Julie felt the blood drain from her face. She hadn't even had time to mourn her love and now she was being told this. It was too much.

She took a menacing step forward, fists clenched. "Every word from your mouth is a lie. Ian would no more betray his country than he would betray me."

"I am only telling you what is being said."

Pulling herself up sharply, she asked coldly, "Precisely *what* is being said?"

"That he went to a rendezvous without telling anyone else. He was found with a knife in his back, a note clenched in his hands. Apparently, he'd been contacted and told to come to a meeting place where he would be supplied with erroneous information for the British. Papers were found on him containing information that would lead them down the wrong path."

Julie's mind whirled. Her stomach felt as though she'd drank curdled milk, sour and full of bile.

The sound of the door opening kept her from gagging. It was Ian's parents. She had to be strong for their sakes.

"I didna think this was a social call," Lachlan Macfie said before Julie could explain, his blue eyes taking in Julie's blanched face and Dubois' defensive stance. "But neither did I think it would be this bad."

Mary Macfie moved to his side. Her face paled until her black brows and lashes were in stark contrast to the white of her skin. "It's about Ian, isn't it."

Julie nodded, unable to speak; to put into words the horrible truth, a truth she had not yet come to terms with. If she ever would.

In a few concise words, Dubois repeated everything he'd already told Julie. The Macfies went from chalk white to brick red.

Lachlan roared, "My son is nae a traitor. And I'll kill with my own hands any man who says so." He took a step closer to the Frenchman.

Julie watched in fascinated horror. The two men were of equal size, but Dubois was a generation younger with no fat padding his stomach. The Macfie would be hurt in any contest, if his heart didn't give out first.

She stepped between the two men. "A servant can show Mr. Dubois to a room. This discussion is getting us nowhere."

Dubois, his face impassive as though a hand had wiped it clean, turned to her. "Thank you, but I will not impose on your hospitality. It is bad enough that I brought you such news."

She didn't have the heart to argue with him. Having him under the same roof would be like harboring Ian's murderer. Even though she knew the man wasn't responsible for Ian's death, he'd brought the news—and the accusation.

Apparently neither Lachlan nor Mary cared to have him remain, either. The three of them drew tightly together as they escorted Dubois to the door.

No sooner was he gone than Lachlan said, "I'll not

have my son's name blackened further. Alive, Ian could fend for himself. Dead, we must fend for him."

The Macfie's face was a mottled purple and Julie began to fear for his health. Mary put a hand on her husband's arm and guided him to the chair behind the desk.

"Please, Lachlan, doona fash yourself. Remember your heart."

He sank into the chair, looking crumpled, as though a giant had taken him in hand and crushed him. If Ian's death was like experiencing hell for her, how much harder must it be for his parents? On wooden legs, she went to them. Reaching out, she took the hands they each extended. She must help them. Later she would grieve.

Lachlan coughed. Mary rushed to a table where a decanter and glasses sat. Pouring generous portions of Scotch whiskey, she brought them back.

The liquor burned all the way down Julie's throat to her stomach, where it exploded out in artificial warmth. She doubted that she would ever feel warm again. Her limbs were frozen. Perhaps it was better this way. The pain might be endurable.

Into this melancholy, Lachlan's raspy voice intruded. "He canna rest."

"Dear," Mary interjected, "don't fash yourself."

He shook his great, shaggy head. "The lad canna rest. His soul. He died in violence and until his murder is avenged his soul will roam the earth."

Julie listened with fatalistic resignation. She realized where this was leading.

"My son," The Macfie moaned. "His name must be cleared. But more importantly, his murderer must be brought to justice. His soul must be freed from the bonds of earth."

The words were so perfect. Even knowing they were superstitious nonsense, they made sense to Julie. At least the part about clearing his name. She knew that while Ian had maintained the outward appearance of not caring about his smirched name, it had bothered him ... bothered him greatly. She remembered the look on his face the day in Hyde Park when Farley had cut him.

She couldn't allow him to carry this greater burden to his grave, wherever that might be. This was something she could do for him. Something she would do for the man she had loved ... still loved ... and had lost.

And she would do it for Ian's parents. To have lost a beloved son was tragic enough; to have lost him and to know that his name would be remembered with scorn would only make his loss unbearable.

Yes, she decided, she would clear Ian's name. She would find out who his killer was and let Ian depart in peace. It was the only thing she could do and live with herself.

"I'll go to London—to France if need be. I'll avenge him." The words tumbled from her mouth.

Both of Ian's parents looked at her. Lachlan Macfie nodded his head in approval. "Aye, as his wife that would be fitting."

Mary was appalled. "Doona be daft, Lachlan. Julie is only a woman. Traipsing all over the world to find Ian's killer is no job for her. It should be Duncan."

"Aye," the Macfie agreed, "but by the time we get a message to his ship, wherever that might be, the

275

trail will be stale. No, 'tis better for Julie. She's a strong lass."

Julie's gaze went from one to the other. "This is my job. I want it. Otherwise," she paused to take several deep breaths, ". . . otherwise, I think I'll go mad. To have lost him just when I'd found him." Her voice dropped and she choked on the tears she'd refused to shed earlier. "To have found love with him where I'd never expected it, and then to lose him and the love . . . I . . ."

Her glance rested on the little jade man. He still sat on the desk where she'd placed him what seemed eons ago. Finding him had been for naught. Ian would never see him.

Carefully, she picked up the jade figurine. Without a word, she placed him on the top shelf of the display case. Then she turned and left the room.

Much later, she woke with a start. Exhaustion weighted her limbs. Her eyes were crusted with dried tears. Her throat was scratchy and swollen. Staring at the ceiling, she tried to gather her wits. Why had she woken? Why did she feel so horrible?

Then she remembered.

Her chest heaved in painful gulps. Her fingers dug into the sheets beneath her. It was too much. Tears flowed from the corners of her eyes.

"Meow!"

Pumpkin Cat's plaintive cry caught Julie unawares. Rising on her elbows, she searched for the animal. The fire burned low in the grate, and the candle that she'd brought up with her was only a stub. It made finding the cat difficult.

"Meow . . ."

This time Pumpkin sounded as though she were greeting someone. But there was no one in the chamber.

Julie strained her eyes to see better in the murky shadows of night that filled the room. A shimmer of light caught her attention. It came from the top of an oak chair pulled up to the fire.

"Meow . . ."

Pumpkin's cry came from in front and to the side of the chair. Squinting, Julie could see the outline of the cat where she sat before the fire, her glowing yellow eyes trained on the seat of the chair.

Julie's fingers turned cold and her palms clammy. "Who's there?" she whispered.

No answer, but the air around the chair seemed to swirl and a cool draft wafted over her face. Still, it didn't feel as though someone were in the room with her, but neither could she explain the unease that settled over her.

Julie reached for the tinder box with fingers that trembled slightly. It took several tries for the flint to catch. The yellow glow of the candle emphasized the shifting of dark and shadow, throwing the reflection of the oak chair onto the wall behind it. There was no outline of a person sitting there.

Julie put her feet firmly on the floor, the cold from the stone seeping through her stockings and making her whole body shake. Every bone felt like wax and it was all she could do not to sink back into the comfort of the feather mattress. But Pumpkin was now on her hind legs, her front paws resting on the chair's seat . . . as though someone were stroking her chin.

Julie took several stumbling steps until she stood directly in front of the chair.

Particles danced in the light that seemed to be concentrated on the chair's seat. The glow didn't come from the fireplace, or even the candle she was holding aloft. The particles coalesced, taking on color and shape.

Her eyes widened. One hand went to her throat. The hand holding the candle tilted so that hot wax ran down her arm, jolting her out of the shock that held her stationary. Hastily, clumsily, she plopped the candlestick on the hearth.

"Ian?" she whispered.

He smiled, sadness turning his eyes black.

"Ian," she repeated, joy beginning to course through her limbs. She moved forward. "Love, they told me you were dead."

His lips moved. *"I am."*

The words felt as though they were forming in her head. But that couldn't be right. They didn't make sense.

Taking another step forward, she reached out for his hand that lay on the armrest of the chair. Her fingers went through it.

She jerked away. "What . . . ?"

What was happening? Nothing made sense. Her head started spinning.

The figure, Ian, shook his head slowly. Pain and disillusionment drew the lines of his face in harsh planes. *I'm dead, Julie. This,"* his hand waved at the body reclining in the chair, *"is only a manifestation of ether."*

Chills wracked her. Her head felt light. There was no air coming into her lungs. Sound rushed in on her. Lights exploded . . .

The next thing she felt was Pumpkin Cat's sandpaper tongue on her cheek. Julie turned into the animal's caress, grateful for any warmth. Cold seemed to have penetrated to the deepest parts of her body. Her head ached.

Bewildered, she realized that she was in a crumpled heap on the floor. The fire was nothing but embers. Focusing on the candle sitting on the hearth, she saw that it was still lit and had quite a way to go before burning out.

Then she *had* gotten out of bed. She *had* lit a candle and walked to this spot . . . where she thought she'd seen Ian and heard him tell her he was dead. She must have fainted.

That was it. She had hallucinated, scaring herself so badly that she passed out. A perfectly logical explanation for someone who'd just been told that her husband was dead.

Perfectly reasonable.

Pumpkin continued to lick her cheek, and Julie scratched absentmindedly at the cat's ears. Picking herself up, she glanced once at the chair, fully expecting to see it empty.

Ian watched her with eyes so dark they made her feel truly haunted. His hair was a little long, curling around the collar of his black jacket. His legs were encased in black pantaloons and Hessian boots. He lounged at his ease.

279

Her tongue clove to the roof of her mouth. She blinked, thinking to dislodge the fantasy that way. He was still there.

Bending all her concentration toward the effort, she told herself he wasn't there. It was only her need for him that made her think he was sitting in front of her.

Dust motes filtered through the air, caught in the warm yellow of the candle. They seemed to dance in the space occupied by his body, making him glimmer. The rich tartan upholstery of the chair was apparent through his form. The next instant he was solid, the swarthy shade of his skin contrasting sharply with his white shirt. His boots even gleamed as though polished with blacking and champagne.

She gulped, but there was no moisture in her mouth and the air caught in her throat nearly choking her. His words came back to her.

"Ian . . . you . . . surely . . ."

His mouth twisted in a resigned smile. *"I'm a ghost, Julie."*

Once more, the words seemed to form in her head, not come to her ears. She stared at him, horror knotting her stomach. "Or I am deranged."

But she knew she wasn't. Somehow this all seemed to be part of her existence since coming to Scotland. Things like this happened here. Hadn't she heard enough tales?

She reached out, more cautiously than before, and touched his arm. Again, her fingers went through him to rest on the rough weave of the wool upholstery. Her eyes met his.

"You can't touch me, but you can see and hear me."

She nodded, not trusting herself to speak. Not yet. She was afraid she would scream if she opened her mouth. Yet she wasn't afraid. Close to hysterical, but not afraid.

Pumpkin, who'd been sitting patiently at Julie's feet jumped onto the chair, seemingly into Ian's lap, and curled up into a ball. She lay directly on the seat. Around her, Ian's ghost shimmered.

With one finger, he scratched under Pumpkin's chin. The cat stretched as though she truly felt the insubstantial touch.

The sight unnerved Julie and she took an unconscious step back. A nervous giggle escaped her stiff lips.

He came to her. His hands reached out as though to cup her face. Julie felt a cool breeze waft over her skin. Wonder settled in her heart that he could do this.

Words came to her, hopeless words for a hopeless situation. "What is to become of us?"

His face softened. *Nothing, love. Our time together is past, For now. But you are still alive, and I want you to stay that way. That's why I've come to you. You must not hunt for my killer. Whoever put paid to my earthly existence would just as coldly do the same to you. Don't try to avenge me."*

The strain she felt, the love she wanted to shower him with made her voice tight. "Not try to avenge you? How could I do otherwise. I love you, Ian. To think of you bearing this dishonor for eternity is unbearable."

His face creased with sadness. *"Sassenach, I couldn't bear the thought of your dying like I did."* With visible effort, he controlled the emotions ravaging his countenance. *"I can't even tell you who killed me so you could be on your guard. I can't protect you."*

Thoroughly confused, she blurted, "You don't know your killer? But I thought ghosts knew everything."

His hands dropped away, leaving her feeling bereft of even that ephemeral contact. Instinctively, she reached for him, her hand going through the sparkles that made up his form.

He chuckled, the unhappy, disembodied sound echoing through her brain. *"At one time, I would have agreed with you. Human beings think ghosts know everything, but no, even ghosts have limitations. At the time of my death . . ."* He paused at her uncontrollable flinch. *I'm sorry, but it seems like a dream to me now. Life, that is."* He shook his head as though to clear it. *"Anyway, when I left my body, I didn't suddenly become omniscient. When I left my body, my soul remained bound to it. I couldn't wander more than twenty feet, and there was no one in that radius."*

More confused than ever, Julie sank to her knees. Her brow furrowed. "If you were bound to your earthly body, why aren't you . . . that is . . . your soul, still in France? That's where they buried you."

A soft sigh came from him, drifting over Julie like a cool breeze. Goosebumps broke out on her exposed arms.

"I'm sorry, love," he said softly. *"It seems that one*

old wive's tale is true. Ghosts bring the coldness of the grave with them. But that doesn't answer your question. I don't know the answer. However, I think I'm able to manifest because of you."

"Because of me?"

As he had in life when troubled, Ian rose and began to work off his anxieties through action. His shade paced across the room, going through furniture as though the heavy oak pieces were water; in that his progress slowed perceptibly when he passed through them.

"But I have a theory. Tonight is Samhain, the last day of October and the time of year when the door between earth and the spirit world opens. In Highland legends, anything can happen now." His eyes blazed into hers. *"I love you, Sassenach, and whether I'm dead or alive, that love permeates everything I do or think. It binds me to you. Soul to soul, heart to heart. It enabled me to materialize because of that— I had to warn you not to avenge me. Yes, somehow, I think that is the explanation. But don't ask how I knew what you intended. Because I don't know. I only know that I'm attuned to you."*

He stopped in front of her and squatted down so that their faces were level. His darkened eyes looked into hers and for a moment, she could believe he was as solid as she. Intense longing swept over Julie. This was her Ian, her husband, the man she loved.

Leaning forward, she pressed her lips to his. She would swear that she felt something: a soft pressure, much like a heavy fog when it presses against the skin. The next instant, her face passed through the effervescent particles that made up her perception of him.

The urge to touch him, feel him was so great that her entire body shook with it. Frustration engulfed her. A single tear stole down her cheek. "Ian . . ."

Sorrow looked at her from his ephemeral features. *"Don't cry, love. This won't last forever. Someday you'll join me, but not prematurely. That's why you can't go to France. That's why I forbid this foolish journey you're contemplating."*

The arrogant command of his final words, rang painfully in her head. The futility of her love for him, a disembodied figure she couldn't even kiss, ignited into a furious anger. It spread like wildfire through her, warming her in spite of the chill that pervaded the room even into the hearth where the flames had died.

Jumping to her feet, arms akimbo, she glared at him. "You are in no position to dictate to me, Ian Macfie." Her voice rose an octave. "You can't stop me, because you can't even touch me."

He stood, seeming to tower over her. *"Dammit, woman! You'll do as I say.*

His words were a dull roar in her mind, fueling the flames of her fury and pain. "I won't. I refuse to allow your shade or ghost or soul or *whatever* you want to call the part of you standing in front of me to roam the earth for eternity. I won't let you continue to suffer shame in death as you did in life. I won't."

Never had she felt such overwhelming emotion, not even on their wedding night. The force of the feeling rioting through her now was overpowering. In her heart, in her soul, in the part of her that bound her to him in death as it had in life, she knew that this was the only decision she could make.

Yet even as she realized this, the stability of his manifestation began to waver. Where minutes before she'd been able to delude herself into believing that he was solid enough to kiss, now she could barely convince herself that she saw him.

Reaching out, she murmured, "Ian? Ian, please don't leave."

He sparkled, like millions of dust motes dancing in a sunbeam. The black of his coat diffused into the white of his shirt, blended into the tartan tapestry hanging on the wall behind him, until only his eyes remained, glinting silver in the darkness of the cold room.

Chapter Sixteen

"The child should bury the parent," Lachlan Macfie muttered. "Not the other way around."

Beside him Mary Macfie stared resolutely into the cold gray morning, the Atlantic Ocean lapping at her heavily booted feet. They had come to bid Julie farewell.

Julie hugged and kissed each of them, lingering in the warmth of Mary Macfie's hold. "Mary, Mother," Julie hesitated, smiling bashfully, "I hope you don't mind if I call you that now?"

Mary Macfie hugged Julie closer, a warm smile breaking through the rigid lines of grief on her cheeks. "No, child. I asked you to do so before. As Ian's wife you were always my daughter, now my wish to be yer mother is even greater."

"Aye, Julie," The Macfie added his second. "'Tis never easy to lose a child; 'tis doubly precious to gain one." He rested a large, freckled hand on Julie's shoulder. "God bless you and bring you back safe."

Looking at them and the love for her that they so obviously felt confirmed her decision to clear Ian's name. If she hadn't wanted to do it for Ian, she would have had to do it for his parents' sake. They had given her so much love and acceptance that ameliorating some of the pain they felt at Ian's death was the least she could do for them.

Unable to take more without crumbling, Julie disengaged from their loving embrace and clambered into the small boat that would take her to the mainland and the first leg of her journey to London, where she hoped to find Louisa, Comtesse de Grasse. Scooting over to make room for Susie, who would accompany her, Julie turned her face purposefully into the bitterly cold breeze blowing in off the North Atlantic.

Jamie, unwilling to let Susie leave him and determined to accompany his master's wife, helped push the boat off. Two extra men traveled with them. They would bring the boat back, laden with grain for the coming winter that couldn't be grown in the overworked soil of Colonsay. Julie's mouth twisted. At least her money would feed the people Ian had given his life to help protect.

The noise of waves and wind almost drowned out Mary Macfie's last words, but like an echo Julie heard: "Doona worry aboot the cat. We'll take care of her for you."

Julie waved one last time to acknowledge what she'd never for an instant doubted.

"Lady Kiloran," Jamie interrupted, "those clouds dinna be a good omen fer our journey."

He pulled his wool hat down and hunched his shoulders inside the heavy jacket he wore. Julie felt Susie, whose thighs rubbed against hers, imitating Jamie's precautions. If she were smart, she'd do the same. The journey over the choppy water wouldn't be pleasant.

But she had her thoughts to occupy her, very likely to the exclusion of her body's discomfort.

There had been no further visit from Ian's shade. Two days had passed during which she'd packed and discussed her plans with Lachlan and Mary . . . and nothing. This morning she'd finally decided that the whole thing had been her imagination. She had conjured him from the yearnings of her heart. That he'd been a very logical fantasy, explaining the whys and wherefores of his appearance, meant only that she was an inherently logical person. That was all.

And yet, the sight of him wavering from insubstantial to substantial had helped to ease some of her grief. Almost as though for a brief instant in time she had been with him, and his love had given her the strength to continue on. Knowing that he existed somewhere, even if only in her own heart, gave her comfort in the long, dark hours of early morning as she lay in bed remembering how it had felt to have his large, hot body curved around hers. She blinked away the moisture blurring her vision.

Just then the boat lurched. Caught in the well between white capped waves, the bow slapped down hard, sending Julie a foot in the air. She landed with a crack that convinced her that her thighs would be black and blue before this trip was over.

Shortly after, they landed and transferred to horses that would convey them to the place where they would spend the night—the same place she and Ian had stayed on their trip to Colonsay. It seemed an eternity ago instead of four short months, and the most eventful period of her life.

Dark came suddenly and early now that winter was approaching. No lights shone to guide them the last mile. No sound broke the silence that hung in the air. No one spoke to break the sense of isolation engulfing them.

But Jamie knew the path they traveled, and it wasn't long before Julie climbed gratefully under the covers of a bed ... the same one she and Ian had shared more than four months before. They had laid like two stick figures on their respective sides then. Now she regretted every moment she hadn't been touching him, loving him.

As sore and stiff as her muscles were, it was a long time before Julie fell asleep.

A fragrant breeze caressed her cheek, smelling of wild roses. The sweet scent of newly scythed grass filled her lungs. A large rowan tree, as massive as the one planted in front of Margaret Fraser's new cottage, stood before her, the orange berries a rich contrast to the lush, dark green leaves.

Under it, in the cool shade, stood a man.

His face was turned toward her, but the shadows hid his features. Julie didn't need to see. Her heart knew her love without sight or words.

Silently, they came together. Their bodies melded into one.

Love looked at her from his gray-black eyes and rained down on her from his warm lips as the touched her cheek, her chin, her mouth. Desir curled in her stomach and spread outward over her skin like a cool mist before the scorching heat of day burns it away.

They were naked; she knew not how and cared less. Ian feathered kisses on her. His hands molded the full flesh of her breasts and she arched into him. He took one of the aching orbs into his mouth and sucked gently.

Her arms clung to him, wrapping around his shoulders, her fingers threading through his hair. She held him flush to her body, molding herself to his hard angles and hollows that seemed made to accommodate her curves and swells.

Heat, so intense it burnt the coolness of minutes before into steam, coursed through her. She twined her legs around his hips, urging him forward.

He lifted his head from her swollen breast and smiled down into her eyes. His mouth took hers, his tongue plunging in to ravage her senses. She lay beneath him, her head reeling, her loins aflame.

She fitted herself to him, felt the blunt velvet of his shaft against the moist need of her woman's sheath. She slid her hands down the ridged muscles lining each side of his spine until she reached the hard swell of his buttocks. Cupping her palms around the twin mounds, she pulled him inside her.

He slipped slowly, exquisitely, into her warm depths.

A sigh of total completion flowed between her parted lips into him. She inhaled the musky scent of his desire deep into every fiber of her being.

He pulled slowly out, slid slowly back in. A piercing tension began to build in Julie. Her loins quick-

ened. With her hands still holding him, she urged him deeper, faster.

Whimpers escaped her to be swallowed by his mouth. His moans filled her with exultation.

Waves of blistering heat rolled over her, only partially cooled by the shade of the rowan tree harboring them. Delicious tremors started in her belly and radiated out to every inch of her body.

Ian's pace increased, his skin slicked with sweat and gleaming with excitement. Julie felt his muscles bunch beneath her fingers and his shaft flex within her expanding and contracting depths. A shout of release catapulted from him, echoed in her mind, reverberated throughout every inch of her.

Together they soared. Together they finally subsided. Limbs entwined, hearts beating strongly as one. The love they had consummated flowed between them like waves of shimmering heat rising into the air.

Julie woke with a start, the bedsheets twisted around her legs, perspiration dampening her nightgown. Her hands roamed the bed, searching for Ian. They'd just made love. *Where was he?*

Memory returned. Ian was dead. It had all been a dream.

Exhaustion, the relaxing, delightful tiredness of physical consummation held her in its sheltering arms for several minutes more. Then it was gone, leaving in its wake a poignant regret that left her vulnerable and shaking. It didn't matter that her muscles were languid and her skin flushed as though he truly had been loving her. That wasn't enough.

Staring sightlessly at the ceiling, still dark in the early morning, she let the tears flow unchecked. Chills began to ripple over her exposed arms, the fire long dead and the air frosty with November's cold.

It would be impossible for her to go back to sleep. She hurt too badly to lose herself in the possible recurrence of love's dream.

Pushing back the covers, she reached for the tinder box and candle she knew were on a nearby table. Soon the faint yellow light and acrid smell of the tallow candle filled the small room.

Julie pulled the coverlet about her shoulders, stuck her feet into slippers and rose. They would be on their way shortly and she needed to dress.

She was in her chemise and pantaloons, deciding to forego the corset when the voice spoke into her head.

"Beautiful."

Whirling around, trembling, she saw him. He reclined on the bed, hands behind his head, as naked as in her dream. Dark pools, his eyes watched her. His chest glowed, the white of the sheets barely discernible through his body. Black curling hairs formed a T on his torso, the bar connecting the dusk of his nipples, the tail arrowing down between his ribs to the flat tightness of his stomach. Julie licked her dry lips when her gaze reached his loins.

Turgid, his manhood stood erect. It seemed to her as though specks of light pulsed through it.

Aroused and yet unable to accept this vision, Julie

made herself look back at his face. His mouth curved in a rakish grin.

Come here, Julie. Come back to bed and sleep and my loving."

Her chest rose and fell in shallow breaths, but she took a step toward the bed. "Why are you back? You haven't come to me in three days. Why now?"

"To love you. To give you pleasure."

Shifting, he rose from the bed. Julie would swear his feet didn't touch the ground as he moved to her. Behind him, the outline of the white sheets was a ghostly blur.

She squeezed her eyes shut and mumbled, "You aren't real. You aren't. This is my imagination."

A chuckle reverberated through her nerve endings, leaving her tingling as though he'd touched her. Her eyes snapped open. He was less than a foot from her.

"I'm as real as I can manage, love. It isn't easy maintaining this form, particularly when you fight against me. Relax and accept that I'm here."

She stared at him, hearing his words but failing in the belief he asked. Fascinated, she watched him reach out. His finger, one minute solid, the next wavering, hovered above her heaving bosom. Like a leaf floating on the wind, it lowered to the line where her chemise met her flesh. It skimmed along her skin.

Darts of electricity sparked through her. It was as though she stood in a thunderstorm and her skin tingled as though lightning struck close by. This apparition seemed more solid than the first one. It wasn't the solid warmth of a man, but still desire licked through her. Her breasts ached and swelled, the nipples rock hard.

His hand cupped over one mound and she could swear that she felt him caress her.

A moan sighed through her. She wanted him to be real.

"Julie," he reiterated, *"come to bed. Sleep. Enjoy this extra time we've been blessed with. In your dreams I can love you. While you sleep I can touch you, caress you, feel the heavy sweetness of your breasts pressed to me. I can taste the womanliness of your desire."* His eyes bored into her, tiny flecks of light in their depths mesmerized her. *"In your dreams, I can enter you and pleasure you. Anything is possible. In your dreams, I'm as real as any man."*

She couldn't look away. He held her with promises, and she was glad of it. He offered her paradise. To be with him again, to feel him beside her, was all she could ask of existence.

She reached out for him. She knew that if he touched her in her most secret part, he would find her smooth and slick as cream, eager for his love.

"Come, Julie," he murmured, backing away from her, drawing her with him.

It was as though an invisible cord united them, and when he moved away she had to follow. Soul to soul, heart to heart, they were one.

"Milady?" Susie's voice penetrated Julie's concentration.

Chagrin, irritation, flashed over Ian's face, hardening his jaw. Then he was gone.

Limp like a shirt that's been washed but not starched, Julie staggered to the bed. There was no sign that Ian had lain there, no indentation, no lingering hint of his smell. Yet it had been so real. Did she belong in Bedlam, or was Ian's ghost actually materializing?

The door opened and Susie bustled into the room, effectively ending Julie's conundrum. Within the hour, they were on the road to Glasgow.

Stark, bare landscape companioned them. The glens were still green, the heather no longer purple. Trees, their leaves changing colors and falling, marched beside them. Lochs with water a bleak gray often had to be circled on horseback. Cloud shadows chased across the rolling land, advancing and retreating with the sun and the wind.

It was a bleak, somber country, with a stark beauty all its own. Scotland was a place of harsh reality and brooding melancholy. Yet, like the hint of whiskey underlying and strengthening a hot toddy, belief in things unseen pervaded the Scottish landscape and saturated the Scottish character.

Anything was possible here, and she was beginning to believe that anything happened. On one hand, she felt apprehension at things unexplained. On the other hand, knowing that the inexplicable was possible gave her comfort.

Comfort, however, was far from her mind as she settled into the lumpy mattress and damp sheets that were the best offering of the solitary farmhouse where they'd taken shelter for the night. Compassion stiffened her resolve. This was the best these people had, she wouldn't offend them by implying that it was less than munificent. In the morning, she'd insure that Jamie left a good token of their appreciation. The winter would be hard.

In spite of her discomfort, exhaustion from the long, cold ride and poor rest from the night before acted like laudanum on her. She quickly fell into a deep slumber, hope blossoming in her heart.

They walked hand in hand along the beach of Colonsay. It was high summer and a salt breeze bathed them in coolness, keeping at bay the blistering heat of the noon sun.

Wonder and confusion warred for supremacy in Julie as she kept pace with Ian. "What are you doing to us?"

He stopped. Taking her shoulders in his hands, he turned her to face him. "I'm taking us down the path we would have trod had I not died. For a little while."

The sadness he made no effort to hide tore at her heart. She reached up and pushed a midnight strand off his forehead. Her fingers lingered to trace the upper line of his black brows.

"How are you able to do this?"

"I don't really know. Much of it is wanting to be with you so badly. Some is your desire to have me." He shrugged.

Releasing her, he strode away. A sure sign that he was bothered. She hastened to catch up.

"But there's more, isn't there?"

He turned back to her. Wind whipped his hair around his head, concealing his features so that she couldn't tell how he felt.

"Yes. You must not try to clear my name. It's too dangerous."

Her lips formed a lopsided, dejected grin. "I could be with you always."

He grabbed her, shaking her hard until she thought her teeth would rattle. Her chignon fell out so that hair streamed down her back and fanned out behind her, the wind lifting and carrying it like silk.

"Don't ever say that again, Julie. That's not the way to join me."

Her head dropped in defeat. "I know, Ian, but it hurts so much not to have you near me. All I want is to be with you, to savor the love we found together. Is that asking so much?"

His voice softened, swirled around her on the warm currents of air. "I know, love. I feel the same, but it can't be. Not yet. Live your life. I'll be waiting for you when it's time."

She raised her head to look him in the eye, bitterness twisting her words. "Like now?"

Gently, he touched his fingers to her lips. "No. Much more than now. This is a pale imitation, a shadow of what we will someday share." He grinned, though his eyes remained serious. "But this is better than visiting you when you're awake. At least here I can touch you and you can feel my touch. Don't let bitterness ruin this, Julie. It's all we have."

The breath caught in her throat as his hands slid down her arms to her fingers. He pulled her close. As though they'd never existed, the clothes disappeared from their forms. Her nipples rubbed his chest hair. Her breasts engorged.

Startled, she pulled away. "What happened?"

"A little trick I've learned."

He laughed just before his mouth took hers. Nibbling, he traced the full pout of her lower lip. Taking her hands, he circled them around his waist and then trailed his fingers back along her arms and up to her neck. Cupping the base of her head, he tilted her back, parting her lips.

His tongue surged in and he bore her to the ground, and she let him. If this was all they could have, sensation and burning need, then she was greedy for it.

Beneath her back, the shifting white sands became their bed, rubbing against her skin and welcoming her at the same time. She willed every sensation to be greater than humanly possible, to become part of the magic they were weaving together.

Kissing her with a depth and passion that scorched to her toes, Ian held her captive. One hand tip-toed down the delicate bones of her spine, rubbing each slight mound. Like nerves brought to life, her response to his massage radiated outward.

At the indentation of her waist, he paused, his thumb gliding across her skin to the projection of her hip bone. He was so close to her hot core and yet not there; the implied promise tightened the muscles in Julie's stomach.

His voice rumbled in her mouth, across her cheek to her ear. "I can feel you trembling beneath my hand. Shall I go lower, love? Shall I stroke across the milky hills of your buttocks and into the shallow valley between?"

The blatant language acted on Julie like a caress.

Her legs weakened, parting for him. She dragged air into her laboring lungs.

His tongue flicked out and rimmed the shell of her ear. Tingles of delight shivered through her. She turned into his kiss, her tongue questing for entry.

He allowed her to trace the outlines of his lips, dipping into the hollow between. While his palm smoothed over her skin and down her flank, back up and around, slipping between the delicate flesh of her inner thighs.

"Open for me, love," he whispered into her mouth. "Let me stroke your moist heat."

Her eyes felt heavy, her limbs like softened wax. All she wanted was here; in his arms. She melted into his embrace.

Ian pressed the engorged length of his manhood into the soft pillow of her belly. Skimming upward, his fingers teased her swollen, silky flesh. Gliding over her thick cream, he slid in.

The breath caught in Julie's throat, and she tightened around him, pulling him deeper.

He pulled out and a whimper parted her lips.

"Easy, love," he murmured, "I won't disappoint you. We have eternity."

Eternity. It resounded through her senses, giving her patience and quiet happiness only to be shattered by the intense enjoyment of Ian's questing fingers.

"That's it," he said, his voice a groan, "let me feel you."

She lay half beneath him, his weight supported on one elbow, his mouth plundering hers. He did things to her that sent wave after spiraling wave coursing through her. Arching her back, small choking cries coming from her throat, she strove for that second of fulfillment that is almost pain.

"You're so soft and tight," he said, burying his face in her neck as he buried his fingers. "I can't take much more."

Delight filled her at the raw need in his voice. To have him want her as much as she did him sent her over the edge. A cry of joy accompanied the pulsating waves that tore her apart, sent her scattering in multitudinous directions.

Only the heavy warmth of his palm massaging her quivering abdomen brought her back. Dazed from the intensity of her reaction, she had to force herself to focus on his face poised above her.

A wry grin showed his white teeth. "I'm glad you liked that."

She blushed, seeing in the black of his eyes her own dishabille. Her hair was spread like liquid gold over the sand, her eyelids were half closed, and her lips were puffy. Her embarrassment was short lived as he chose that moment to thrust himself against her thigh.

"But I have a small problem."

Laughter bubbled up in her. Wrapping her fingers around his demanding instrument, she said, "Not so small, but certainly nothing I can't handle."

He groaned at her pun, but allowed her to push him onto his back.

Straddling him, Julie felt the cooling breeze stroke her skin, taking with it the heat of minutes before. It was as though her body was refreshed. Distantly, dimmed by the rush of blood in her ears, she heard the waves of the Atlantic break on the beach.

"A penny for your thoughts," Ian said, tucking a strand of golden hair behind her right ear.

She smiled down at him. "I love you."

Quietly, he answered, "I know."

Inexplicably, tears came to her. Everything was perfect here. In this moment out of time, she was with the only man she would ever love and she knew he felt the same. All the pains and hurts of life were nonexistent. But this was fantasy.

"Don't, Julie," he said softly, as though he understood how she felt. "Don't tarnish the beauty of this moment. Enjoy it."

Gulping down a sob, she smiled at him. It was weak and didn't quite reach her eyes, but he returned it, pulling her down to kiss her.

"Love me," he murmured, his lips brushing over hers like butterfly wings. "Lose yourself in this act of joining."

He was right. This was all she had of him and paradise.

Running her palms along the varied texture of his chest, she forced herself to concentrate on the contrast inherent in his male body. Soon she was immersed in the exploration, her inborn sensuality reveling in his untrammeled masculinity.

The hairs on his chest curved like a conch shell, yet were smooth as a bird's feather. His nipples peaked like tiny mountains but were ecru in color, not the barren brown of an unproductive land. And his skin, light where his shirt usually covered him, was unlike the tanned swarthiness of his face.

Musk rose from him where their loins met, a mingling of maleness and femininity. It was a scent she remembered well. Before it had always mingled with horse and leather. This scent was better. This excited her more.

The feel of smoothness against roughness, the sight of light against dark, the scent of familiar against new were all arousing. They spoke to something deep inside her.

Scooting down, she stopped when her derriere rested on his thighs. Her hands trailed slowly along his torso and down his ribs, skimming over his pelvic bones. The sharp indrawing of his breath filled her ears.

Casting a roguish glance his way, she trailed her fingers lower. The object of her quest quivered and pointed straight up.

Ian groaned. "Doon stop now."

She laughed outright, but continued her progress. Slipping her fingers around him like a many banded ring, she marveled in the satin like feel of him. The skin was as fragile as that around her eyes. The head of his instrument was like fine-napped velvet, plush and pliant to her caress.

A tiny bead, like a translucent pearl formed on the tip. She bent and took it on the tip of her tongue.

"God, Julie!"

Startled at the raw pain in Ian's voice, Julie swallowed convulsively. "What's wrong? What did I do?"

Lifting his head he stared at her as if she were crazy. "Nothing. But I can't take much more of this."

Her hands stilled. Comprehension dawned. "Oh. You like this . . ."

A grin of pure feminine power lit her face. Stroking up and down, she drew each motion out, watching *the emotions riot across his face: pleasure, excitement, even a grimace of pain ... that exquisite pain that was the opposite side of ecstasy's coin.*

Bending forward, she took him into her mouth, sucking gently, not wanting to hurt him and not knowing what would hurt. The hiss of his expelled breath eased the tension holding her back.

"I like that very much," he groaned.

Thoroughly delighted, she increased her ministrations. This was as much fun as having him do similar, yet different, things to her. She quickly found that her imagination, as fertile as she thought it to be after seeing his ghost, was even more productive than she could have ever envisioned.

Ian's thrashing hips and clenched hands told her that he found her imagination wonderful, too.

Before she knew it, his hands clamped down on her waist, lifted her and positioned her above him. He released her and she sank slowly onto his shaft.

Tremors pulsated outward from where he caressed her inner flesh. Her head dropped back, spilling her long hair onto his thighs. His hands cupped her jutting breasts and squeezed in rhythm to their melding loins.

Together they climbed to the top of the volcano and exploded outward. Release, like molten lava, coursed through their nerves to the ends where it sparked into the ocean breeze still wafting over them.

Only later, as she lay in his arms, wondering when she would awaken, did she ask, "Why did you bring me here? Wherever here is."

He stroked her raised hip, sending shivers through her. "Did that feel good?"

She frowned at him and pushed his hand away so that it fell into the crack between their bodies. "Answering a question with a question?"

"Trying to prove something to you, love. You enjoy my lovemaking. We have a very limited time to be together like this. Don't waste it by trying to find my killer."

Looking into his eyes, she saw determination. "So," she mused, "you're offering the delights of your body in exchange for my compliance with your demands."

His lips quirked up. "In a manner of speaking." Tweaking her breast so that the nipple pouted up at him, he added, "You can't deny that you like it. Your body gives you away."

This time she swatted his hand away, annoyed at the betrayal of her flesh. "There's more to life than pleasure."

Soberly, he answered, "I know. That's why I want you to stop this stupid quest. There's more to life than revenge. Life is to be lived each day, not haunted by the past. You can't change what happened. Leave it be and get on with your life."

Understanding came to her, much as the sun's morning light moves slowly over the Eastern horizon. Not blindingly, as lightning, but gently as daybreak.

She caressed his cheek, feeling the stubble that even this unearthly body could produce. It gave her a sense of solidity.

"My life is nothing without you, Ian. I've nothing else to live for. My father cares nothing for me. The money I brought to you is being well used by your father. There will be no child from our union."

305

With the last words came a misting of tears. She had pushed that disappointment into the recesses of her heart, but now it was out. Now that he was gone, the comfort of a child from his loving would have been welcome.

He wiped one tear away, drinking its salty moisture from his finger. "Don't cry, love. Your whole life is before you. Find someone else to love and give him a child. I want your happiness. Pursuing this vendetta will only cause you grief."

She stared at him, hurt by his words. "You want me to love another man? Let him touch me?"

His eyes met hers. In one fierce move, he pulled her face into his chest so that her cheek rested against the strong beat of his racing heart.

"No, Julie. I can't bear the thought of another touching you. But . . ." He took a deep breath and let it slowly out, the air whistling through his lungs clearly for her to hear, "but I want you to be happy. If that will give you some joy in the life remaining to you, then I want that for you."

Pushing away, she stared deeply into him, seeing the pain those words caused him. Very simply, she spoke what her heart bade her. "You spoiled me for any other man, Ian, and I'm glad of it."

He smiled even as he began to fade.

Hands shook Julie roughly. She batted at them wanting to return to Ian. But the hands were relentless.

"Milady," Susie's voice pierced through Julie's rejection.

Forcing her eyes open, Julie could barely make out the outline of Susie's white face in the darkness that was lit by a single candle the maid had set on the floor.

"What is wrong?" Julie didn't try to keep the irritation she felt from her voice. Susie's intrusion had ruined everything. Ian might never come to her again.

Susie's hands fell away and she backed from the bed. "You . . . thrashin' an' moanin'. Like to wake everyone." She gulped, her throat bobbing. "Sounded like you was p-possessed."

Hysterical laughter bubbled up in Julie. She clamped down hard, biting her tongue in the process. She stifled her exclamation of pain. Susie's description was so appropriate it was uncanny.

"A nightmare. Nothing else." She ran fingers through her tangled hair. Wearily, she added, "Go back to bed, Susie. Try to get some rest."

Not waiting for Susie's reaction, Julie rolled to her side, away from the maid. It was a cold night, and it would be a lonely one.

Chapter Seventeen

They reached Carlisle without mishap. At least no
mishap that the others could see. Julie, however, was
permanently deranged. She believed in ghosts.

Julie stared fiercely at a corner of the rented coach.
Ian, attired in the same black jacket and pantaloons
of his first manifestation, lounged at his ease against
the seat. The worn purple velvet squabs showed
through his shirt much as a woman's skin would
show through a diaphanous gown. It would have
been unsettling if she hadn't become inured to it
through repetition. He grinned at her.

Julie knew he was trying to provoke her. His nocturnal visits hadn't deterred her so now he was haunting her waking moments as well.

His voice rang in her head. *"What do you intend to
do when you reach London? You're not a spy. You
have no skills."*

She glowered at him, wishing him at the devil. She
caught herself immediately. For all she knew, he
might already be there and this haunting was the result.

Under her breath, she muttered, "Oh, do go away. You've done nothing but bother me."

From her seat beside Ian's shade, Susie watched her mistress from under lowered lashes. Julie felt the pressure of Susie's regard and flushed. The maid must think she was daft.

"Do you feel anything unusual, Susie?" Julie asked, curious for the umpteenth time about whether anyone else could see Ian.

"No, milady," the maid mumbled, quickly averting her eyes.

Ian's rich laughter rang like a bell in Julie's mind. *"You're the only one who can see me, love. You're the only one with a bond to me that will allow it."*

And so it went through the long days of travel. Still, his needling made Julie think. He was right in that she didn't have the least idea of how to start or whom to contact beyond Lord Liverpool, the Prime Minister.

But that might be a mistake. The letter Dubois had delivered made it clear that the Home Office wished nothing further to do with the situation. Perhaps she should find the Comtesse de Grasse. Supposedly, she had been with Ian and Dubois, and she had certainly sent Ian enough letters. She might know something.

There was really no other place for her to start. And she already had a source of information to help her locate the comtesse. Julie looked pointedly at Ian's shimmering body.

Stepping from the hackney coach, Julie picked up her black velvet skirts and mounted the steps of the

Comtesse de Grasse's London townhouse. Today no ghostly escort accompanied her. Angered by where she intended to go, he'd stomped off, disappearing into the walls of the very fashionable and very proper Pulteney Hotel. The memory amused her still. But it didn't erase the faint sense of bereftness that his absence created in her.

The door opened and Julie imperiously handed her card to the butler. Bowing, he showed her into a small room off the central hall.

It seemed an interminable time before the door was reopened.

"Darling." The comtesse swept into the room, hands outstretched. "Such a terrible fate. So sad."

Distaste at the woman's effusiveness made Julie wonder what Ian had ever seen in her. Still, the Frenchwoman was beautiful, with her heart-shaped face and hourglass figure, and men put great store on looks.

Allowing jealousy to enter into this situation would thwart her purpose, so Julie drew herself up straight and extended her hand. "Comtesse, thank you for seeing me so quickly. I know my arrival must have come as a surprise, and I wouldn't have blamed you if you'd asked to meet at a later date."

"Tut, tut." Louisa led Julie to a chair, taking the one opposite. "Now, Lady Kiloran ... or may I call you Julie?"

Julie had no desire to be on such familiar terms with the other woman, but to refuse would be bad manners, and possibly even interfere with getting the information she needed. Gritting her teeth, she nodded graciously. "Of course. May I call you Louisa?"

"Certainly, darling. What precisely did you need to know about dear Ian's time in France?"

Julie nearly gaped. The comtesse didn't beat around the bush and seemed much more inclined to talk than she'd anticipated. After all, spies were supposed to be tight-lipped. Ian had been.

Well, Julie decided, she would be as blunt. There was no sense in not being. "I'm trying to find out who killed my husband, and why."

For an instant, so fast that Julie thought she might have imagined it, the Frenchwoman's eyes narrowed. "That is a big job," she answered in a voice devoid of any emotion.

"Yes, but one which must be done." Julie cleared her throat. "I want to clear Ian's name. He was not a double agent."

Clicking her tongue against small, pearlescent teeth, Louisa replied, "How can you be so sure?"

Indignation flew red flags on Julie's cheeks. "Because I knew him." She paused, her eyes boring into the comtesse's. "So did you."

The words fell between the women like a blade. Julie had the satisfaction of seeing the Frenchwoman's face turn a delicate coral.

"All I can tell you is that he was found on the docks, a knife in his back, a note clutched in his hands implicating him in a French plot dealing with Napoleon."

"That's nothing more than Jacque Dubois has already told me."

"Jacque?"

Surprise showed in every line of the comtesse'

posture. Obviously, she had not expected this, and from the tightening of her lips, she didn't like it.

"Yes. He came to Colonsay with a letter from Lord Liverpool."

The Frenchwoman began clicking her tongue against her teeth once more. Julie decided it was a sign of agitation.

"It appears that you have already received help. Perhaps I can help you even more. After all, Ian and I were partners long before Jacque Dubois joined us."

The abrupt turnaround was interesting, and Julie was determined to press her advantage. "Is there more? Possibly someone else you could introduce me to. In Paris?" She pressed her wet palms together under cover of her skirts. "Or perhaps I can locate Mr. Dubois and he can tell me more, now that I have some definite questions to ask him."

The comtesse's eyes narrowed and remained so. "You are a shrewd woman, Julie . . . Viscountess Kiloran." As though reaching a decision, Louisa stood up. "Yes, that's what we will do. We will go to Paris. It is the only way."

Julie was momentarily taken aback by the woman's abrupt decision. She hadn't expected this, but she wouldn't refuse it, either. Rising before the comtesse could reconsider her words, Julie said, "Good. Shall we leave in two days time?"

Even as she said the words, a chill of unease drifted over her. The hair on her arms stood up. Glancing to her left, she saw Ian, shoulders propped against the wall. Or seeming that way. The gold Greek key design on the wallpaper showed through the buff jacket he was wearing.

"I'm a little late, Sassenach. What have the two of you hatched?"

The words rumbled through her head, distracting her from the comtesse's last comments. "Pardon me, Louisa? I'm afraid I didn't hear."

"I said, that is excellent. Two days it is."

"Two days what?"

Julie shook her head in tiny motions, trying to ignore his interference. "I'll send my servant around tomorrow morning with the arrangements. That is, unless you would prefer to make them, having done all of this before."

"No, darling. You do it. As far as Paris, I own an hotel near the *Palais-Royal* where I stay when in town. It is closed right now, but it will be only a matter of hours to open it. The housekeeper and butler live there year round." She rang the bellpull. "I'll have my butler show you to the door, Julie. I know that you must be eager to get on with this." She swept from the room, not allowing Julie any comment.

Ian scowled at the comtesse's retreating back. *I'll just nip along and see where she's going. I learned long ago never to take at face value anything Louisa says.* His form appeared to stride after the woman— except that he went through the closed door.

Julie waited long minutes for Ian's return. When the butler came to usher her out, she left reluctantly. As much as she wanted to continue waiting for Ian, she decided that no ghost needed a human being's presence. He would just materialize at the Pulteney Hotel when he was finished. She had too many things to accomplish before sailing to France to worry about

Ian, one of which was to call on her father one last time.

Julie stood beside the heavy mahogany desk where she'd spent so many hours balancing her father's business books. It looked the same, even to the piles of papers in their neat little stacks waiting to be gotten to. But why was it taking so long for the servant to fetch her father?

Nervously, she started rubbing the fingers of her right hand along the highly polished finish of the desktop. She could feel the warmth of the friction softening the beeswax, releasing into the air the slight hint of honey.

"So," her father's voice boomed from the door where he stood with one meaty hand gripping the handle, "you've run away again. Well, you bloody hell won't find refuge here. And don't think that sniveling coward, Reverend Worthington, will take you in, either. He won't. I've seen to that."

"The Reverend Worthington?" she murmured, her mind unable to connect the name to a person. The vague picture of soulful brown eyes and a narrow esthetic face formed in her mind. The memory of a soft voice and gentle hands. Betrayal. "David."

"David," Stockton mimicked. "Weakling. Letting Kiloran bully him into marry the two of you. Sending me the note saying where he was taking you—as though I would have let a paltry thing like wedding vows to that eunuch keep me from marrying you to Kiloran."

It was the same vituperation, the same theme. Julie

watched her father's face go from ruddy to purple as the words spilled from his mouth.

"I made it worth Worthington's while to immigrate to the Americas. And believe me when I tell you he was easy to persuade. Money." He pounded one fist into the palm of the other hand. "When I remember that you tried to throw away a title for that whey-faced parson."

"Poor David," she murmured. Had he always been so weak, or was she just now realizing it?

"Poor David, bedamned!" Stockton's eyes practically popped out in his ranting. He took several strides into the room until he was within arm's reach of the desk Julie stood behind. "And speaking of poor, where's that husband of yours? Left him on that island? Well, I'm sending for a bow street runner and you'll be on your way back within the hour. No bargain of mine is going to be broken by the likes of you."

Julie stared at her father, seeing in his actions a continuation of her last meeting with him just before she'd eloped with David out of desperation. She'd tried to reason with him then, perhaps learn that he truly did care for her. But no.

However, unlike that last time, no pain constricted her breathing and no tears threatened her composure. Ian and his family had given her the love she'd always longed for. Joshua Stockton was just an old man.

"You don't need the bow street runners." Her voice was calm and her hands steady. "I didn't run away from my husband. Ian is dead." Unlike the realization of seconds before that her father still cared nothing for her, just saying out loud the words of Ian's death brought moisture to her eyes and a burning sensation to her throat.

"Ah, so." Stockton rubbed his chin with a large hand. "You're a widow. Well, I suppose there's room for you to move back here. I've been meaning to get a bookkeeper and housekeeper. You would solve those problems for me."

She couldn't believe him. No, she corrected herself, this was exactly what he would do.

Making no effort to conceal the contempt she felt for him, she said, "No, thank you. I have certain things to accomplish, and then I will return to Colonsay where I've been made part of a loving family."

Before he could speak, or even move to bar her way, Julie swept past him, yanking her skirts to one side so that they wouldn't brush his shins. She'd been crazy to come here, and all she wanted was to escape the confinement of this room and the man she'd once hoped to make love her.

Outside, she took great draughts of air. True, it was full of soot and heavy with fog, but it was cleaner then what she'd been breathing.

Concentrating on calming herself, she set off on foot in the direction she knew the Pulteney Hotel to be. She set an easy rhythm, and the swish of her silk-stockinged legs soothed the remains of her agitation.

No matter what had occurred between her and her father, she felt no bitterness toward him. He'd given her to Ian and kept her from making the biggest mistake of her life by marrying David. For that, if nothing else, she would be grateful.

* * *

Many hours later, worry for Ian drove her to pace the limited space of her hotel room. He hadn't returned since disappearing after the comtesse twelve hours ago.

It was late and the fire was burnt down to embers, but Julie knew that she wouldn't be able to sleep. She feared that Ian had completely disappeared this time. Not since the two days on Colonsay when he didn't appear had he stayed away this long. He said he'd be right back. One thing about Ian: when he said he'd do something, he did it, regardless of the consequences.

"Did you miss me?"

She jumped. Whirling around, she saw him lounging on the bed. He looked tired. His eyelids were dark and there were lines of strain around his mouth.

"How can a ghost look like he's been through hell?"

His smile was wan. *"Because that's exactly where I've been."*

It wasn't the answer she'd expected. "What do you mean? I thought that until your killer was brought to justice you couldn't leave earth."

He sighed, the force of it whistling through Julie's mind and sending cold shivers down her back. *"It was a turn of phrase. I've spent an interminable amount of time trying to manifest, and been unable to do so until now. The energy it took has drained me."*

Now that he mentioned it, he did look a little less substantial. The sheets beneath him seemed a little too white.

318

"But I thought you could come and go as you pleased and that only you controlled it."

"So did I. I was wrong." He sat up and ran a hand through his hair. *"There seem to be limitations to what I can do, and we'd better find out what they are."* He eyed her. *"Particularly, if you intend to keep on as you've been."*

Lifting her chin, she said, "I intend to do whatever necessary. Louisa and I are leaving the day after to-morrow for Paris."

"What? Are you daft? Louisa is a trained spy. You're a babe in swaddling clothes compared to her." He jumped to the floor, his feet hovering inches above. Before she could move away, he loomed in front of her, seeming to take up all the space in the tiny room. *"I won't allow you. You're going back to Colonsay."*

She glared back at him. "You can't dictate to me. Not now." Sniffing haughtily, she stepped around him, gingerly, in spite of her brave words. "I suggest that instead of issuing threats you can't keep, that you work on finding out exactly what your limitations are. We may need to know in Paris."

She could hear him grinding his teeth. Good.

"You don't understand, Julie. What you are doing is dangerous."

She sighed. "So you've told me countless times. It doesn't matter. I'm going to clear your name and find your killer, for your parent's sake if not yours. Your father's heart is weak and the strain of knowing that you've been unjustly branded a traitor will kill him if it's allowed to remain. You're going to rest in peace."

319

She grimaced at the pun. "And if Louisa can do this sort of thing, so can I."

He groaned. *"Louisa is a dangerous woman. She's had years of practice and has the cunning of a fox. You don't have either of those traits."*

Julie stared him down. "I have better. I love you."

He sighed pointedly. *"All right, you win. For now."*

"Good. Let's start by having you walk away from me and I'll pay strict attention to you . . . to your hair. It's pretty black right now, but if you lose the ability to be solid, or whatever, with distance then it should turn more and more gray as the separation increases." She chewed on her lip. "That is, if distance is a factor."

Still facing her, he moved away. Julie concentrated on the black hair that framed his face. At first it was almost opaque, but at about ten feet she noticed that it appeared lighter; almost as though the white of the walls had mixed with the black to turn his locks gray.

"You're getting fainter."

He nodded and slowed his progress. *"It's harder to keep everything together, too. I feel as though my body is being stretched too thin."*

At twenty feet, he disappeared.

It appeared that they had solved the dilemma. Ian could not remain visible beyond twenty feet, the same as when he'd been murdered and couldn't go twenty feet away from his body. That would put an interesting twist on their Paris junket.

Julie sat on the bed and waited for him to materialize. When he didn't after an hour, she gave up and got under the covers. If this mimicked his first disappearance, as it seemed likely to do, it would be twelve hours before he would be strong enough to return. In the interim, she needed some sleep.

Once again they were under the protective branches of the rowan tree.

This time, instead of just thinking their clothing off, Ian began to undo the buttons of Julie's bodice. The brush of his fingers against her aroused breasts made the extra time well spent, in her opinion.

But she was curious about his disappearance. "Ian, I thought that once you moved out of the distance, and it was twenty feet, that you couldn't rematerialize for a while."

Before answering, he bent to suckle at the white flesh and dusky nipple of her breast. Shivers of excitement spiraled outward from his touch.

"This isn't the same as materializing. I don't know exactly why, but this is like stepping through a curtain. I don't have to concentrate on keeping together whatever force it is that gives me a body in your time and space. When you sleep, it's almost as though we're on the same plane." He shrugged.

He slipped the dress from her shoulders, and lowered his head. How Ian materialized was suddenly unimportant to Julie.

Part of her, the part that was sleeping soundly in the well-aired sheets of the Pulteney Hotel, knew that in the morning she would be exhausted; her limbs feeling as though she'd walked the length and breadth of Colonsay with full baskets hanging from each shoulder. He was purposely trying to wear her down so that she would be too tired to continue the hunt for his killer, yet even knowing this, she couldn't bring herself to deny them this taste of heaven.

But as her back arched, pushing her loins against his, her will to continue her quest hardened.

Chapter Eighteen

Julie unpacked her own portmanteau; she had insisted that Susie and Jamie stay behind in London. It had been a fight to keep the old Scot from accompanying her, but Julie had finally won by telling him he needed to stay with Susie, and she would not bring Susie to Paris. He had grumbled, but in the end had accepted her decision.

She didn't want to endanger them. It was obvious that they would marry as soon as the mourning period for Ian was over. In fact, she wondered if their first child would be born early. The idea brought a bittersweet smile to Julie's lips.

Instead, she concentrated on her surroundings. The comtesse had said her townhouse, or hotel as the French called it, had six complete suites. It was very luxurious and made Julie wonder where the money came to keep it up. Obviously, the comtesse was extremely wealthy.

This room alone was done in varying shades of burgundy velvet, a good color for the comtesse' dark coloring, but it turned Julie's fair complexion sallow.

The bed was large and canopied, its walnut wood a well-polished golden brown. Next to it, on either side, were matching tables. A dressing table with beveled mirror and heavily upholstered chair finished the sleeping portion.

Julie turned and looked at the second part of the room. Tucked into a window alcove was a sitting area with two dainty chairs and a table. A small empty bookcase stood to one side. She smiled. Evidently Louisa didn't read ... or her guests didn't.

"Nice room."

The words sent shivers down her spine. She didn't think she would ever become accustomed to the deep, penetrating quality of Ian's communication. It was almost as though his voice became part of her body; flowing with her blood, supporting with her bone, and strengthening with her muscles.

"Yes, it is nice, but I don't intend to be spending much time in it."

He scowled, making the tiny particles that always seemed to be dancing within the confines of his form spark where they defined his eyes. *"You're determined in this course to avenge my death and clear my name."*

She met his irritation without backing down. "Would I be in Paris otherwise? You may either help me, or continue to try and hinder me. I know exactly what your nocturnal visits are intended to do."

His face softened. *"Tire you out so you'll not feel like pursuing this folly. But they're more. They're our last opportunities to be together for a long time, my love."*

She smiled wistfully. "I know, and I cherish then

as such. But this is important, too—if not to you, then to your parents."

"Very well." He turned away from her for long minutes. When he turned back, he was resigned. *"I'll stop fighting you."*

The fists she'd made while waiting for his answer relaxed. "Thank you," she said. Briskly she continued, "You're the spy. How do you suggest we proceed? I think we should find Jacque Dubois."

He raised one eyebrow. *"Why?"*

"Because when I first asked for Louisa's help, she wasn't exactly champing at the bit to provide it. When I mentioned that Dubois might be able to help, she suddenly decided to assist." She took a turn around the room. "Now, I don't know her as well as you . . ." When all he did was continue to look mildly interested with no twitch of response to her allusion, she continued. "But she doesn't strike me as a person who goes out of her way for others."

"She isn't. Did her hesitation occur before I arrived?"

"Yes."

It was his turn to pace the room, his figure passing in slow motion through a chair in the process. He didn't seem to notice.

"Dubois is the one who brought you the letter from the Home Office?" She nodded. *"I always liked and trusted him, even after he and Louisa became lovers. And it doesn't surprise me that he would have brought the message. He never skirted what he thought was his duty. If Louisa had continued in her refusal to help, he would have been the logical per-*

*son to contact next. In fact, he might have been my
first choice if he'd still been in England.*

He stopped to look at her, and she could see the
emotions working across his face as he thought about
her words. It was apparent that he liked none of this,
but was determined to help to the best of his ability.
He had been like that in life.

*"It seems strange that Louisa wasn't willing to
help, only to change her mind at the suggestion of
Jacque. I could understand her not wanting to go to
the trouble, but not changing her mind like that."*

"That's only one of the puzzling things about all
this. More importantly, who planted the papers on
you that incriminated you as a double agent?" Her
anger at the injustice showed in the curl of her lip.
"I'd like to know that."

He came to her, one hand out to stroke her cheek.
His palm brushed her skin, leaving a scattering of
sparks on her face in its wake. It wasn't as substantial
as when he caressed her in her dreams, but it was
something.

*"I know, love. You're determined to clear my name
and I thank you for it. But if we find the person who
killed me, we'll very likely find the person who
framed me."*

"Ah . . ." It made sense, now that he pointed it out.
"But where do we begin? Dubois?"

*"Not yet. Louisa has a lot of contacts and it
wouldn't be a bad idea to stick close to her. One of
those contacts might give us a clue. She'll also know
where Dubois is."*

"Do you think she was involved?" Julie hadn't
even thought of this before, but as soon as the words

were out she wondered why not. "She is a spy and she didn't want to help."

Ian stopped pacing, looking thoughtful before shaking his head slowly. *"Doubtful. I was killed by a knife thrown some distance and with great accuracy in the dark. No. Knife wielding isn't one of Louisa's skills."*

"Could she have hired someone to do it?"

He looked thoughtful, then slowly shook his head. *"It's possible, but hirelings can be bought by other people. She'd have had to want me dead very badly to do something that risky. I don't think Louisa had anything to do with this."*

"Then who?"

Turning from her, he headed toward the door. *"That's what we have to find out."* Over his shoulder, he added with a mischievous grin, *"You have to come with me."*

She followed. "Where are we going?"

"I'm going into Louisa's room. You're going as close to it as we can get you without anyone seeing."

"Why?"

"It's the best place to start. Never know what you'll find in someone's bedroom."

She snorted. "I'm sure."

"Don't be sarcastic, Sassenach. Just think about what someone might have found in our bedroom."

Julie blushed at the image created by his words and changed the subject. "Just so I'm not caught. Louisa might easily be coming or going at this time of evening."

He smiled reassuringly at her. *"You won't be.*

You're too shrewd for that and I'm here to warn you."

"You'll be in the room."

"True, but I know that Louisa doesn't allow her servants to roam about in the sleeping wing after dinner. Privacy."

Under her breath, Julie muttered, "I wonder why?" Ian's eyebrows rose in feigned surprise. *"Claws?"*

"Not me," Julie muttered.

He grinned as he disappeared through the closed door. Julie opened it and kept close behind him as they made their way down the dark hallway. Stubbing her toe as they turned a corner, she stifled a cry. She'd known this hall wouldn't be pleasant at night, and neither was skulking through her hostess' house. But she had to admit that Ian had known what he was talking about. No one moved on this floor, and there were no lights coming from under any of the doors they passed.

They didn't stop until well after Julie stubbed her other foot.

Seeming to sparkle in the dimly lit hall, Ian held one finger to his mouth for silence. *"This is her room. Stay right here. Be on the alert in case she isn't in. You'll have to make the decision to leave if you hear someone coming. Don't worry about me. If she comes in before I dematerialize she won't see me anyway. If she's in, I'll come back out if it appears that she's leaving or expecting company."* His eyes laughed. *"Louisa likes company."*

I bet, Julie thought since she couldn't speak it. Ian's gray eyes lightened, as though she'd spoken the words, but he didn't comment.

He kissed her lightly on the lips, a cool brushing of sparks. Then he disappeared.

Before she had time to start worrying, he was back.

"Come on. Fast."

Knowing urgency when she heard it, Julie flew down the dark hall. She was breathless by the time she was safely in her own room.

"Being a spy isn't glamorous," she stated.

He looked solemnly at her. *"I never told you it was. Only that it's necessary."*

"Why did we have to run as though that fairy dog was chasing us?"

Looking startled, he asked, *"The Cu-sith? Why do you mention it?"*

She shrugged. "It just popped into my mind, like your voice. But you didn't answer my question."

His eyes narrowed in consideration before he answered. *"I know Louisa. She was dressed in a very diaphanous gown, and her hair and face were perfectly arranged."*

"A visitor." While the logical conclusion, Julie said the words to mask the sharp dart of jealousy that speared her at the thought of Ian seeing another woman dressed seductively. Had he enjoyed the sight?

Surreptitiously, she looked his body over from top to loins. There didn't appear to be any evidence that Louisa's state of *dishabille* had aroused him.

"She doesn't compare to you, Sassenach."

Julie looked quickly away. Heat moved over her chest, neck and face, and she knew her cheeks were as red as the flames in the hearth.

"No?"

"No." He smiled tenderly. *"Louisa half undressed does nothing for me."*

His accuracy nonplussed her. "Can you read my mind?"

He laughed. *"If I say yes, then you'll never feel comfortable with me again."*

She glared at him. "Do you think it's easy to converse with a ghost as it is? I'm constantly wondering if I've gone insane."

He sobered. *"I know this is hard on you. I wish I could change things, but . . . Anyway, I can't read your mind. I just know jealousy when I see it in a woman's eyes; the way she looks a man over."*

"Very experienced."

"That was before I met you, but knowledge is something you don't lose. Shall we change the subject?"

"Yes."

The unreasonable jealousy that had tormented her eased, but for a brief period, she would have gladly scratched out the Comtesse de Grasse's eyes.

"Back to our purpose. I want you to pull a chair up to your door and sit there. I'm going into the hall. I want to see who Louisa's current paramour is. It might be to our advantage."

Julie did as directed, but she wondered how Ian intended to see the man coming up when her room was so far from the main staircase, closer to the servant's passage. She'd ask when he returned. Right now, her eyelids felt as if they were weighted with lead.

* * *

His touch on her shoulder woke her. She knew instantly that this was a dream because his hand was solid and warm on her skin, sending wafting heat down her arm to tingle in her fingertips.

Stretching and yawning, she said, "Did you learn anything? We're so far from the main staircase I wondered if you would."

He started undoing the pins in her hair and running his fingers through the golden strands as they fell to her shoulders. "I learned not to expect things to remain static with Louisa. Something I should have learned long ago."

Basking in his ministrations, she closed her eyes in bliss. "You're not making sense, and you didn't answer my question."

"Louisa's partners come up the servant's stairs—much more discreet." Burying his face in the heavy mantle of her hair, he murmured, "Your hair smells like roses, even in this fractured reality." Then he sighed, a great gusting rush of air. "I honestly thought Louisa's tryst would be with Jacque."

Julie sat bolt upright, jerking away so that Ian's grip on her hair pulled painfully. Rubbing her scalp, she said, "Jacque Dubois and Louisa, Comtesse de Grasse, are having an affair?"

He stroked the spot her fingers were still massaging. "Don't be a snob, Julie."

"I'm not. I just . . . they don't look as though they belong together. I mean, he's so huge and ordinary—bourgeois—while she's delicate and aristocratic from the top of her hair to the tip of her foot. A mismatch."

Releasing her, he strode away. "Evidently Louisa agrees with you. But I don't think Jacque would."

He crossed the expanse of dune with several floating strides. Reaching the rowan tree, he pivoted on the ball of his boot and strode back.

"I hadn't anticipated this. It could cause complications."

Julie rose and went to him, worry puckering her brow. "How so?"

"Like someone else I know, Jacque is a jealous person. He wouldn't take kindly to being cuckolded."

"Maybe they've called it off. As I said, they don't seem to be a likely pair."

A frown pulled Ian's black brows into a V. His eyes stared off into space. "Possible, but I don't think so. Jacque is very steadfast, and I think he truly loves Louisa. I think it's time we located Jacque."

"Why?"

His attention returned to her. "A hunch." He rubbed the back of his neck. "In this business, you learn to trust your instincts. If I'd trusted mine, I would have turned back that night before I reached the docks. You won't find me ignoring them again."

Goosebumps marched up Julie's arms. "Oh, Ian, if only we could start over again."

He smiled down at her, a lopsided, resigned twist of lips that said more of his regret for things lost than any words could have. "I know, love. But we have this, while it lasts."

She nodded and stepped into his open arms.

* * *

Julie woke to morning sunshine and the rich aroma of fresh chocolate. She sat up and shivered.

Even with the fire, the room was chilly. Paris in mid-November was cold and damp—a thoroughly unpleasant place to be, with a deep chill that seemed to settle in her flesh and refuse to leave no matter how many layers of clothing she donned. Colonsay had just started to be uncomfortable when she'd left, but nothing like this. Its maritime climate kept it temperate through much of the year.

Pulling the covers around her like a shawl, she glanced around the room for the source of the chocolate. It was by the bed. Ian was by the fireplace, staring morosely into the flames.

"I'm going to follow Louisa today."

Before answering, Julie took a long sip of the reviving chocolate. This was a new tack—one they hadn't discussed last night. "Is there any particular reason?"

His glance rested on her face and then slid away. *"A hunch."* He stood and kicked ineffectually at the fire, his booted foot absorbing the orange sparks and doing nothing to the coals. *"And something that happened before I was killed."*

Julie watched him carefully, sensing that he wasn't entirely comfortable with what he was about to tell her. She said nothing.

He came and sat on the bed, his thigh riding hers in sparkling tension. His eyes met hers. *"Shortly before I received the note that sent me to the docks, Louisa invited me here. Thinking that she was involved exclusively with Jacque, I came. I thought she had some information she couldn't entrust to a note."*

333

His mouth twisted bitterly. *"I should have known better. She wanted to take up where we'd left off years before. I refused. At the time, I thought she'd accepted my decision. Now I'm beginning to wonder."*

Julie's stomach twisted. The jealousy that had been laid to rest during the long hours of the night resurfaced, a snake rising up above the grass. But he'd refused, and she believed him—trusted him implicitly. She beat down the jealousy.

She forced herself to focus on the issue of Ian's murder. She said, "You told me you don't think she killed you. You said she can't use a knife. And you said she's too smart to hire someone to do it."

"I said that I didn't think she wanted me dead badly enough to take the risk." His eyes held her, his gray irises shining like well-polished silver. *"But I don't dare ignore this hunch. It's too strong."*

A chill moved over Julie like a lover's caress, making her shiver even under the heavy blankets from the bed. This was all so cold-blooded: so vindictive.

"Aren't you jumping to conclusions?"

He rose and stalked to the window where the curtains were pulled back to reveal the early morning sunlight. *"I don't know, but, even if I am, I'd still trail Louisa. She's our best source of information no matter how you look at it."*

Julie had to concede the truth of that. She took a sip of chocolate: it was cold. With a sigh, she put it down and rose to start dressing. "You'll have to show me how to follow her without being seen."

He turned back to look at her, and for the first time

that morning he smiled. *"Be sure that I'll do my best to keep you from being caught."*

An hour later, Julie ducked into the alcove of a store, afraid that she'd just been caught. Having sneaked down the stairs in time to hear Louisa give the butler her destination to relay to the driver of her carriage, Julie promptly caught a cab to the same destination; the *Palais-Royal*. Louisa was two stores down from Julie at a coffee shop. Before going in, the Frenchwoman had checked behind herself and on both sides. To Julie, it seemed that Louisa had been looking for possible followers.

"Calm down. That was a normal precaution. One that Louisa takes without even thinking about it."

"I'm glad to hear that," she answered with some exasperation.

A man passing by the doorway at that moment stared strangely at her. Julie caught his look and flushed. It was obvious he thought her demented, and in a way, she was.

Ian laughed. *"You'd best be careful how and when you speak."*

Julie grumbled under her breath, but managed not to respond. Her comfort level was low. A light sleet had started and even with a heavy wool cape, she was damp and chilled. But she didn't allow it to stop her from leaving the relative comfort of her alcove to relocate in front of an unprotected shop window next to the coffee shop. This way, Ian would be within twenty feet of the coffee shop door when Louisa left. He would be able to hear her next destination.

"She's coming out."

Relief at not having to remain in the bad weather much longer warmed Julie right up. She hoped Louisa wouldn't recognize her cape. She pulled the hood further up and hunched her shoulders.

As though pre-arranged, the coachman drove the carriage up at just that moment, and Louisa stepped regally in.

"She's headed home. There's a brown parcel under her arm. A book perhaps."

Julie grunted when her calves, half frozen, protested as she attempted the brisk walk necessary to keep up with Ian's retreating figure. The last thing they needed at this moment was for him to dematerialize.

"Hail a cab."

She frowned at his autocratic tone, but did as directed. It was the best thing to do, and getting out of the sleet would be welcome.

"Tell him to hurry. We have to get back right after her so I can see what's in that package." He sat across from her on the worn and torn squabs of the smelly carriage. *"In case you haven't noticed, Louisa isn't much of a reader."*

Julie had to smile. "That's an understatement. There's not a book in the entire house, not even the library."

Ian joined her in a chuckle. *"Louisa prefers physical recreation."*

"Yes," Julie said dryly.

The cab lurched to a halt and Ian sped from the carriage, going through its side. Julie, hampered by her solidity and damp skirts, fumbled with the door handle, trying to keep within twenty feet of Ian's impatient form.

He disappeared through the front door. Julie didn't bother to knock, knowing it would take too long for the butler to answer, and followed behind. He was running up the stairs and she had to take them two at a time to keep up with him. It necessitated lifting her skirts well above her ankles. By the time she reached the landing, she was panting and Ian's figure was a dim fluorescence down the hall. She redoubled her efforts to keep up with him. What she would do if Louisa came unexpectedly upon her she didn't know and couldn't pause to consider. She'd have to prevaricate.

She came to a screeching halt one door down from Louisa's bedroom. Ian stood just outside the comtesse's room. He beckoned Julie toward him.

"You have to come closer. There's no telling how far into the room I'll have to go. If she comes out, just think up something to say. She's undoubtedly suspicious of you—it won't matter if you make her more so."

Julie didn't even get to nod her understanding before he disappeared into the door. She stood stock still, her ear to the door for any sound that might warn her of Louisa's approach. In for a penny, in for a pound, she thought.

It was a thick door and strain as she might to hear, there was nothing. Her ear was still pressed tight when Ian appeared beside her.

"Let's go."

The curt coldness of his voice, and the stiff way he

337

held himself, told her that he'd found out something unpleasant. Just then the door opened.

Julie jumped. Green eyes wide, she looked into the comtesse's narrowed brown ones.

"Uhm, hello, Louisa." Mind spinning frantically, Julie coughed to give herself time. "I came to see if you had time to help me—I know you're going to get in contact with the people you know, but I'd like to look at the spot where Ian was killed and is buried." It was true enough, and she could see that Louisa found it to be a good reason for standing outside her bedroom door.

"Darling, I'm so sorry. I forgot that you would naturally wish to do so. I will take you."

Julie didn't really want to see either place with this woman. She didn't want to have anyone with her when she saw where Ian had been killed. His grave would be a little easier. She intended to have his body sent to Colonsay anyway, so the place here in Paris wasn't really his final resting place.

Keeping her reservations from showing, Julie replied, "Thank you. When do you think we might go?"

"I'm busy this afternoon and the docks aren't the best place to be at night. Tomorrow morning, late would probably be best." Louisa smiled, showing her perfect teeth.

Julie noticed that the warmth of the comtesse' reddened lips didn't extend to the expression in her brown eyes. They were as cold and unemotional as velvety brown eyes could manage.

Another thank you, and Julie was on her way down the hall, away from the Frenchwoman who was

338

beginning to make her skin crawl with dislike. Ian was a shadowy specter leading the way. Entering her own room with a sigh of relief, she found Ian roaming from one end to the other. He was agitated.

"She has a safe built into the headboard of her bed. The brown package was a sheaf of papers. I couldn't read them because the top sheet was blank, but I saw the combination that opens the lock." He paused and stared straight at her. *"I don't like this, but it's too late to turn back. There's more at stake here now than redeeming my name."*

Julie's eyes grew wide as meaning dawned on her. "You think she's a double agent." It was the only logical explanation. "She had you framed."

He nodded. *"Possible. But until we read those papers I can't be sure."*

The blood froze in Julie's veins as the import of his words sank in. "I'm going to have to break into her safe and read those papers."

"Yes."

Chapter Nineteen

Julie gulped, her fingers clenching and unclenching automatically at her sides. Ian had been right—she wasn't cut out to be a spy. But at least Louisa hadn't locked her room. She hadn't had to break in.

"Easy."

Her head jerked up and down to show that she heard. He was trying to calm her, but sweat broke out on her forehead anyway. It didn't matter that she knew Louisa was at a ball and that her latest paramour was with her. It didn't matter that the servants had orders to stay away from this part of the house. She was still nervous as hell.

There was nothing like being in someone's bedroom uninvited. When you added burglary to it, it became unbearable. But it had to be done.

Julie took a deep breath and sat on the bed. The faint candle light wasn't strong enough for her to see anything distinctly, but Ian had explained that sometimes touch was more sensitive than sight.

Julie felt along the smooth wood of the headboard.

Her fingertips skimmed the surface lightly, then repeated the process, pressing harder. Was that a crack? She slowed and traced the line. It went down then right then up then left. A perfect rectangle.

Excitement made her giddy. A buzz started in her ears. So close.

"Let's hope Louisa is well entertained."

Ian's echo of her own fears made her hand shake. She picked up the candle to get a good look. The orange flame danced, throwing macabre shadows on the bed and wall. Sure enough, a faint line showed where the safe was supposed to be.

"Press on the upper right hand corner. It should push in and the wood panel will open out."

She did as he instructed. Sure enough, the panel did what he predicted, revealing a metal door with a lock. Ian told her the combination. Anxiety made her fingers clumsily and it took several tries before she was able to line up the sequence of numbers with the required precision.

She heard the final click.

Ian's excited voice ordered, *"Open it. We haven't much time."*

Inside was a packet wrapped in oiled cloth. *"I guess you can't see through objects."*

"Right. Hurry up."

"Shouldn't we just take it with us?"

"No. Never let a double agent, if that's what she is, know that you're onto them. This way, if the Home Office wants, they can feed her erroneous information and Napoleon will be none the wiser."

She undid the string. Laying the package on the

bed, she spread out the sheets. Holding the candle aloft, she read the first page.

"My God!"

"There are people in British intelligence who'd kill for this information on Napoleon's plans. I wonder who Louisa's supposed to pass this on to?"

Hearing the concern in his voice, Julie rounded on him where he floated beside her, his body divided by the bed, torso above the covers, loins and legs somewhere in the mattress. The incongruity made her stomach flip.

"I'm not here for any reason but clearing your name. If the British government never gets this package, then that's too bad. It won't keep me from sleeping at night."

"So fierce . . ."

He leaned forward and kissed her. It felt like the effervescent bubbles of fine champagne.

Pulling back he said, *"This will serve the purpose of clearing me as long as it's found on Louisa."*

"You said a double agent was best used when she didn't know she was discovered."

He shrugged. *"That's true, but if they don't know she's a double agent the only way we can prove it is for someone who's trusted to find this packet and relay the information. And I know the perfect person."*

"Jacque Dubois."

"Exactly."

She lost no time in wrapping the papers back up and replacing them in the safe. Just as quickly, she moved to the closed door, pausing only long enough for Ian to precede her out and scout the area for anyone close by. When he told her it was all clear, she sped to the haven of her own room.

Safe, or as safe as she could feel in the Comtesse de Grasse's Paris house, Julie said, "But how do we find Dubois without Louisa's help?"

"I know some of his haunts. I can't imagine that Louisa has stopped seeing him completely. She likes variety in her love life. Given time, Jacque will probably show up here one night. Then we simply stay alert and follow him when he leaves."

Sarcasm dripped from her reply. "Nothing simpler. After all, we have all of my life to resolve this."

He had the grace to look chagrined before his face hardened. *"This isn't exactly a picnic for me, either. Knowing that any moment you could be revealed. If my murder was instigated by Louisa and she thinks that you've found her out, she wouldn't hesitate to have you disposed of."*

"As she did you?"

"We don't know that for sure."

"Defending her because she was once your lover?"

One brow rose. *"Preserve me from jealous women who don't think. I'm not defending her. I'm not jumping to conclusions, because once you think you've found an answer you become careless. This business is too dangerous to be careless."*

Before she could retort, he winked out of existence.

It was the first time he'd lost his patience with her and it hurt. Part of her wanted to sleep in the hope that he would visit her and everything could be made right between them again. Another part of her longed to have him come to her while she was awake.

344

least awake they would be able to discuss his murderer without getting caught up in their need to make love.

There were too many unanswered questions. Had Louisa really arranged for someone to kill Ian? Why did he want to wait for Jacque Dubois to show up here instead of tracking him down, since he already knew several places the Frenchman frequented?

Curled up in one of the sitting area chairs, she watched the dawn through the window. Sometime between the muted purple shades that foreshadowed the demise of black from the sky and the full yellow of a triumphant sun, she fell into slumber.

"I thought you'd never come," Ian said, a lazily triumphant smile curling his mouth.

Disgusted with her weakness, she turned away from his knowing look. Already, from just watching his eyes move leisurely over her body, she felt herself warming and dewing for his lovemaking. Soon, he would have her where he wanted her: in his arms, agreeing to everything he wanted, right down to how they handled the rest of their quest.

She broke the thread of desire spinning out between them by moving away so that her back was to him. With one hand on the trunk of the ever-present rowan tree, she gazed into the distant landscape of this dream. It was Colonsay.

Clouds scuttled across the blue sky, their shadows skimming over the moors and rolling hills. Gulls flew overhead. Only it was late summer now, instead of the early winter of reality, and heather in full purple bloom blanketed the ground.

Ian's hands settled on her shoulders, sending messages of warmth and desire and satiation speeding to her limbs. Her knees melted, and she had to grip the trunk of the tree until the bark bit into her palm.

"Are you still fretting over Louisa?"

His breath wafted against the back of her bare neck. She could feel the tendrils of hair that had escaped from her topknot stroke her flesh. She didn't want to answer his question because she wasn't sure she wanted to hear his reply.

"Love," he murmured. "That one word is the key to all of this, Julie. I'm not defending Louisa because I loved her. I never loved Louisa. I'm hesitating to condemn her outright because I fear what will happen to you if it's true or if you let on that you believe it's so." He took her face between his palms and gently kissed her, a mingling of flesh that spoke of a union of spirit. "I don't want you hurt, because I love you. I'll never stop loving you."

She wanted to believe that, and did . . . deep down. But, somehow it wasn't enough to keep her doubts at bay when he refused to believe what was so obvious to her. Louisa had planned his murder.

"Then why won't you believe that she had you killed?"

Running his finger along the top of her shoulders, he said, "Perhaps I'm afraid that once we avenge my death I'll lose you again."

"I . . . I hadn't thought of that." She turned into the comfort of his embrace and raised her head to meet his gaze. "What's to become of us?"

His eyes clouded over, turning the color of tarnished silver. "You asked that once before, Sassenach. I don't have a different answer. We'll be together in the end. We just have to endure the separation until then."

She allowed her head to rest in the hollow of his shoulder. He was right. "We have to be strong."

He nodded, holding her tightly to him. She wouldn't cry, she told herself. She wouldn't.

The next morning, Julie's body was languid and satisfied, but her head felt as though every spy in the world was using her brain for a knife target. Sharp, jabbing pains made her want to crawl back under the covers, but this was the day Louisa was taking her to Ian's grave.

The grave was in a desolate, poor section on the outskirts of Paris. Anger and pain warred in Julie as she realized the disgrace and animosity Britain had dealt her love. The government he'd left her for, given his life for, had put his body in a pauper's grave in a country removed in distance and meaning from the land he'd loved whole-heartedly.

She stared down at the raw plot of ground, no head stone marking it. Only a rough wooden cross showing that a person lay buried here. Ian's name was hacked into the cross beam. That was it.

Tears burned her eyes and choked her throat.

"Let it go, Sassenach. It doesn't matter."

He stood in front of her, blurring the cross. His feet seemed planted in the chewed earth. She gulped hard. "It's so unfair."

He reached for her, enveloping her in a cocoon of misty unreality. Even though she couldn't feel him, she sensed his presence and his love. It was a healing balm on her ravaged heart.

One transparent hand raised her chin as though he truly were touching her; they were that much attuned to one another. *"Let's go, love. The day isn't over yet."*

Nodding, unable to look any longer, she gritted her teeth and turned her back on the sight. Blinking rapidly to clear her sight, she strode back to where the carriage waited on a rutted road no better than a rocky path.

"Darling," Louisa's voice penetrated Julie's anguish, "I'm sorry. This is the first time I've been here. I didn't know it would be this bad."

Julie glared at the Frenchwoman. She *knew* Louisa was responsible for this. She knew it in her heart, and she hated her for it. She balled her hands into fists around great wads of skirt material to keep herself from scratching out the comtesse's soulful brown eyes.

Julie swallowed an angry retort. She couldn't let Louisa know she blamed her for this, not yet. "Thank you. I'm going to the English Ambassador today and make arrangements to have Ian's body removed and shipped to Colonsay."

Stepping into the plush carriage, the coat of arms of the Comtesse de Grasse blazoned in gold above the door and on every piece of equipage inside, Julie pulled out her handkerchief. One good blow and she disciplined herself to gaze impassively at the scenery rushing by the window. She wouldn't collapse i front of Louisa. That would come later. Right now, she had things to accomplish.

There were still the Paris docks to get through.

They were dirty and smelled of brine and rotting fish. Ocean-going vessels rocked in their berths, and smaller boats bobbed up and down in time to the currents of the Seine. Sailors milled about on decks, unloaded cargo, and crowded the narrow streets. Activity seemed to fill the narrow confines until it seemed to Julie that there wasn't a calm port to be had.

Louisa signaled the coach to stop in front of a large wood-sided warehouse. The smell of tobacco permeated the air and bales of cotton propped open the two large loading doors.

"An importer from America's southern states," Louisa explained, waving her hand in the general direction of the warehouse. "But that's not why we're here."

Briskly, she stepped out and to the front of the carriage, diagonal from the warehouse's doors. Pointing with one enameled nail, she stated, "This is where Ian's body was found. It was surmised that his assailant hid in that alleyway." She pointed to a narrow alley beside the warehouse.

Julie watched the comtesse's face carefully, alert to any fleeting change. There was nothing. Louisa looked very much as though she were discussing the weather.

Louisa would not be a source of information. Julie turned her attention to the surrounding area. If the assassin had thrown the knife from beside the warehouse, then he was extremely skilled. As Ian had already told her.

The very idea that someone could deal out death at that range made her skin crawl. Any minute she expected to feel cold steel between her shoulder blades. It was a very disconcerting sensation. To dispel the feeling and to gather data, she carefully paced off the distance from the spot Louisa had pointed out to the side of the warehouse where the attacker was thought to have hidden. It was well over twenty feet. Too far for Ian to have seen his murderer after the fact.

"Have you seen enough?"

Ian materialized at her side, breaking her concentration. "Yes," she answered before thinking. A quick glance around showed two sailors eyeing her as though she were bewitched. Flushing, she hurried back to Louisa.

"Have you seen everything you wanted?"

Louisa's echoing of Ian's question was unsettling, and Julie found herself clenching her teeth and pulling the soft kid leather of her gloves through one hand. "I've seen more than enough."

"Good, because I don't like the feel of returning here. It brings back too many things." He actually seemed to shudder, and the brilliant lights that always danced within the outline of his ghostly body flickered in and out as though each and every one was agitated. It added to her unease.

"Good," Louisa unknowingly seconded Ian. "I never have liked docks. Smelly, dirty places." Fastidiously lifting her skirts to miss a puddle of who knew what, she stepped into the coach.

Julie followed with relief. She was reaching the end of her emotional endurance and she still had to visit the English Ambassador.

The English Ambassador was cool, but at least he agreed not to hinder her plan to have Ian's body removed. The visit to him was the most pleasant thing she'd done the entire day. For that she was thankful. She couldn't have withstood any more battering.

As she left the Ambassador's house, she waved away Louisa's carriage. The fresh air would revive her. The late afternoon was chilly, but the sky was clear. The sun hadn't gone completely down, and if she hurried she'd reach Louisa's townhouse before it got dark. The Frenchwoman only lived three blocks from the Ambassador's residence.

But the fresh air only magnified her melancholy. It contrasted too sharply with her memories of the dock stench, and the elegant homes and buildings she passed reminded her of Ian's shabby grave.

As though sensing the precarious hold she had on her emotions, Ian spoke. *"We've only a short way to go, Sassenach. Hold on till then, love."*

She nodded and turned her face into the shoulder that only she could see. While she couldn't feel anything physically, she sensed his love and support. Without him she wouldn't have made it.

At last she stood in her room. Collapsing on the bed, head bowed, Julie let the long suppressed tears come. They flowed freely, as though trying to compensate for all the times she'd refused to shed them. Her shoulders rose and fell in great heaving sobs that she did her best to muffle even though she didn't try to stop them. The relief of letting out the pain and horror was too great to stop.

Enveloping her like a great wool cape, Ian's earthly body, with its insubstantial flickering, brought her emotional comfort even though it couldn't take away the hurt that wracked her heart like a hurricane. She turned into his invisible warmth.

"Ach, love. Don't do this to yourself. I should never have allowed you to come here. It doesn't matter where my body lays. It's only a perishable vessel for the part of me that lives eternally."

"I know, but it's all I have left of you."

"I'm in your heart."

She realized that what he said was true. No matter what befell her, in her heart she would always remember Ian. He would be with her the rest of her days, and beyond.

Chapter Twenty

That evening Julie wavered between sleep and wakefulness as she lounged in a chair pulled close to the wall separating one of the guest rooms from Louisa's. The opening and closing of a nearby door brought her to instant alertness.

Simultaneously, Ian's figure moved from the window he'd been staring out of toward Julie and through the wall, one black brow raised. This is what they'd hoped for. That Louisa, upset from the day's doings, would summon a lover. They had prayed he would be Jacque Dubois. Now they would find out.

He was back in seconds, his face red but triumphant. *"It's Dubois."*

From what he didn't say, Julie surmised that the two had been in a compromising position. She smiled. Surely, that could be turned to their advantage.

At a more leisurely pace, she returned to her room, where they could talk without fear of alerting the two lovers to their presence. Julie could barely contain herself when the door to her room closed behind them.

"This is it. As soon as he leaves, we'll follow him."

Without waiting for Ian's agreement, she put on a sturdy pair of boots and started changing her light-colored clothing for dark ones. She didn't need Ian's expertise to know that she'd do better following Dubois home if she blended in with the night.

"You aren't following Jacque tonight."

She ignored him, taking her cape out of the wardrobe and laying it on a nearby chair.

"Julie, I said you aren't following him."

This time she looked at him. "I am, and there isn't anything you can do to stop me."

He stomped toward her, his feet landing a hairsbreadth above the floor with each step. *"Damnation, Sassenach, I said no. You can't follow him through the Paris streets at this time of night, and that's final."*

A thin smile stretched her lips. "I can, and I *will.* It was your suggestion in the first place."

He groaned. *"And a stupid one."*

"I'll be careful and you can range ahead and warn me of danger."

"As simple as that." Sarcasm dripped from each word as his shade towered above her.

Julie refused to cower. "Yes."

"Then at least take a weapon of some sort."

She knew he was right. Scanning the room, her gaze alighted on the fire implements. In minutes she was hefting the poker, wondering how tired her arm would get carrying it.

"That will do."

She grimaced at him before moving one of the chairs next to the door where she could hear Dubois passing her room on his way to the back stairs. She didn't have long to wait. She followed him out of the house.

Dubois moved stealthily, amazingly quiet for a man of his size, but with Ian's help, Julie trailed him unnoticed. Once she had to stop and press herself tightly against a darkened door they were passing. Ian said several drunken men were reeling down the street she'd have to cross. As soon as the carousers passed, she sped across, the poker gripped in white-knuckled hands.

After what seemed all night, with her heart pounding like a bass drum in her chest, they saw Dubois turn into the alleyway beside a tailor's shop. Several minutes later, they saw a candle's golden glow in a second story window.

Ian let out a whistle of relief. *"Good thing we followed him. He's changed living quarters."*

Back pressed protectively against a building, Julie whispered, "Now what?"

"Get you back to Louisa's. This is all we need tonight."

She pushed off from the wall with alacrity. Being on the streets of Paris in the small hours of the morning wasn't inclined to make her feel safe, but it had been necessary.

Julie retraced her steps quickly, Ian ranging ahead. There were no people about, not even thieves. Occasionally she would see the shadow of a lump in a doorway which she took to be a beggar seeking shelter of any kind, but nothing more. Even the drunks had retired.

Once she veered toward one of the sleeping figures, intending to drop a franc on the ground nearby. When the man or woman or child awoke, there would be money to buy something warm to eat. It wasn't much, but . . .

Ian's voice stopped her. *"What are you doing?"* He took in the glitter of her green eyes. *"No, don't tell me. You were going to leave money. Don't. There's the very likely chance that if you approach one of them they'll wake up. Not all of them would take kindly to you."*

He was right and she knew it. Was leaving a few francs worth the possibility of having to use the poker to defend herself against the very person she was trying to help? That might not happen, but it wasn't worth the risk. With a sigh of resignation, she continued on. As they neared the more fashionable area where Louisa's townhouse was located, Julie noticed more and more windows were lit by candles. The wealthy played into the small hours.

She was rounding the corner on Louisa's street when she heard it. She started, perspiration breaking out on her neck. "What was that?"

Ian's ghostly face seemed paler than usual in the darkness. *"Only a hound baying at the moon."*

"Only a hound?" she echoed, shuddering at the eerie sound that seemed to resonate through her flesh.

"Yes. Hurry, Sassenach. You've been lucky so far. It may not last."

Ian picked up speed so that Julie had to run to keep up with him. She was panting when the

356

reached the back door that led to the servant's section of the house. Ian was already inside."

"Hide!"

Reacting instinctively, Julie pulled back, sliding her feet along the ground as she wedged herself between two shrubs, and not a moment too soon.

The dark shadow of a man appeared in the lighter gray of the opening door. There wasn't enough light for Julie to make out his features, but the long cape he wore and the proud way he carried himself told her he was no servant. He didn't bother to try and leave stealthily. Another one of Louisa's lovers, no doubt. That made two in one night, within hours of each other.

Shaking her head in wonder at the Frenchwoman's insatiability, Julie counted till twenty as Ian had told her and then entered the house. Only when she was safe in her room did she allow herself a deep breath. It filled her lungs and helped to relax the muscles in her neck that she hadn't realized were rigid with tension. The next thing she did was replace the heavy poker.

Ian was prowling the room in a crisscross pattern. *"We have to approach Dubois tomorrow. Bring him back here while Louisa's out. That will probably make it evening. She always goes out."*

Julie nodded. "Thank goodness I'm in mourning and she doesn't expect me to attend these parties with her."

He paused, then came to her. Reaching out, his hand brushed her face, leaving a trail of exploding bubbles along her cheek.

"I wish you weren't in black, Sassenach." His eyes

softened and he held his arms out. *"But enough of Louisa and this damned business. Come to bed, come to me."*

Again they were on Colonsay, and it was summer. Clouds cavorted overhead, casting their shadows onto the heather-covered moors. A gentle breeze brought the tang of salt water and the sweetness of growing plants.

Ian walked beside her, his hand warm and solid in hers. They stopped under the shading branches of a giant rowan tree.

"Why are these always in our dreams?" Julie asked, reaching up and stroking a cluster of the orange berries adorning the tree.

Ian smiled down at her. "Don't you know? My Gran told you."

Incredulous, she said, "To protect us against witches?" She expected him to laugh at her, sharing what she was sure was a joke.

Solemnly, he said, "Better to be safe than sorry. What we're doing—these meetings—I don't know how they're accomplished, but I do know most people never have them."

Her stomach fluttered. She hadn't thought of that, just as she'd refused to dwell further on their final conclusion. "Soon they'll end."

"Yes."

Her hands clenched in fists of fury. Tears coursed down her face, anguish bowed her shoulders. "Why, Ian? Why? We had so much to live for."

He took her into his arms and cuddled her against

his chest. "I know, Sassenach. I know. But we have to be grateful for this. It's more than most have."

Sobs wracked her body, her words coming between them in breathless spurts. "We were meant for each other. You brought me the love I'd always wanted and I brought you the means to save Colonsay. Why did you have to die?"

He stroked her back, holding tight to her convulsing body. "I don't know, love. But it's done, and we can't change it."

When the tempest in her heart began to ease, he lifted her chin and kissed her gently. With a finger, he brushed away a tear that trembled on her lashes.

"Always remember, Julie, that I love you. You did more than save Colonsay for me: you brought me a love that few men are blessed to find."

She stared into his eyes, memorized every line and crease on his face. "Why is it so hard?"

He smiled sadly. "I don't know, Sassenach. I don't know."

Sighing, she laid her cheek on his chest, in the hollow between his breast and shoulder. It was her favorite spot. She fit as though his body had been designed to accommodate her. Beneath her ear was the strong, steady beat of his heart, but this time it didn't reassure her. Nothing could ease the dread creeping over her as the final moments of their stolen time together drew near.

Ian stroked the long tresses of her hair. "When the time comes, love, I'll be waiting for you."

Chapter Twenty-one

Louisa had been gone an hour when Julie slipped from the house into the cold night. At the nearest corner she hailed a hansom cab and gave the driver her destination. Ian sat across from her, his eyes hooded.

Julie shivered. This might be their last night together. If Dubois believed her when she told him Louisa was a double agent, he would tell his British contacts. It would clear Ian's name.

But they still wouldn't know who had murdered him.

"Ian, we still don't have any idea who killed you."

He stared at her as though considering before speaking. It made chills run up her arms to think that he might know something he wasn't telling her.

"But we have a good idea of who arranged it."

"Louisa."

He nodded.

"But—"

"One thing at a time, Julie."

Further discussion was curtailed by the carriage's

abrupt halt. Julie paid the driver, got out and looked around. A smattering of people walked the street. On the second story a window glowed warmly—the same one as last night. They were incredibly lucky.

It was a matter of several coins passing hands before Julie knocked on the door that she believed Jacque Dubois resided behind. Seconds later he was staring at her.

"Lady Kiloran," he said, his pale blue eyes showing nothing of his thoughts.

"Mr. Dubois," Julie said calmly, meeting his look coolly. "May I come in? I have something to discuss with you in private."

Ian had already entered. Julie could see him traversing the cramped corners, alert to anything that might help them. Seeing her love boldly examining everything gave her courage.

Dubois continued to study her, his body blocking her. Then he shrugged. "As you wish."

Did she detect a hint of surliness? Julie wasn't sure, and it didn't matter.

Not giving him an opportunity to change his mind, she sailed in. A quick glance showed the room to be spartan in its furnishings, nothing like the sumptuous house of the comtesse. Once more Julie was struck by the disparity between this middle class, at best, Frenchman and the comtesse.

"You came to tell me something," Dubois prompted, his mouth thinning at her obvious scrutiny of his surroundings.

Julie felt the moisture on her palms that had already dampened her gloves. "Yes." She licked her dry lips.

"Go ahead, Sassenach," Ian encouraged her.

Her eyes flicked his way, but she instantly brought them back to the massive Frenchman. Her spine stiffened. "Yes. It's about the Comtesse de Grasse."

Dubois' face hardened into a sharpness that Julie had thought him incapable of. "What about her?"

The words tumbled out before Julie lost her nerve in face of this formidable man. "She's a double agent, working for France."

Dubois looked incredulous, then he started to laugh, great belly shaking sounds that grated on Julie's raw nerves. When at last he could speak, he said in a cold voice which was the complete antithesis of the deep laughter of seconds before, "You are deranged."

The insult warmed Julie's blood, easing some of the dread with which she'd watched his mood change. "I can prove it."

"How?"

"Easy, Sassenach," Ian warned, *"don't tell him how. Make him agree to accompany you back to Louisa's. Otherwise, you can't prove anything to him. He's going to have to see it for himself—he's that kind of man."*

Julie nodded, signaling that she'd heard. "I'll show you, but you must come with me."

"What if I refuse?"

She took a deep breath as she gathered her wits. Lifting her chin, she said haughtily, "Then I will have to go to the English Ambassador on my own. If what I say proves untrue, Louisa's reputation will still have been besmirched. If what I say is true, then she'll be caught and it will be brought out that she and not Ian is the double agent."

Dubois eyes narrowed to glittering slits. "You would risk ruining Louisa's reputation because *you* think she's a double agent?"

"Yes. Because I have proof she is."

"Then why come to me?"

On her right, Ian smiled encouragement at her. She needed it. Not once since concocting this plan had she imagined it would be this difficult to convince Dubois.

"Because in order to make the Ambassador believe me, I would have to provide the evidence, and that would entail exposing Louisa. But there is a better way. If you believe it, and I'll show you the evidence, you can convince your superiors. Then Louisa can be used without her knowledge to plant erroneous information."

Dubois took a menacing step closer to her. "Why are you trusting me with this? For all you know, I could be in on this with Louisa."

Julie gulped down the fear rising in her throat like bile. "Ian trusted you."

The simple words stopped him. "All right. Say I come with you, you show me the information and I believe it. What is your purpose?"

Julie expelled her breath. "I want you to have Ian's name cleared, and—"

"Stop."

Bewildered, Julie's attention faltered.

"Don't tell him about wanting to find my killer, Julie. Not yet."

She wanted to question Ian's motives, but he ha

364

her at an impasse. It would have to wait until this business was finished.

"—and this will do it," she finished lamely.

Dubois rubbed his chin as though he saw nothing amiss in her hesitation. "When?"

"Now."

"As you wish."

Relief turned her knees to jelly. Julie had to hold the back of a chair to keep from sinking to the ground. She prayed that Louisa had not returned early.

"Good job." Ian passed through the door ahead of them.

The return cab had just pulled up a block from Louisa's front door when Julie heard the sound again. Her eyes widened in recognition. Her gaze shot to Ian, who sat up straight on the squabs next to Dubois.

"It's just a hungry dog howling. Nothing more."

It was the logical explanation, the only explanation, but it didn't prevent shudders from wracking Julie's limbs. The hound's voice was too mournful.

Meanwhile, Dubois hadn't waited for her. By the time she was out of the carriage he was circling around to the back of the house, his large bulk blending with the night shadows. In the murky light of the servants' stairs and the hallway leading to Louisa's bedroom, Dubois was even less visible.

Ahead of them was Ian's shade, a translucent entity the shifting color of milky moonstones. He disappeared through the door to the comtesse's room.

Julie ran to catch up, not knowing what to expect but feeling her heart pound in anticipation. Dubois hesitated before reaching out and turning the knob. As usual, it was unlocked.

The first thing Julie saw was Ian, standing just inside. The second thing was the comtesse's startled face followed by the blur of a man's pale body jumping from the bed.

"Oh, my, God," Julie breathed. "Her other lover!" Never had she imagined that Louisa would be here with another man.

Simultaneously, Dubois barged into the center of the room, his shoulders hunched forward but his hands hanging loosely at his sides. He looked dangerous.

Julie's eyes riveted on him. What would he do?

The other man gathered his clothes and disappeared through another door. Louisa sat up in bed, full breasts heaving, magnificently indignant at the interruption and without a trace of shyness at her nakedness.

"How dare you!" the comtesse said imperiously, just as though she'd been interrupted having tea instead of in the act of copulating. Her brown eyes flashed as they moved from Julie to Dubois and back to Julie.

Julie, dismayed at this turn of events, wanted to sink into the floor. Embarrassed, she sought Ian's presence. He was just coming back from the room the strange man had fled to.

"He's gone. And a good thing too," He saw the knife in Dubois's hand and his face blanched. *"Dear God! Julie, get out of here!"*

The breath froze in Julie's throat. Instead of the reassurance she needed, Ian was acting as though there were danger here for her. Wide eyed, confused, she looked back at Dubois.

The Frenchman held the knife casually, as though he knew how to handle the weapon and did so frequently. Everything fell into place: Louisa's indignation, Dubois' cold, glittering eyes. Julie blanched.

"Louisa," Dubois said in a soft voice, all the more menacing because its very reasoning tone revealed the true depth of his emotions. "You promised to be faithful to me. Do you remember?"

The color drained from the comtesse's high cheeks. "Nonsense, Jacque. I agreed to see you more than anyone else."

Mesmerized, Julie watched the tableau unfold.

"For Christ's sake, Julie, get the hell out of here."

Ian's agonized words grated down her spine, breaking her concentration on the two lovers. She turned her attention to him. His entire body sparked, the particles dancing as though they were a nest of angry hornets.

But she couldn't leave. She had to get proof, something to show that Louisa was a double agent and that Dubois, as she now suspected, had killed Ian. But what?

"Louisa," Dubois spoke again, drawing Julie's mind back to him. "I killed a man for you—a man I respected."

Julie's feet rooted to the spot. He was admitting it.

"You killed a man you were jealous of," Louisa spat at him. "Don't try to be noble with me."

Dubois took a step closer to the bed, the flexing of

367

his shoulder muscles evident even through his coat. "You promised, Louisa."

Like a consummate actress, the comtesse changed tactics. Her eyelids lowered, her body reclined until she resembled a sultry siren. "I promised you many things, Jacque. What I'm offering you now is only part of them."

Under the cover of the sheet, she spread her legs provocatively. Dubois' sight lowered, lingered.

Julie's gasp of disgust quickly changed to surprise as the comtesse pulled a small pistol out from under her pillow.

"Julie, get out now!"

Ian's frantic order distracted Julie. When she looked back at Louisa, the comtesse was sitting in bed with the gun trained on Dubois.

"Don't move, Jacque," Louisa said, her voice colder than the November night. "I'm as good with this little beauty as you are with that."

"Now!"

Belatedly, Julie realized that there was real danger in this room. A sense of violence permeated the air, hanging with a heavy stink. She took a tentative step backward.

"Don't move," Louisa said, holding another pistol in her other hand as though conjured by magic.

Julie gasped, but she stopped moving.

Dubois' impersonal gaze flicked to Julie then centered back on the woman still sitting in bed without a stitch of clothing to mar the perfection of her flesh. "Let her go, Louisa. She has no evidence to implicate either one of us. This is our fight."

Louisa laughed, her rouged mouth opening into a

gaping dark hole in the magnolia smoothness of her face. "Let her go? After killing her precious husband and framing him as a double agent, you want to let her go to spread that kind of gossip?"

Julie cursed her own curiosity that had held her here. Now she would not get away. She could see it in the hard brown of Louisa's eyes, and the thin cruelty of her red lips.

Louisa continued. "You are a stupid peasant, Jacque." She laughed harder, but her hands, holding the pistols, remained steady. "You stupid, stupid imbecile. She's part of the aristocracy. Do you think that if it came to your word against hers that any court would believe *you,* a peasant?"

Dubois's entire body stiffened at the insulting taunts. "I loved you, Louisa. I would have done anything for you."

Julie listened to the man expose his soul and felt pity for him.

Louisa laughed again. "But you did. You killed Macfie. You even made me forget him for a while." A dreamy look came over her face. "You were good in bed. A big animal with a tool to match." She licked her lips hungrily. "You always satisfied me, but," her eyes hardened again, "you're nothing. I would never have married you."

Julie saw Dubois' fingers tighten on the hilt of the knife and wondered if Louisa saw it too. The Frenchwoman was pushing him too far.

"You used me," he accused her.

"Of course." She waved one of the pistols toward Julie. "Now move next to her. When the two of you are found, it will look as though she shot you and

369

you knifed her. Very neat and tidy, don't you think?"

Julie's heart stopped.

"For all that's holy, Julie, listen! When Dubois moves, you bolt for the door. It's your only chance."

Julie felt numb. It was all she could do to nod enough for Ian to see.

Everything happened too quickly. Dubois moved, the knife flashing from his hand toward the bed. A bright flower of crimson blossomed between Louisa's heaving breasts. Two shots rent the air back to back. Dubois slumped to the floor. Julie felt as though her chest were burning. She crumpled.

"Julie, love, listen to me."

Ian's frantic words penetrated the fog blanketing her mind and Julie gazed upward. He was kneeling beside her, his hands reaching for her. But she couldn't feel them. This aching, painful sensation in her chest wasn't part of a bad dream. Ian would have been able to touch her if it were.

"Julie, you've got to get up! Get out of here! The English Ambassador is only a few houses away. He'll get you a doctor." His face twisted in agony. *"For Christ's sake, love, get up!"*

Julie reached up to touch him, to comfort him. Her hand passed through his face. A single tear trickled down her cheek.

"Please, Sassenach, for me! Get up!"

She nodded. It was a struggle, and she had to hold onto a chair, but she managed to stagger to her feet. She smiled triumphantly at him.

He returned her smile, the agonized lines of his face easing. *"That's my love. Now move."*

Ian's love and need gave her the determination she needed. She had to do this for Ian. The English Ambassador was the person to tell. He would be able to clear Ian's name once he knew what had happened here. Her love would be free, no longer disgraced. It gave her strength.

She stumbled and fell down several steps, wondering vaguely why no one came to her aid. "Where are the servants," she muttered.

"Easy, Julie. They're in their quarters. This house could fall down around their ears and they wouldn't budge. They fear Louisa too much."

Julie nodded, understanding exactly why they would hesitate to anger the comtesse. "Is . . . is she dead?" It took all her breath to ask that question as she struggled with the front door.

"Yes. So is Jacque, but never mind them. It's you we must think of."

Like a marionette, she nodded, nearly falling into the street. The next minutes were a blur of pain and frustration and determination as she made her way to the English Ambassador's residence.

"Here you are, love. Just one loud knock and someone will help you."

She fell to her knees, banging on the door, the last of her energy gone. A little longer and she would clear Ian's name, free his soul. A little longer.

The sound of a great dog howling came low and piercing to her ear. It seemed as though the beast were directly behind her. Twisting around, she peered into the dark night but could see nothing.

"Cu-sith," Ian whispered.

A smile of happiness transformed her pain-ravaged face as the meaning of the dog's howl sank in. Then there was light and voices and movement, and she forgot. Someone picked her up, carried her at what seemed a dizzying height. She was laid gently on something soft. A drink was put to her lips and tipped into her mouth. It burned down her throat and exploded in her stomach.

Her eyes fluttered open. She recognized the English Ambassador's face. He was dressed in formal clothes.

"I'm sorry to detain you," she murmured inanely. Then remembered her reason for being here.

She tried to sit up. It seemed that she couldn't get enough air to tell him the story. Her chest hurt. Looking down she saw red all over her bodice and spattered on her skirts.

"Funny," she muttered, "I wasn't wearing red." Then she remembered the pistols and the shots. One had gotten her. She was dying.

"There, there, take it easy." It was the ambassador speaking. "We'll have a doctor here immediately."

"Must ... must tell you ..." Julie trailed off. She had so little time. She had to clear Ian's name.

Above her Ian hovered, the room's chandelier visible through his ghostly form. *"I'm here, Sassenach.* She smiled at him.

"Must ... tell you all of it." Drawing from energy reserves she hadn't known she possessed, Juli told the story, leaving nothing out. "... they're i

Louisa's chamber. In the headboard of the bed is a panel . . . and a safe behind it. The papers are there."

A great relief held her as she finished. She had done what she'd set out to do: save her love. But she was so cold, so tired. She would close her eyes and rest . . . just for a moment.

It seemed like only an instant before she felt refreshed and warm and full of energy. In fact, she felt so good that she wanted to go with them to Louisa's.

Opening her eyes, Julie sat up, feeling better than she'd ever felt in her life. She'd never felt so alive. She must have been mistaken when she'd thought she was dying. The baying hound must have been a poor dog crying for its dinner.

Laughing at her fears, she stood up and smiled at the ambassador who was standing beside her with another man. Neither man noticed her. She walked toward them and said, "Gentlemen, thank you . . ." but they didn't seem to hear her.

"What a pity, doctor," the ambassador said. "But if what she said is true, a man's name has been cleared tonight, his senseless murder exonerated and his soul put to rest."

The doctor shook his head. "But what about her? Who will exonerate her?"

The ambassador smiled and looked at the woman both men were discussing. "I don't think she's unhappy."

Bewildered, Julie turned to see who the men were talking about. Her mouth opened, her hands rose to her throat. It was her. She was lying on a settee, a smile on her lips. She was dead.

Dead. That meant . . .

Joy such as she'd never known existed spiraled up in her. She was free, free to join her love.

Excitement bubbled up in her, escaped as a trilling laugh of exultation as she looked up. There he was, near the ceiling. But instead of being transparent, he was solid—as solid as he'd been in her dreams.

"Ian, Ian," she called, rising up to him. "I'm free now. Nothing will ever separate us again."

Taking her outstretched hand, he pulled her into his arms. "Welcome to forever, my love."

> *Fast this Life of mine was dying,*
> *Blind already and calm as death,*
> *Snowflakes on her bosom lying*
> *Scarcely heaving with her breath*
>
> *Love came by, and having known her*
> *In a dream of fabled lands,*
> *Gently stooped, and laid upon her*
> *Mystic chrism of holy hands;*
>
> *Drew his smile across her folded*
> *Eyelids, as the swallow dips;*
> *Breathed as finely as the cold did*
> *Through the locking of her lips.*
>
> *So, when Life looked upward, being*
> *Warmed and breathed on from above,*

What sight could she have for seeing,
    Evermore ... but only LOVE?

> *Elizabeth Barrett Browning*
> *Life and Love*

AUTHOR'S NOTE

In writing the story of Ian and Julie, I've taken some liberties with history. During Ian and Julie's time, Colonsay no longer belonged to the Macfies, it belonged to the MacNeills and had done so since 1710.

Also, there is more than one way to spell Macfie. I chose the one that seemed the most natural to me. However, some of the other spellings are: McPhee, MacFie, and MacDuffie.

But no matter what changes are made or what names the characters use, a romance is the tale of two people whose love surmounts all obstacles . . . even death.

ABOUT THE AUTHOR

AMBER KAYE is the pseudonym for a talented and prolific writer, who is also the author of the Zebra historical romance ENDLESS SURRENDER.

Ms. Kaye also authors Zebra Regency Romances under the name Georgina Devon, including AN UNCOMMON INTRIGUE, THE SCARLET LADY, and her Golden Heart Award-winning LADY OF THE NIGHT.

Aside from her successful writing career, Amber has had an interesting life. She was born in 1952 while her father was stationed in San Antonio, Texas with the United States Air Force. After receiving her B. A. in Social Sciences from California State College San Bernardino, Amber followed in her father's footsteps and joined the USAF. She met her husband, Martin, an A10 fighter pilot, while she was serving as an Aircraft Maintenance Officer.

The mother of a young daughter, she now serves as a major in the USAF Reserves. She resides with her family near Langley Air Force Base in the Hampton, Virginia area and is an active member of the RWA's Richmond, VA chapter.

DANA RANSOM'S RED-HOT HEARTFIRES!

ALEXANDRA'S ECSTASY   (2773, $3.75)
   Alexandra had known Tucker for all her seventeen years, but all at once she realized her childhood friend was the man capable of tempting her to leave innocence behind!

LIAR'S PROMISE   (2881, $4.25)
   Kathryn Mallory's sincere questions about her father's ship to the disreputable Captain Brady Rogan were met with mocking indifference. Then he noticed her trim waist, angelic face and Kathryn won the wrong kind of attention!

LOVE'S GLORIOUS GAMBLE   (2497, $3.75)
   Nothing could match the true thrill that coursed through Gloria Daniels when she first spotted the gambler, Sterling Caulder. Experiencing his embrace, feeling his lips against hers would be a risk, but she was willing to chance it all!

WILD, SAVAGE LOVE   (3055, $4.25)
   Evangeline, set free from Indians, discovered liberty had its price to pay when her uncle sold her into marriage to Royce Tanner. Dreaming of her return to the people she loved, she vowed never to submit to her husband's caress.

WILD WYOMING LOVE   (3427, $4.25)
   Lucille Blessing had no time for the new marshal Sam Zachary. His mocking and arrogant manner grated her nerves, yet she longed to ease the tension she knew he held inside. She knew that if he wanted her, she could never say no!

FEEL THE FIRE IN CAROL FINCH'S ROMANCES!

BELOVED BETRAYAL (2346, $3.95)

Sabrina Spencer donned a gray wig and veiled hat before blackmailing rugged Ridge Tanner into guiding her to Fort Canby. But the costume soon became her prison—the beauty had fallen head over heels in love!

LOVE'S HIDDEN TREASURE (2980, $4.50)

Shandra d'Evereux felt her heart throb beneath the stolen map she'd hidden in her bodice when Nolan Elliot swept her out onto the veranda. It was hard to concentrate on her mission with that wily rogue around!

MONTANA MOONFIRE (3263, $4.95)

Just as debutante Victoria Flemming-Cassidy was about to marry an oh-so-suitable mate, the towering preacher, Dru Sullivan flung her over his shoulder and headed West! Suddenly, Tori realized she had been given the best present for a bride: a night of passion with a real man!

THUNDER'S TENDER TOUCH (2809, $4.50)

Refined Piper Malone needed bounty-hunter, Vince Logan to recover her swindled inheritance. She thought she could coolly dismiss him after he did the job, but she never counted on the hot flood of desire she felt whenever he was near!

Available wherever paperbacks are sold, or order direct from the Publisher. Send cover price plus 50¢ per copy for mailing and handling to Zebra Books, Dept. 4204, 475 Park Avenue South, New York, N.Y. 10016. Residents of New York and Tennessee must include sales tax. DO NOT SEND CASH. For a free Zebra/Pinnacle catalog please write to the above address.

PASSION BLAZES IN A ZEBRA HEARTFIRE!

COLORADO MOONFIRE (3730, $4.25/$5.50)
by Charlotte Hubbard

Lila O'Riley left Ireland, determined to make her own way in America. Finding work and saving pennies presented no problem for the independent lass; locating love was another story. Then one hot night, Lila meets Marshal Barry Thompson. Sparks fly between the fiery beauty and the lawman. Lila learns that America is the promised land, indeed!

MIDNIGHT LOVESTORM (3705, $4.25/$5.50)
by Linda Windsor

Dr. Catalina McCulloch was eager to begin her practice in Los Reyes, California. On her trip from East Texas, the train is robbed by the notorious, masked bandit known as Archangel. Before making his escape, the thief grabs Cat, kisses her fervently, and steals her heart. Even at the risk of losing her standing in the community, Cat must find her mysterious lover once again. No matter what the future might bring . . .

MOUNTAIN ECSTASY (3729, $4.25/$5.50)
by Linda Sandifer

As a divorced woman, Hattie Longmore knew that she faced prejudice. Hoping to escape wagging tongues, she traveled to her brother's Idaho ranch, only to learn of his murder from long, lean Jim Rider. Hattie seeks comfort in Rider's powerful arms, but she soon discovers that this strong cowboy has one weakness . . . marriage. Trying to lasso this wandering man's heart is a challenge that Hattie enthusiastically undertakes.

RENEGADE BRIDE (3813, $4.25/$5.50)
by Barbara Ankrum

In her heart, Mariah Parsons always believed that she would marry the man who had given her her first kiss at age sixteen. Four years later, she is actually on her way West to begin her life with him . . . and she meets Creed Deveraux. Creed is a rough-and-tumble bounty hunter with a masculine swagger and a powerful magnetism. Mariah finds herself drawn to this bold wilderness man, and their passion is as unbridled as the Montana landscape.

ROYAL ECSTASY (3861, $4.25/$5.50)
by Robin Gideon

The name Princess Jade Crosse has become hated throughout the kingdom. After her husband's death, her "advisors" have punished and taxed the commoners with relentless glee. Sir Lyon Beauchane has sworn to stop this evil tyrant and her cruel ways. Scaling the castle wall, he meets this "wicked" woman face to face . . . and is overpowered by love. Beauchane learns the truth behind Jade's imprisonment. Together they struggle to free Jade from her jailors and from her inhibitions.

Available wherever paperbacks are sold, or order direct from the Publisher. Send cover price plus 50¢ per copy for mailing and handling to Zebra Books, Dept. 4204, 475 Park Avenue South, New York, N.Y. 10016. Residents of New York and Tennessee must include sales tax. DO NOT SEND CASH. For a free Zebra/Pinnacle catalog please write to the above address.